AN AGONY OF PLEASURE
COURSED THROUGH HER

"You are some woman, Caroline Blaine."
Hunter's voice was ragged, but his eyes
were steady.

"And you're not like anyone I've ever known,
Hunter Victor Pierce," Cary whispered.

She held fast to those midnight eyes looking at
her, even though she felt afraid. Was she
mistaking what she thought she saw there? Was
she really more than just an unexpected bonus to
his investigation?

"Hold me," she pleaded, trembling.

Hunter put his arms around her and snuggled
against her hair. "It's all right," he whispered, as
if to a child. Then he began a slow hypnotic
movement, swaying with her in his arms.

"You're the loveliest, smartest woman I've ever
met," Hunter said. "I've been looking for
someone like you for a long time."

Donna Saucier

AMETHYST FIRE

Harlequin Books

TORONTO • NEW YORK • LONDON
AMSTERDAM • PARIS • SYDNEY • HAMBURG
STOCKHOLM • ATHENS • TOKYO • MILAN

For Annette, who gave me the dream, and
for Rita G., who showed me how to make
it come true. Thank you.

Published March 1984

First printing January 1984

ISBN 0-373-70109-8

Printed in Canada

CHAPTER ONE

"WHAT I NEED is a forty-hour day!" Cary Blaine groaned with weary frustration in the silence of her rented Cutlass. One slender, white-knuckled fist banged the steering wheel irritably, because she was already tired at only eleven-thirty in the morning—and she had so much more to do today.

Long before dawn, Cary had been in Willingham's regional-headquarters office in St. Louis, distributing a stack of last-minute notes for the staff, trying to stave off chaos and tie up as many loose ends as possible before she had to leave town. There was no way to know if or when the senior partners might ask her to return, or when the region's manager, Mary Ellen Hughes, would be discharged from the hospital to resume her regular duties.

Cary had spent the last thirty minutes in the quiet early-morning emptiness of the manager's office, fruitlessly trying to find employment leads for Jimmy Copeland, an exceptionally bright young forestry graduate. Mary Ellen had been working overtime to place him when hemorrhaging ulcers had disastrously struck her down. But Cary had not found enough time in the last few days to compile a satisfactory prospect list for him. She'd finally been forced to abandon the placement effort entirely in order to catch her plane to Kansas City for the first leg of her trip back to Topeka. It was upsetting to know she was leaving Jimmy to the awkward ministrations of an unsupervised junior staff member, but there was nothing more she could do about the situation without seriously compromising her own assignments in Kansas.

Jimmy Copeland's continued unemployment, however, had proved to be only the first of many frustrations. Cary's early-morning flight took off on time, but it was not a breakfast flight as she had supposed. Her stomach growled in empty protest later, when her plane was required to circle the airport a half hour before being granted landing clearance.

Ravenously hungry after her unintentional fast, she'd bolted down an undercooked hamburger at a coffee shop near the turnpike entrance, nearly choking on the flat, greasy meal. Then had come the fast, sixty-mile drive on to Topeka. There, two engineering applicants were waiting for interviews with her, and Willingham had scheduled her to speak at the Career Day activities at Central High School.

In this all-too-brief moment before she had to resume her hectic schedule, Cary sat tensely in her assigned parking space outside the offices marked Willingham Personnel Services and Executive Recruiting. It was time to slow down, be outwardly calm, forget the unfinished paperwork and the disillusioned young man in St. Louis. She must go inside to face her clients as the perfectly serene consultant that just now she did not resemble at all.

Cary unclenched her hand deliberately and slowly, trying to quiet her racing heart and churning emotions. What would happen to the region if Mary Ellen was not able to return to work soon? Not a single one of the regional recruiters could be spared from fieldwork to step in as interim manager—except herself. She was the only one on temporary assignment and the only one with training in supervisory skills. But did she want the hassle and tension that went with a management job, tension that had driven strong, capable Mary Ellen Hughes into the hospital? Could she handle the stress of running the largest, fastest-growing region in the Willingham empire—even for a few months?

Some small part of her thrilled at the idea. Despite her weariness and Mary Ellen's ulcers, she had to admit the prospect of running the central region was an exciting one. There were so many things that could be done, so many new projects that could be started—if she had the time and the authority!

But she did not have the position yet and might never have it. Knowing she must relax, Cary tried to force all her speculation, all her aching tiredness and idle hopes into a tidy box to be opened some other time, in private.

Breathing deeply, Cary closed her eyes and focused on imaginary soft clouds floating against an azure sky, untroubled by even the October Kansas winds. After a few moments she was able to get out of the car, moving purposefully, with only a slight nervous anticipation tingling somewhere deep inside to remind her of the possible chances opening magically around her.

Calm at last, Cary went around the Cutlass to unlock the trunk. She had borrowed several pieces of audiovisual equipment from headquarters and would need to sort through the slides and charts in her office before the speech at Central this afternoon.

Outside the limestone office complex, a chill capricious wind ruffled her midnight-black hair across her shoulders and whipped several piles of fallen leaves into a frenzied dance around her. Beside the building, elm and cottonwood were shifting their massive branches and shaking off thin, rusty orange leaves. The remaining leaves shimmered in the full glare of noonday sun, glowing with shades of crimson, saffron, and defiant emerald, seeming almost as transparent as stained glass in the colorless daylight. The winking, changing brilliance of the leaves lifted Cary's spirits, and the carefree wind heightened the color of her fair, delicately tinted complexion.

Unloading the equipment, Cary watched absently as a woman and a small boy got out of a station wagon across the street. The woman pulled her jacket tightly around her and began to walk toward one of the plaza office buildings. But as the boy started after her, the wind lifted his bright blue cap and sent it spinning across the parking lot into a field of sunflowers and tall grass. The boy whooped and ran after it. After a moment's hesitation the woman joined the chase. They ran shouting, then swooping, to catch the elusive cap, then crying out and running again.

Cary was almost tempted to join them. Somewhere in her memory she watched herself as a little girl running after a hat in the wind, laughing and swooping. The memory was sweet and as refreshingly clear as the skies were today. It was good to be back in Topeka for fall. This was where she'd been born, where her sister still lived. Perhaps a whole new future was waiting for her here, waiting to be born fresh and new from the ever-changing Kansas winds.

But she would be late for her appointments with the two engineers if she did not hurry. And so she forced herself to finish unpacking her equipment and move it to the doorway of the Willingham offices.

Cary pushed the heavy oak door to one side and tried to maneuver her Ringmaster slide projector and two briefcases through the opening. As she bumped her way into the vestibule, a dozen faces, some bored, some nervous, turned to regard her progress.

Knowing her face was flushed with the autumn cold as well as the exertion of carrying such bulky equipment, Cary did not flash her greeting smile— that professional gesture of good-natured poise she had learned on her first assignment. She was afraid the smile would turn into a grimace if the Ringmaster slipped even a fraction of an inch from its precarious perch on her hip.

I could use an extra hand, she silently admonished the room's occupants. *Can't anybody see this stuff is heavy?*

As if in answer to her thought, Cary felt the Ringmaster grow suddenly lighter. She looked around quickly to discover that a handsomely suited man was cushioning the weight of her projector with the support of one strategically placed hand. He was strong. Capable.

"You look like you could use some help." The man's statement was almost artificial in its polite, deferential phrasing. But he *had* been the only one to offer any assistance.

Cary looked up with the genuine smile of friendly pleasure she usually reserved for after hours.

Her years of practice made a catalog of his superficial qualities automatic. Intelligent eyes framed by dark gray metal-rimmed glasses, a very quick and penetrating glance. Well-groomed, a conservative haircut. But his smile! Only a professional smiler like herself would have recognized the impersonal nature of his friendly but bland expression. Cary felt her own face harden into a mask of cool reserve.

"Thank you. My office is just inside that corridor to the left."

He swung the projector away from her easily and strode away. Lithe, like a dancer—or an athlete. Cary found herself watching him approvingly. Then she shifted her remaining load and followed him, away from the fluorescent brightness of the waiting room to a short hall whose maroon-carpeted walls seemed to absorb both the light and the sound of their footsteps. The hallway had been designed as a buffer to ensure that the conversations in each of the offices opening from it were undisturbed and private. As a buffer, it worked well; but its dimness always seemed to dampen Cary's spirits a little. It was definitely not the way she would have chosen to introduce clients to the office, had the decision been hers to make.

The stranger stopped just inside the door of Cary's temporary office.

Two of the walls were also carpeted, in a steel blue hue. Their color was calculated to set off the third wall, which was paneled in gray weathered wood. Its sheen reflected light softly, smoothly.

Cary strode quickly to this lightly textured wall and reached for one of the barely perceptible silver knobs protruding from it.

"The Ringmaster goes in this closet, please." She swung the concealed ceiling-to-floor door open, revealing shelves, partly full of equipment and boxes, above rows of black steel filing cabinets. Then she moved aside while the man lifted his burden and stowed it on an empty shelf. He was tall, several inches above her own five feet seven and a half. But not so tall that she missed the cool scent of his aftershave, lime crisp and tantalizing in its clean freshness.

"Thank you again, Mr.—"

"Thompson. David Thompson."

His voice was unusually melodious.

"I appreciate your help, Mr. Thompson. I was just about to drop that projector, and I would have hated to do that."

"Right. Most unprofessional. Not to mention the hole in the floor when it hit." His tone was playful, and his smile was no longer bland. But if anything, it had become more artificial, thought Cary, like the broad grin of the Cheshire cat. Perhaps she was only seeing the awkward exterior of a nervous man. But no, his voice and manner were so controlled, so very perfect. He didn't really seem ill at ease.

"Of course the floor was my primary consideration all along. I'm so glad you saved us from such disaster." She grinned back at him, then turned away to close the closet door. Cary wished he would speak again. Was it perhaps an imperceptible accent of some sort that made his voice seem so hauntingly full and rich? But before she had dropped the latch knob, the sound of her office door closing signaled his departure.

What a strange encounter! Why had Mr. David Thompson seemed so utterly perfect that she was left with an impression of either fraud or mystery?

Cary had always enjoyed a good riddle or puzzle. The challenge excited her and gave her a chance to use the excellent analytical skills that had once prompted her study of mathematics and the applied sciences. Those days of classroom competition and youthful exhilaration were more than four years behind her now. Her job as regional executive recruiter–technical for one of the nation's top personnel consulting firms generally supplied her with enough day-to-day challenge and stimulation so that she did not have to go inventing mysteries where none existed.

Cary shook her head as if to shed her fancies. Perhaps it was only midlife restlessness hitting too early—she was only twenty-eight, after all. Yet here she was, inventing a complication, when she *surely* faced enough of those already! On this temporary assignment in Topeka, she had to find several of the very best, most talented professionals in the country and work out a campaign to improve Willingham's public image in Kansas at the same time. As if those two directives hadn't provided plenty of everyday puzzles to solve, now there was the added difficulty of covering for her absent supervisor in St. Louis in her "spare" time.

Actually, the present demands were no greater strain than the frenetic pace she'd been forced to maintain since March on her previous assignment. Jetting constantly from Denver to St. Louis to Casper, Wyoming, on that hopeless American Paper Company deal had been more than just exhausting and frustrating. It had been futile from the start.

But the American Paper fiasco was all over now. The senior partners and Mary Ellen had set up special screening procedures for all new clients. Each of their current clients was a well-established, respectable firm with legitimate personnel needs. No one at Willingham was wasting time chasing wild geese anymore.

And Cary was *home* for at least a few months in Topeka, in a gray-paneled room, looking out from a window-wall whose expanse of glass was the only thing between her and the brisk wind and falling leaves that reminded her of a happy childhood.

This is only a temporary assignment to find a handful of specialized engineers, she thought. *So enjoy it while you can. And forget the wasted work of the last six months. Think instead of David Thompson and his unusually beautiful voice, or Omega Aircraft's hypersensitive personnel director—or your first appointment.*

Moving resolutely to her desk, Cary picked up the folders on today's two interviewees. The top name jumped out at her. Thompson, D. So she would see him again! How nice. How very, very nice.

Thirty years old, unmarried. An aerospace engineer from U.C.L.A., currently senior design engineer for Burkham Air Labs in Tecumseh. Moved up quickly from staff engineer through project detail work and into advanced design work in less than seven years. Ready for "new challenges." All in all, a very impressive résumé. He was exactly the sort of person Omega Aircraft had hired her agency to find for them.

She pressed the intercom lever beside her phone.

"Marian, please send in Mr. Thompson."

"Yes, Miss Blaine."

In a few moments, the receptionist was knocking on her door and then ushering in the handsome man who had only just left. Cary rose to shake hands.

"Mr. Thompson. I'm so glad we're meeting again. I'm Caroline Blaine, the executive recruiter assigned to help you in your job search."

"I had noticed your name on your door earlier, Miss Blaine, and I'm very happy to know you'll be the one working with me." His handshake was firm and self-confident. "It's nice to share a common, um, projector with your recruiter. I feel like we're old friends already."

What a suave line! It seemed to Cary that he was trying to put *her* at ease. For some reason, that thought made her bristle.

She was in charge of this interview, not he!

She opened the file in front of her and scanned it quickly. She would begin some routine questioning—the innocuous questions usually necessary to put the interview on a comfortable basis.

"I see you graduated from U.C.L.A. Did you ever work with Winfred Holly there?"

"I don't believe so. But I was a bit of a loner in college, so it may be that I just never met the man."

He was smiling, with a relaxed professional smile that Cary could imagine would work wonders on stuffy managers. He was the perfect picture of a junior executive destined for greatness. It was hard to believe that he'd ever been a loner. No, he seemed more the type to have been class president and center for the varsity basketball team.

"How did you find the course work...tough? I've heard comments that the school of engineering is one of the roughest." She thought fondly of her own semesters in that school and the stimulating courses she had taken from Professor Holly.

"Oh, the courses were certainly thorough. They gave me a good background to begin work at Burkham. But not especially rough."

Cary glanced again at the résumé. Magna cum laude. Of course. But she wondered why he had never taken a course from Winfred Holly. Even exceptional students were required to take basic physics courses, and until the professor died just three years ago, U.C.L.A. students had been known to wait in line to register for his classes.

"Why don't you tell me a little about your reasons for wanting to leave Burkham." She got a pen ready to take notes.

Across from her desk, the tall man seemed to settle firmly into the overstuffed armchair, as if he was now more at ease. Cary examined his appearance once more as his melodious voice began a recital that, more or less, went word for word along with the statements in his résumé. His hair was a deep, rich black lightly flecked throughout with gray. Large dark brown eyes behind his glasses dominated his face. Heavily fringed with black lashes, his eyes seemed warm and liquid. Like a cocker spaniel, thought Cary, suppressing a giggle. Such an elegant figure, so perfect in manner and voice, with the eyes of a devoted lapdog! Trying to stifle her wandering thoughts before the giggle burst out, Cary tried to listen more carefully to the man's words.

There was something definitely missing. Those eyes were intelligent, even caring. Yet there was little of either obvious brilliance or emotional content in his carefully articulated recital.

"Mr. Thompson—David," she broke in. "What sort of projects have you been working on recently at Burkham?" Was it her imagination, or did his posture now betray a certain tenseness?

"Well, my shop has been working two separate but related problems. The first is a new stress test for midsection stability in commercial airliners, and the second is a final-phase testing program for our new engine-mount design."

"What type of stress testing are you using at this stage on the midsection—physical or radioisotope? Are you working with scale models or full-size mock-ups?" Cary was genuinely curious. There were so many ways to test the strength and flexibility of metal.

David Thompson sat up straighter in his gray tweed suit. His eyes narrowed slightly, showing emotion for the first time since the interview had begun. Cary read surprise there, mixed with suspicion.

"You're a very smart lady, Miss Blaine, I hadn't expected such detailed technical knowledge from a personnel counselor."

She laughed. "No? Perhaps not. I don't usually mention it, but I was working on a master's degree in civil engineering before I switched to business. I'm really very interested in your job, and I'm sure any prospective employer would ask the same questions."

"But wouldn't I be violating the contract I have

now with Burkham if I answered them?'' He leaned forward, as if confronting her.

"Of course you would, if you went into enough details to compromise your project. But I am neither a competitor nor was I asking for proprietary information, David.'' Intelligent and capable he might be, but Cary mentally added the label ''cagey'' to his file description. So far, he had avoided answering her questions, and she was fairly convinced he would continue to do so unless she pressed harder. And that would be difficult to justify during a preliminary interview. Henry Crandon at Omega could pursue the matter.

"Let's change the subject, shall we?'' She skimmed again through the résumé and checked off points she would expand upon.

Her applicant answered all of the next few routine questions about salary expectations, relocation problems and long-range career plans. He did not volunteer information that was not specifically requested. He did not refer to his work projects, even indirectly. Cary was disturbed by his reticence. With his suspicious almost paranoid attitude she wasn't sure if she should recommend him to Omega or to anyone else. But then his record proved he was by far the most qualified candidate she had interviewed so far.

"Why have you been so concerned to avoid discussing your work?'' she finally asked.

"Why do you want so many details?'' He was challenging her again, leaning forward as if their verbal joust were a physical battle.

"Mr. Thompson, a prospective employer has the right to expect that a man I recommend as a competent aerospace design engineer is, in fact, both competent and an aerospace engineer. A certain risk is expected, but we try to minimize it by prudent screening of applicants without betraying the confidentiality of your job search."

"Then will you be calling Burkham for references?" He was tense, she was sure of it, though the only evidence was his posture. His tone was still even, his hands relaxed. Perhaps he just didn't want to jeopardize the job he already had. That was understandable.

"No, we won't do that. Not unless you authorize it," she answered.

The man across from her smiled, and his eyes narrowed once more. "But you will discuss my background with whatever employers are interested?"

Cary was getting impatient with his cross-examination, but her professional smile, like his, remained intact. "Yes, of course. How else would we be able to decide if you're the right candidate for the job?"

"So an employer sees only the candidates you choose, Miss Blaine. Is that right?"

"More or less. Surely you knew most of these things when you left your résumé with us. Didn't you, David?"

"Let's just say. . .Caroline, that I'm interested in knowing more about your job, too."

A perfect tit-for-tat response, thought Cary.

Round one goes to David Thompson. "Would you also be interested in a job as chief design engineer for Omega Aircraft Corporation in Wichita?"

The man in the chair before her leaned back in a fully composed, self-satisfied manner. He crossed one leg nonchalantly and rearranged a lapel of his stylish tweed suit.

Preening himself! Cary tried to smother the irritation she felt might be only too apparent in her expression. Unconsciously, her fingers tightened on the pen she held in her right hand.

"Yes. I would be very interested indeed."

"Can you be free all day on Thursday? Omega is flying several potential candidates down to Wichita for a full day of interviews. I warn you, though. They'll ask even more questions than I have about your work."

David Thompson took a deep breath. "Yes, I can be free."

Cary closed his file folder. "Good. That makes six of you on the flight."

"A quota, Miss Blaine?"

Don't let him get to you, she silently admonished herself. What a suspicious, antagonistic character he was!

"No," she replied. "I was merely thinking of the plane's capacity. The Omegajet B10 holds only eight passengers—you and I with the other five candidates I found two weeks ago will make seven. We'll be leaving at seven-thirty Thursday morning from Municipal Airport, Mr. Thompson. Have a good day."

She rose and moved to open the office door for him. But he was quicker. With his hand on the silver doorknob, he turned back to her. His eyes swept across her face, then down, as if to measure her. He looked again directly at her, his dark eyes somewhat hidden behind his glasses. But she was certain they were looking, unwavering, at her own brownish gray ones.

"Do you have a question, Mr. Thompson?"

"No." Still he stared at her. "No. Unfortunately, I think I've found the answer to at least one of my questions." He frowned and turned. The heavy oak door sighed shut behind him.

Cary was disturbed. Her first impression of the man had been of a successful, self-assured, competent professional—very attractive, with pleasant manners. Hmm, not just attractive—downright charismatic.

I'll bet heads turn when he walks through a room, she speculated. But some inner devil led her to the next thought, that anyone who spent five minutes with the man would soon forget his good looks. There was something so phony and put on about David Thompson.

Should she have included him in the group for Omega? His academic record and job history were outstanding, but with his paranoid, secretive nature.... No, better to let Henry Crandon at Omega Aircraft make that decision. Cagey David and Nervous Henry deserved each other! Perhaps Henry could find a job for Thompson that didn't involve much interaction with other people.

She had begun to dictate from her interview notes when a horrible thought crossed her mind. It couldn't be! But what if this was all some kind of hoax—if there was no such person as David Thompson! That would explain her impression of fraud. But the last thing the Willingham agency needed was another client playing self-serving charades—just like the vice-president at American Paper had been doing.

She thumbed quickly through her telephone directory and dialed the general information number for Burkham Air Labs.

"I'd like to speak with David Thompson, please."

"That extension is 6124. One moment and I'll connect you."

Cary breathed a sigh of grateful relief and flicked away the tendril of dark hair that had fallen across her eye. She'd been so upset for a second that its presence hadn't even disturbed her.

She chuckled softly to herself. The idea that someone had played a stupid joke on her had been a rather fanciful one. Paranoia was probably the answer, after all. He's just suspicious and sneaky and afraid the world will steal some important secret from him, or maybe he's jealous of a . . . .

She was about to hang up when a flat, unmusical voice answered, "Thompson here."

She was so surprised that she almost stuttered.

"*David* Thompson?"

"Yes. Can I help you?"

"Um, personnel is just verifying telephone extensions. Thank you.'' She slammed the receiver into its cradle.

So there actually was a David Thompson. But that elegant, well-dressed man who'd been in her office a few minutes ago was not the real thing!

For several seconds, Cary stared out the window at the multicolored woodland scene behind her office building. Then she resumed her dictation. Early this evening she would call the bogus engineer at the number he had given for his home in nearby Tecumseh—if he had such a home—and she would cancel his trip to Wichita. It was a shame.

CHAPTER TWO

CARY INCHED HER WAY lower into the steaming tub, until her nape rested on the cold blue porcelain just a few inches above the water. Her long hair was piled up in looping curls on top of her head. She closed her eyes, willing away the day's tension.

Steamy water lapped at her milk-white skin, imparting a faint, false sense of motion. She could almost be floating in some secluded sunlit lagoon, separated from the rest of the world by miles of sandy tan beach and colorful coral. The South Pacific, perhaps. Her own palm-ringed Bali Hai.

And striding across the glittering sand should be a tall, dark stranger. Cary positioned him in her fantasy, watching as he executed a perfect racing dive and swam with easy strokes to meet her. His head emerged from the clear deep water beside her and he turned to look at her with sky-blue eyes... wrong! They should be dark brown, like David Thompson's beautiful spaniel eyes.

Her own lids flew open. This was just plain ridiculous! That man, whatever his real name was, had no place in her imagination at all. Yes, he did have a physique worth a movie star's ransom and, yes, he did look cultured and distinguished, and, yes...

no! She forced away the hungry devil inside her, which reached out toward that perfect idol, that gold-painted forgery. He was not brilliant, not a graduate cum laude, not a successful career engineer. Not anything except a fake. Certainly not worth another minute's thought.

Somehow, the pleasure and hoped-for relaxation of her bath had been spoiled. She was tense again, the coiled tightness reaching her mind from somewhere deep inside her.

She was reliving today's problems all over again—that was it. As soon as she called that cheap fraud to tell him he'd been exposed, then she could forget him completely. Mary Ellen would be proud of her, spotting his little game and spoiling it so quickly.

The students at Central High, though, were a problem she would not be able to solve as easily. The fear-born hostility in their pointed questions was not a charade that could be shrugged aside and forgotten. Even now—hours after the Career Day speech was over—she still felt a cold, hard knot grip her stomach at the memory of those insistent, questioning teenagers crowding around and challenging her to defend her career, her ideals, the whole capitalist system, even....

No, that wasn't true. All they really wanted was a reassurance she couldn't give them that there would be jobs, good jobs, out there in business when they graduated. They were afraid. So many of them had parents laid off, and some who had counted on a college education were scared that their dreams were evaporating in their parents' fears of a new recession. She didn't have any magic answers for their questions, and it tore at her soul to be standing before them, representing a personnel agency and yet unable to promise them jobs.

Closing her smoky topaz eyes, she tried to put aside the taunting faces, so hard and mocking in their fear. There must be a way to help them, her reason argued. She had a reputation for creative, imaginative problem solving, but just now her mind was not functioning at its best; she could not think of a single, brilliant plan to erase the students' worries and give them back their dreams of the future.

It wasn't her lack of ideas that worried her,most however. She felt confident something could be done in time. There were so many possibilities, really. She wondered if the schools had tried job hotlines for teens, or work-study programs with local businesses. She'd check out those ideas right away—if only she had enough time. On a temporary assignment such as this one, time was not something to count on. She would have to work fast.

But first the necessary phone call to the fake Mr. Thompson.

She sat down comfortably beside the telephone and dialed, mentally rehearsing the brief speech she would use to end his little masquerade. The phone rang once, twice, eight times.

Perhaps he hadn't given her a legitimate number, either. Why, he might show up on Thursday morning and create quite a scene when she tried to send him away. She slammed down the receiver in impotent anger.

Thoroughly disgusted, Cary prowled aimlessly around her apartment, clad only in an orange print beach towel. What she needed to fight this restless, unproductive mood was some pampering. She debated calling her sister, but Tuesday was Louise's bowling league, and Cary would feel guilty spoiling that. Good food—a steak, perhaps?

But there were no steaks in the refrigerator, and no sour cream for the mandatory baked potato, either.

Suddenly full of purpose, Cary returned to the bathroom and began to reapply her steam-dampened makeup. A touch of violet eyeshadow, fading out near her arched brow, seemed to enlarge and emphasize her smoky brown eyes, warmed near the center by hints of golden glow. She put a light mauve color on her lips and smiled.

With an even deeper smile she selected an elegant black silk dress and jacket. It was one of her sister's exclusive designs, with delicately embroidered Chinese chrysanthemums and amethyst dragons trailing around the jacket's mandarin collar, down one sleeve and along the same side of the dress. Of all the many exotic and unique outfits Louise had designed for her, this was Cary's favorite. In it she felt like an Oriental princess, a descendant of some magnificent royal dynasty.

She slipped on patent-leather sandals and brushed her glowing black waves to a rich, shimmering fullness. There! Now she looked pampered.

Soon she would be waited on, coddled and treated like a real princess.

At the Holiday Inn's glass-ceilinged Holidome, a pretty young woman ushered her to a small table. Her waiter came immediately. Yes, she mused, the dress was working again. Louise's designs all looked as if they cost a small fortune, and this one especially seemed to carry a sign that told waiters to expect a generous tip from such an expensively garbed lady.

But after "My-name-is-Gene" had left to place her order, Cary's restlessness returned. There weren't many stars visible through the glass-domed ceiling, and no other interesting diners near to watch. She tried to focus on the problem of the kids from Central High, but it was no use. She felt restless. A good long run around the apartment complex before the bath would have been a lot better for her, she decided, than this meal, high in calories and full of self-pitying purpose.

"Are you by any chance alone this evening, Miss Blaine?"

Startled, she turned toward the familiar voice. The pseudo engineer himself! No wonder he hadn't answered his phone. He was still in Topeka! An intense surge of adrenaline stunned her with its sudden force. Good grief, she must be tense to react like this!

He smiled smoothly, and the tension increased. Without giving her an opportunity to reply, he swung into the chair opposite her own and continued, "May I join you, then?"

Cary's eyes were wide with astonishment. Was he *really* that bold?

"I don't think—"

"Please! I really don't know very many people in town, but since I stayed in town to...look around, a dinner out seemed inevitable. I detest eating in public places alone, though, and I'm not enjoying my meal at all." His eyes were bright, glittering behind gray-framed glass. "Please say yes," he concluded on a low, seductively pleading note.

Was this acting again? If so, the man could certainly play the relaxed, gregarious bachelor-on-the-make role perfectly! His puppy eyes positively glowed with erotic magnetism. His arrogance was unbelievable! Should she confront him immediately with her knowledge of his fraud? No, the other way would be much more...satisfying. Umm, what a nasty thought!

"Of course you may join me. We had such a short interview this afternoon, perhaps we can talk some more about your job search." She smiled very sweetly.

"Oh. Of course. Yes, that would be nice," he answerd with only the briefest of hesitations. "I'll just go get my coffee," he added with a frown.

There! His facade of seductive charm had been cracked. For a brief moment, Cary regretted seeing the fiery warmth in his eyes fade so, but then she reminded herself that it, too, was probably an act.

So. Let him worry a bit first. A man as cocky as he was needed to be brought down to earth slowly.

She smiled. Then a little nagging doubt intruded

on her thoughts. What if his act was something more sinister than merely using someone else's credentials to obtain a job. He was so very, very smooth and cagey. What if his purpose was theft, or—sabotage! Would he see her as a threat if she attempted to expose his disguise? Could he be dangerous?

"I assure you I am not in the habit of strangling my dinner companions."

Cary started violently, causing the table to tremble noisily as silverware and glasses tinkled against each other, mimicking her internal agitation.

"What?" she whispered. Then, "What did you say?" she asked more loudly as her courage returned.

"I said that I do not ordinarily strangle my dinner partners. Especially when they are as lovely as you."

He must have been making an ill-timed joke. Of course he couldn't read her mind! She tried to laugh, but the shaky squeak sounded more like a giggle.

"No, I didn't read your mind," he continued, mirth only a twitch of his mouth away. "Look at yourself and tell me how you would read that body language."

Cary realized first that she was clutching her own throat and, second, that her eyes were wide with trepidation. Her heart was thumping wildly, and her other hand was gripping the edge of the table. *Now my imagination is working just fine*, she though bleakly. With a rapid shifting of internal gears, she forced herself to be practical and semirational.

"Excuse me. I've swallowed something...an ice cube...wrong." She winced with mock pain and hurriedly left the table, heading with shaky steps for the ladies' room.

Once inside, she all but collapsed. *That man almost gave me a heart attack*! She leaned in a daze against the mirror, not seeing her own pale reflection but only the smiling face of her tormentor. Would her performance as a choking victim convince him she was not terrified by him?

Minutes later her brain began to function somewhat normally again. She could almost laugh at the foolish fancy her tired imagination had concocted.

It also occurred to her at last that this man was deliberately trying to put her off balance. She'd been constantly on the defensive today during the interview. Now this evening he had appeared out of nowhere and rattled her so badly she had reacted like a teenager at a horror movie. Well, the sages claimed that forewarned was forearmed; she would not need another reminder to be on guard.

She reached into her tiny purse for the mauve lipstick and used a touch of it to give her pale cheeks some healthy color. Forcing both an inner and outer calm, she was determined he would have no clues to think her scared again.

When Cary returned to her table, the enemy had risen gallantly to hold her chair. Undaunted, she led the first attack.

"Why don't you tell me, Mr. Thompson, about your first assignment for Burkham? I always enjoy

hearing about those right-out-of-school adjustments one has to make. They're so indicative of a
person's ability to face a challenge and accept
change, don't you think?'' she asked brightly.

"Absolutely. If you can't move forward from
idealistic expectations to form meaningful goals
within the context of reality, you can't expect to be
successful in any aspect of life." His voice was like
a resonant melody, and his shadowy eyes examined
her closely as he spoke. Too closely. She found her
heart was beating inexplicably faster under his gaze.

"My, what lovely words! But you haven't answered my question."

"I will, Miss Blaine. May I call you Caroline? I
was merely agreeing with your perceptive philo-
sophy. And marveling at your quick recovery from
such a frightening...accident." His smooth voice
slid along quickly. "But, yes, of course I had my
share of adjustments to make when I graduated,
like everyone else. I guess the hardest thing for me
to take at first was that my ideas were subject to
other people's constant revisions. My ego was badly
bruised for a while."

"Not seriously, I'm sure," returned Cary, becoming annoyed by his steady, measuring look and
artificial conversation. "But what exactly—"

"No, not seriously. I don't think any of us is ever
truly hurt by temporary setbacks if we are doing
something we really believe in. Tell me something,
Caroline. Do you believe in what you're doing or is
it just...the easiest way to make a lot of money?"

"I'm afraid I don't understand," she said. His

sudden question puzzled and troubled her. What did he mean by "a lot of money"?

"What I really intended to say," he went on, "was that I know you traded an interest in engineering for the business world while you were still in college. You mentioned that decision this morning with a wistful look on your face. Was it the right decision? Are you happy with what you're doing now?" He was leaning forward as he spoke, looking earnestly into her eyes again.

"Yes. I love what I do. Sometimes it's quite frustrating work. Sometimes individuals make the job harder than it has to be," she added pointedly. "But, in general, the rewards are sufficient. And I've been very lucky and successful."

"I can see that," he commented dryly, his eyes now traveling over her unique dress. "You must get a hefty. . . commission from your client corporations. What is Omega Aircraft paying you for each of us—or is that a secret?"

Her eyes flashed, and her teeth clamped down on the instinctive, angry reply that jumped to her mind.

"I am paid by Willingham consultants, Mr. Thompson! I receive a commission on actual placements, but I resent the innuendo in your question." *I resent your questioning me at all*! Wasn't *she* supposed to be questioning *him*? She took a deep breath and continued, "Applicants are not sold to the highest bidder, Mr. Thompson. I do my best to provide each of our client companies with the specially skilled people they need to succeed. But I make sure the applicants are happy, too."

"I'll bet you do."

"*I beg your pardon?*"

"Forget it. I was just speculating how far someone in your position would be willing to go to satisfy a job-seeker or a corporation. For instance, what would you be able to offer me if I were to tell you that I was rather hard-up right now?"

Cary felt a hot rush of anger—and something that was far from anger—flood her face with crimson. She had a fleeting vision of David Thompson, his junior-executive suit gone, bending over her with a hungry look in his eye. *How dared he*, she asked herself even as her body's heat continued to rise. Her hand moved a barely perceptible inch toward her opponent's face, but she checked the motion as she remembered their very public location.

This verbal war had gone too far. She must get rid of him for good. She did not want him on that Thursday flight!

"Mr. Thompson. I'm really very sorry, but I've changed my mind about dining with you. And I don't believe you should bother to show up at the airport on Thursday, either. I have decided that you are not really the type of professional that Omega has asked me to find for them."

He smiled—no, smirked!

"Was it something I said?" He showed no intention of leaving the table.

"I will not sit here listening to implications that I

conduct my business in the bedroom. Now please leave!''

"Bedroom? Did I ...." He appeared genuinely puzzled.

Suddenly his expression cleared, and he looked at Cary with a softer light in his eyes. A faint color in his cheeks might have been embarrassment.

"May I apologize, Caroline? I wasn't thinking about sexual satisfaction. But it was rude of me...."

Cary did not hear his next words. Not sex? Then what had he meant by—oh, what had he said, anyway? Something about ....

"Can we do that, Caroline?"

"What . . . what did you say?"

"I said I was sorry for unintentionally insulting you. I would like to just sit here with you and enjoy my meal and not talk anymore about business. Yours or mine. Is that all right with you? You haven't even touched your steak."

Cary looked down at her plate. When had the waiter brought it? How did this man keep her so off balance? Sudden lethargy hit her, and she was conscious of a headache beginning to form behind her eyes.

"I'm not very hungry, after all." She sighed. Her strategies to give the impostor a difficult time were not going well at all.

"Well, I intend to finish this delicious chicken. I would really like you to stay, even if you don't eat. I'm very sorry you misunderstood my remarks. But I'm sure I can convince you I belong on that flight, if you'll just give me a chance." He paused and showed her again his charming, too-perfect smile.

She needed nothing more to remind her that everything about this man was phony.

"No, I won't be changing my mind," she said quietly.

"Why, Caroline?"

"Mr. Whoever-you-are," she answered with a flat, resigned voice. "I know you're not David Thompson. I've already decided to cancel your interview in Wichita. Now please excuse me; I'm tired of this little game we're playing, and I think I'll just go home." She bent to retrieve her purse.

Above her, David whistled. "I knew you were one smart lady, Caroline Blaine, but...."

In dull surprise Cary turned her head and watched as the bogus engineer threw back his head and laughed. It was an easy, infectious laugh. Not an intimidating or sadistic laugh that would have sparked her fear, but a relaxed expression of good humor and pleasure. The remnants of anxiety behind her tension disappeared at the sound. He seemed to be enjoying the exposure—as if it were some private joke.

With a flourish, he rose from his chair and made a sweeping bow toward Cary. He extended his hand and declaimed with stagelike exaggeration, "May I present myself? Hunter V. Pierce, investigative reporter *extraordinaire*, with KMKX-TV in Kansas City, at your service, Mademoiselle Blaine."

Bewildered and feeling foolish as she caught the interested looks of nearby diners, Cary reached to take his outstretched hand, but received instead an elegant, light kiss on her fingertips. It was as soft as the caress of a butterfly bringing pollen and promises of new life. Above his lips, those warm eyes glowed again with an intensity she did not understand.

"Oh!"

"And now I'll tell you all about the *real* David Thompson and why I've been impersonating him," he whispered sotto voce. "You see, I'm a spy!"

"A spy?" This was outrageous—and uncomfortably close to her earlier speculation! But for the first time, the man's voice and carriage rang true. This time he was being sincere, she was certain. She looked at him cautiously. What kind of game was this television reporter playing? And what did he want with her?

Hunter laughed again. "Here, let me prove my story to you. I guarantee that I am who I claim to be—this time." He took out a wallet and withdrew several cards.

"My press card, my driver's license, and my Social Security card. Do you want to see anything else?"

"N-no. I believe you really are Hunter Pierce. At least my brain tells me I probably ought to believe you. But a spy!"

His expression grew serious. "Yes, I'm afraid so. But before I tell you why and how, I must ask you one question, and you must answer it truthfully."

"I'm rarely untruthful, Mr. Pierce."

"I'm beginning to realize that, Caroline. But this

question is very important to me. And it may be even more important to you.''

''Well, ask!''

Still he hesitated. Cary wondered if he was purposefully trying to heighten the drama of the moment.

With a gesture of annoyance, he pulled off his glasses, revealing black brows knit in worry. He looked at Cary, his deep, earnest eyes searching hers. ''What exactly did Omega Aircraft Corporation hire you to do for them?''

Cary had not realized that she was holding her breath, that she was afraid of his ''important'' question, afraid, too, of the intense emotion in his eyes. She was still irrationally leery, uncertain of this man's purpose. But what an innocuous question!

''I can't see why a reporter would want to know, but there is no reason why I can't tell you the more obvious aspects of our deal. Omega has been losing money—even *Fortune* magazine has reported that fact. They need some fresh ideas, new blood. Willingham has been hired to find some new engineers for them. That's about all there is.''

''And a new head of research, too?''

''Well, that part of the job has already been completed. How did you know about it?''

''In a minute. Are there any other facets of this recruiting job that you haven't told me about? I warned you that you must be completely truthful.''

''I *am* being truthful. I can't tell you more without violating our client's confidence. Have you ever heard of industrial espionage?''

"Yes, I have," he answered grimly. "That's what this conversation is all about. One company stealing secrets from competing companies."

Cary felt her stomach tighten in horror. "That's a very serious charge, Mr. Pierce. Who are you accusing of such theft? Me?"

"Wait. Please call me Hunter. It's my real name, and I'm sort of used to it. I'm tired of being someone else—and I am no longer an interviewee talking to a consultant, am I?"

"No, Hunter. You most definitely are not an interviewee anymore." She was equally grim. Mary Ellen would blow her stack, and her ulcers would literally explode. A *television* reporter with some off-the-wall story of spies!

"There is a rumor, Caroline, that Willingham is mixed up in a very nasty piece of industrial espionage. Now, before you get started denying any and everything, let me say that I'm now convinced you did not know about the more crooked aspects of the deal. I think you believed you were screening legitimate candidates in good faith."

His large hand suddenly was resting on her clenched fist, its heat searing her cold hand. She jerked her hand away and glared at him. "That's just exactly what I—"

"Let me finish. The story goes that Omega is nearly bankrupt. In order to bail out they need something new, something better than anyone else has. And they need to get it on the market first and fast. The story goes further that they are buying the services of top design engineers and the plans for any new designs that those engineers had been working on for their former employers.''

''Oh, no!''

''And, my dear innocent consultant, the story concludes that all of the potential defectors are being carefully selected and groomed by Will-ingham. In fact, the new head of research for Omega was found by your firm and offered special incentives to switch his allegiance, and his current invention project, to Omega. Is that true?''

''That's not fair! There are so many half truths in what you've said that I can't deny them completely. But what you've concluded is all wrong!'' She was drawing away, her spine pressed against the chair. If she could have escaped she would have. But she couldn't run away; she had to hear everything.

''Okay. You tell me how the story goes.'' He, too, leaned back but it was not retreat. It was a challenge.

''Well, *of course* we searched for the new re-search director. So did a half dozen other head-hunter firms. Mary Ellen Hughes, our regional manager, found him. He's a brilliant but shy Ph.D. in physics, looking for demanding new work. He felt stifled at his old job.''

''She found him at Burkham Air Labs?''

''Yes. But it was up to Omega to woo him away. We just set up the negotiations. Willingham didn't offer the man anything. We couldn't!''

''Then it's entirely Omega who's responsible for the financial ruin faced by Burkham now. Your new research man stole the plan for an important project when he moved over to his new job—a project that would have put Burkham out in front in the industry.''

"Then call the police! But quit calling him *my* research man.''

"I'm sorry, Caroline. I didn't mean to imply I still think you had anything to do with this. Believe me, I know you didn't.'' He leaned closer and she caught again the fresh scent of his after-shave. Cool—like the man.

"And this affair is not so simple that a phone call to the police would work. Racine didn't steal pieces of paper and leave his fingerprints behind. He stole ideas, and that's a lot harder to prove. But now we have a report that Omega is offering other young engineers a chance to double their salaries by actually stealing—''

"No! You must be wrong! Mary Ellen and our senior partners checked out the Omega business thoroughly. Mary Ellen, of all people, would have been cautious about approving their methods, their financial position. The company's been burned once, and—this just couldn't happen. You don't understand the headhunting business, and you're seeing pirates and criminals everywhere, just to make up a sensational story for your television program.'' She was almost out of breath with her urgent speech. She was leaning forward now, across the table. Her face reflected her troubled spirit. Was he capable of understanding what she said?

"Listen to me, Hunter. Things like this just can't happen. No consulting firm would ever knowingly cooperate in such a scheme, even if the corporation offered outrageous premiums. I assure you we—I— have not been asked to do anything unethical. And it would be almost impossible for Omega to attempt what you describe without our becoming aware of it. What about the honest applicant who is offered such a bribe? Wouldn't he or she come back to us and report the matter?''

''No. She was too scared.'' His voice mirrored the contempt on his face. Contempt for the timid applicant or for Cary?

''Who was?''

''Jeannie Whitaker. You sent her down to Omega two weeks ago. Three days later they telephoned her with their 'bribe' as you call it. Jeannie was afraid someone might think she had already told them more than she should about her projects. She's young and sensitive about her prospects, and after she realized what the job at Omega entailed she got scared. She didn't want to jeopardize her career at Burkham by admitting she'd gone looking for another job.

''But she did confide in her boyfriend, David Thompson. He had already received your firm's letter inviting him to Topeka to discuss his career, and he decided to accept your invitation. He and I sail together in the summer, and we got to talking about the whole messy deal last weekend. I persuaded him that I should go in his place and expose the entire scheme without actually involving him or Jeannie.''

''How noble.''

''You don't believe me?''

"I believe you believe this story. But it can't be true," she concluded hopelessly. How could she convince him? He had already made up his mind.

"Would you be willing to help me prove what you say?"

"Me? How?"

"Will you help me uncover the truth about these rumors? Let me continue with my masquerade until I know for certain if Omega is corrupt. We think they got a little nervous after Jeannie refused their offer, and they may have stopped making their bribes before hiring people. I may have to actually take a job as an engineer at Omega in order to expose them. Help me, Caroline. Please."

"Does it matter so much to you?"

"Yes, it does." His hand again covered her own, but this time she did not try to pull away. She wanted comfort, even if it was only the steady warmth of a stranger's hand. She was upset and overtired. Neither her brain nor her emotions were functioning properly.

"I . . . I don't know. I need time to think."

"All right. Why don't I take you home, and you can think about it until tomorrow?"

Numbly, Cary followed him out to the parking lot where he paused beside a racy little Audi.

"Let me drive you home," he said, putting his hand on her arm protectively. "You looked bushed."

"My car. . . ."

"You can take a cab over here to pick it up in the morning, can't you? Really, you shouldn't drive when you're this tired."

"All right," she sighed, losing.

All consideration for the Cutlass and tomorrow's inconvenience drifted away. Her thoughts were a confused whirl of "what ifs" centering around her participation in an undercover investigation of her own client. She asked herself two million questions but had no answers ready. The tension and bewildering accusations she had faced this evening had taken their toll, leaving her body exhausted and her mind almost paralyzed.

During the ride to her apartment, Hunter asked very ordinary questions about directions and the sights. He commented briefly on the weather. She responded when necessary, longing for this night to be over, yet somehow vaguely excited by the stranger beside her and his tale of secret immoral dealings.

The small Audi was almost intimate. In the dark, with her eyes closed against the world, Cary could sense the warmth of the male body next to hers. As he reached down to shift gears, his hand would brush against her silk-skirted thigh. His melodic voice spoke, he paused, then resumed, using words that might have been ordinary if anyone else had uttered them.

Hunter Pierce had turned her very prosaic world into a fantasy tonight. Drowsily, Cary wondered if he would also turn into a prince.

At her door, she hesitated before turning the key. Hunter had laid his hand on her arm, insistently.

"You're a very beautiful woman, Caroline Blaine. And a very intelligent one. Will you think objectively about what I've said? Will you look at the facts and not just at your loyalties?''

He was so near. He was not wearing his glasses, and she could see his eyes. They looked black in the evening darkness. She sensed he would come inside if she invited him. But what would that prove? Only that she was a fool, and he needed her help most desperately.

"I promise to think about it. Good night.''

"Good night, Caroline.''

His soft words whispered to a hunger somewhere low in her abdomen.

He turned as if to go. Foolishly, confused by the signals she was receiving from her body, Cary stood still a moment too long, watching as he turned. Watching as he halted and came back to her, slowly, searching her eyes in the darkness.

She suddenly knew he would kiss her if she didn't move. One part of her, the purely physical part, wanted to reach out for that kiss. But another part wondered if he was capable of sensing her desire and using it—using it to gain her full cooperation in his dubious scheme. She warred with herself. But her feet were firmly rooted to the balcony floor, in the physical world, and her eyes were soon held fast by his questioning look.

Then his lips brushed hers. They were soft, warm and electric. Twice they touched her. And then his arms swept around her, pulling her up into the midnight blackness of hunger. She was shaken to her very core by the intensity of the need that surged through her.

"Good night again, Caroline," he whispered.

"Cary," she corrected.

"Good night Cary," he said softly, smiling. "Until tomorrow."

She entered the even deeper darkness of her apartment and closed the door. Her whole body felt relaxed. She sank onto the couch and stared at the inky rectangles of her window.

Should she. . . could she afford to get emotionally involved with Hunter Pierce? Her power of reason seemed to be letting her down. Had her body just made a decision for her?

She pushed away the questions revolving like carousel horses in her mind, but they kept returning around the circle to torment her. Again and again the query formed, "Why?"

Why is my life suddenly so complicated?

CHAPTER THREE

CARY HAD HAD THREE MAJOR BATTLES with Hunter by seven o'clock the next morning. And since the real person was not there to defend himself, she detailed Mary Ellen's high performance standards, then accused the TV newsman and his entire industry of being sensationalists. Even so, she was no more confident of winning an *actual* argument with Hunter when she had finished.

She prided herself on being able to judge sincerity and honesty. After all, she *had* seen right through Hunter's little impersonation. But unfortunately the new Hunter—the real one—seemed genuinely concerned and earnest. The doubts he had put in her mind at dinner had grown during the night until she, too, began to see as suspicious many previously unremarkable dealings with Henry Crandon at Omega.

But in the clear light of day she refused to examine the strange magnetism she had sensed was charging the air between herself and the reporter. That had been last night, and she had been tired. Today was a new day, and now she could see the phenomenon was just a physical attraction.

In the early dawn, a taxi took her back to the

Holidome for her car. While she sat in the impersonal quiet of the cab, with nothing to do but stare
at the morning traffic, she reflected on her options.

Always sensitive to others' pain, Cary knew she
could not go to Mary Ellen and tell her that someone had accused the woman and her newest big
client of unethical conduct. Right after the brutally
cruel ending of an ill-fated romance, her supervisor
had been hurt again, both personally and profes-
sionally, by the shady maneuverings of a completely
unethical client—American Paper. Cary believed
that fiasco, following so closely on the heels of a
broken affair, had probably started the ulcers that
were now out of control. No, since nothing had
been proved yet, relaying mere suspicions would be
cruel.

Yet she could not deny that Hunter's allegations
deserved to be checked out.

When Cary reached her office, she would call the
real David Thompson and perhaps even Jeannie
Whitaker. If they confirmed the reporter's story,
then she would probably have to obtain approval
for Hunter to continue his investigation.

Unfortunately, the two Burkham engineers completely corroborated Hunter's tale. Both were filled
with admiration for the reporter's determination to
bring Omega to justice. Now Cary had to decide
who in the Willingham organization must be told—
and how to tell them.

The most logical thing to do, in Mary Ellen's continued absence, was to approach the next man up
the totem pole, the senior partner responsible for

the entire Midwest region. But Dennis Forsythe had worked closely with Cary in St. Louis since her supervisor's hospitalization, and Cary hated to put such an outlandish proposition before the very self-contained, conservative man. She underestimated, however, the older man's outrage.

"Willingham must be completely vindicated, Miss Blaine." His voice fairly blazed with fury over the phone.

"Yes, I agree," Cary answered.

"Do you think this reporter can carry off the investigation? Would you be willing to assume responsibility for him?"

Cary felt uneasy, but she answered firmly, "Yes." She couldn't very well propose to have Willingham sponsor Hunter's activities and then admit she didn't fully trust him. Besides, it wasn't his talents as an investigator that she had qualms about.

"And what will he do with the evidence when he gets it—assuming Omega is indeed guilty of espionage?"

"I...I don't know for certain, Mr. Forsythe. I would imagine he'll want to put it on the air and expose Omega as publicly as possible."

"What will he say about Willingham? You know these television reporters have a tendency to exaggerate, to sensationalize everything. We can't have any of that!"

"No, of course not, Mr. Forsythe. But what can he say? We assisted in the investigation, that's all." She hesitated. Here were her own fears brought out into the open, magnified by the worried voice of management.

"He can't involve us," she said, trying to sound as if she believed her own words. "We didn't have anything to do with the buying of secrets, and he knows it."

Cary heard a deep sigh, and the knot in her stomach tightened.

"Very well, Miss Blaine. I'm forced to trust your judgment. But it's your responsibility to keep our name as far out of this as possible. I want you to keep a tight rein on this reporter's activities—make him give you periodic progress reports."

"Yes, Mr. Forsythe, I understand. Should I leave some kind of report on all this for Miss Hughes— when she gets back?" She would really prefer to share this burden with practical, levelheaded Mary Ellen.

"No, no. Let's just keep this between us for now."

There was a pause. When he spoke again, David Forsythe's voice sounded less formal, more personal than Cary had ever heard.

"You're a very remarkably sensible young woman, Miss Blaine. So far, you've kept your head in this outrageous business. I'm sure you'll be able to see it through with a minimum of trouble for Willingham. But if you need me, just call."

"Thank you. I will." Cary put down the receiver, wondering just how much "responsibility" she had actually agreed to assume.

She certainly hoped Hunter could act well enough

to carry off the impersonation of an engineer for Omega's personnel manager. If Henry Crandon really was buying secrets, his guilty conscience would probably make him suspicious of everyone who walked into his office.

But of course creating a professional identity for a mass audience was Hunter's forte, just as screening and evaluating people was hers. She congratulated herself again on having been able to see through his masquerade. She had even spotted—belatedly—his acting when he'd pretended an interest in her at her apartment door last night. She sighed, thinking of his midnight eyes, so full of feigned concern for her.

At eleven-thirty, she was thinking of Hunter's eyes again. She was wording a cable to Omega, giving them the roster of applicants who would be coming down on Thursday. Would Henry Crandon read sincerity in those warm, bedroom eyes—or would he spot the charade immediately?

Her intercom buzzed."

"Yes, Marian?"

"Mr. Thompson is here for your luncheon engagement."

"Mr. Thompson!" Cary exclaimed, feeling her abdomen fill with wild butterflies. "Send him in, please," she said calmly.

The door to her office opened, and simultaneously, Hunter's liquid honey voice began speaking.

"Now I know that we didn't have a date. But your calendar was empty and Marian...."

"Well, we do have a date now!" she said matter-of-factly, moving toward the door. She slipped around him and walked out of the office, hearing him follow behind.

Cary led the way to her Cutlass, unlocking the passenger door for him. After only a moment's puzzled frown, Hunter had begun grinning with pleasure. He took his seat silently, turning his obnoxiously beautiful smile on her as she started the motor.

"Before you get too sure of yourself, Hunter, there are a few things we need to get straight. I'm willing to cooperate with you—to an extent. But there are conditions to my agreement."

Hunter continued to flaunt his dazzling smile.

"I have confirmed your story with David Thompson and Jeannie Whitaker. I must reluctantly agree that there appear to be some grounds for suspicion. But I am not convinced there isn't some other explanation, and I insist that not a word of these rumors be mentioned on your program until you have documented proof."

"Agreed."

She glanced briefly at him in surprise. "I also insist that you keep me informed of everything you do and say at Omega when I'm not around. And you have to guarantee to be fair to Willingham when you put together your report."

"Also agreed."

Cary couldn't think of anything else to say. She had rehearsed several persuasive arguments in her mind only to find, now, that they were unnecessary. Perhaps this situation would not be so difficult, after all. Hunter had her cooperation now, and there would be no more need for him to pretend a romantic interest in her. She could keep a very tight control on him and not allow him to go overboard in his enthusiasm for what might turn out to be a nonexistent story.

"You know, you are really very beautiful when you're insistent."

Cary outwardly ignored his remark, her chin firmly pointed ahead. But it had set her stomach to spawning butterflies again at a frightening pace. He was still flirting, even though she'd agreed to work with him! Her hands turned suddenly clammy at the realization.

She couldn't let herself be attracted to a reporter, a public image who probably didn't even have a private life. As far as she knew, reporters were inordinately concerned about their careers, their appearance and the rest of the world—in that order. Anyone who craved to be the center of attention every day for thousands of people obviously must have a strong desire for adulation. Well, she wasn't about to join the adoring throng around Hunter Pierce!

Nevertheless, her body was behaving traitorously, and she would have to double her guard. Before it was too late!

At the sandwich shop, Cary guided Hunter to a table in the middle of the crowded room. It would be impossible for him to flirt here, and it was so noisy that no one could overhear a syllable as they discussed their plans for sending him to Wichita. But Hunter chose to misunderstand.

"Very cosy and comfortable. We can be as personal as we like, and no one will notice."

"I have no intention of being 'personal,' Mr. Pierce."

"Oh, heck. Are we back to being formal again, Cary? This really isn't the place for it, you know."

Cary buried herself behind a menu.

"I dare you to smile. Double dare!"

In spite of herself, Cary found herself grinning.

"Ah, that's better. We really don't have any more business to talk about, do we? I'm going to be a good boy and do whatever you say tomorrow. I promise not to get either one of us in trouble. David's been coaching me for a week on engineering terms. So what's left to discuss?"

"Nothing, I guess. I had planned on arguing with you for hours about being reasonable," she admitted.

"You thought I would be...unreasonable? No man in his right mind would even consider refusing to go along with you, Cary. You're the boss. You know much more than I about this aircraft business. Of course we'll do it your way." He paused long enough to give his order to the waitress. "You don't believe me, do you?"

"You're a television reporter," she said, as if that fully explained everything. "You do exposés of big crime. I don't think you'd care very much who got hurt if this little story turned out to be trumped-up gossip and nothing more."

"So. You don't think I'd care." He had returned again to the professional smile that removed him light years from her. "And you thought *I* was willing to believe rumors without evidence! Well, you're pretty quick to jump to conclusions yourself, aren't you?" He had folded his long, strong arms across his chest and was watching her with the stern cold glare of a parent reprimanding a naughty child. His voice was chilly, and Cary shivered in its coolness.

"You've become judge and jury together and passed sentence already," he continued. "Haven't you? Just what makes you think I wouldn't care about innocent people who were hurt by my actions?"

Cary felt her cheeks begin to burn, in sharp contrast to the ice that pierced her heart. This was all wrong! She hadn't meant to insult him so cruelly, just put him off. Now he was flinging her barbs back at her, and they stung far worse than she could have imagined.

"I'm sorry," she offered.

But he said nothing more until the waitress brought their sandwiches. Cary's guilt stewed in the silence. She hadn't given him the benefit of the doubt, it was true. She had only made a natural assumption, however; surely he was used to that. She was even willing to concede she might be wrong. But he was making her apology difficult.

"Haven't you ever been wrong?" she asked irritably.

"Not yet. That may sound egotistical, but I assure you it wasn't meant to be. I do my job thoroughly, and I have a manager and staff who pass judgment on everything I submit."

"Oh."

"They wholeheartedly approved this assignment."

"Oh."

She burned inside with shame at her doubt and narrowminded words. He would never let her forget it, either. Lunch was going to be very uncomfortable.

"Cary, look at me."

She looked up at his face, avoiding his mesmerizing eyes.

"I wanted to take you to lunch today because I like you and want to know you better. Truce?"

She looked doubtingly into his eyes and that was her second mistake of the day. For those luminous, deep, mysterious eyes were not filled with cold scorn but with something much hotter. His gaze moved from her parted lips to her long, arching neck, to her breasts hidden beneath the starched prudery of an oxford-cloth shirt. She knew he saw her skin and not the fabric. Knew it as surely as she knew her own heart had begun to skip and race in a mad rush that colored her cheeks and made those hidden breasts swell against the bonds of cloth and propriety.

"If we had met at a party or a concert, it would have been the same for me, Cary. You're a beautiful, clever woman, and something inside of me has been doing weird little flip-flops since last night. You're also a courageous woman, willing to risk her career to pursue the truth."

She lowered her eyes quickly. Suddenly he'd gone

back to his old game! He was making it so hard to remain impersonal, detached. How could they possibly manage to work together, if he continued like this?

When he paused, his eyes continued their roving—over her rich black curls, her fair complexion and dark topaz eyes. His voice dropped to a low murmur, increasing the intimacy of the moment. "We're going to be working so close together, that I wonder if. . . ." His voice trailed away.

"If?"

"I wonder if you can guess just how close we will need to be. We're not working on an ordinary business deal here, you know. I can't let you keep your usual professional distance from what I'm doing."

"So what are you trying to suggest?" she asked, attempting sarcasm. "That we live together or something while you infiltrate Omega's operation?" That seemed to be exactly what his look implied, and Cary shook inside as if she was afraid of his answer. She hadn't succeeded in getting him to abandon his flirtation, and now she was losing control of her responses. What if he . . . .

"No. Although I kind of like that idea. I may come back to it later. No, I only meant that in an investigation like this, we each have a lot to lose. I'm totally dependent on you," he said, reaching for her hand, "for my cover—for my success. And you have to take my word that I won't jeopardize your company's reputation. That's a lot of trusting, Cary. Can we do it? Can we work. . . together?"

"Y-yes." She was confused. He was putting his

heart and his job together in such a misleading, bewildering way. And if Cary had learned to read his sincerity level correctly, something about that last little speech was false—or perhaps forced.

Cary finished her sandwich platter amid a whirl of jumbled speculations. Had she misread the message in his eyes? So much depended on establishing a high degree of trust between them, but they just had to keep their emotions out of this. There was too much at stake for. . . .

"Dessert?"

"Oh, no. I'm too full."

"Then I'll order only one banana split, and we can share it," he announced.

When the enormous confection arrived with one spoon, Cary's bewildered thoughts were given another confusing puzzle piece to ponder. With his gaze locked tight to her own, Hunter fed her the ice cream and topping as though he offered ambrosia that might satisfy another hunger. Every bite became a shared experience.

"More?" he asked, drawing out the simple word.

"Mmm," she answered, her mouth full of sweet cream.

So he took the next spoonful, licking it slowly from the silver. She could almost taste the cold vanilla on his tongue, the bittersweet chocolate flavor that he wiped from her cheek and then licked from his finger. Her mind swam with a heady intoxication that had nothing to do with liquor.

"Enough?" he asked, finally

"Yes," she said. *No!* she thought.

He paid for their meal and then walked with her to the Cutlass. "May I drive?"

She gave him the keys wordlessly. Her mind was numbly remembering something he had said earlier, wondering, *what did he mean about doing flip-flops inside? What is he doing to my head? Why?* But she knew instinctively it would be impossible to approach those questions directly. Perhaps she would not want to know the answers because then there would be something concrete she would have to face. Her thoughts skittered around nervously.

"Where are we going? This isn't the way to my office."

"We deserve a break, don't you think? I hear you have a beautiful lake out in this direction."

"Yes," she answered. "Lake Shawnee. You've never seen it?"

"No. I was hoping you'd show it to me today." He turned his eyes from the road to smile at her.

"Well. . .just a quick look, then." She told herself that she deserved some time off, considering the uncountable extra hours she had given Willingham in the past. And she needed more data to try to figure out who this Hunter Pierce really was inside.

At the lake, she led the way to a small pagodalike structure on a promontory overlooking the water. The enormous oak and elm trees crowding around gave them protection from the chill autumn wind.

Uncertain of Hunter's motives for wanting to come here, Cary remained silent, waiting for him to make the first move.

"You really don't trust me, do you?"

Now, how could she answer that? How could she say, *No, I began by not trusting you, and now I even have doubts about myself. You've robbed me of something, Hunter Pierce, and I'm not even certain what it is I've lost.*

"I need your trust, Cary. I want you to believe in me—and not just for the sake of my project with you. What would it take to win you?"

To win me? Please, please don't ask! She stood still, facing out toward the water.

Under the shadowy roof of the shelter, the world seemed to come to a gentle stop. The sunlight made a single glittering brightness of the myriad waves in the water, and the sighing leaves around them ceased whispering while Hunter talked.

"I want you to know why," he said. "Why this investigation—my career— is important to me." He pulled at her shoulder and turned her to face him. "Maybe that will convince you my motives are honest and sincere."

He told her about a childhood that had been happy until his father's business partner embezzled $40,000 from the corporate account and fled to Mexico. About the friends who came to tell his family they had "seen it coming," or had known of other petty crimes the man had committed elsewhere.

"My father had been blinded by the charming personality and shrewd business expertise of a man he trusted too far. But the real crime against him was the silence of all his 'friends.'

"Six years later an old lady who lived next door

told my mother all about the fabulous amount of money she and a stranger had found on the bus. The man had offered to invest the windfall for her, along with several thousand she had saved from her husband's insurance. Mother suspected the whole thing was a fraud, but she didn't think it was 'her place' to say anything. So the old lady lost her fortune.

"Well, I've made it my place to speak out. To warn the old ladies and gullible businessmen about the greedy people, about the desperate men and women who don't care about rules, and about the lawless ones who believe they're entitled to anything they can take. Sometimes, people listen." He shaded his eyes against the glare and looked out over the shining lake.

"So you're like an unofficial policeman or something, out to catch the bad guys in the black hats?"

"Don't mock me, Cary."

She wanted to cry out, *but I feel safer when I laugh at you!* Instead she closed her eyes against a possible future pain. What was she afraid she would feel if there were no more doubts, no more questioning of motives?

Abruptly, he changed the subject. His voice was flat. "Do you want to leave now?"

Cary was torn between wanting to flee the temptation of his nearness and a swelling longing for the sparkle of this moment to last forever.

She took a deep breath. "No. I found my seventh applicant this morning. I was just going to help one of the other consultants with a client survey. But he can handle it alone."

"Then you'll stay here...with me...for a while?"

Oh, it was impossible to make the next logical move to utter that simple word, yes! But he seemed to understand her wordless response, for he made no move to leave.

The silence between them was a palpable thing, connecting them together in its sweetness, yet separating them. Did he understand that her staying meant she accepted what he had told her? Was he aware that the sunlight that caught on his glasses made his eyes unreadable, invisible?

Cary was aware, as if from some point of view outside herself, that dry leaves and bits of broken twigs had fastened themselves to her herringbone wool slacks and jacket. She saw her hand lying relaxed on the fullness of her hip. She felt her body yearn toward his, with an almost overpowering ache for his touch. But she did not move. Her hand lay still.

She knew what her body craved. But should she let herself be drawn even a tiny bit close to this astonishingly handsome and provocative man, this reporter—at whose side she was now committed to lie and deceive? What did *he* really expect from her?

SHE WOKE LATER when a falling leaf kissed her cheek on its way to earth. Her hand had fallen from her hip to rest against the ground, and her head had slipped back into a soft pile of crumpled leaves.

"Awake at last, beautiful?"

"Um hmm. I...didn't mean to fall asleep."

He was sitting beside her, one leg pressed against her shoulder. Or had her shoulder moved to lie comfortably against his lean, long leg?

She sat up and began picking at the pieces of leaf in her hair.

"I didn't mind in the least. Here. Let me." Hunter moved around behind her and began to slide the dry bits out of her curls.

The back of her neck tingled when he touched her, sending shivers down her spine. "Thank you," she managed breathlessly.

"Will you return the confidence, Cary? Will you tell me about yourself and your dreams—why you abandoned engineering? I want to know all there is to know about you."

There was magic on the county lake that day. Nothing else could have explained Cary's sudden, deep daytime sleep. No one but a sorcerer could have stolen her away from her work, with no regrets, no worries. And nothing but a spell could have made his request seem like a caress.

Lazy gray clouds were beginning to fill the autumn sky, turning the lake into a shimmering silver basin. She stared at the patterns of dark and light on the water and remembered all that he had said about himself. He had become a crusader. What had she become?

Her words spilled out into the waning sunshine. She told him how she had loved physics and math, but had eventually become bored by the restrictions of her curriculum. She described worrying for two long semesters whether she really wanted a career in science. She enjoyed accounting and literature, but there was no time to indulge those whims. She wasn't sure she wanted to be tied to just one field for the rest of her life. And then she had gone to the school's placement office and found her vocation. The counselor there had spoken knowledgeably about many, many different careers.

"I asked her how she knew so much about them all. She told me she studied them constantly, to keep up with what was happening in every field she could. I knew at once that was what I wanted—to keep on learning new things for the rest of my life.

"And I could help other people, too. It wouldn't be just a selfishly ego-rewarding job." She had almost run out of words. "Sometimes, though, I just can't seem to help at all."

"Can't?" He went straight for her hesitation, her failure.

"I'm an executive recruiter. I look for executives and for top-level professionals. It's been years since I worked the regular placement jobs, and I didn't really realize until yesterday how hard it is for ordinary people to find work today."

"What happened yesterday, besides me?" His voice caressed her mind soothingly.

Though there were no longer any leaves in her hair, his hands continued to stroke through the mass of curling tresses. No longer were there tingles along her neck from his touch. Now there was a fire wherever his fingers brushed against her skin. It was becoming harder to concentrate.

"Yesterday I gave up on a very bright college

graduate—a forestry major. I couldn't find anything for him, anything at all."

"Is that it? One person without a job?" He said it lightly, as if he knew that was not what troubled her most deeply.

Cary told him about the students at the high school and about having had no answers for their questions.

The words just seemed to tumble out on their own, releasing some of her pent-up frustration into the cloud-covered day. At times she seemed to forget the presence of the man beside her. At last, with a sigh, she lay still and spent on the leaf-strewn floor of the pagoda.

With a gentle movement, Hunter leaned across and brushed a soft kiss across her cheek.

She looked up with a weary smile. There'd been no hint of danger in his touch, no passion she need fear in her response.

"What was that for?"

"For caring."

His words haunted her during the elegant dinner they shared back at the Holidome. For the time being, he was staying there at the Holiday Inn as David Thompson. After tomorrow, Thursday, he would return to Kansas City and his life as Hunter Pierce, reporter.

Wistfully, she searched his face as they ate, looking for evidence of that tender compassion he had shown earlier. But it was as if he was wearing another mask, a falsely gay one that was neither sincere nor sensitive. Light, darting glances around the room betrayed that he was overly conscious of the presence of other diners. Did he think they recognized him? Did he want them to?

A more serious question tugged at her conscience. Had she made a mistake believing in him?

At her apartment, Hunter asked quietly if he might come in for a drink. Cary agreed without enthusiasm when he suggested that he might need some advice about how to act during the Omega interviews tomorrow.

"Just play the part of the rising junior executive," she recommended wearily, "You do it very well."

"Do I?" he asked brightly.

"Yes, you play your parts well, Hunter. Brandy?" she asked, moving off toward her tiny kitchen.

"Please. But you saw through me, didn't you? Aren't you worried that someone at Omega might, too?"

"No. Their management won't be looking too closely at little mannerisms. If you can fool them with your pseudo-engineer's jargon, you'll be all right. As for Henry Crandon...."

"He's not as smart as you. Right?"

Cary didn't reply to that. If all Hunter wanted was reassurance, he could have probed for it earlier. Right now, she was beginning to wish she hadn't agreed to fix him a drink.

But as she was pouring the liquor into glasses, he stole behind her and slipped his arms around her waist. Off guard, she set the decanter of Courvoisier down and turned into the embrace, finding all of the warmth and caring in his eyes that she had seen earlier at the lake. This was the Hunter she believed in, the one whose eyes looked only at her, the one who shut out the rest of the world. She was relieved and suddenly smiling, too. Yet she remembered that she had to work with this man on an assignment that was important to her agency. She had decided not to get emotionally involved with him—hadn't she?

She tried to pull away from him.

"Hunter, I don't think we should...."

"Hush. I only want to hold you. Just for a moment."

He pulled her head to his shoulder, running his hand from her hair down to the small of her back. His strokes were soft caresses, hypnotizing her with their sensuous rhythm. His other hand still cradled her waist, his touch light on the swell of her hip. Her own hands held the filled glasses, warming between their bodies.

She wanted to melt against him, merge her rising heat with his. *This wasn't right!* She had to get things back on a professional level before it was too late.

"About those interviews tomorrow—" she began. But the question was never finished.

Instead, he inclined his head that small fraction necessary to reach her lips, which were upturned to meet his. Unlike that first tentative, searching, testing kiss of last night, this touching was strong and possessive. She tried to draw away from it, but

Hunter pulled her back for more until her reluctance was only pretense.

Surrender was not something Cary had ever dreamed of feeling, but in Hunter's arms just now she seemed to have no will of her own but to drown in the swirling passion he provoked in her. At first, she was not even aware of how utterly lost she'd become.

His hands roamed up and down her spine, pressing her against him, heedless of the hard glassware held between them. The suffocating urgency of their kiss was astonishing. It was as if they were not strangers but lovers with an age-old lust that sought fulfillment desperately.

"Mmm, I want you so, Cary. Let me love you. Now," he whispered, reaching behind her for the clasp on her bra.

Cary felt her body grow hot beneath his hands and that, even more than the feeling of need, warned her. He wanted too much too soon.

She withdrew quickly inside herself, feeling her senses grow suddenly cold.

"No, Hunter!" she cried, pushing at his unmoving chest. "Please, no," she whispered.

But he held her fast, until tears of defeat began to shimmer in her eyes.

To her surprise, she suddenly found herself standing alone, as Hunter walked back to the couch, breathing deeply. She felt caution float around her. Hunter was awakening long-dormant fires inside her, fires she was not lucid enough just now to decide whether to quench or fan.

She followed him to the couch but remained standing before him, silently offering the glass. Hunter smiled and took the liquor from her, sipping its smooth heat ever so slowly.

She sipped also, still standing. Her eyes questioned his and eventually he broke the silence, indicating he accepted her unspoken withdrawal.

"I really don't think I'd better stay—even for advice about the interview," he offered. "I need a clear head in the morning, sweetheart, and what you do to me is more unsettling than this brandy. Good night, Cary. I meant every word I said." He set down the glass and was gone.

Her heart cried into the stillness, *every word?* For even in her turmoil, she knew that it was not what had been spoken that hung between them now. She felt as if she was playing a dangerous game with unwritten rules, and Hunter had just made aseries of bewildering moves. It was her turn now, but if she guressed wrong, she would lose—everything.

CHAPTER FOUR

"I MEANT EVERY WORD."

What a perfect practiced line! It shouldn't have been so, but in that weary hour last night Cary's heart had responded alarmingly to the corny, empty phrase Hunter had spoken as he left. Now, with the energy of a new day to freshen her mind Cary could judge Hunter's words, and her reaction to them, fairly.

He'd said very little yesterday that needed the emphasis of that parting phrase. So what had he meant every word of? Surely not the story of his childhood or his prosaic comments on the scenery. His promise to do as she instructed during the interview, then? Or perhaps his earnest words about mutual trust.

Not his kiss. No, he'd said nothing at all about that. It was time for her to examine his words and actions, and her response, objectively and make some decisions for the future.

The first conclusion was easy. Hunter wanted her total support. Very well. That much was understandable and straightforward.

Next possible conclusion. To achieve his goal, Hunter might try to involve her feelings as well as her sense of responsibility. It was an excellent ploy—make your accomplice believe she is helping you for the sake of love as well as justice, and she will do anything you want, even lie or cheat or steal.

Yet Cary had sensed earlier that his smile was the key to recognizing when he was sincere. And his smile had been so warm and perfect just before they'd kissed. Was it possible that she *did* stir something inside him, something other than a desire to manipulate her for his professional purposes?

It had certainly seemed so. But then, Hunter was so self-confident, so practiced and smooth, he might be able to convince her just because....

No. It seemed it was Cary herself who needed investigating. At the age of twenty-eight, she would have thought she could be sure about her feelings. But she wasn't. She was afraid they were clouding her judgment, that she might be seeing honesty in his eyes and in his smile only because she wanted to.

Because it had been so long since anyone had come close to her in the hurly-burly, helter-skelter life she led.

Another recruiter, Jason French, had almost broken through the barriers she'd erected around her heart. She had once thought she could love him. But then their jobs had interfered, and Jason had been transferred and had gone his separate way.

She would have to watch herself more closely, truly be on guard. It would be best to consider Hunter Pierce as nothing more than a business associate. In fact she would not try to read anything at all in the reporter's expressions, lest she lead herself merrily down another garden path.

Though his story about David and Jeannie had checked out and she was committed to allowing Hunter on the flight this morning, she would keep her eyes open. She would conduct her own investigation and find her own answers—for Omega and for her heart.

The kettle on the stove whistled its shrill, commonplace alarm, and Cary hurried to finish dressing and eat breakfast. There wasn't much time, if she was to be at the airport before the others arrived at seven-thirty.

Only two bites into her oatmeal, however, Cary was startled by the sound of the telephone. Who would be calling at this hour?

"Cary, where were you yesterday? We were worried about you."

"Mary Ellen? I had... some business to take care of before the Omega trip. Did you need something?"

"Yes I did, but no one in your office knew where you had gone."

She didn't have to remind Cary that unexplained absences were poor business practice. Cary felt her face grow hot.

"I'm sorry you missed me, but ...."

"I'm sure you had a good reason. Just keep the staff informed in the future. I understand you've spent the last two weeks up here, doing my job. I wanted to thank you for leaving everything in such good order. But I wish you had called about some of it—just to make me feel needed, you know." She chuckled, but the sound seemed strained to Cary.

"The doctor told us not to worry you with anything at all. And Dennis Forsythe was afraid you might—"

"Some idiotic medic tells me to relax and stop worrying—and then puts me in a *hospital*! Just being there made me more upset and worried. So I checked myself out and came in here ready to go to work. But when I got to my desk, it was clean. My calendar was empty, and even my own clients didn't seem to realize I'd been gone."

"Except for the forester. He's really looking forward to your return."

"Oh, him. Poor guy. I'll take care of him as soon as I can. I'm sure I can turn up something for him. But, Cary, I just...I just wish you had called me and we could have worked out some of this together. I feel a little like a fifth wheel."

Cary was sure the slight chuckle this time was forced. Of course, she should have considered that Mary Ellen would feel bad if no one seemed to need her.

"Oh, you've got that all wrong! We have only just now found out how much you do for Willingham. I didn't get half of your normal workload done—even working in the evenings! But Mr. Forsythe told me specifically not to bother you. He said the doctor told him it might be quite a while before you were able to come back if we disturbed your rest. And we *did* want you to come back soon." Cary didn't mention that the doctor had said surgery might be required. She didn't know if Mary Ellen was aware of that possibility. "Does anyone at the hospital know you're back on the job?"

"They do now!" the older woman replied, laughing. "Stop changing the subject, Cary. We are not going to discuss my health. I called because I can't find some of my files, and I thought you might know where they are." Her voice sounded confident and sure again.

"Which ones are you missing?"

"Right now, I'm looking for the folder on Joe Hartman. Tell me, did you use that one?"

"Why, I'm certain we put it back in the American Paper Company file," Cary answered, puzzled. "Isn't it there now?"

"Oh, I didn't look there. Let me check."

She didn't look in the client company file? Well, where else could it, should it, have been?

"It's here." Relief echoed in the words. "I'm sorry. It wasn't where I usually keep it on my desk, and I was worried. That's all. Why did you refile it, anyway?"

"I just thought it belonged with the rest of the Americian Paper materials. When we got the check in the mail last Friday...."

"Check?"

"From Mr. Hartman. It was for far more than we had billed. So Anita and I found the folder on your desk, looked up the address and sent back a voucher for the difference. Then we refiled the folder. It's all there in your log."

The stillness on the other end of the line seemed

ominous, and Cary began to worry that she had indeed overstepped her authority and seriously displeased her supervisor. But there had been no way of knowing when Mary Ellen would be able to take care of her normal duties, and none of the other regional recruiters could leave their assignments. Cary had been glad she could help relieve the worried staff in the main office. She had even felt she'd done a good job there.

At last her supervisor spoke, calmly and in measured tones. "I appreciate what you did, Cary. But I must ask you not to make policy decisions in the future. If I am ever absent again for any length of time, I will make my own arrangements for whatever decisions must be made."

"Certainly, Mary Ellen. I was only trying...."

"Yes, I know. I'm sorry if I sound ungrateful. I'm not. I'm sure I would have done the same thing. It's just that you don't know everything about the politics of this job and you might have inadvertently rubbed someone the wrong way or caused us to lose a client. And then my ulcers would be even worse than they are now! You understand, don't you?"

"Of course," Cary replied. But she did not. She was as qualified as anyone else to take over the routine part of Mary Ellen's job, and she would never presume to interfere in its politics. She had thought Mary Ellen trusted her.

"Well, that's all I called for. I really do appreciate what you did while I was out. Let's hope I never have to implement any of those contingency

plans, shall we? Have a good day, Cary. Goodbye.'' The tinny voice rang off without waiting for
Cary's reply.

Good day? After that I should have a good day?
The flush, which earlier had invaded her cheeks,
was gone. *Lord, I hope she gets rid of those ulcers
soon!*

Glancing rapidly at her watch, Cary shoved her
upset emotions to one side; she would have to deal
with Mary Ellen's defensiveness later. She couldn't
afford to be unnerved by it or irritable today. Not
today when she was already late—and anxious
about the part she would have to play in just a short
time. She tossed the cold oatmeal into the disposal
and grabbed a can of juice to drink in the car. Never
had calm serenity seemed so impossible a goal.

Indian summer still lingered over the Midwestern
plains, its golden mornings just barely cool enough
to spark an autumn response form the many different deciduous trees native to the creeks and river-
beds of northeastern Kansas. Only a month ago,
green lawns and pastures had been covered with the
thin white fluff from cottonwoods, making heat-
weary folk yearn for an early snow. Now the
ground was littered with dry leaves, and it seemed
unlikely they would be blessed with any kind of
moisture soon, frozen or otherwise.

Cary could feel a dusty dryness in the air as she
sped toward the airport. After a near drought this
summer and scorching temperatures, a kind of
urgent expectancy seemed to hang over everything
as the world waited for rain. To Cary, it also

seemed that the sense of expectation was spilling over into her feelings about the trip to Omega Aircraft.

In spite of her misgivings, or perhaps because of them, a growing excitement was filling her as she neared the hangar. Before it, in gleaming silver, gold and black, was the Omegajet that would take them to Wichita. Cary could hardly wait to be airborne in the sleek, elegant plane. It was truly amazing how her adrenaline was surging at the thought of beginning this investigation. It was possible, after all, that it would end in disaster. But just now, only breathless anticipation filled her. If Omega and Willingham were proved innocent, Mary Ellen and Dennis Forsythe would be so proud of her!

The six applicants and Hunter were all waiting for her outside with the copilot. As she drove up, several people came to greet her.

"Good morning!" she called. "Sorry I'm late!"

Hunter's long athletic stride brought him to her car first. He reached out to help her, and Cary saw his eyes twinkle as if he was sharing a private joke with her. She tossed her head as if to banish the suggestion of any intimacy. She must remember to be on her guard every moment she was with this man!

"We were worried about you, Miss Blaine. Did you forget to set your alarm?" he asked, grinning.

"No, I didn't...David." She smiled sweetly. "I had to speak with my supervisor in St. Louis about a few little problems that came up yesterday." She noted the slight frown that creased Hunter's brow when she finished her explanation. He was wondering if she had discussed his real identity with anyone at Willingham! Well, let him worry a bit. Perhaps a little uncertainty would roughen the edges of his too-perfect self-confidence.

For a brief moment she was visited by a feeling of déjà vu. Once before she had thought to put Hunter off balance—the night he had come upon her so unexpectedly in the Holidome. How quickly he had turned the tables on her then, changing her serene world into a topsy-turvy one of masquerades and lies and heart-stopping kisses over warm brandy. Her resolve faltered. Could she really maintain control over this investigation, especially if she let her emotions get involved? Would she be able to rein in if Hunter tried to race ahead in foolish pursuit of an imagined wrong?

Hunter was smiling again, any concern he might have felt gone—or hidden behind his professional mask and camera-ready pose. One hand was outstretched to assist her getting out of the car. She could not refuse in front of the others. As her cold fingers met his warm ones, he bent down to whisper, "We begin!"

"This isn't a game!" she answered furiously. He was pulling her up and close to him. Too close.

"I know. That's what makes it exciting." His words were bright and traitorously echoed her own emotions of a few moments ago. Suddenly she saw how childish her anticipation really was. She could lose her job! Hunter's cheerful disregard for the risks ahead almost succeeded in unnerving her completely.

The copilot checked them quickly on to the plane. Inside, luxurious padded armchairs were arranged by the windows in two rows of four, with small tables down the center of the aircraft.

In only a few moments, the jet had taxied down the runway and was aloft. Cary showed Hunter and another applicant how to unlock and swivel their seats, moving them on a little track in the floor to cluster around the tables. The other passengers were familiar with the procedure and had soon established comfortable groups where nervous, animated introductions were taking place.

Jeremy Slade and Peter Holcombe were NASA engineers from Houston and the Kennedy Space Center in Florida respectively. Suzanne Foley was also a civilian government employee, programming aircraft simulators for the air force in Colorado. The other three applicants had been working as design engineers for an automobile-parts manufacturer in Chicago and hoped to transfer their skills to aircraft design. They were Mark Goodrich, Tommy Ghiberti and Stan Brooker.

Though naturally the three friends from Chicago were quite talkative, Cary had expected Hunter's gregarious nature would move him to the center of the group's attention. Instead, she saw that he kept his distance, listening and watching as the others joked about their jobs, politics and the future of aviation.

Reluctantly, she admired his good sense. Listening to the legitimate candidates, he could pick up on a lot of the casual jargon thrown about by engineers. If the real David Thompson had also suc-ceeded in coaching Hunter about current research projects, the reporter could surely fool Omega's management during the series of brief interviews he must attend today.

The prospect of success was not altogether com-forting, however. Cary's troubled gaze returned again and again to the dark gold leather seat where Hunter sat, silent and watchful. She wondered how much of the playful excitement he'd exhibited earlier was still with him. Had the reality of their si-tuation finally sobered him, also?

His chin rested on the knuckles of one hand, thus placing a black onyx signet in close proximity to his deep black-and-gray-flecked hair. Tiny coils of silver light twisted among coarser coal black locks: midnight and stars. The evening metaphor came un-bidden as she watched the play of setting against stone, light against dark, in his ring and in his hair—gray strands shifting in abstract patterns against darker waves with each quick, searching movement of Hunter's head. The signet's steady, deep intensity shone against those shifting patterns as a perfect counterpoint—its dead black a foil for the living, changing darkness above it.

Hmm. Gray hair. David Thompson was only thirty.... *I wonder how old Hunter Pierce is?* she found herself speculating.

Her hands unconsciously stroked the soft leather-clad armrests beside her. She felt the coolness of the hide, smooth but not slick, and mentally touched the smooth forehead of the man she watched. The light fingers of her imagination slid down his freshly shaved cheek and chin to his neck, shadowed above the hard crispness of his collar.

She crossed her long legs, rubbing the silken, slippery softness of her hose and imagining the faintly rough texture of his thighs on hers.

A tenseness had begun to wind inside her, sprung partly from anxiety and also from the visions seen by her inner eye. Cary was not aware of the tight coil forming within, because she was completely mesmerized by the seductive presence of the man who had walked into her life only two days ago.

It didn't matter that he was looking at others. She felt and sensed his nearness, and that was enough to spark this...this wild imagining. She shook her head, but the bond held, drawing her eyes back to him.

And then Hunter turned. His eyes rested on hers and read some message there. His head tipped slightly in silent questioning. Slowly, he took off the gray-rimmed glasses and his large dark eyes widened further.

A thrum of high-powered electricity sang across the space between them. He grinned and nodded his head, challenging her to deny the secret excitement that had sparked the charge of energy.

She smiled back weakly. No, she couldn't deny it. The risk, the mystery, the challenge all were still there. All were alluring. Her body tingled from the shock of the admission, and a prickly warmth crept over her as Hunter's expression altered subtly. The engaging grin was softer, his gaze heavier as his eyes moved down her figure. She felt his glance pause at her suddenly taut breasts, then move down across her stomach. He was looking at her... *the way she had been looking at him!*

Last night, Cary had been merely entranced. Now she found herself completely enthralled, a captive of those dark eyes. His appraising gaze returned to her face. What message did he read there? Had she laid open her soul, and was she now lost? It seemed so. Some vast emptiness had opened up and she felt as if she were falling, that she had somehow surrendered a vital part of herself.

Hunter frowned, then smiled tightly. He nodded distantly and put the glasses back in place on his nose. His gaze returned to their fellow passengers.

Still, he had not quite released her to reality. She might look away now, but all she saw was Hunter. Frowning?

She stood up and walked back to the plane's tiny galley. With sudden clarity, she knew why she had trembled beside Hunter in his car, why his form and face had intruded on her fantasies and why her legs were weak now. It was not the anticipation and thrill of adventure she had felt sing between them but something much more dangerous—raw desire. And Hunter had felt it, too! She couldn't have misread that blatantly seductive look, which had stripped away the layers of wool and lace clothing to touch her very skin.

But why had that look changed suddenly to a frown and a tense, hard smile?

For the first time, she wished that Hunter's ruse

would succeed. If Omega offered him a bribe, then he would have to stay around—at least long enough to finish his story. Long enough for Cary to find out for certain why her heart raced at the sound of his voice and her head swam with a spinning torrent of confusing, contradictory needs whenever he was near.

A loud, static-filled voice from the plane's intercom finally broke the spell, and she felt suddenly as if the last few minutes had never happened. "Please return your seats to their locked position and fasten seat belts. We'll be landing at the Omega Aircraft private airfield in just a few minutes."

Cary was shocked and vaguely uneasy. Had she really spent the entire flight watching Hunter Pierce and speculating about him? Had they really exchanged such looks, so full of innuendo and promise? *That's not very smart,* she warned herself as she returned to her seat. She must remember; she couldn't afford to allow Hunter to gain complete control of her or the investigation. She couldn't afford to lose any chances to restrain his ambitious enthusiasm. Willingham was counting on her. She must keep her priorities straight.

Now she, too, was frowning. "All right, everyone. Some last-minute instructions." The intercom had scarcely disturbed the noisy conversations on board the plane, but her own firm voice produced instant quiet.

She looked around at the now silent people before her. For everyone but Hunter, these next few hours might mean the beginning of a whole new life, a change of both career and location. The eyes turned toward her were anxious and excited.

"Two cars will be waiting outside to take us to the main administration building for a tour. Afterward we will be met by Henry Crandon, Omega's chief personnel officer. He has an orientation film to show you, and then you will begin your round of interviews. Each of you will be taken to lunch by the executive who is scheduled to see you at noon. We'll meet back at Henry's office at four o'clock and then come home. Any questions?"

Seeing that there were none she glanced at Hunter, who solemnly winked back. A nervous giggle tickled inside her throat, but Cary managed to quell the reaction before her laughter escaped. He was still treating this whole investigation as if it was a game!

A sudden doubt crossed her mind. If this was only a game for him, how did she fit in? Was she merely the king's pawn?

CHAPTER FIVE

A TALL, ELEGANT YOUNG WOMAN emerged from one of the waiting silver gray limos and gracefully crossed the runway to greet them.

"Hello, Miss Blaine. Is this our group of engineers?" Her smile was especially approving of the six male passengers. "My name is Adrienne Marshall, from public relations. I'll be your guide today for our tour of the Omega Aircraft Corporation jet-assembly plant."

She handed each of them a brilliant silver-gold-and-black visitor's pass and then stowed Jeremy Slade and the three Chicago friends in the first car. Cary took Hunter, Suzanne and Peter with her to the back seat of the second car. A two-way radio allowed them to hear Adrienne's running commentary and even to ask questions.

This was Cary's third tour of the Omega facility, and she didn't pay much attention to Adrienne's soft, ultrafeminine voice as she described the function of each building on the Omega site. Cary was seated next to Hunter, and for all her resolve to concentrate more closely on the investigation, he filled her thoughts.

His knee was close to hers, pressing gently against

the fabric of her skirt. She did not turn her head toward him, but she could sense that his chin was several inches above her own, thrusting forward in concentration as he listened to Adrienne.

"Which are the mock-up garages?" Suzanne asked as they cruised by several wide hangars.

Cary turned to point them out, and her movement shifted her body closer to Hunter's. Adrienne's soft voice floated around them in the car.

"The long building on your far right contains the mock-up testing facility. Unfortunately, it is off limits to our tour today. We do all our own testing here on the site, except for wind tunnel tests, which are run at Wichita State University."

Suzanne and Hunter twisted in their seats to see more of the secret facility, and the action pulled Hunter's body away from Cary. She knew an unreasonable sense of loss for an instant, and then Hunter was back beside her, his warmth comfortably close again.

Why did she feel excited about this adventure only when he was near? Because Hunter was part and parcel of the game, she realized. In fact, she had to admit that she probably wouldn't have allowed herself to get involved had the investigator been someone other than the very self-assured, smooth-talking Hunter Pierce. Unsettled by her discovery, she concentrated on pulling her scattered wits about her.

Finally the group pulled up in front of a two-story structure facing Omegagate Drive. Once inside the building, Adrienne led them past elaborate display cases holding scale models of the most famous Omega planes, the Sunrise, Cloud King, Omegajet B10, Milky Way 4000 and Sunspot T45. They followed her from building to building, past machine shops with giant Verson presses and rows of quality-control equipment, to the paint shops where an electrostatic primer coat and infrared bake turned out assembly-ready parts with antistatic or antiradar "stealth" finishes, or simple undercoatings ready for a buyer's personal colors and markings to be painted on.

They watched as polarized windows were installed in the cabin of a partially constructed Sunspot and then mesh netting was wrapped around the body so that the jet's cabin could be safely pressure-tested.

"By the time it is fully assembled, each Omegajet will have undergone nearly six thousand inspections," Adrienne said, above the roar of fans and the whine of drills.

Hunter, who was never more than a hand's breadth away from Cary, looked at her in amazement.

Cary laughed. "That doesn't even count the testing you 'engineers' do on new designs," she whispered. This talk of testing and design was much more her territory than Hunter's, and that knowledge gave her a small measure of confidence and restored control.

"Umm." Hunter's attention returned to Adrienne and the massive planes behind her. Cary could sense his awe and she shared it. Building one of these was indeed a monumental task.

Their final stop in the assembly hangar was a small turbojet whose body was covered with tiny white cotton tufts. Adrienne explained the tufts helped in checking aerodynamics during test flights. The other engineers nodded acknowledgment of this method, but Hunter's brow creased in a puzzled furrow.

Don't ask! Cary signaled silently.

Hunter caught her message and shrugged, moving on with the others outside to look at some of the planes that were ready for delivery.

Cary sighed gratefully. She hoped Hunter would save most of his questions for later, when they were alone. One question about a topic any engineer should understand would sabotage the entire masquerade.

After a brief stop in the pilot's lounge, Adrienne took the group to the central management offices and Henry Crandon.

"Good to see you again, Caroline." Henry Crandon was a small, pencil-thin man, fairly bubbling now with his customary hyperactive enthusiasm. "So these are our applicants! Well, you look like a great bunch of folks. Come on in and sit down for a while."

The applicants filed in to the enormous office silently, good behavior radiating like halos around them all. Each of the candidates was smiling, but Hunter's smile was the friendliest, the most open, the most appealing. Cary watched in admiration as he walked up to Henry and shook hands.

"David Thompson here. I was really impressed with the tour of your facility."

"Thank you, Mr. Thompson. That means a lot coming from someone like you at Burkham Air Labs." Henry beamed at the reporter and bobbed his head several times. "This is a great group," he continued as he shook hands with Phil Hanson. "A really great group. It's a real pleasure to meet such high-powered people. I'm probably as excited as any of you today."

I can believe it! thought Cary as she watched the older man pat his hair, straighten his tie and scamper around the room offering ashtrays and coffee.

"I hope you'll enjoy your visit with us today," Henry said to Hunter as he passed. "Just call my office if you need anything at all."

The excited personnel director dashed over to the window and closed its pale green blinds. As the dim sunlight continued to filter through, he thanked them all again for coming and then switched on a slide-and-sound projector, which began a story of the Omega Corporation's history. Then Henry motioned for Cary to join him outside in the hall.

"Yes?"

"This group is very talented, Caroline. You've really outdone yourself this time."

"Thank you, Henry. I think they're all really fine candidates," she lied.

"Especially that David Thompson. The file you sent me on him reads like a blueprint of the kind of man we're looking for. I think we've hit the jackpot with him."

Cary should have been thankful Henry had

formed such a good opinion of "David." She should have been relieved that there had been no suspicions raised so far. But her enthusiasm had been ebbing slowly since early this morning, and now that the adventure had actually begun and their plan was really working, Cary was being hit by little annoying pangs of guilt. Was she right in deceiving Henry? He seemed so nervous and gullible—not the kind of person who could carry off a high-stakes espionage racket. Suppose this insecure little man was really innocent. What chance did he have against the smooth-talking con devised by Hunter Pierce?

Yet she remembered that she had sensed something false about "David Thompson" almost immediately. With a rapid intake of breath, she realized how much she had counted on Henry's not having that same perception. She had counted strongly on his gullibility. Couldn't someone else, someone for instance in upper management at Omega, have depended on that same credulous flaw to win Henry's cooperation for something quite unethical? Perhaps Henry didn't even realize how he was being used!

Poor Henry!

"Aren't you moving a little fast on this one, Henry? He hasn't even been to his first interview yet."

"Oh, I'm sure about this one, young lady. I've got a feeling right here." He thumped his chest meaningfully. "I can tell he's gonna fit right in."

Cary's hands were clammy. "I hope you're right, Henry. I just—"

"Now, now. He's got to be good—*you* pickea him out, didn't you?" He slapped Cary gently on the back in good-ole-boy comradery.

Yes. She had done that all right. She was in this thing now as deeply as Hunter, up to her neck. And with her in the investigation was the reputation ot Willingham. Was it a crime to impersonate an engineer?

When the slide show was over it was time to begin the interviews. Adrienne and six other pretty young women arrived to escort the candidates to the first round of questioning.

Cary watched as Hunter followed a petite blonde and gave her his most charming smile, a confection of gleaming teeth and sincere dimples. She felt a pang of irritation.

Suddenly depressed by the realization that this investigation would require continual, perhaps distasteful role-playing for both herself and Hunter, Cary wandered out to the foyer where the scale models hung in a graceful simulated flight. Hunter apparently was enjoying his charade as an engineering applicant; Cary was just beginning to find out how difficult and complicated her role would be.

"Would you like to get some coffee with me, Caroline?" Henry Crandon's normally excited voice was just a soft murmur.

"Yes, that would be nice," she answered, surprised by his presence. Perhaps coffee and a social chat would take her mind off Hunter and their wild, reckless scheme.

The coffee bar was brilliantly lit with a colorful mural of famous Omegajets and other aircraft and their owners. It covered the far wall. Cary sipped the hot liquid and tried to identify some of the faces in the mural.

"You know, Caroline, that I only have spots for three more engineers. What's the big idea of bringing me a whole planeload of outstanding applicants?" Henry tittered lightly. "My managers will go bananas trying to choose!'

"Oh, Henry." Cary smiled at his attempt at humor. "What a tough job you have!'

A frown replaced Henry's good-humored grin. "It really is rough sometimes. You can't even guess how rough it can be here."

"Why, Henry! What is it? The budget? Have they started to cut costs in your department?"

"No—no. Nothing like that." Henry's eyes danced around the room. "They're really pushing, Caroline. They need somebody exceptional to pull them through, and so far they don't feel any of the new people fill that bill."

"But, Henry, we've sent you the best we could find."

"I know you've tried, Caroline. But I just wanted to warn you that Jack Beale, our senior vice-president, is talking about asking another headhunter firm to step in."

Cary sipped her coffee silently. Henry merely played with his cup, turning it round and round on the table in front of him.

"How much more time have I got?" she asked quietly.

"I just don't know," answered Henry, avoiding her eyes. "This planeload you brought here today may be the last. If there's no one in this bunch, well. . . ."

Cary's heart skipped, and she felt her face drain of color.

"Of course, I'm personally convinced that David Thompson will be perfect for us. For all of us." Somehow Henry's assurance did not make her feel better. Omega was counting on the engineering skills of a man who had none!

"Have you discussed any of this with Mary Ellen Hughes?"

"No. They told me she was in the hospital, and you were in charge until she got back."

She expelled the breath she had been holding in. Cary decided not to mention that Mary Ellen was very definitely back—against her doctor's orders and obviously in pain. After all, it was Dennis Forsythe who knew all about Hunter's scheme, and he could tell Mary Ellen if he thought it was wise. If they didn't lose the Omega account.

"Well, thanks for warning me, Henry." She set the coffee down and pushed it away. Its warmth was no longer comforting. Suddenly she wanted to talk to Hunter and suggest that maybe they should wait until—

No! she realized miserably. It was too late for that. Hunter was trying right now to convince Omega management he was an exceptional candidate, willing to sell his brilliant ideas to the highest bidder. If he succeeded, and Omega offered him a lucrative salary, they would have every reason in the world to dismiss her and Willingham when they discovered he could not give them the engineering expertise and creativity they so despiratley needed.

What should she do? She picked up the coffee again, but not even its warmth could lessen the chill that had invaded her soul.

"I did want you to know, Caroline. But you don't really have to worry," Henry continued. "I just know this David Thompson fellow is everything we need. I know you were impressed with him, too. Weren't you?"

Dully, Cary realized she had no choices left. She had begun this thing, and now she would be forced to follow through with it. She was committed, for what it was worth.

"Yes, I thought he seemed just right for you." She almost choked on the words.

"I knew it! Don't you fear. Jack Beale's gonna love our Mr. Thompson!"

Cary stood, her heart quaking. "I hope so. Thanks for the coffee, Henry. I think I'll go on into town for a while."

"Sure, Caroline. Go take one of the company cars out for the day with our thanks for a job well done. And don't worry."

I'll scream if he says 'don't worry' again. Cary turned away from him with a tight smile.

Once she'd found a car, Cary drove until she came to a shopping mall packed with cars and people. The rest of the morning and early afternoon, she walked up and down the mall, hardly seeing any of its shops or wares. She agonized over a decision she had thought was already made. As Hunter had explained it, their mutual objective was simple: vindicate the right and expose the wrong.

That hadn't changed. Discovering the truth *was* important. But was it the most important thing of all? Weren't honesty, integrity and trust necessary, too? And what of the people who might be hurt—poor worried Henry, vulnerable Mary Ellen, Dennis Forsythe and even herself? How did human beings' lives compare with principles—were they of equal value?

A sudden flood of illumination washed over her. She and Henry and Mary Ellen were not the only ones who could be hurt. They were simply the only ones she knew personally. There were all those other faceless individuals at both Burkham and Omega—the innocent ones and the guilty. One could look at it that way, too. It wasn't only abstract principles at stake.

One company or the other was destined to lose in this battle and the losses would be heavy indeed. One of the two would probably never recover. She and Hunter were trying to make certain it was not the greedy who triumphed.

Yes, Cary could now see the picture from Hunter's perspective. His certainly wasn't the only point of view. She had to overlook the possibility that some people might get hurt, but Cary could see that Hunter's way of looking at things was essentially valid. Her tension eased a bit. She had examined her conscience and confirmed that her first instinct had been right. Cary felt as if she could reach out and touch the truth. Together, she and Hunter must finish the investigation. And the half-truths she must tell Henry Crandon were undoubtedly justified.

At three-thirty, Cary returned to Henry's office. The seven candidates were not due back for half an hour, but Cary wanted to sound out the personnel director on the type of assignment Hunter might receive if he was hired.

Henry greeted her with an energetic handshake. "It's in the bag, Caroline. We've got David Thompson, I just know it."

Cary smiled with satisfaction. So Hunter had fooled them completely, had he? Phase one complete! "You've made him an offer?"

"No. Oh, we couldn't do that yet. We need Jack Beale's approval, you know. But my managers love him! Jack wouldn't dare deny them a chance at the golden goose."

"Golden goose?"

"Profit, my dear. David Thompson means money in the bank. He's really got a head on his shoulders, hasn't he?"

Cary thought of Hunter's lean, strong jaw, his dimples, his puppy eyes. "Yes, he has a good head," she agreed.

"And your Miss Foley has really made an impression on some of the managers, too. Of course, she's a woman and . . . well, you know how some men are."

Cary raised her eyebrows questioningly.

"I mean, umm, some of our supervisors and managers don't like to, umm, work with high-level professional women. You know." He paused and his face began to color an unhealthy shade of red. "Of course, that won't influence our decision whether to hire her at all."

"Of course not." Cary's voice was firm. Sharing such a confidence wasn't typical of Henry. He knew the rules as well as she did, and his last comments were totally out of place. If Suzanne was not hired now, the reasons would certainly be suspect. Henry must be even more nervous than usual to let such a remark slip out.

"And of course she'd be a real asset to Omega, if we did hire her," Henry added, looking down at the floor.

"Of course she would. She is a good engineer."

"Yes, yes. Though not as good as David Thompson." Henry paused. "If we were to hire both of them—just *if*, I say—then we would only need one more engineer to fill the roster."

"That's right. Only one." Was Henry trying to tell her something? If so, she was too dense today to catch his meaning. She decided to ask her own questions. "Henry, what kind of assignment did you have in mind for David?"

"Assignment? Oh, just design work. It depends on exactly what he's been working on for Burkham."

"It does?" She hadn't expected her questions to be answered so easily. Had she stumbled in on

Henry's bad day, when he would give away store secrets free? "How does it depend on Burkham?"

"Is. . . is that what I said?" Henry nearly jumped out of his chair. "I meant it depends on his experience. What he knows. What he's familiar with."

"Oh." Of course. Cary had been so ready just now to believe in Hunter's theory of Omega's complicity that she'd seen guilt where perhaps none existed at all. Henry was just being Henry. He was nervous and a little rattled about the uncalled-for comments he had made about Suzanne.

Naturally the first assignment will depend on what "David" already knows. Nothing sinister there. Cary told herself she had to be more careful about jumping to conclusions.

Just then Jeremy and Suzanne arrived, and Cary cut short her talk with the personnel director. The other candidates wandered in one by one within a few more minutes—except for Hunter. Finally, Henry Crandon buzzed his secretary and sent her to look for the missing applicant. She returned with Hunter.

"Sorry I'm late. Jack Beale and I were just trading stories about our favorite vacation spots in South America," he announced with a wink at Henry.

The other candidates stared at Hunter with ill-disguised envy. None of them had gotten around to discussing frivolous matters of personal taste in the presence of the august Mr. Beale!

After his initial shock, Henry had begun beaming

with self-confidence. Cary knew he was reading between the lines of Hunter's announcement. He was imagining a burgeoning friendship with this newest engineer and the powerful senior vice-president who could make or break Henry's own career.

"Umm. I'll be right back." Henry scooted out of his chair and was gone almost before anyone noticed.

Hunter and the other candidates looked to Cary for an explanation. But all she could do was shrug. The room was tensely silent. After a few minutes, Cary decided her presence was inhibiting the others and perhaps increasing their nervous speculations, so she went out to the secretary's desk and stood there, waiting for Henry to return.

The personnel director was gone for almost twenty minutes, and Cary was beginning to worry. Finally he appeared, scuttling nervously along the hall.

"Henry, is something wrong?"

"Huh? Oh, Caroline. No, not at all." He tried to smile brightly, but made a rather lopsided mess of it. "As a matter of fact, it's going just fine. Just fine indeed."

He lowered his voice and motioned her to join him around the corner from his office. "Cary, we'll have to wait until Monday to finalize this, but—" he paused and looked over his shoulder "—I think I can promise you we will be offering Miss Foley a job *if*—"

"If what?"

"If you can guarantee that David Thompson won't take anyone else's offer in the meantime."

Cary thought of the unique status of "David's" employment position. "He has no other offers that I know of. But Henry, you—"

"*And* if you can help us with the negotiations. I've got orders, Cary. 'Get Thompson.' If I need your help, I want to know you'll give it."

Cary was struck dumb. She had truly believed, somewhere in her heart, that Henry Crandon was too simple and too insecure to be dishonest or unethical. This little "deal" astounded her and changed the outlook of the entire investigation. Suddenly it seemed likely that Hunter could be right about Omega's alleged espionage.

"What kind of help are you talking about?" she asked, trying to keep her voice neutral.

"Oh, just help. I'll let you know."

Henry was being evasive. Cary decided to accept his answer, unsatisfactory as it was. She would find out more later, she was sure.

Henry went back to his office and said goodbye to the applicants. Adrienne Marshall was sent for to accompany the group back to the waiting plane.

In their car, Hunter grasped Cary's hand and squeezed. Excitement radiated from his dark, shadowy eyes. Surrounded by people who really *were* the people they claimed to be, he and Cary engaged in a dialogue that was outwardly innocuous but carried messages of far more import than the others could guess.

"Did you have a good day?" Cary asked.

"Outstanding! I was really pleased." Hunter squeezed her hand again under the cover of her handbag.

"I take it you feel your interviews went well?"

"Oh, yes. Especially the one with Dr. Howard Racine, the new head of research. He was pretty much a recluse at Burkham and none of us knew him."

"Oh?"

"Yes, he asked some very interesting questions about my work at Burkham. It would be a real challenge to work for him."

I'll bet! thought Cary, with an outward grin and inward quaking. "How about you, Peter? How did your interviews go?"

"Oh, fine, Miss Blaine. I'm going to have to think about whether or not I'm really interested, though. I've gotten used to the informality of NASA, and I'm not sure I want to move into such a...structured atmosphere."

"Me, I'm used to structure," commented Suzanne. "You can't get more structured than top-secret military programs testing and training air force pilots to fly experimental planes. I'm looking forward to being able to talk about what I'm doing at work without worrying that some CIA man might be in the crowd."

They all laughed a little nervously. It had been a very exhausting day, and now they would all have to wait and worry until Monday.

Peter was sitting in front with their driver. As Suzanne turned around to get a last glimpse of the testing hangar, Hunter leaned close to Cary and whispered, "I'm so pleased I could hug you! Dinner tonight?"

Suzanne had begun to turn back before Cary could do more than nod once. But when they climbed out of the limo, Hunter held on to Cary's arm, delaying her.

"What about your day? Did you find out anything?" he asked.

"Only that our Mr. Crandon is not a very nice man. He wants me to influence you."

"How? In return for what?"

"I don't know how. But he's promising to hire Suzanne as payment."

"Do you particularly want her hired?"

"He thinks I do."

"Why?"

"She's a woman."

"No kidding!" Hunter looked out over the runway where Suzanne was just climbing up into the Omega-jet. "Well, well. Isn't that lucky for all of us."

Cary wasn't sure what he meant, but they couldn't risk any more chatting. They had to get moving.

Later, she began to understand what Hunter meant by lucky. It was certainly lucky that Cary's comment about Henry Crandon's promise had given Hunter a chance to pay lavish attention to the only candidate with a better-than-average possibility of success. And it was also lucky that Suzanne was a woman, susceptible to those magnificent charms Hunter used so cunningly.

Cary watched as the two paired up in the rear of the cabin, talking in low voices, occasionally laughing, sometimes touching casually. They looked animated, friendly. She could believe that Suzanne was hungry to talk to someone about her work, and Hunter would make sure he was the one she confided in.

A bleak winter wilderness eclipsed Cary's previous excitement. Phase One was complete. Now began Phase Two and the involvement of innocent people. Of course Hunter would need informers. How else could he get the evidence he needed?

And while Cary had been able to justify not telling the truth to Henry Crandon, could she just as easily justify lying to Suzanne Foley—and all their other unwitting accomplices?

Just thinking about the possible pain she and Hunter might inflict made her stomach feel hollow. Indeed, every part of her felt hollow, emptied of all the rich fullness she'd known in Hunter's arms.

Cary went to the plane's narrow galley for coffee, trying to forget Hunter and his quest. She filled a large ceramic mug with the hot drink and turned to go back to her seat.

In a startling replay of last night's embrace, Cary found herself in Hunter's arms, the coffee pressed between them as the brandy had been. She gasped and tried to move back.

Hunter put his arms around her and pulled her tightly against him.

"Fancy meeting you here!" he whispered, grinning.

"Hunter! The coffee—it will spill if you—"

"If I what? I won't wiggle if you won't."

Then he bent his head and began to kiss her slowly, oh, so softly. She could feel the coffee mug against her abdomen, but its warmth was nothing compared to the intense heat that spread through her entire body at his touch. If ever Cary had needed confirmation that the attraction between them had little to do with the investigation, this moment provided it. Why, at this point she positively hated the investigation! Yet she couldn't deny the arousal of her body.

But she should! This was not the time or the place—and she had only just begun to admit what was happening between them. She needed time!

She couldn't move or she might ruin the pale blue wool suit she was wearing. Hunter had neatly made her a captive, but she could show him how unwilling she was. She forced her mind to concentrate on their fellow passengers. She became as unresponsive and limp as a rag doll.

Hunter pulled back then, a puzzled look in his eyes.

"What's the matter, Cary? Last night you weren't so distant. . .at first. And on the flight out this morning I thought you—"

"Last night was last night, 'Mr. Thompson,' and it was private." She rushed on. "Aren't you worried someone like Suzanne Foley might come over and see us now?"

"You're right, of course." He grinned again. "I guess I just couldn't wait until tonight to celebrate our victory. You're such a temptation, woman!"

"If you will stand aside, I would like to go back to my seat now," she said coldly.

As she sat once more in the leather-covered chair, Cary saw Hunter going back to bend over Suzanne. Their heads seemed to blend into one in her misty-eyed vision.

Cary turned away from them to stare out at icy white clouds too high to bring rain to a moisture-starved earth and too much like fragile dreams to fill the emptiness in her heart. Suddenly, she had a splitting headache. Was she really sure about anything? About what was right or wrong? Could she trust her own perception and judgment?

One man had turned her neat, rational world topsy-turvy. How powerful he was! And how lost she felt without him close beside her!

CHAPTER SIX

WHEN THEY HAD LANDED, Hunter walked with Suzanne to her car, which was parked at Topeka's Municipal Airport. His salt-and-pepper hair contrasted strongly with the short woman's carrot-red curls. With helpless fascination, Cary watched as he bent to offer a last good-luck wish to Suzanne.

Then Hunter strolled over to Cary, nonchalantly grinning with all the good spirits of one who had spent a sunny day at the beach.

"We've sure got a lot to talk about. Shall I pick you up about seven, or is that too early?"

Cary stared at him while the headache pounded. *More* plotting? Hunter appeared to look forward to the intrigue but Cary knew she was already in deep water, way over her head. All day she had been tense and...and even frightened. But not until the plane was headed home had she begun to realize how much that tension had affected her. She was numb, although her thoughts continued to reel around so fast she couldn't concentrate. Her muscles were sore, yet she was restless.

The last thing she needed was the unsettling presence of Hunter Pierce and more talk of conspiracy. She shook her head. "Not tonight, Hunter. Please."

"Is something wrong, Cary?" Hunter moved to put his arm around her shoulders, but she drew away. "You look terribly pale. And...your hands are cold. Are you getting sick?"

"I feel...umm, yes. I do feel a little sick just now. It's probably only tension. I think I'll just go on home and get some rest."

"Will you be all right? Can I take you to your apartment?" His tone was once again caressing and she trembled at her traitorous response.

"I'll be fine! Go on. I'm sure you can find some-one else to eat dinner with you. I know how you hate to eat alone." She smiled crookedly.

Hunter looked puzzled. "No," he said quietly. "I wanted to eat with you. No one else will do."

Those were not the words she wanted to hear right now! She pressed her fingers against her temples, then turned her head away.

"I just...need to be alone now, Hunter. Good-bye."

He was silent for so long that Cary turned back to face him. She tried to interpret his expression, but a trick of the failing sun rendered his glasses into mirrors, reflecting only her own troubled face. She looked away, to hide the pain in her heart.

Hunter sighed. "Goodbye, then. I hope you feel better tomorrow."

She didn't answer. In a whirlpool of conflicting desires and questions, she went to her car and began the long, lonely trip home.

At the corner of Seventeenth and Kansas she thought of Louise. Maybe an evening of mindless games with her sister's infant daughter would be the perfect diversion. As a matter of fact, that might have been what she'd been missing for months—family and noisy relaxation. Perhaps Hunter's overtures had seemed so appealing only because she had been lonely for so long.

Cary pulled up in the carport beside Louise's large frame house and knocked on the back door.

"Oh, Cary! I'm so glad to see you! Come in and grab Lynette for a minute, will you?" Louise opened the screen door and then hurried abruptly back inside.

Cary followed her through the kitchen and down a short hall to her sister's sewing room. The house had once been a funeral parlor, with a large room full of empty caskets and the paraphernalia of interment. Now that room was filled with sewing machines, yard goods, dressmakers' manikins and drawing boards.

Louise often joked about the headless, legless manikins that crowded around the walls and the many customers who crowded in, also, for fittings. "This old house has seen a lot of bodies come and go," she would say, laughing. Her husband, Tommy, would then make a comment about the body that belonged in a bedroom upstairs, and Louise would blush like a new bride.

Sitting alone at one of the machines, Louise was stitching rapidly now on some pale dusky rose crepe. Lynette was in a bassinet nearby, crying. The sound of the infant's wail cut through Cary's own misery. She reached for the tiny six-week-old girl and held her close.

"Hush, Lynnie. Hush, now. Everything's going to be all right." Gradually, the baby's cries subsided into hiccups. She snuggled against Cary's shoulder and began to pat around gently with her tiny fists.

"Will you see if she needs changing, Cary?" Louise asked, her words oddly distorted by the row of pins she held in her teeth.

"She's just fine. All dry and warm, aren't you, little Lynnie?" Cary closed her eyes and let her senses drink in the scent of baby powder, the feel of soft down on Lynette's scalp, and the lightness of the tiny warm body nestled against her own. Yes, this was what Cary needed. It was almost easy to forget the world and the pain and confusion in it when she was holding such a small, fragile bit of innocence.

"Thanks, Cary," mumbled Louise. "I'll be finished here in just a few minutes. Today has been positively frantic."

"What's the big rush?"

"Emily Morgan is coming at six-thirty for her last fitting on this dress. It's for her retirement party tomorrow."

"Emily is retiring? I didn't think she would ever quit voluntarily!"

Louise looked up and smiled. She took the shiny pins from her mouth and said, "Well, I offered her a little inducement."

"You?"

"Yes. I asked her to work in my new boutique."

Cary almost dropped the infant in her arms. "Louise, you didn't—!"

Louise got up and danced over to her sister, a broad grin nearly splitting her face. "Yes, I did! I got the loan and the Belle Dame Boutique is on its way!" She reached out her arms and the two women embraced, Lynette wriggling between them.

"Oh, Louise! I'm so happy for you. I just know your store will be a big success. You'll have to tell me all about what you're going to do, and when."

Louise pulled away and looked at her watch.

"Cary, I'd just love to. But I'm going to have to kick you out in only a few minutes. It's almost time for Emily to get here. And after she leaves, Tommy is picking up a babysitter and taking me out some-place nice and expensive to celebrate."

"Oh. No problem. I'll just stop by sometime this weekend to hear the details." Cary hid her face near the baby's blankets, knowing her eyes might betray the bleak emptiness that had suddenly returned. She would be alone tonight after all. Alone with her doubts about the masquerade she was playing at Omega. Alone with her unsettling desire for a man she had met only two day ago.

Just then, the back door slammed and Tommy Shiplett breezed in, waving an armful of long-stemmed roses and singing, "Tonight, Tonight" from *West Side Story*. He pulled Louise into an ex-aggerated waltz and then crushed her in a happy bear hug.

Cary watched, and the emptiness inside her grew. Tommy wasn't a handsome man. He was very tall and blond, but his hair was thinning on top, he wore thick glasses that magnified his pale eyes, and he had the beginnings of a beer paunch. Louise was tall and slender like her husband and Cary. She had her sister's fair complexion and black hair. She and Tommy were perfect light and dark complements, Louise exuberant and flamboyantly creative, Tommy quiet and practical. But tonight, Tommy was caught up in the excitement of their future, and his face was boyishly alive with happiness.

The future. Cary had imagined one for herself only two days ago—stepping in for Mary Ellen and running the entire central region. A crazy dream that now seemed very far away. Perhaps impossibly far. She laid the squirming infant down and moved away.

"I'll be going now, Louise. Bye, Tommy. Congratulations again to both of you!"

"Good night, Cary. Pleasant dreams!"

By the time Cary pulled into her apartment parking lot, she was even more emotionally exhausted than she'd been at the airport. She was also unreasonably and uncharacteristically depressed by her sister's happiness.

She must be awfully tired or something to be reacting this way, Cary told herself. Surely she could handle being part of an investigation without falling apart. The combined tension and anxiety of not only today, but also of the past two weeks worrying about Mary Ellen and of the six months before that in Colorado must have taken their toll. What she needed was a good night's sleep Everything would look different tomorrow.

Yes, all she needed was sleep. She could deal with anything, anyone—tomorrow.

As she climbed the stairs to her second-story apartment, Cary felt a growing sense of peace and calm. The sun was down now and the raw, unfinished wood siding of the complex was full of intricate patterns of shadow in the growing dusk. Insects were beginning their evening serenade, and Venus could be seen glowing brightly below a faint new moon. The world was settling down quietly, and Cary willed her soul to silence, also.

But there in the deepening shadows beside her door sat a man, holding something bulky on his lap. Hunter.

Inexplicably, her exhaustion evaporated. Suddenly the birds of sunrise were singing somewhere, perhaps only in her mind, but their song echoed all around her in the evening dark.

"Cary?"

"Yes."

"Are you feeling better now?"

"Yes, much better." How could she tell him that a great wound had instantly been healed the moment she had recognized him, and her heart had realized that she wanted, more than anything, to be with him? Miracles were for other times and places and had nothing to do with her life.

He rose from the darkness and came toward her. "Good. I was worried about you. Now how about that dinner?"

Yes, oh, yes! A flood of energy washed over her. She was even hungry! How could she have thought his presence would only make her feel worse?

"Well, I'll have to change. I . . . stopped by to visit someone, and her baby just gurgled milk all over my shoulder."

"I'll wait. May I come in?"

In the dusk, his face was plains and valleys of shadows, some dark, some light. But the shape of one longer valley led her to believe Hunter was smiling. She knew she was.

He reached for her keys and unlocked the door. Inside, the lamp from her living room cast a realistic light on everything. He was definitely smiling. And he was holding a small plant of purple hothouse chrysanthemums.

"For you." He handed her the flowers. "I've never seen you in purple, but this color just seemed to be right for you. I hope you like them."

No, she had not worn purple the last three days—except for the amethyst dragons in the Chinese silk dress. So how had he known of her fondness for the color? A sudden idea brought a sparkle of dark gold to her topaz eyes.

"Oh, I like the flowers very much. Thank you."

Cary walked in to set the plant on the coffee table. Hunter followed. When she offered him a chair, he sat down and stretched his long, lean legs out toward the hearth. Slowly, he laid his head back on clasped hands, and it seemed to Cary that he was as comfortable on her old rented couch as if he had sat there a million times before.

Looking back at him and smiling in secret satisfaction, Cary went into the bedroom. She knew exactly what to wear tonight.

Gone was the feeling of exhaustion and the emptiness. If she had bothered to question their absence, she might have felt a remaining pang of doubt, for she and Hunter were still bound more by the crime of industrial espionage than by anything else. But she didn't want to question anything right now. She just wanted to be alive and to be with the man who was sitting on her couch in the next room. This feeling inside her was too simple for questions.

In her closet, her hand traveled across a multitude of shades of amethyst, lilac, purple and indigo. How had he guessed?

At last her hand paused and drew out a satin-smooth blouse of pale amethyst with matching lace-knit skirt and jacket. It was one of the first things Louise had ever made for her and—now she was remembering, with surprise—Louise had said this was Cary's special color. She would have to ask her sister why that was so.

She only took a few moments to dress. Hunter was standing by the cold fireplace when she returned to the living room. His eyes widened with admiration when he saw her.

"Mmm. Purple does look good on you."

"I don't know how you guessed, but my sister thinks so, too. Almost everything I own is some shade of this color."

"Come here and let me look at you."

Slowly, Cary walked closer, until she could smell

the lime-cool scent of him, until she could almost touch him.

He had said that he wanted to look at her. But after one flickering, brief drop of his glance Hunter looked nowhere else but into her eyes. And she into his eyes. They were so dark that pupil and iris seemed one. So steady and strong that Cary felt mesmerized by their intensity.

Hunter stepped toward her, his look unwavering, and she felt her own eyelids growing heavy with a languorous, sensual surrender.

His hands reached out, then touched her shoulders. Oh, so slowly, they slid down the lacy covering of her unresisting arms. He pulled gently at her hands, drawing her body close to his. . . as if drawing her soul to a union with his before she'd had even the grace of a kiss.

Cary knew now that she wanted him, with all the same longing she could read in his eyes. This was real; it was no fantasy. Heart to heart they stood, and promises were exchanged with each look. Her heart beat wildly, waiting.

Hunter wrapped his arms tightly around her and she was crushed against him, exulting in the heady feeling of victory and reward that swamped her mind so unexpectedly.

She had been right to think she meant more to him than an accomplice, after all!

Now he kissed her and she kissed him, again and again. But this was only a beginning. Some things would come later, in the now imaginable future.

Eventually, their kisses became slower, less

hungry and frantic, more satisfying, and at last her head rested against his thumping chest.

Cary smiled. They were still dressed! Yet she felt as if they had made a kind of silent, passionate love. She trembled from its aftermath, awash with its heat.

Hunter's voice rumbled close to her ear. "It's after seven. Are you hungry?"

It was time to pull away, to break the spell. She looked again at his eyes and knew that he would forego dinner if she said the word. *Hold on!* Cary warned herself silently. *Neither one of us is ready for lovemaking.* "Yes, it is late. I'm sorry I had to change clothes."

"Cary, I waited for you a long time. Another ten minutes didn't matter."

"Oh! How long did you have to wait? I was only at Louise's for a little while...."

"Honey, I've been waiting a lot longer than that for you. All my life, I think."

All she could do was look at him and drown in his eyes and his words. Some frightened part of her whispered that his words were only another way to win her cooperation, but her heart knew the truth. She'd been waiting, too. And now the tide had come in, bringing this love on its crest.

"Shall we go, then? I made reservations for seven-thirty." He gave her his arm, again playing the courtly knight. High color filled her cheeks as she walked with him out into the warm, starry night.

IT WAS A FRENCH RESTAURANT on Sixth Street, gracious and continental, redolent of garlic, onion and other tantalizing herbs.

"This is beautiful, Hunter. I didn't know this place existed. I don't remember it...."

"Perhaps you just never asked a bellhop to recommend the most romantic restaurant in town."

"No," she agreed, laughing. "I never did that."

As they talked, the planet spinned and the tides ebbed. But everything outside of themselves was only a framework, a necessary construct to support the true reality—Hunter and Cary.

The evening was a mystery, full of miracles. Time stood still while they looked at each other, yet time was also racing by them, hurling them headlong into circumstances too inevitable to be resisted.

Somehow Cary knew that tonight was magically different from any other. Strange things were happening to her tonight, unfamiliar feelings welled inside her every time she looked at Hunter.

Hunter Pierce, investigative reporter *extraordinaire*, was sitting across from her, making love to her with his spaniel eyes and his musical voice. And she knew her own eyes were drinking in that love as thirstily as if she had been parched for a thousand years.

It was dangerous, playing this game. Double dangerous, for romance was not the only high-stakes wager being offered at this table.

A man with the power to disrupt her ordinary world was sitting here with Cary, tamely listening to her jokes and offering anecdotes about people and places she had never seen. He might destroy her world eventually. She might lose out on all the opportunities that so recently seemed to be opening up before her. But then again, he might—he just might—be offering her a priceless chance at love that would make any loss worthwhile.

For together they might succeed. United, they might discover the truth and show it to the world. Theirs was a golden bright vision of a better world. And in this dream the *together* part was more important than all the rest.

"You're a very courageous woman, Cary. Not everyone would risk a good job to catch a thief, especially if that thief is not hurting her personally."

"You make me sound like a saint," Cary protested.

"No, you're just a very special lady."

He was silent, watching her, but she was not embarrassed by his praise. Cary was earning it the hard way. There was certainly a risk that Willingham, and she herself, would be hurt, even if Hunter and she were right. And if they were wrong. . .!

"Hunter V. Pierce. I know all about your *nom de guerre*, David Thompson. I've read his résumé very carefully. But I don't know nearly as much about you."

"Okay. What will you have? Age, height, weight and marital status first?" He looked at her sharply.

She laughed. *Yes, that's exactly what I want to know!* she thought.

"Thirty-four, six feet even, one hundred eighty pounds, never married." He grinned. "Satisfied?"

"No," she answered, grinning back. So he thought he knew which question she most wanted answered! This evening, his cavalier manner merely amused her. She wasn't about to let him see he was right, however.

"Where were you born? Where did you go to school? How long have you been in broadcasting? What's it like behind a camera? That's what I'm dying to know."

"Oh, you mean you're not just interested in my good looks?" He put on a pout and pretended to sulk for a moment.

"Ah! I have it!" He brightened. "You think I might be rich—the long-lost scion of some immensely wealthy —and conveniently dead—ancestor, like Texas's Shanghai Pierce. You're going to hold me for ransom and make your fortune with my undeserved millions, right?"

"No, you silly!" Cary was laughing and smiling so hard her cheeks began to hurt. "I've never even heard of Shanghai Pierce, but I certainly wouldn't want to kidnap you! That would be a disaster, I'm sure. I'd have to pay the station to take you back!"

"Oh, I'm not all that bad, am I?" His expressive face became the very picture of affronted pride.

"No, you're not half bad at all, Mr. Pierce." Her voice was husky, though she hadn't meant it to be. "But I think you're making it a habit not answering my questions."

"I'll happily break that habit because I think I've got a new one to replace it—you." His voice, too, was low and loaded with innuendo. They were saying so many things on so many levels, Cary could barely think straight.

"Like Shanghai, I'm from the South. Biloxi, Mississippi."

"So that's what I hear in your voice! I wondered...." She recalled the way she had first heard him say her name, softening it to "Caroline."

"I got my degree from the LBJ School of Journalism at the University of Texas. But a few years in Texas is my only connection to the infamous bandit Pierce. He was a cattle baron who built an empire on stolen herds. Whereas—"

"If you'd been born back then, you would have probably signed up to be a Texas Ranger, white hat and all."

"Are you making fun of me again?"

"No." This time she meant it. "I admire your principles."

"Thank you, ma'am," he replied, doffing an imaginary Stetson. "I reckon you know all there is to know about me now. As for television, it would mean more to you if I could take you to the station and show you how I work."

"Yes, I'd like that very much. By the way, what does the *V.* stand for?"

He grimaced.

"I was afraid you'd get around to asking that. My mother swore I owed my career to that name. When I was born, she wanted me to be a policeman, a nice respectable Irish policeman. She thought Hunter would be an appropriate name for a cop.''

"And the *V.*?" she reminded him.

"Victor. To insure I would always get my man." He looked embarrassed.

"Hunter Victor Pierce. It sort of rolls off the tongue, doesn't it? I like it. It suits you.''

"Hmm. I think I'll have you explain why sometime. In private, of course."

Hunter reached for her hand, but Cary scarcely noticed. The message in his eyes was far more physical than the mere touch of his fingers. She knew he would have made love to her earlier, if she had asked. And she knew she wouldn't have to wonder later, when they returned to her apartment. He was seducing her right now with his eyes.

"What do you think about . . . .''

"Life? It's pretty good, isn't it?" He pressed her fingers tightly.

Was that what she had started to ask? Funny, but Cary couldn't remember any of the things she probably ought to be saying, or thinking.

Somehow they finished eating. Hunter drove back through the dark streets, his hand now changing gears, now holding Cary's slim fingers. At her door, he waited until she actually asked him to come in. The invitation wasn't forced, yet it almost seemed she had no choice—this night was as inevitable as the tide.

Cary went to fill the brandy glasses and cut a fresh wedge of Brie cheese. Hunter lit a fire, though neither of them was cold. When Cary came back into the living room, he was standing in front of a print near the bookcase.

"That's my talisman. My Indian spirit. She goes with me on every assignment." Cary handed a glass to Hunter and stood beside him at the picture.

The woman depicted—surely a princess, for her bearing was regal, her pose beyond elegance—had an expression suggesting considerable pride. Her face was full, not fat but not hardship-thin, either. The firm features might almost have been a man's, but for the feminine softness of the eyes and mouth. From the woman's ebony hair hung a long, sleek feather, and near her waist were blossoms, the name of which was unknown to Cary but which evoked for her a pungent perfume and soft, succulent moisture-laden petals.

Cary was glad Hunter had been attracted to the Indian print, because she felt a strange affinity with the woman portrayed. Whenever she could not take the picture with her on a trip, it occupied a place of honor back in her apartment in Topeka.

"She's like you," said Hunter softly. "Proud and brave and beautiful. A princess."

He set aside the brandy and pulled Cary to him. His lips, tasting of liquor, brushed over her own, then swept on to caress her cheeks, her eyes, her hair. When his mouth reached her arching neck, she groaned with the heavy, heady pleasure of his touch.

Cary's fingers stole up his back, so broad her hands could barely meet across his shoulders. Her lips parted for his kiss and drew from it the honey sweetness of the brandy mixed with the taste of his desire.

Hunter was so powerful. And yet she had so much power over him that his arms trembled at her kiss, and his breath was quick and shallow. Cary recognized her dominion over him even as she surrendered completely to his easy control over her.

He turned and she moved with him, to the cream-and-cocoa couch before the fire, where he lifted her gently and placed her against the cushions. Slowly, he knelt beside her, leaning across her to lay his glasses aside and to turn off the lamp. She reached up and caught his hand as it left the switch and brought it down to kiss it. Then she touched his hair and pulled him to her.

Hunter kissed her lips again, then began those roving feather-light kisses that had aroused her so before. He caressed Cary's neck, her eyes, her ears—and then suddenly he was kissing the white skin above her bra, though when he had loosened her blouse Cary couldn't say. His hands were caressing her, but her mind was unable to realize at once all of the sensations he created, and each new touch was so distracting that she found herself dizzy.

This experience was so much fuller than she had ever imagined lovemaking could be.... Never had she been so overwhelmed with desire!

Her first love, Jason, long-ago Jason, in his casual, abstracted tenderness had never aroused in her such a fever. She had never longed for his touch the way her body ached now for Hunter's slightest caress. His tongue was gently teasing her nipples, and she wanted to scream with the agony of pleasure that coursed through her.

Drunk on sensation, Cary became aware that mixed with the lime scent of him was the hot breath of his desire. Cary's pulse raced wildly.

She opened Hunter's shirt and found the short curling hairs of his chest. They were bristly yet soft underneath. She reached up and slid the shirt off his shoulders to reveal smooth tensed muscles.

He stood and pulled her up against him. "You're some woman, Car'line Blaine." His voice was ragged, but his eyes were steady.

"And you're not like anyone I've ever known, Hunter Victor Pierce," she whispered.

She held fast to those midnight eyes looking at her, suddenly afraid. Was she making a horrible mistake in interpreting what she thought she saw there? Was she really more than just an unexpected bonus to his investigation? Was his hunger for her as special, as completely new and wonderful as her need of him?

Cary shuddered, feeling a strange chill. "Hold me!" she said, trembling.

Hunter put his arms around her and snuggled against her hair. "It's all right," he whispered, as if to a child. "It's all right."

Together they began a slow, hypnotic movement. It was almost a waltz, yet they did not move their feet. Cary swayed to his unsung melody as he continued whispering in her ear.

"I've been looking for someone like you for a

long time. You're the most lovely, witty, strong woman I've ever met. I want to hold you in my arms and feel your strength wrap around me.''

Cary could feel him harden against her and her breasts ached in instinctive response. They felt swollen, tender, unfulfilled. She arched back and his mouth came down to touch their fullness and to increase, rather than relieve, her need. Every molecule of her being was yearning for an end to this rising torment. She could hear her heart pounding, sending rivers of hot blood to increase the ache.

She was falling into space and only Hunter's arms saved her. He reached around her and pulled the quilt from her rocker and spread it on the floor beside them. Then he gently released his support and she slipped down to the quilt.

He stood for a moment longer and loosened his pants before he bent to slip off her skirt. As he looked at her, his breath quick and heavy, Cary's breasts rose and fell rapidly. She watched the look of hunger on Hunter's face and marveled that she was the cause of it.

Then he lowered himself beside her and resumed kissing her. She pulled him to her, rocking with a motion that matched the rhythm of his heart. And then they were lost inside each other; there were no more games, no more questions.

A roar like the ocean breaking on a million rocky shores echoed around her as she was lifted and then cast down in ecstasy. Waves of passion crashed through her again and again, at last subsiding as the tide does.

Cary's eyes opened wide in astonishment, seeing clearly in the darkness. *This* was what she'd been missing, what she'd craved. This was what her body had been made for.

"I'm so glad I found you," whispered Hunter. "I always knew I would."

"Oh, Hunter! I waited a long time for you, too."

"Was it worth it?" He grinned, teeth flashing in the dark night.

"Mmm!" She tried to lift her head high enough to kiss him once more, but her strength was gone, stolen from her by that sweet receding passion they had shared.

"Better watch it, woman." Hunter laughed. "The slightest movement on your part might trigger a repeat performance. And you haven't critiqued the last one yet."

"Was that what it was? A performance?" she whispered softly.

He must have sensed the tiny, almost-hidden fear behind her question, for he kissed her again, lightly, and whispered back. "There are no cameras, no script here, darling. Just the two of us, alone."

Cary tried to glimpse Hunter's eyes in the flickering firelight, but he had closed them, bent to her and silenced her with a kiss.

CHAPTER SEVEN

LATER, Hunter pulled on his "David Thompson" suit coat and glasses.

"Do you really need them?" she asked, pointing to his gray-rimmed glasses, as she gathered the thin purple blouse around her shoulders.

"No, but here in Topeka I run the most risk of being recognized. Wichita cable companies haven't picked up on KMKX yet, so I'm safer there. I can't run the risk of one of my many ardent fans here running up to me and asking for my autograph, now can I?" He grinned. "Besides, the glasses and all do help remind me of who I'm pretending to be. When I walk out that door, in a sense I really am David Thompson."

"Who am I saying good-night to, then?"

"Me. Hunter." He put a hand under her chin and tilted her face to the moonlight. "Don't worry. I won't ever be anyone else when I'm with you."

The melody of his voice made the promise into lyrics fit for a song. At that thought, Cary smiled. "You should have been a singer," she said.

"Not me! They have to work too hard. And they never get any time to just...be." He fiddled with the neck buttons on his shirt. "I'm really lucky, you know. I didn't expect you to be someone I could trust—someone I could really share with.''

Cary nodded. ''I didn't trust you, either, at first.''

''And now?''

But Cary dodged the question. Her remnants of doubt were probably only the product of strain and the suddenness and intensity of this experience. Nonetheless, something held her back.

''You know, don't you, that I'm falling in love with you?'' Hunter's voice was so soft, Cary almost missed his words. Now the tiny fear in her leaped up and raced through her, sending her thoughts spinning feverishly. She closed her eyes and covered them with her hand. But Cary couldn't shut out the echoes of Hunter's words.

''Too much, too soon?'' Hunter walked quickly to her side and put his hand on hers. ''I'm sorry if I rushed you, Cary. I knew you were tired tonight, and I shouldn't have taken advantage of that to press you into something. . . .''

''No! I. . .wanted you, too, Hunter. Very much.''

''Mmm, I thought so.'' He nuzzled her cheek contentedly. ''Then there's nothing wrong at all. Is there?''

''N-no. It's just that I'm still not sure about. . . .''

But Cary couldn't put a name to the uncertainty still lurking somewhere inside her. Perhaps it *was* their rapid move to lovemaking, but maybe it was the nature of the investigation that disturbed her. Or perhaps it was merely an inclination to stay away from entanglements while she was on a temporary assignment.

Something held her back uneasily. Something in Hunter's tentative declaration of love made her draw back. Perhaps she shouldn't have given in to her need tonight. Not with so many questions still unanswered, still unrecognized. It hadn't really been fair to either of them.

But then her body remembered the passion that had raged inside her when Hunter had touched her. Cary realized that, given another chance, she would have made the same mistake again, if mistake it was.

"It will come, princess. Give it time. We'll make a great team." He held her close. "And, if it's all right with you," his beautiful voice continued, "I'd like to work on getting to know you...well enough to chase all the goblins away the next time."

"Yes, I'd like that," she whispered, turning to kiss him lightly.

He was silent for several seconds.

"You know I have to be going now, Cary. I have a lot of work to catch up on tomorrow and arrangements to make for the future." He pushed her away gently. "But if you don't get some more clothes on soon, lady, you may find yourself under siege again, ready or not."

Cary laughed and rose. No, she definitely wasn't ready for more. Not yet. She picked up her clothes and went to the bedroom. There, she pulled on a mauve quilted robe and came back to find that

Hunter had donned his tie and was getting ready to leave.

"I have three shows to tape this weekend," he said at Cary's door. "I won't be able to get back here before Monday."

"I'll miss you."

"I was hoping you'd say that, princess." Then he was out the door and starting down the balcony stairs. "I'll phone you. This investigation is gonna be fun!" he called from the bottom, just before he disappeared into the darkness of the courtyard.

It was still a game for him, she thought with a slight frown.

Wearily, Cary returned to the bedroom. She was so exhausted now, there was no question but that she would sleep tonight!

IN THE MORNING she woke refreshed for the first time in what seemed to be ages. She had slept well and soundly.

Cary's feelings of lightheartedness were still mixed with uncertainty all day on Friday. In every dark head of curling hair, she saw Hunter's. In the measured tones of other voices, she longed for the special music of his.

It was difficult to concentrate on reading résumés and filing reports when the wind whistled outside her window, and Hunter was sixty miles away in Kansas City. Each time the phone rang, her pulse quickened.

At noon, he called. "Hello, princess. I just

wanted you to know I've got all the arrangements made here. I'm ready to start work at Omega whenever Henry calls.''

"Well, that's good to know. You're a little overconfident, don't you think? Is that the only reason you called?''

"No, but it seemed like a good excuse at the time. Will you have dinner with me Monday night after I settle things with Crandon?''

"There you go, getting even more arrogant. Pretty sure you're going to get that job offer, aren't you?''

"Yep. And if Suzanne told Omega anything like what she told me, she's a cinch, too.''

"What did she tell you?''

"That she's money-hungry. She likes the excitement of working for the government, but not the pay. She figures she can make at lease twice her current salary by moving to the private sector. That speaks of greed to me. And Omega is looking for greedy people.''

Cary drew a deep breath. "Hunter, I know you may not understand this, but I hope you're wrong.''

"About Suzanne? It would sure make my job easier if Crandon offered her a special deal right off the bat. I think she'd tell me about it if he did, too. She thinks I'm a good listener. Uh, you're not jealous, are you?''

"Be serious! I meant that I hoped you were wrong about everything connected with this charge of espionage. I just can't believe all these people can be so willing to sell secrets that belong to someone else. I guess I don't want to believe it.''

"Cary, honey, you need to be protected from your own naiveté. And I know just the man for the job. Are you going to have dinner with me on Monday or not?''

Cary sighed. Hunter's voice was so seductive, even when he was joking. She really couldn't resist him.

"Of course I'll have dinner with you.''

"And afterward?''

"Maybe we'd better hold off on the afterward for a while. Okay?''

"Mmm. I'll call you before I leave the station. Bye.''

And that's what you call a noncommittal answer, Cary thought ruefully.

She had hoped that after Hunter phoned, as he had promised her last night, she could concentrate on work. But Hunter invaded her mind. She tried to focus on the charity contributions' budget for Kansas, but the words and numbers couldn't fill her mind.

The other half of her assignment was to make some long-range recommendations for the Willingham operation in Kansas and to get the firm more actively involved in community relations in Topeka. So far, all she'd had time to do was make that ill-fated speech at Central High. Now she needed to come up with a whole lot more quality activities. This challenge had really excited her when she'd been given the job two months ago. Today it seemed mere drudgery. Would Monday never come?

Her buzzer indicated a message from her secretary.

"Yes, Marian?"

"Miss Hughes is here. She would like to see you."

"Mary Ellen? Of course! Send her in."

Cary got up to open her office door just as Mary Ellen reached it. The two women shook hands cordially.

Mary Ellen Hughes was quite petite. Even with her silver blond hair fluffed up in curls on top of her head, she barely reached Cary's shoulder. She was wearing a dark green suit, which emphasized the sallowness of her complexion.

When the older woman had been seated, Cary asked, "How are you feeling?"

"Great. Just great." Mary Ellen's smile was broad and confident, but Cary had noticed that she sat stiffly.

"Coffee?" she asked.

"Wish I could, but no. They won't let me touch it."

"Oh, that's a real hardship for you, I know. You were a 'ten-cupper,' weren't you?"

"And now I'm a teetotaler, too. But enough of that. It's good to see you again, Cary. Now I can thank you in person for helping out at the main office while I was ill." Still keeping the broad smile, Mary Ellen carefully altered her position in the chair a bit.

"Surely you didn't come all this way to thank me!" exclaimed Cary.

"No, no. Just passing through. I've got to check on all my divisions at budget time, you know."

Cary nodded. But surely this wasn't a regular budget-planning trip. No one had been notified. The Topeka office wasn't prepared to present plans yet. Cary wondered what Mary Ellen's real purpose might be.

"By the way, you've done great work, Cary, on the Omega job. Henry Crandon tells me you've got him two more people."

"You've talked to Henry today?"

"Yes. He's ecstatic, as only Henry can be, and I'm really proud of you."

"Well, thank you. But Henry told me he wouldn't know for certain until Monday. Did they reach their decision early? Can I call the applicants?"

"Hold on, young woman! You sound as excited as Henry. No, the decision is final, but not official. So you can't call anybody yet. But you haven't even asked me who the successful candidates are! Don't you want to know?"

"Yes, of course." Cary's heart began hammering, and her hands were damp with anticipation.

"Suzanne Foley and David Thompson."

Cary breathed again.

"Henry says they were all especially pleased by Thompson. Good for you!"

"Th...thanks. I hope he works out for them."

Lying to Henry had been difficult, but lying to Mary Ellen was going to tear her apart!

"Sure he will, don't you fret. How's the community-relations program coming?"

Cary winced. "To tell the truth, Mary Ellen, I haven't spent much time on it. But I'm working on it right now, and I plan to make a preliminary report by the end of the week. Is that all right?"

She expected a reproof after having spent a whole afternoon away from the office, but Mary Ellen surprised her. "Fine," came the cheerful, jovial response. "Just fine. But don't forget Henry still needs one more engineer." Though Mary Ellen still smiled, Cary thought she was showing signs of pain in her posture and her over-bright eyes.

"I won't forget. Is there anything else you need?" Cary waited for another reminder to keep her nose out of headquarters' affairs. But it did not come.

"No. That's it. Everything seems to be going very well here. I probably won't be back again until it's time to talk serious money plans." She rose slowly. Cary was sure she was in considerable pain, but Mary Ellen kept smiling. "Have a good weekend!" she offered, shaking Cary's hand.

With a worried frown, Cary closed the door behind her supervisor.

What a complete change from yesterday! They both knew why Cary had not worked on the community-relations program, but Mary Ellen hadn't even mentioned Cary's afternoon absence or her own illness and Cary's unappreciated trip to St. Louis. On the contrary, Mary Ellen had been careful to say only positive things, encouraging things. She had denied her very obvious pain.

And Cary didn't believe for a moment that her supervisor was just "passing through," or that she had made the trip from St. Louis just to commend Cary for the good job she was doing at Omega.

Nevertheless, it was great to be back in Mary Ellen's good graces. And Hunter was as good as hired!

Cary's spirits soared, transporting her through the rest of the day on a cloud high above the mundane world of Willingham, paper and people. She wanted to share her good feelings, but there was only one person she could safely talk to. And he wasn't available until Monday.

Cary picked up the telephone and dialed outside.

"Louise, I know you went out last night, but can you get a babysitter for tonight, too? I'll pay."

Her sister sounded tired. "No, hon, I don't think so. It's Friday night and all the high-school kids have football games or dates. What's up?"

"Well, don't put anything on for dinner. I'll bring all the fixings. I want to celebrate my only sister's fabulous news."

"That's a great idea. I could tell you were too busy last night to join Tommy and me." She sounded a little miffed. But that wasn't like Louise.

"Last night? Oh, no. I came over hoping to have dinner with you, but you didn't invite me.

Remember?'' Had Louise wanted her to invite herself?

"Oh, really? Well, you must have gotten a better invitation then, later, didn't you?''

Now Cary could hear suppressed laughter in her sister's voice.

"What are you talking about?''

"We were sitting just two tables away from you at Le Flambeau all evening, but you didn't even look our way.'' Louise chuckled and paused to let Cary absorb that information. "That's really some guy you've got there, Cary. Where have you been hiding him?''

"It's a long story, Lou. You probably won't believe half of it, but I'll tell you all about him tonight. Six o'clock?''

"Fine. But don't bring any wine. We've still got plenty of champagne left from last night.''

At five o'clock, Cary stopped at a grocery store on her way to Louise's house and bought thick sirloins, ears of corn, a cheesecake and charcoal for grilling. It wasn't as grand fare as she would have liked to provide, but on short notice Louise would appreciate not having to cook, she knew.

"Cary, you look radiant!'' Louise hugged her warmly as soon as she had set down the grocery bags.

"You too, Lou. How does it feel to be in business for yourself?''

"Absolutely grand! And a little scary. Oh, just a minute.''

From the rear of the house came a soft cry and

Louise spun quickly at the sound, her patchwork skirt whirling around her. Today, she looked like a Gypsy in her multicolored skirt and embroidered blouse. A bright crimson scarf held back her long black hair.

The two sisters had identical coloring and were nearly the same height. Cary knew if she was wearing the same Gypsy outfit, they would look almost like twins. But while Louise always chose pale pastels and muted, dusky colors in the clothes she designed for Cary, she sewed only vivid hues and color mixtures for herself. And each of the two women looked perfect in her own way.

Louise had such great, natural taste! If only the women who came to her would listen to her advice about style and color, her shop was sure to be a success.

Smiling to herself, Cary started a fire in the grill on the patio and shucked the corn. Louise came out in a few minutes with Lynette and began to nurse her daughter by the fire.

"Okay. I'm all settled now. Who is he, Cary?" Louise had tucked a shawl around herself and Lynette, sheltering them both from the chill evening.

"Oh. His name is Hunter Pierce and—"

"Not the Hunter Pierce from KMKX!"

"Why, yes. Did you recognize him?" Cary asked quickly. If Louise had known him, perhaps others would!

"Oh, no. I've only seen him on television, of course. And he doesn't dress like that or wear glasses on TV. I'm impressed. Now, how do you happen to know him?''

''I'm part of his latest investigation.''

''No! Really?''

Louise was not shocked at all, bless her. In fact, her expression seemed to be one of great satisfaction. She lifted Lynette and began burping her.

''You don't seem to be very worried, Lou. I said Hunter Pierce is investigating *me*!''

''Well, he has obviously decided you're totally innocent, hasn't he?''

''Yes, he has. But how could you know that?''

''I watched you both all evening, you remember?'' Louise smiled with just a touch of smugness. ''I can recognize infatuation when I see it, dear.''

''You...you think Hunter is infatuated with me?''

''Uh-huh. And the feeling is mutual, isn't it? Congratulations, sis. You've hooked yourself a winner! Here.'' Louise handed Cary the fussing infant. ''You burp her. You might as well start practicing.''

Cary blushed and took Lynette up to her shoulder. ''Now Lou, don't start counting chickens yet. The only thing that's hatched so far is a weird little plot to spy on Omega Aircraft.''

A tiny hollow noise signaled the baby's successful burp, and Cary reluctantly handed her back to Louise. The fire was almost ready for the steaks.

''Where's Tommy?''

''Oh, he'll be here. Sometimes he works late at

the office. But he's almost always here by six-thirty. If he's not . . . I'll take his steak!''

''Heartless!'' Cary went back inside to get the meat. While she cooked it over the bright flames, her heart kept skipping to a beat that echoed the words in her head. *Take care! Take care! It's too fast, too soon. Didn't we agree on that?*

Cary repressed her pounding sense of anticipation and stared at the orange glare in front of her with calm eyes. But the flames continued to leap, and a part of her struggled to join their wild, uninhibited dance.

When Tommy finally arrived, he looked less exuberant than he had the evening before. Louise put it down to his being a new papa and the accompanying late nights. But as Cary was preparing to leave, he caught her alone in the living room.

''Cary, can I come see you at your office on Monday?''

''Sure, Tommy. Anytime. Just tell my secretary who you are and come right in. Is anything wrong?''

''Maybe. But I don't want to worry Lou just yet.'' He laughed, a strained chuckle that died too soon. ''Maybe it's nothing. But I would like to talk about it.''

''Of course. You know I love you both. If there is anything I can ever do, just name it. And I'll see you whenever you like on Monday.''

''Thanks, Cary. Thanks.''

It had not been the best way to end the evening. Tommy had never talked to her much about anything. He was a very quiet man. But Cary could sense he was worried about something, and she was upset that there would be no explanation forthcoming for days. She hoped Tommy's concern was nothing that could affect Louise's new business, now that her sister was finally achieving the success she so deserved!

Sunday morning, Cary want to church with Tommy and Louise. He said no more about his worries, but he looked as if he hadn't slept at all. Cary noticed that he seemed pale, also. Too pale for having spent a summer under hot Kansas sunshine. Was he ill?

A knot of fear clenched inside Cary. If Tommy was ill, Louise didn't know of it—she was certain. *Dear Lord,* she prayed. Don't let something terrible happen to them. Not now!

The silence in her heart, though, as she watched Tommy, was a cold winter emptiness frosted with fear.

As she was fixing dinner that evening, it occurred to her for the first time that her cable-TV system probably included Hunter's channel. She flipped to station after station until she finally hit upon the right one. Peeling carrots, she listened for the special voice she had not heard since Friday.

"And now, here's Hunter Pierce on 'Lineup' with a report about some special children who may be losing their home soon."

Cary let the carrots slide down into the sink.

"This is the Good Hope Orphanage in St. Joseph, Missouri. Today it houses...."

Yes, it was Hunter. Cary watched his image on the flickering screen curiously. There seemed to be no trace of gray in the rich black mane that surrounded his face. A trick of the camera? He was wearing slacks and a bright red cardigan sweater, embroidered over his left breast with the KMKX news logo. Louise had said the sweater was Hunter's trademark. He was not wearing the gray-rimmed glasses that hid his spaniel eyes, either.

But it *was* Hunter. Her heart raced. She would have known his voice, the way he smiled, even if he had been wearing a clown costume. Surely anyone who had seen this program and heard him speak would recognize him as David Thompson!

Cary barely listened as he related the financial problems faced by the orphanage. His report ended with a plea for private contributions. Too soon his voice and face were replaced by the station's news logo and the bland tones of the anchorman.

"Beginning on Monday, KMKX and Hunter Pierce will examine in depth the alcoholic-beverage industry in Missouri and Kansas: Two Systems of Control. How big is the drink business? Who makes money and who loses? Just how much control is there? Some of the answers may surprise you."

Cary turned off the set and fumbled around the counter, looking for her carrots.

Everything about Hunter Pierce surprised her. His sensitivity, his anger, his passion. Tonight his appearance had startled her. Gone was the immaculately dressed, perfect businessman who had been David and then Hunter—the man who had looked like a model junior executive behind sedate spectacles.

Tonight she'd seen a younger-looking Hunter, more casual and less dignified. And infinitely more attractive. In his scarlet cardigan and with his professional coolness, he seemed so remote from her. This image on the screen could be a magician or a famous celebrity, someone wholly apart from the very special but very ordinary man who had whispered, "I'm falling in love with you."

Cary had argued that they should get to know each other better, but how many versions of the public Hunter Pierce would she have to learn to live with?

There was just one single man at the private core of him. The man who was simply Hunter. But he enjoyed being all those other people, too. Would he always be able to keep his private life separate from the work he loved, or would he someday find himself forced to mix the two? It was one more troubling question she would have to find an answer for...soon.

CHAPTER EIGHT

UNEXPECTED AND UNPREDICTED, vast hordes of dense and mighty stormclouds formed over the Midwestern plains during the night. By Monday morning, northeastern Kansas was being drenched with long-awaited rain. The moisture-laden air smelled clean and good, but the dark daytime gloom was vaguely depressing.

Hunter hadn't called all weekend. He'd said he would be busy. Cary had waited in vain until late each night, but he hadn't phoned since Friday. It was discouraging to realize how much she had counted on hearing from him. Cary hadn't even been able to tell him Mary Ellen's news.

Her formal morning schedule was completely clear. That meant she had no excuse to dawdle any longer on the community-relations program. She had only until Friday to pull together some kind of preliminary report.

Nagged by this deadline, Cary still sat with several open files and a blank note pad before her, staring out her window wall at the downpour. If the sky was any kind of omen, this was going to be a bad day. But she could sit and worry about the weather, her feelings for Hunter and his investiga-

tion, she could even worry about Tommy's health—
or she could go to work and get something done.

The Career Day speech had been one way to
make the Willingham name public, but it was only a
beginning. Mary Ellen wanted her to find some
fresh new ways to get the office involved in the life
of the area it served. Pulling open the files, Cary
went over the list of charities and agencies that had
asked for and received money during the last five
years. A few of them no longer existed, victims of
bureaucratic neglect or poor management. A few
new ones had sprung up to fill the gap. But in
general, the list was a deadly dull one, full of good
causes and money spread tissue thin among them.
Cary wondered, for the hundredth time, if such tiny
amounts of cash could really do any good.
Wouldn't it be more effective if a lot of money
could be channeled into only a few first-class projects?

How to select the privileged few, however? That
was the problem. Obviously, those who had worked
the budget before had encountered the difficulty and solved it by continuing to allocate minuscule amounts to every worthy organization in the
area.

Spurred on by the constant dismal chatter of
raindrops on her window, Cary made her decision
and began to cut at the budget, ruthlessly crossing
out all the tiniest sums, then the next smallest
amounts, until she was left with only twelve major
contributions and more than three thousand dollars
in excess funds. So far, so good. Now she had to

decide whether to split up the excess among the dozen, or look for one more project to bestow the whole amount upon.

Cary read through the list of twelve again. Good charities, all of them. But not a one could be singled out as needing the special attention of a personnel agency. What she felt Willingham should try to find was a cause it could stand behind that related directly to employment—some cause that could serve as the basis for a community-involvement program, too. But what?

The high-school students who couldn't get jobs!

It was a perfect, important problem with no ready-made solution. Willingham money would be well spent if they could come up with a successful program to find jobs for these local kids.

Her intercom buzzed.

"Yes, Marian?"

"Dwight Miller from the school board wants to know if he can see you as soon as possible. He has a proposition he would like to discuss with you."

What luck, Cary thought. *Here comes my special project, right on cue.* The fates seemed to be working on her side today, despite the foul weather.

"Tell him I'll be happy to see him whenever he can get here."

Quickly, she raced through her figures again and made sure of the total amount available for donation. She would not mention it to Miller, but she needed to know the size of the project they could begin planning.

Her buzzer sounded again. This time it was Tommy. She went over and opened the heavy oak door for him.

"What is it, Tommy?" she asked, dreading the answer.

He walked slowly over to her window and stood there, staring out at the dripping trees. But he said nothing. Cary felt rather than saw that his shoulders were sagging as if he bore an incalculable weight.

"It's my job, Cary. I'm going to be laid off in two weeks."

"Oh, no! But Tommy, you've been working for Hanson Development for more than ten years! Why you?"

He turned around and Cary saw he was trying to smile. He had a sardonic expression that looked out of place on his normally bland features. "It's not just me. They're cutting forty percent off the payroll and they're doing it by function. My whole department is being abolished, except for one junior accountant."

Cary sat down behind her desk. Before her danced visions of Louise's shop, glowing with color and life. All lost dreams now.

"Can you help, Cary? You're the only one I can ask. I...can't tell Louise. Not yet."

"No, of course you can't. I'll get to work on it today. You're an excellent financial planner, and you have lots of good experience. We'll find something, don't worry." Cary's words hid her own personal panic, but she maintained a facade of calm assurance with her best reassuring smile.

Tommy sighed. "I know things are tight right now, but I'll appreciate anything you can find. Anything." His shoulders were still drooping, and he looked lost as well as weary. "I just can't destroy Louise's chances now. She's worked so hard—"

He turned back to the window, and Cary knew it was to hide the glitter of tears.

She came to stand beside him, her arm around his waist. "It isn't that tight, Tommy," she hedged. "We'll find something real soon. Something good, I promise. Now get that defeated look off your face and go fix up your résumé."

"Thanks, Cary. I don't know what I'd do if I didn't have you just now."

Cary felt tears beginning to cloud her own eyes, and she shook her head to chase them away. "Just be cheerful and happy for Louise. We don't want her to worry, do we?"

"No, we don't. I won't let her down, Cary. I promise."

Tommy shrugged into his raincoat and went out into the ugly gray day, leaving Cary to sit in shocked silence inside her brightly lit office.

Just when the world seemed to be beginning a whole new turn, when her own future was starting to look brighter, this had to happen to Louise!

She thought of the disillusioned young forester who still didn't have a job, and her jaw hardened with resolve. She would find Tommy something good, and soon. If she had to beg for it, she would find him a job!

The meeting with Dwight Miller was another disappointing surprise. His "proposition" was nothing more than a meeting he had scheduled in a few days to discuss the problems brought up during the Career Day activities. No, he had no ideas. Yes, they had tried conventional work-study arrangements, apprenticeships, teen job hotlines, everything. Nothing had worked. Now he wanted as many area employers as possible to sit down with the board, a couple of student-council members and some interested professionals for a brainstorming session.

It sounded to Cary as if the idea would involve far too many people to produce anything but chaos, but she couldn't refuse to attend.

By lunchtime, she had developed a slight nausea, with anxiety and frustration warring for dominance in her emotions.

At two, she received a message to have Suzanne and Hunter call Henry Crandon for salary negotiations. She called Suzanne, but Hunter was out filming and couldn't be reached. Cary was uncertain who at KMKX knew of Hunter's investigation, and she decided to leave a cryptic message for Hunter to call "the nervous man in Wichita." A very young-sounding, enthusiastic receptionist took the message and said she would be sure to give it to Mr. Pierce "the very minute he walks in the door."

Cary sighed. She had been hoping to talk to him directly, to let the sound of his voice banish the real world for a while and allow her to see some sunshine.

But the day continued to be gloomy and unlucky. There were no current requests for accountants, controllers or financial analysts in the Willingham files for Topeka. And she knew Tommy wouldn't consider leaving—now that Louise had a loan for the store here—unless it was a last resort. In desperation, Cary checked the regular personnel-placement file requests for bookkeepers, but the salaries were less than half what Tommy would need to make the first few loan payments and feed his new family until the store began paying for itself.

When her phone rang at four o'clock, she was aggravated and irritable. "Hello," she snapped.

"Hey, that's no way to greet the man who's going to buy you dinner, ma'am."

"Oh, Hunter. I'm sorry. It's been a very bad day."

"Well, cheer up! It can only get better. I'll be there in an hour and a half. And be prepared to smile, or I'll tickle you silly!"

"You wouldn't!" she retorted, grinning in spite of herself.

"Is that a dare? I never pass up a dare."

"No. I'll bet you don't. But in that case, it is most definitely *not* a dare."

"Aw, shucks. I was looking forward to making you helpless with laughter. I like my women helpless."

"That's not what you said the other day," she reminded him softly. He'd called her strong and brave and told her he had waited a long time to find her. The memory of his words sent a warming glow through her, a glow that had the power to light even the dim evening outside.

"No, that's not what I said when I saw you. You changed my life, you know." His voice was lower now, not bantering. "Until later, princess."

"Later," she echoed.

IT WAS ALMOST SIX when he finally arrived. The rain had stopped, and the world had taken on a curious, hollow feeling. The sky was still cloudy but a sickly yellowish glow pervaded everything. There was no wind at ground level, but high gray masses of moisture roiled and whirled across the heavens.

Cary stood on her balcony, watching Hunter's long stride as he came up to meet her.

"How are you feeling now?" he asked after they had kissed—a light, gentle hello kiss.

"Just fine now," she answered and meant it.

"I heard the weather forecast as I was pulling up. A tornado warning has been issued for our area. Does that mean we shouldn't go out to eat?"

"I think you must have heard them wrong. The last forecast I listened to mentioned a watch, not a warning."

"What's the difference?"

"How long have you been in the Midwest, anyway?" she asked, laughing.

"Nine months."

"And you don't know about tornadoes? Amazing, Mr. Newsman. Tornado watches happen all the time in the summer; they just mean that weather conditions are right to form tornadoes. Usually, nothing happens at all—and I would really be surprised if one even formed this late in the year.

"A warning means a tornado has been sighted somewhere nearby, and everybody should be prepared for an alert."

"I guess an alert is when a funnel is actually coming down on your head, right?"

"If you can't make it big with crime and corruption, you can always try rain and snow. Everybody loves a handsome weatherman."

"They do?"

"Absolutely. Now I'm famished. How about that dinner?"

Hunter extended his arm, and Cary slipped her own around it comfortably.

As they were talking, the sky began to lose its eerie yellow glow and turn dark.

"At least it isn't raining anymore," commented Hunter as they started down the stairs.

"Little does he know!" Cary exclaimed. "You never start to worry about tornadoes until it stops raining."

As if her words were prophetic, the Civil Defense sirens began their loud wailing, echoing in the hollow air.

"This is it!" cried Cary.

She pulled Hunter with her down the stairs and into the apartment complex's laundry room in the basement. Within five minutes they were joined by the rest of the building's occupants. Some brought food, lawn chairs and lanterns, others hauled down radios, portable TVs and Monopoly games. In short order, the laundry room became a neighborhood recreation center and the sound of laughter and conversation rose above the howling winds outside. Hunter found them both seats on a long narrow table where they could watch all the activity.

"Why doesn't anyone else but me seem to be worried?" asked Hunter.

"Well, for one thing this is the first week of October," said Cary, smiling. "I don't ever recall hearing of a major tornado this late in the year."

"But I thought you said—"

"I'm sorry. I didn't mean to imply that we would definitely be hit if a warning sounded. Chances are very high that we won't. There's nothing to be worried about. Besides, what else can we do but laugh and pass the time? You can't let the weather give you ulcers."

"But if there's a tornado up there—"

"Oh, there might actually be one up there, of course. But it may not come all the way down to the ground, or it may skip over us, or it may not cause much damage. We're probably perfectly safe."

"Probably," Hunter repeated. He tilted his head to listen to the shrill whistling wind and looked at her questioningly. Suddenly, the lights went out. In the darkness, he leaned closer and whispered, "I think I'd feel much better if I had someone warm and soft to hold onto."

His arm snaked behind her, and suddenly Cary was lifted into his lap. His face came round to hers and he was kissing her deliberately, moving as she moved so that she had no choice but to allow his insistent caress. Even here, even surrounded by strangers in the pitch black he could provoke a response in her that defied all logic, all reason. What did the presence of strangers matter anyway? All that was real was this feeling of lassitude in Hunter's arms and his honeyed kisses raining down on her. Had she really thought she could resist him?

Someone jostled against their table. Startled, Cary opened her eyes to see candles being lit around the cavernous room. As the winds howled outside, a mimicking draft brushed all the tiny flames to flickering stars and people rushed to protect their bits of light. They totally ignored the man with the woman in his lap.

Hunter's arms wrapped around Cary more tightly than before, as if he would never let her go. He lifted her hair and kissed her cheek, then the tender spot on her neck behind her ear. He touched his lips lightly to her eyes, while he shifted her weight across his lap. Suddenly, Cary knew the strength of his desire was increasing dangerously.

"Hunter, not here," she protested weakly.

"Mmm. Why not? No one's looking, and if I'm going to die, I want to do it holding you."

She shoved at his chest gently but firmly. "You're not going to die."

"But I might. I might die of wanting you, right here and now," he whispered in her ear. "My cool, calm princess sitting there so regally. Don't you know what you do to me? It's more dangerous than any storm, I promise you.''

''But—''

His kisses began roving over her neck and throat, starting the pattern of her downfall again. He knew so well the words of love, how to summon her physical surrender with his silken voice alone. But Cary would call her heart's defeat a partial victory for she could feel him tremble when he spoke to her and touched her.

Old-fashioned Jason had never trembled so, had never made her shiver and lose control. Nor had anyone else ever tempted her like this. Only Hunter could lead her to these dizzying heights of sensual bliss with just the whispering touch of his warm, delicious lips.

She and he were transformed when this awesome power surged through them, primitive lovers in touch with the heavens, the only people on a paradise planet where work and worry and pain had no hold. The howling wind and the darkness had been banished.

Then the lights came back on. Cary was not startled, mesmerized as she was by Hunter's touch. Gently, she drew away from him, her eyes full of regret. Yet she stayed on his lap, comfortable and untroubled, until the sirens at last wailed the all-clear signal.

They were the last to leave the basement, walking hand in hand up the steep wooden stairs.

Outside, the sky was a deep Mediterranean blue. In the West where day was dying, its cerulean brightness was streaked with gold, scarlet and purple. The only clouds were wisps of fluffy white against the brilliant color.

"What a magnificent sunset! It's hard to believe the sky is this clear," remarked Hunter. "Only a while ago, it was black with threatening stormclouds. It's like the calm in the eye of a hurricane."

He turned to her with a frown. "Is it like that? Will there be another, worse storm right behind this one?"

"No, the storm has passed completely. Summer storms here are often like that—dumping tons of rain and bringing wind very quickly and racing on."

The frown gradually left Hunter's face as he looked around at the gently dripping trees and flowers that swayed in a cool breeze.

"After all that menacing gloom and those howling winds, the world can look like this paradise! It's truly awesome. Well, one storm down and one to go. How about your doubts?"

"Doubts?"

"About us. Where we are and where we're going. It's been three days, Cary. Have you had enough time to accept what's happening between us?"

He was facing her, outside in the courtyard where branches ripped out by the storm littered the grass and concrete. His dark eyes were so intense with feeling that Cary knew a moment's panic.

She'd let it happen again! In the darkness and the

urgency generated by an approaching storm, she had once more lost control, given in to lust. How could she!

She was no sex-starved wanton rushing headlong into bed with every handsome stranger who propositioned her. And certainly not with a business partner. She had thought she knew better than that!

Besides, there was so much more to a relationship than bedroom fun. She wouldn't want to find out too late that there were parts of Hunter she couldn't live with. Jason French hadn't wanted to know her. He'd been content to make love to her—until the time came when he wanted something else she had to refuse to give.

She felt her fingers curl tightly into fists of nervous frustration. She wouldn't make that mistake again, with Hunter or anyone else.

"I...I'm not sure what you want from me, Hunter," she temporized, trying to pull her wits together. "We're supposed to be working together."

"I want you, Caroline Blaine. All of you. Not just the part that's helping me in the investigation." He took her hands and gently uncurled the fingers, slipping his own around her palms. "What are you afraid of? Hasn't anyone ever wanted to make love to you before?"

"Is that...what you meant by 'where we're going'?" she asked in a low whisper.

"I meant tonight and all the tomorrows. The future. Our future together, princess."

"Hunter, please! The future is not something we just decide on like that. It depends on—things. Don't you want to know me first?" Her voice trailed away. The something that wanted her to run away was strong now, warning her to retreat.

"I know you, Cary, and you know me. That was me in that laundry room tonight. The real me. What else do you need to know? I drink coffee black, I run four miles every day, my favorite color is red. Do you want to know my salary and bank balance, too?"

"No. Please," she repeated. "Let go of me. Those aren't the questions I'm talking about. I haven't had time to—"

"Look at me!" he said quietly but firmly.

She looked, and his soft spaniel eyes were glittering with some suppressed emotion. Anger? Or desire?

She had her answer quickly, for his head bent down to hers and his lips pressed hungrily against her mouth. Cary's legs trembled weakly. Torrents of feeling washed over her, urging her to surrender. Her breasts pressed against him, and there might as well have been no fabric at all between her skin and his. Her nipples hardened against the heat that blazed through from his chest.

Hunter had raised her arms, pulling her up to him. Now she wound them feverishly around his neck, drawing support for her weakness. Every movement of his lips made her stomach tense. She should stop this, but, oh, it was far too difficult!

Suddenly, Hunter gently pushed her away. Her eyes searched his, questioning.

"Cary, listen to your body. You *know* what you're feeling! I know it, too. You want me now, but you won't admit it. Why?"

"I...know what my body feels, yes," she admitted. *Yes! My body is empty without you!* "But that's not all there is—just physical feeling. There should be more...inside." Her eyes were wide with appeal. The night's still strong breeze had blown her long black curls wildly around her face. She felt as if she should take flight on that wind, flee from his questions and his kisses.

"Can't we slow down?" she pleaded, denying her need. "Why don't we wait...until your investigation is over?"

"For what, Cary? What we've got is here and now. Don't fight it so. I know you as well as I need to. You're like me, princess. We go after what we believe in right away, no matter what it costs." He held her closer in the growing dark. "I know that, just as I know what your body wants right now."

The fierce desire in his midnight eyes was changing, slowly, softening into something else. He began to trace the outline of her face with his fingertips. Then his hand slid down to touch her neck to circle her breast, and then to cup it gently as he bent to kiss her.

"I know what I feel tremble inside you, Cary. You do want me, too."

"Yes," she whispered, still on fire with yearning. But out of the heat she could still draw some reason, some sanity. Or was it reason that held her back? "I want more than that. Don't you see?" Breathing rapidly, she pulled away.

"No. I don't." Hunter sounded hurt and angry. "You're trying to deny what's natural and real inside of you! Why?" He reached for her again, but this time she pulled away. "Princess, I'm all through playing games. I want it all, too. The grand prize. The brass ring. And that's you."

Cary took a deep, ragged breath. "No. You're wrong when you say you know me. You don't know anything about me at all, Hunter Pierce. It isn't fair to either of us this way. Can't what we have wait... just a little more while we learn the truth about each other?"

"Sure. It can wait." His eyes glittered with anger in the dying light. "Take all the time you want."

He turned, walked to the edge of the courtyard and stopped. "Let me know when you grow up, Cary Blaine, and learn to live in the real world."

That was his answer, then. He wanted it all now or not at all. Well, she had certainly learned one more thing about Hunter Pierce.

Cary went to the stairs and slowly began to climb back up to her apartment. Perhaps she had thrown something important away just now, something that could have been saved, but just now the loss hurt too badly for her to judge whether the pretense and lies that would have saved it were too small—or too high—a price. If he was unwilling to take the time. . . .

With just a few quick strides however, Hunter

had turned and caught up with her, forcefully pulling downward on her shoulder.

"I can't let you slip out of my hands like this, Cary!" He dragged her back down the steps and crushed her to his chest. Cary's heart began beating again, as if it had never stopped, though now she knew it had begun to die a little when he walked away. The world began to move again, too, according to its age-old pattern. She listened to Hunter's whispered words and heard in them the sounds of life returning after the storm.

"Yes, Cary. I'll play your game and wait until you're sure, if you'll play fair," he said. "But there will always be an investigation—that's my job. I won't wait weeks and months until this one's over. Do you understand?"

"But this one...." She saw the warning glitter in his eye and sighed. She didn't really want to win that argument, anyway. "All right."

"And don't ever tease me with your kisses and your soft touches if you don't intend to follow through. I'm only human, princess. I can't just turn it off with a smile when you stop me like that."

Cary thought of the exchange between them in the darkness and groaned. *But I hadn't meant to tease. I hadn't planned to kiss you at all!* "But you always start it!" she protested. "And you must know by now that I...don't seem to be able to resist you until...it's too late."

"Really? A very good sign. I won't press you, Cary darling, any further than you want to go. I promise." He hugged her closely once more.

She pulled away slowly from the addictive drug of his embrace. He was still one step below her, his beautiful eyes looking up to hers. No, she didn't want to let him go, either. Not when—sometimes—she sensed that her mysterious inner warnings were growing weaker against Hunter.

"All right," she said, smiling. "I can't refuse an offer like that. You should have been a salesman, Hunter Pierce."

"Nope. Wouldn't have worked at all, my dear." He grinned up at her. "I can only sell what I believe in. But I do believe in us, and I aim to stick closer to you than a shadow until you believe it, too."

"Then let's go eat!" she said brightly. "You can convince me and feed me at the same time."

Hunter sighed and then grinned again. "Certainly, princess. I can recognize a plea for neutral territory when I hear one. Shall we?"

They walked across the courtyard to the parking lot and the tension inside Cary began to ease. He was still here; he still wanted her. And he would give her time. Her heart was almost as clear as the storm-cleansed air around them. Tomorrow hadn't been lost after all.

"What did Henry offer you?" she asked later, sipping coffee.

"Nothing in the way of evidence, I'm sorry to say. Looks like I'll have to take the job and hope they make their move before I fall flat on my face as an engineer. One good thing—the real David Thompson is going to take a paid leave of absence from Burkham to live with me in Wichita and help me keep up the facade as long as possible.''

"How is he going to do that?''

"Oh, you'd be surprised at the amount of effort that's going into this investigation, sweetheart. This is the big time! We've got a computer terminal for the apartment, so David can work on stuff using Burkham's big computers in Tecumseh. We'll set up a drawing board and everything he needs. During the day, I'll do a lot of reading and fussing with David's work and pass it off as my own.''

"What do you do when somebody asks you questions?''

"I'm going to stall. It's the best I can do. David will write up all the answers, and I'll send them off as memos.''

Cary looked dubious. "I hope it works.''

"Have faith, princess. It will. David's dreamed up this really great 'invention' for us to bargain with if they come seeking some illicit plans.''

"What is it? Or may I ask?''

"It's a variation on a bleeding bolt.''

"A what?''

"Gotcha! And you call yourself an expert.''

"Oh, Hunter! I can't know everything. Quit teasing and tell me. Quickly!''

"A bleeding bolt is something new that some of the airlines use on engine mounts and other places where vibration puts a lot of stress on the bolt. The core of this new bolt is filled with red dye. If it cracks, or breaks, the dye 'bleeds' and a visual inspection can pinpoint the weak spot.''

"Sounds like a terrific invention. How can David improve on that?"

"He can't. But he's going to make them think he can. We have all these fake documents that prove the current bleeding bolt is so weak that it breaks down faster than a regular bolt. David's got drawings for a modified bolt with a slimmer core and the dye to be injected under extreme pressure. It all sounds good to me, but David says it's really a bunch of hogwash."

"Well, he should know," Cary replied, hoping he did. But if David's plan was hogwash, how would it fool the experts at Omega?

As they talked, a sad wailing had begun in the distance. Sirens. Cary realized she'd heard them several times during the meal. Perhaps lightning from the storm had started a fire somewhere.

"When do you start work?" She tried to set aside her worries about the sirens and David's spurious invention and to absorb some of Hunter's enthusiasm.

"Next Monday. I'm going to go down to Wichita this Saturday to find an apartment. Will you come with me—just for the day, to help me look?" he added quickly, grinning. "I promise, no heavy overtures."

Cary grinned, too. He really was taking her seriously. Her spirits began to rise.

"Yes, I'd like that very much. Wichita is a nice place to visit. But how can your station afford to have you gone for...what, several months, perhaps, and even pay for an apartment?"

"I thought you knew. Burkham is paying most of my salary and all of the expenses—including this dinner." He waved his hand expansively.

"Oh. That's awfully generous of them."

"Well, we all hope this won't take several months as you suggested. But whatever money they spend on me is nothing compared to what they lost when Dr. Racine stole those plans and sold them to Omega. When my station manager realized the enormity of the problem, he contacted Burkham and suggested we help with the investigation. They were positively overjoyed."

"But why is your station so willing to let you be gone? And why didn't somebody just hire real detectives?"

"My dear, I am a detective—of sorts. And I don't think you realize the publicity potential of this whole thing. If KMKX can not only get an exclusive story, but can say they unearthed the whole rotten mess themselves, we've got a really hot promotion number."

"I see." The worse the situation turned out to be, the better for Hunter's purpose. Was this what her inner voice was trying to warn her of? That she might not be able to live with Hunter's professional distance from the world and its pain?

The wary look in her eyes was an open book. Hunter laughed.

"Honey, listen," he said. "I'm after truth first and a good show second. That's always true."

"I'll try to keep that in mind," she answered evenly.

Now he'd see her pulling back again, the fact that she couldn't accept what he was doing totally, without question. After that scene in the courtyard, he might take this as the last straw. But she wouldn't pretend to accept his words at face value. She had to know him.

Right now, "the great crusader" seemed as if it might be just another tactic he used to get ahead, the crusade itself just another news story for the six o'clock show. Maybe a billboard slogan would come of it, too. But she would have helped destroy a lot of people—for the sake of one of Hunter's dubious principles.

"Can't swallow that one easily, either. Can you? Here I am, trying to let you get to know me, and you sit there demanding some kind of proof of everything I say. That's what this silence is all about, isn't it, Cary?"

He wasn't angry. He was just very serious. Almost sad, she thought.

"You'll get your proof in time, Cary. I really am looking for justice first. But if I can make a living doing it for television, is that so bad?"

Put that way, anything she might reply would sound absurdly exaggerated. "No, I guess not."

"I'll make you believe me, princess. I'll show you." He reached across the table to hold her hand.

His touch was magical, as always. But Cary knew she couldn't think straight now. "Wanna bet?" she asked, laughing lightly and trying to draw her hand away.

He released her and leaned back. "On a sure thing? Of course. Name your stakes—no, I'm the challenged. I name the stakes."

His eyes held hers fast. *Beware!* the cautious part of her cried. He did not need to touch her to ignite flames of passion. The look now in his eyes was more than enough.

"But you know what I want, don't you?" he whispered.

"Yes."

"Shall we seal the bet with a. . . handshake?"

Cary laughed. Subtlety was definitely not his strong suit. She reached across for his hand, and it was several minutes later before she thought to let go.

"How about going out to look at Lake Shawnee in the moonlight?" Hunter asked as they were leaving.

"We can't stay long," she warned. "It's closed and patroled at night, I think."

"A little moonlight is better than none," he quipped.

"For what?"

"Oh, you know. The usual."

She laughed easily, confident just now of her self-control. After all, he had promised. "You reporter types never give up, do you?"

"No, ma'am. And remember, my mama made sure when she christened me I would always get my 'man.' "

They laughed together, enjoying the light banter. Suddenly a police car swung in front of the Audi from a side street. Lights flashing, it made a wide arc in front of them and came to a halt, blocking both lanes of traffic.

Hunter braked to a stop. In the glare of his headlights, Cary could see two policemen getting out of the patrol car and walking toward them.

"What's wrong?" Hunter called out.

"Power lines down up ahead. Got to close these roads."

"Any other way to get to the lake?"

"Nope. Not from here. I wouldn't go up there tonight, anyway. Looks like a tornado may have ripped up some trees out there. Houses, too, along the golf course."

"Oh! Was anybody hurt?" Cary asked.

"Haven't heard of anyone. Better get going now, before traffic piles up behind you. Wait just a minute." The officer was waving to a large van coming up behind Hunter. The van pulled around beside the Audi and Cary saw its WIBW logo.

In a split second, Hunter had the door open and was heading for the van. He'd seen the logo, too. "Pull over and wait for me!" he shouted to her.

Cary slid over to the driver's seat and fumbled with the unfamiliar gearshift. Finally she found first gear and eased the small car over to the shoulder. In only a few minutes, Hunter came hurrying back.

"Go on back to your apartment, Cary. I'm going to help these guys with their camera work. We're going to take a look at the storm damage for the morning news." His voice lowered. "I think I can talk them into letting me have some of the footage for our news, too.''

"But what about your car?"

"I'll have them drop me off at your parking lot when we're done. I'll call you from Kansas City tomorrow. Good night now." He bent to her window and kissed her upturned face.

"Be careful, Hunter!"

"I will," he called, already halfway to the van.

Cary searched for reverse gear and began to make her way home.

Always after a story, she thought, disappointed and a little annoyed. *Reporter first and just plain Hunter last.*

CHAPTER NINE

IN THE EMPTY DARKNESS of her bedroom, Cary lay without sleep, thinking about Hunter. They hadn't talked at all about what would happen if Hunter found his evidence at Omega. How ruthless would he be? How cold? What would he do about all the innocent people caught in his trap?

Somehow, they hadn't talked about anything else of importance, either. Was that her fault? Only she knew what was crucial to her. If she wanted answers, she would have to ask questions.

She'd made herself a promise. If, *if*, she came to him again, it would be because she was ready to believe in his motives and accept his words of love, ready to risk loving him in return. Maybe that was why she hadn't asked more about him—she wasn't ready to take that particular risk.

Cary's thoughts drifted off and sleep stole around them, turning her questions into answers. In her dreams, she found Hunter's face smiling down at her, and she rose to meet his kiss with all the passion of a raging tide that has been roused by the inevitable, inconstant moon.

"THANK heaven!" breathed the husky voice on the telephone.

"What? Who is this?" Cary's mind was still numb from sleep. She glanced at her grandmother clock and groaned.

"It's Tommy. This is the third time I've come out to call. When you didn't answer before, we were afraid you'd somehow been caught in all this mess."

"What mess? Tommy, it's one o'clock! Has something happened to Louise—or to Lynette?"

"No, they're fine. Lynnie's with our neighbors and Louise is down on Thirty-seventh Street with the emergency Red Cross shelter people. The tornado, Cary—it's just terrible here."

"Oh, Tommy! I didn't know. I've been out and...we knew about the lake, but you're so much farther out, I didn't even think of you. What's happened?" As she listened, Cary reached for her robe. Her eyes teared from the sudden glare when she finally turned on the table lamp beside the couch.

"Well, we've got reports, or rumors, that there are one hundred families homeless. I don't know how bad the damage is. Our house is only half a block away from the edge of the destruction, and I've been working with National Guardsmen and paramedics to dig people out of their basements. Right where I am now, I'd say the destruction is complete; there's nothing left of some of the houses near me."

"That's awful! Is there any way I can help?"

"Not tonight. All our streets are blocked off. No one can get in except the National Guard. Got to go now. Sorry I disturbed your sleep. But Louise will be glad to hear you're all right. We've heard such rumors...."

"Call me again, Tommy, and let me know what I can do. In the morning?"

"Sure, Cary. Bye."

Cary switched on the lights and went in to the living room to the television. Every local station was covering the tornado's horrible aftermath. She flipped to WIBW and watched in stunned silence as aerial shots showed street after street filled with the debris of blasted houses and twisted cars. Many homes were no more than concrete holes in the ground, with a bit of flooring above and a few pipes sticking up. The film had been shot immediately after the storm hit, when there was still a little daylight. Now, with no electricity, those areas were lit only by the flashing lights of police cars, fire engines and ambulances. So far, no one had been reported killed.

The announcer gave the locations of temporary shelters and updates on which streets were closed and which subdivisions were without phones or light.

Cary was shocked. She and Hunter had passed off the storm as a joke. Who ever heard of tornadoes in October! Of course it was just barely October, and last year there had been two freak storms in September. But this! This was a nightmare—and she hadn't even known it was happening; she'd laughed at Hunter's concern.

The announcer cut to scenes of wet, dirty crews digging by spotlight in the rubble of a brick house.

Fascinated, Cary watched as crewmen began yelling and then converged at one corner of the house. One child after another emerged, and finally a whole group of tired, scared people crawled out of the protected basement. Tears were streaming down Cary's cheeks as she watched the scene. Hunter was out there somewhere. She should have stayed with him—helped out some way. Now it was too late. There wouldn't be anything she could do until morning.

Tommy and Louise were helping, though. Thank goodness they had been spared the terror of having their house blown down on top of them!

Cary turned off the TV set and went back to bed. In the morning she would see what could be done. She knew there would be lots of help needed for several days. But she'd be no good to anyone if she didn't get some sleep now.

Images of stormclouds and wailing winds, with flying bricks and crazy cracked stones, haunted her dreams. Suddenly she awoke to a thunderous knocking at her door.

Instantly awake this time, her heart hammering in fear, Cary grabbed her robe and sped to the door. Through the tiny cylinder peephole she could make out the dark curling hair around a familiar face.

"Hunter!"

She fumbled for the lock and chain, her hands shaking in alarm. He was covered with mud and grime. Both sleeves were missing from his shirt, and only a large jagged tear marked the spot where his pocket had been.

"Please, can I sleep here for the rest of the night? I'm too tired to drive back home." His beautiful melodic voice was hoarse.

Cary reached for him with fearful hands, but he pushed her away. Her eyes were round with fright and concern.

"I'm all right. All right. Just tired and dirty from digging. So much rubble." Hunter's sigh spoke volumes for his exhaustion. He pushed past Cary toward the bathroom.

She closed her eyes for a moment to steady her reeling brain and followed him. Surely he didn't get that dirty operating a camera! He must have joined a work crew trying to clean up the streets so emergency vehicles could get through.

Hunter was so tired, he could barely lift his arms to slip off the torn shirt. He didn't protest when she reached to help him take off his clothes and turn on the shower for him. Neither of them was even aware of his nakedness. All Cary saw were the scratches and cuts that covered his arms and legs, and the mud that had caked in his hair and skin.

"What happened, Hunter?" she asked softly, guessing only some of the answer.

He climbed painfully into the shower enclosure and slid the translucent glass doors closed. Through them, Cary could see that he stood still, simply allowing the water to pound at his layers of grime.

"The tornado. I just had to stay. I couldn't leave. Oh, Cary! I never guessed it would be like that! So many people trapped. Everything gone." His voice rasped and cracked.

"I know," she answered, so softly he could not hear. *But nobody can describe what it's like,* she said to herself.

A tornado is sudden annihilation, she thought. But one learns to live with it. She'd been in the fourth grade when a massive tornado had plowed through miles and miles of this beautiful city, leaving death and complete destruction in its wake. Her own house had been leveled and she had lost her beloved cat, Timothy. Her mother had lost all the little treasures and belongings of a lifetime. But they had gone on, as had all their neighbors and friends. After a while, the horror became just a memory. There were stories to top other people's stories, tornado tales that seemed exaggerated only because the reality kept slipping farther into the past.

Cary watched Hunter for a moment more and then removed her robe and gown. She slipped into the shower with him and began to scrub his worn-out body. He accepted her presence and purpose wordlessly.

She shampooed his hair and wrapped him in towels as she would a child, and led him unprotesting to her bed.

"Thanks, princess." He smiled when his head touched the soft pillow. And then he was instantly, deeply asleep.

She drew her gown back on and climbed in beside him. If she had asked for evidence of Hunter's honor, she had been handed it tonight, neatly scribed on dirty cotton with the mud from a town he did not know and wrapped with the pain of helping people he had never met before. Who was she to question his motives further?

If she was honest with herself, she had never wanted to question him at all. From that first evening at the Holidome, she'd wanted to believe in his reasons for pursuing her.

Perhaps Hunter had been right—it was she herself Cary hadn't believed in. She'd been afraid to love. But no longer. Her heart ached with emotion now, as she watched the damp coils of hair on Hunter's chest move slightly with every breath he took in sleep. Certainty and contentment filled the space in her where doubt had lodged before, and she, too, slept.

When Cary's alarm shrilled its wake-up signal she was lying curled against Hunter's chest. One of his large, tanned arms lay across her, his hand lightly cupping her breast. She had to pull away from him slightly to shut off the alarm, but she did so reluctantly. She'd never wakened like this to the warmth of a man lying sleeping close beside her. His breath tickled softly at her neck and his knee was crooked up against her thigh, gently nudging with an indescribably sensuous pressure.

If he whispered her name or kissed her now or merely moved his hand closer to her heart, she would tell him that she had no more hesitation. She would show him she believed in his love without reservation.

But Hunter lay sleeping soundly, his exhaustion so great that he had not heard the alarm and didn't move when she slid out from beneath his arm to dress.

Before she left for work, she took the phone off the hook. Bending over Hunter's still, relaxed face, she left a soft kiss on his brow. But he didn't feel the feathery touch and slept on.

"Mmm. What you missed!" She smiled to herself and gently closed the door.

At Willingham's she called KMKX in Kansas City to explain why Hunter was not there this morning.

"Typical," was the flat response to her story. "Tell him to try and make the six o'clock broadcast, if he can break away. Oh, and tell him thanks for the film. It was real good."

"Which film was that?"

"The message we got was he ran a camera for some guys at WIBW, and they let him send us some of their footage. Actually, I don't care how he got it. Just say 'thanks, and get back to work.'" The unemotional voice broke off and a dial tone replaced it.

So Hunter had managed to get a story out of last night's heroics, after all. Cary laughed, and there was only admiration in the sound.

Quickly, she moved on to another important task. She asked Elma Garcia, the office manager, to call a general staff meeting for eight-fifteen to find out how many of their own people were affected by the storm. Amazingly, none had been directly hit. Cary and Elma took offers of canned goods and clothes, made arrangements to pick up the items for delivery to the Red Cross centers and gave those who had close friends or family involved time off to help them find temporary shelter. Everyone contributed. Some of the counselors and recruiters offered to take on additional work loads so others could volunteer to help the victims.

Spirits were high, and good will absorbed everyone's energy. Willingham had united to help. In the back of Cary's mind sprang hope for the high-school kids who were also victims, in a way. If Willingham could rally after a storm, surely they could find a way to work together and accomplish something equally special for the students.

Cary didn't worry that Tommy hadn't called. He had probably gone home for some well-deserved sleep, just as Hunter had done. He would call later and tell her where the food and clothing were most needed.

What she should be doing now was looking for a new job for him. If she could relieve his mind on that score, he would be better able to handle the disaster all around him and be a support to his own family and neighbors. That was something positive she could do right now.

But, just as before, Cary had no luck. Everyone she contacted was sitting tight, waiting to see what interest rates and the economy were going to do in the new year. No one was hiring senior staff or middle management unless it was absolutely necessary. As necessary as it was with Omega Aircraft.

Miserable about her lack of success on Tommy's

behalf, Cary returned to her primary task of finding one more engineer for Omega. Until Hunter could prove the company's lack of ethics, she must treat it as a legitimate client. Mary Ellen expected as much, and Cary was still under orders not to tell her supervisor about the investigation or her part in it.

The phone buzzed a welcome interruption.

"Hello. This is Caroline Blaine."

"Good morning, princess. How about sharing breakfast with the man who shared your bed last night? The coffee's on the stove right now."

"Sounds like an offer I can't refuse, as long as you let me call it lunch. I've been up for hours, you know."

"Call it whatever you like, but be here in twenty minutes, or I can't promise there will be any bacon left. And thanks, princess, for calling my office. I really needed the sleep."

"You sure did. I hope you look better today than you did last night."

"Not much, unless you have an extra man's suit stashed in your closet. What's left of my David Thompson costume looks like it belongs to Bo-Jo the Clown."

"Oh! I forgot about that. Make it thirty minutes for the bacon, and I'll have a change of clothes for you."

"Look, I can get a new suit in Kansas City when I get back. Don't bother—"

"Hush up and take your charity like a man. I'm not getting you a tux! But Tommy won't mind letting me have some of his work clothes. See you later!"

"FOR HUNTER? Of course!" said Louise with a smirk. Cary had a feeling Louise did not believe that Hunter had come over to her apartment merely to sleep after working with the cleanup crews. But if she had any questions, Louise did not voice them. She put the Red Cross donations Cary had brought from Willingham on the kitchen table and took Cary down the hall to the master bedroom to pick out something that might fit the lanky reporter.

According to Louise, Tommy had gone to the office early, after resting only a few hours. Cary guessed the reason he'd gone in—to make certain Hanson Development had no excuse to lay him off earlier than planned. But Louise still didn't know about the expected staff reduction, and she was angry that her husband seemed to be pushing himself too hard.

"He can't do everything himself!" she complained. "He's trying to be father, husband, accountant and savior of the world all at the same time. At least your Hunter had the sense to get some rest! Would you believe Tommy promised the Guard he'd be back out there with them by seven o'clock this morning?"

"How late did he work last night?"

"Until four o'clock in the morning, that idiot!"

Cary smiled at her sister's indignant words. "But you're proud of him for it, aren't you? I know you, sis."

"Of course I am. But...." Louise sat down on the bed, holding the slacks and shirt she'd gotten out to give Cary. "I have a feeling something's been bothering him lately, Cary. I think he's working so hard in order to avoid facing it. Oh, I wish he'd just talk to me about it!"

"What do you think it is?" asked Cary, keeping her voice carefully casual.

"I'm afraid...that he's upset about my new success. As long as sewing and designing were just a hobby, everything was fine. But the day I got the loan for the dress shop, something seemed to change. He's so...distant now." Her hands clenched the fabric of the denim pants convulsively.

"Oh, no, Lou! I'm sure you're wrong. Tommy's not like that. Believe me, he's not jealous of your success." *Oh, dear,* she thought in panic. *The truth would only make Louise feel worse!*

Cary couldn't let her sister go on believing Tommy was so insecure. Louise had always been strong, and Tommy had loved her for it. Now was no time for her to lose that precious courage—or her self-confidence.

"He's probably just worried about something at work," she said carefully. "Maybe it's audit time or something, and his boss is making heavy demands on him."

Louise appeared to consider the idea. "But if he's under so much pressure at work, why volunteer for such hard labor in the evening? He's going to kill himself!"

"Do you really want him to ignore the plight of your neighbors, Lou?" Cary asked softly.

"N-no." Louise threw her arms around Cary and began sobbing. "I'm just so worried about him— he's changed just since last Friday. And he won't talk to me!"

Cary tried to comfort her sister without breaking the promise of secrecy she had made to Tommy. When she finally left, Louise was cuddling Lynette, trying to believe that she had imagined the new tension she sensed in her husband.

When Cary knocked at her apartment door, Hunter opened it. He was wearing one of Cary's quilted winter robes. The sleeves of the rosebud-print wrap were too short, and the open, frilly lace collar revealed a mass of curling black hairs below his neck.

"Don't laugh, woman!" Hunter warned her in a mock ferocious voice. "A man's gotta wear what a man's gotta wear. After the bacon spit at my bare skin a couple of times, I decided anything would be better than nothing."

"Don't worry, I'm not laughing. You look lovely, darling," said Cary sweetly. "So. . . domestic."

"Grrr!" Hunter advanced on her with a greasy spatula.

She sidestepped him and laid Tommy's work clothes on the couch.

Hunter gave her one last fierce look, grabbed the clothes and disappeared into the bedroom to change. When he came out, Cary couldn't stifle the giggle inspired by the sight of his makeshift outfit.

"Hey! You didn't laugh at me when I was wearing your robe. What's so funny now?" Hunter asked, annoyed.

"Your pants!" She giggled again helplessly.

Though both Hunter and Tommy were tall, Tommy's waist must have been at least ten or fifteen inches larger than Hunter's lean athlete's stomach. He had pulled his own belt tightly through their loops, but the stiff denim ballooned around his hips like bizarre culottes.

"May I respectfully remind you these are not my pants. They belong to someone you affectionately call Tommy. If you could love pot-bellied Tommy in these baggy jeans, why not me?" His voice was bantering, but underneath it Cary sensed an edge of suppressed anger in his voice.

She laughed delightedly. "Tommy is my brother-in-law, silly!"

Hunter brightened, and Cary glowed with the knowledge that he cared enough to be jealous.

"You mean that ravishing woman I met last night in the Red Cross shelter is married? Heck! I thought maybe I could share both of you. Start a harem or something." He smiled that charming brilliant smile that sent Cary's pulse racing wildly.

"I'm afraid Tommy is far too possessive. Tough luck." Her own smile threatened to crack her face. *No wonder Louise acted so peculiarly secretive when I told her you were sleeping here. I wonder what you said to her!*

"There!" Cary took the grimy clothes Hunter had worn last night and threw them in the trash as she spoke. "I'm so glad you and Louise know each other now. She and Tommy are the nicest people I know—present company excepted, of course."

"Of course. And this nice person has cooked breakfast—or lunch, if you prefer—for another nice person he knows. But we'd better eat quickly before we all drown in our own niceness!" Hunter took her arm and led her to the small dining table.

The sun was shining, sparkling in from the window on dust motes that floated in the air. The table was set with crockery and stainless—no roses and candles or bone china and silver. Hunter spilled some orange juice on the kitchen floor, and they had to mop it up. In short, it was such a prosaic meal, so completely devoid of magic and romance, that Cary knew for certain she was falling in love with Hunter.

It felt so right to share with him, to listen and talk without self-consciousness or pretense.

"I really enjoyed sleeping in your bed, princess," he teased. "I'll have to figure out a way to do it again some time when I'm less sleepy." He made an exaggerated wink in her direction.

Cary's mouth was full of toast just then, but she winked back.

"As a matter of fact," he continued, "I had a great morning altogether. How was yours?"

"Like always, a little good and a little bad."

"Meaning? Tell me about your life, Cary. I'm supposed to be getting to know you, remember?"

"Well, this morning was a little different because of the tornado. We talked a lot about that and got together some volunteers to help. Fortunately we don't go through that every day!''

"Once would be enough for me, thank you. I hope I never see anything like that again!'' Hunter shook his head for emphasis. "Such awesome, unbridled power!''

"And I thought you admired power!'' Cary teased.

"Nothing doing. We're talking about you now. Not me.''

"It's awfully boring. I spent the rest of the morning trying to find a job for my brother-in-law.''

"Tommy?''

"Yes. Oh, I shouldn't have even mentioned it. If you ever see Louise again, don't say anything about it. Please.''

"Why, did he get fired in deep disgrace, and she hasn't been told?''

"No. He's going to be laid off. But he doesn't want to worry her.''

"Ahh. The loan for the boutique that just came through. Bad timing for a layoff.'' Hunter frowned.

"My! You two really must have talked up a storm in that shelter!''

Cary was touched that Hunter seemed to have such a genuine interest in her family. But she was surprised that Louise had opened up to a stranger.

"Talking kept our minds off. . .other things for a while,'' Hunter explained. "I liked your sister very much. I hope things work out for her. You'll find her husband a good job soon, won't you?''

"It's not that easy, Hunter. The economy was tight already—before the disaster." She looked down at her coffee.

There was silence for a moment, and then Hunter reached across to lay his hand on hers. He didn't say anything, but she felt his sympathy and appreciated it.

"So, when am I going to get the big tour of your station?" she asked brightly.

"That's going to be hard. This weekend I'll have to go to Wichita, and every weekend after that—for a while at least—I'll be working my tail off to film segments for the next week. I hate to say it, but you'd just be in my way then."

"Oh." She looked down at her coffee again.

"I'm really sorry, honey. But that's the way it is right now. When this investigation is over, I'll have more time, I promise. I've been thinking over what you said about waiting, and...maybe we should. Wait, I mean. Until after this Omega thing's all over. You were right that it's not fair to either of us now."

Cary continued staring at her cup.

"That *is* what you wanted, isn't it?" He was still holding her hand, squeezing it gently now.

She looked up and smiled brightly, concealing the emptiness she felt inside. "Yes, that's what I wanted." *Once, but no longer!*

"Good. I want this thing we've got between us to grow, princess. I think you were the wise one to slow it down. Give it time to blossom naturally." He smiled, too. A tired, soft smile that seemed to break her heart.

What made
Marge
burn the toast
and miss
her favorite
soap opera?

HARLEQUIN SUPER ROMANCE

Rachel Palmer

LOVE BEYOND DESIRE

...At his touch,
her body felt a
familiar wild stir-
ring, but she
struggled to
resist it. This is
not love, she
thought bitterly.

A SUPERROMANCE™
the great new romantic novel she never wanted to end.
And it can be yours

FREE!

She never wanted it to end. And neither will you. From the moment you begin... *Love Beyond Desire,* your **FREE** introduction to the newest series of bestseller romance novels, SUPERROMANCES.

You'll be enthralled by this powerful love story... from the moment Robin meets the dark, handsome Carlos and finds herself involved in the jealousies, bitterness and secret passions of the Lopez family. Where her own forbidden love threatens to shatter her life.

Your FREE *Love Beyond Desire* is only the beginning. A subscription to SUPERROMANCES lets you look forward to a long love affair. Month after month, you'll receive four love stories of heroic dimension. Novels that will involve you in spellbinding intrigue, forbidden love and fiery passions.

You'll begin this series of sensuous, exciting contemporary novels... written by some of the top romance novelists of the day... with four each month.

And this big value... each novel, almost 400 pages of compelling reading... is yours for only $2.50 a book. Hours of entertainment for so little. Far less than a first-run movie or Pay-TV. Newly published novels, with beautifully illustrated covers, filled with page after page of delicious escape into a world of romantic love... delivered right to your home.

A compelling love story of mystery and intrigue... conflicts and jealousies... and a forbidden love that threatens to shatter the lives of all involved with the aristocratic Lopez family.

← Mail this card today for your FREE gifts.

TAKE THIS BOOK
AND TOTE BAG FREE!

Mail to: **SUPERROMANCE**
2504 W. Southern Avenue, Tempe, Arizona 85282

YES, please send me FREE and without any obligation, my SUPERROMANCE novel, *Love Beyond Desire*. If you do not hear from me after I have examined my FREE book, please send me the 4 new SUPERROMANCE books every month as soon as they come off the press. I understand that I will be billed only $2.50 per book (total $10.00). There are no shipping and handling or any other hidden charges. There is no minimum number of books that I have to purchase. In fact, I may cancel this arrangement at any time. *Love Beyond Desire* and the tote bag are mine to keep as FREE gifts even if I do not buy any additional books.

134 CIS KAK6

Name	(Please Print)	
Address		Apt. No.
City		
State		Zip

Signature   (If under 18, parent or guardian must sign.)

This offer is limited to one order per household and not valid to present subscribers. We reserve the right to exercise discretion in granting membership. If price changes are necessary you will be notified. Offer expires December 31, 1984.

PRINTED IN U.S.A.

SUPERROMANCE ™

EXTRA BONUS
MAIL YOUR ORDER
TODAY AND GET A
FREE TOTE BAG
FROM SUPERROMANCE.

Mail this card today for your FREE gifts.

She certainly didn't feel wise now.

The glow of noon's brilliance began to deepen into afternoon's slanting light as they got up to wash the dishes.

"Did you read the paper this morning?" Hunter asked seriously.

"No, I didn't have time."

"The damage in Tecumseh was just about as bad as it was here. Burkham lost the roof off one of its hangars, and a half dozen of their test craft are just twisted junk today."

"Will. . . will that change anything for you? For us?"

Hunter gave her a quick quizzical glance.

"It just means they'll be more anxious than ever to settle this espionage thing. They really needed the prestige and publicity of that invention Dr. Racine stole. Now they'll need goodwill even more. And they can't afford to have any additional secrets stolen while they're trying to recover from the storm."

"Yes. It seems really unfair that this tornado should have struck them right now when they're so vulnerable anyway. I hope their resources will hold out until you can give them the evidence they need to prosecute."

Hunter took a quick breath and smiled. "So do I, princess. But with you on our side now, I know we'll make it," he said lightly. He didn't pursue the topic any further, but switched to desultory questions about Willingham. Had she heard from her supervisor? How were the ulcers doing? How long had Mary Ellen been working for Willing-ham?''

His line of questioning surprised Cary. ''Forever, I think,'' she answered jokingly. ''Some of the staff in St. Louis think she was born in the company's medical department!''

''You like her, don't you?''

''She's had a rough time getting where she is. And lately she's had a lot of bad luck. The man she was going to marry—a high-school basketball coach—was offered a college job in California and wanted her to go with him. But she had worked so hard to make supervisor, and Willingham doesn't have any offices in California. She had to tell him no. I feel sorry for her. She told me all about it because she knew I would understand. Someone asked me to give up my job, too, once.'' Would he see that this was another of her hesitations, her fears?

''Someone who...mattered?''

''Not after that!'' she said lightly. ''I realized then he just didn't mean very much to me at all.''

''I'm glad,'' said Hunter abstractedly.

She waited, but he didn't pursue that topic either. Instead, he returned to the safer subject of Mary Ellen. ''Sympathy isn't the same thing though, is it? I think you really like her.''

''Yes, I suppose I do. Why?''

''Oh, just wondering how you get along with your bosses, I guess.'' Hunter shrugged and reached up into the cupboard to put away a glass.

While they finished, Cary waited for some caress-ing words of flirtation, for a light touch or a sensual glance from those dark-forest eyes, but Hunter remained casual. Perhaps too artificially casual. Was it what she said about her first love, Jason? Hunter was taking her request for time very seriously—except now she did not need any more time.

How could she just come right out and say, "I'm ready now. Please love me"?

Finally, it was time for her to go back to work and for him to drive to the station. He hadn't made a move to touch her. They had not even held hands. So she was relieved when he came to her and pulled her close.

Cary wrapped her arms around his neck, feeling the coarse coils of his hair through her blouse of thin georgette. Below her hips, his hands tightened to bring her body nearer to his. They were drawn together like magnets; even the atmosphere around them seemed charged with their attraction.

She rose to receive his kiss, a sweet tender touch that barely caused their lips to meet. Hunter loosed his hold on her a fraction, but Cary communicated wordlessly that he did not need to. She pulled with her arms around his head, crushing his mouth to hers with fiery passion.

For a moment more he held back, making sure of her response. Then all at once he accepted it, and his kiss was hungry, demanding. His hands moved convulsively up and down her spine, kneading the tense muscles of her back. Her arms loosened around his neck as she felt her body relax.

Bright currents of joy coursed through her. *Yes!*

her heart sang out as Hunter's kisses plumbed some hidden wellspring of happiness within her.

"You're still coming with me to Wichita this weekend to help me find that apartment, aren't you?" he murmured when they breathed again.

"Yes, of course."

"Would you object to staying over Saturday night, if we couldn't find anything right away?" He looked at her searchingly.

She smiled, steady and sure. "That would be very nice."

In sudden, surprised response to her answer, Hunter's mouth came down quickly to cover hers and to pull away, kiss and tease, kiss and smile. Cary arched into his embrace, yearning for more of his sweet seductive touch. Her lips parted and he took their offering with his tongue, each of them tasting fully the other's hunger.

Distantly, Cary was aware that Hunter's hands had moved up from her hips, touched the waist, then moved beside her breasts. "Ahh!" With a panicky jerk, she pulled away from him, her arms whipping down from around his neck to wrap around herself protectively.

Hunter stared at her with anger in his eyes. "Is this another attack of regret, Cary? I warned you before, I can't take much more of this."

Cary giggled. "No, not regret. I'm just... ticklish underneath my arms. I'm sorry," she added, returning to his embrace. "I really am."

"Now why are you so suddenly ticklish, I wonder?"

"Silly. I've always been—but the last time you held me, you didn't really do that much exploring. We were sort of in a hurry. Remember?"

"Mmm. Yes, we were, weren't we? And I promised never to rush you again, didn't I? We'll just have to see where else you're ticklish, won't we?"

Cary squirmed against him in mock anguish and felt his body's natural response to her movement.

Hunter groaned. "Oh, don't, Cary! We don't have time to finish that particular game now, darling," he whispered hoarsely against her cheek.

"I know," she sighed against his morning beard. "I know."

"I'll see you early Saturday morning, princess. Save your teasing little body until then, okay?"

"How about Friday night, instead?" she asked, and marveled at her boldness. "No teasing."

He squeezed her tightly in answer. "Do you mean that? You're sure?"

"Yes. Now I am."

In the background, her grandmother clock chimed twice.

"Hell!" Hunter swore. "You'd better be sure this time, you vixen. You've made love to me with your beautiful topaz eyes and then put me off, teased me with a taste of heaven and then kept me waiting when I couldn't wait. And now—now when there isn't any time for either of us—you come to me and say yes! I warn you, Cary. If you agree to go on Friday, you'd better be prepared to satisfy this hunger I have for you. Oh, princess, I want you so!"

She glowed with the power of his words. *I want you, too,* she sang silently to the melody of his voice.

"Friday," she promised. "I'll be waiting."

Hunter kissed her once more, and then it was truly time to go.

They both had lives to live outside this room, duties to people besides each other. That would probably never change, but after Friday they would have a special sharing, too. A physical closeness that could only lead to mutual respect and love.

Back at the office, Cary listened to starry-eyed applicants and hard-nosed employers. As she sat by her dictating machine and tried to summarize their needs and aspirations, and later at night when she sat alone beneath the portrait of the Indian woman, she felt a new promise in the world—an optimism born of her contentedness.

When Tommy called to say Hanson Development was giving the staff a ninety-day reprieve because of the tornado's damage to the Topeka economy, Cary saw it as proof that the tides had truly turned.

Everything would turn out perfectly. Now.

CHAPTER TEN

AT FOUR-THIRTY on Thursday, Cary's secretary came into her office, wearing a puzzled expression.

"I think I may have just caused some trouble for your school board—unintentionally, of course."

"What is it, Marian?"

"We just received a call from KMKX—the regional cable-TV station out of Kansas City, you know. They wanted instructions on how to get to the gymnasium for tonight's meeting."

Hunter, of course! But how had he known of the meeting? Cary hadn't mentioned it. There'd been no particular reason to.

"Did you give them instructions?"

"Yes, I'm afraid so. I thought it was one of our local firms calling—the woman didn't identify herself until after I had told her how to find the building. I'm sorry, Miss Blaine."

"Don't worry about it, Marian. If you hadn't given them the information they wanted, I'm sure they would have called someone else."

But why? Cary wondered after Marian had left. Why would Hunter's station be interested in a community meeting in Topeka? And how had he found out she was attending?

She decided to warn the school-board president of the impending publicity. Contrary to her expectations, however, Hal Smith was overjoyed at her news.

"Those press releases have really been working," he gloated. "That makes five local or regional stations coming. Outstanding!"

"But Mr. Smith, do you really think we'll get anything done with TV cameras looking over our shoulders?" Cary was thoroughly dismayed by the president's reaction.

"Sure, sure. No problem. People will be competing with each other to come up with something to say on camera. The ideas will be flying thick and fast. You just wait and see."

Cary groaned. What Hal Smith said might be true, but it could just as easily work against them as for them. Everyone would be vying for the camera's attention. But all some of them would want was free air time to make pompous little speeches about humanitarianism and "the poor kids with no jobs." The projects that did get mentioned would probably be tired old ideas that had been tried and had failed. The group would never get anything constructive done!

"And if we don't come up with any solutions tonight," Hal Smith continued, "the TV audience may send us some suggestions. Think of it, Miss Blaine. 'Public responds to student needs for jobs.' Now *that's* the kind of good publicity we could use for our schools. Parent involvement. Community involvement."

"Well...."

"I tell you this TV exposure can only help us, not hurt our cause. The full board is behind me on this."

"In that case, I must bow to majority opinion, Mr. Smith. I hope the coverage does everything you want."

"How can we miss? We've got people like you, Miss Blaine, to speak up tonight and get the ball rolling."

Suddenly, Cary ceased to perceive the evening meeting as an informal but potentially productive brainstorming session. Now it seemed to be nothing more than a publicity stunt with herself and other unwitting participants cast as the stars. A publicity stunt that would be most successful if the stars fell flat on their faces in front of a few million people and had to be rescued later by John Q. Public.

Cary seriously considered not going to the fiasco, but finally realized her absence would be interpreted as a lack of concern by the entire Willingham agency. She decided she had no choice but to attend.

After a hasty dinner in a Mexican-style restaurant, Cary drove out to the high school. Several cars were already there. The noise level in the gymnasium was high, with introductions and meetings between old friends. A large group of students stood against one wall, talking among themselves and eyeing the adults warily.

The gym floor had been set up with short tables

arranged in a circle, with microphones at every third seat. Each participant in the meeting could see everyone else and speak directly to the whole group over a small loudspeaker system. Each place held a placard bearing the name of a guest, evenly shuffled so that student council members, school-board members and representatives of local businesses were scattered around the circle.

Cary had to approve the planning that had gone into the seating arrangements. Yet her misgivings increased from the evidence that Hal Smith had turned the affair into a major production.

Eventually, when it seemed the noise could get no louder, a booming voice on the speaker system rose above the clamor.

"Please take your seats. We're ready to begin. Please take your seats now." It was Hal Smith, portly and bald, waving everyone toward the tables.

Cary was seated directly opposite the president and between a student and the employee-relations director of a large hospital. Around her were dentists and doctors, officers and managers from banks, the telephone company and insurance agencies and about thirty students from the city's high schools.

The television crews had set up their cameras around the outside of the circle. In hushed whispers they conferred on angles, checked focus and lighting and moved like ghosts around the group of self-conscious participants.

Cary looked for Hunter, but did not see him,

although she did notice that one of the big cameras had the bright KMKX logo on its side. Perhaps this wasn't the kind of story an investigative reporter would cover, after all. There must be someone from the news staff here instead. But where? Did everyone from the station wear a red blazer?

A high-pitched whine called her attention to the tables as individual mikes were being turned on and adjusted to eliminate feedback. Cary began to feel a little nervous. The cameras were aiming around the room, focusing here and then there in no particular pattern. Several times, Cary felt their mechanical eyes turned upon her.

Hal Smith began the meeting with an impassioned statement about the financial plight of the students. He showed a chart outlining projected four-year costs for college and university attendance, a list of discontinued grants and scholarships and another chart giving current and estimated summer employment figures.

"Even last spring's graduates don't all have jobs!" he concluded. "How are these kids going to make it? They need jobs today, during the school year, and they need good summer jobs next year. What we want to do tonight is try to find some of those jobs."

"Now hold on here, Hal." One of the insurance agents raised his hand. "You've already gotten us to pledge as many jobs as possible. I understood we were coming here to explore alternatives, to find some new solutions. We can't just keep inventing unnecessary jobs for kids—we've got skilled adults out there who need work, too. Real work.''

Murmurs of agreement sounded around the table.

"Well, let's hear some alternatives, then," said Hal, sitting down.

The silence around the circle was embarrassing. Cary knew the uncomfortable position most of the business people had been put in. She hadn't been able to come up with any truly original ideas before the meeting, either.

And here they all sat, looking like morons, as the cameras kept rolling to preserve their idiocy for posterity. If someone couldn't come up with a sound, innovated idea soon, it would appear to the audience that businesses were refusing to hire the students and were unwilling to help solve a major community problem.

"Mr. Smith." One of the students had raised her hand tentatively. "I'm Brenda Richardson from Topeka High. I don't think some of the people here realize that we're pretty desperate. We'd do just about anything. Scrubbing floors, running errands...."

"Washing windows. Babysitting. Sweeping up shops." Several other students added their comments.

"No. It's you kids who don't understand," said the hospital representative sitting near Cary. "It isn't that simple. It's not even a question of not having enough money to pay you all. We don't particularly need your kind of help. We've already got janitors, and we don't need babysitters."

"That's right," someone agreed.

"With today's economic problems and the tornado on top of everything, things really are kind of tight," another voice added.

"We'd help if we could," a man said apologetically.

The business people were jumping in quickly, talking over each other, trying to defend their inability to help.

"The only people I need are skilled people or older ones," a chamber of commerce representative interjected gruffly.

"I could hire somebody to sit in a corner, but there isn't any work for them to do. You wouldn't want that, would you?" asked a man Cary recognized as a former client.

Cary watched at first as the cameramen zoomed in on the speakers, pointing their boom microphones around the room. They weren't missing a single sentence, not a single damning word of this tired old discussion. But eventually even she got drawn into the emotional battle being waged around the tables. She forgot all about the intrusive cameras.

"Mr. James, Mrs. Andrews, Mr. Potsky," she broke in. "Do any of you have employees who have some minimal training who could be relieving your professional staff—if they were not doing clerical or cleanup work? I know you do. What if some of these students or graduates could do all your 'dirty work' for you, couldn't you perhaps use your present stock boys as cashiers and stay open later, Mr. James? Couldn't you let some of your mail clerks help the secretaries out with filing and use students to run your mail, Mrs. Andrews? And Mr. Potsky, couldn't you get more building maintenance done if your foremen could simply supervise and didn't have to join in the work—if your teams were larger by one or two students?''

After a moment, some heads began to nod—others to shake.

"Miss Blaine," said Harlan Potsky. "Some of what you say is true. But what you don't seem to be taking into consideration is that we're already trying most of that. The few extra jobs such tactics might scare up at this point are not going to get rid of the big problem.''

"Just a minute," said Hal Smith, booming over the over voices. "How many errand runners, copiers, file clerks and janitors do you all have right now, making more than minimum wage? 'Cause you can have these kids for rock-bottom wages.''

"Putting their parents out of work?"

With that insensitive, unpropitious remark, some of the students began to look even more desperate. Hands flew up, and a dozen young voices cried out to be heard.

"I can paint houses, too," a muscular youth asserted.

"I'm a good mechanic," the boy beside him said.

"I can cut hair," a timid blond girl added shyly.

"I can type seventy words a minute," added Brenda Richardson.

Cary listened as they pleaded to be allowed to earn their own way. There were probably a lot of people out in the community who needed babysitting or house painting or minor car repairs, people who would be willing to hire these teens if they could only get together with the right ones. An idea began to form in her head.

One of the school-board members echoed her thoughts out loud. "There's a lot of talent in our student body, but it's all so fragmented. It's the kind of talent needed in the suburbs, not by business."

A woman from a chemical company agreed. "Can you imagine the amount of work it would take to coordinate all that in the suburbs!" she exclaimed.

"Listen!" Cary cried above the clamor. "Listen to yourselves. These kids are not asking for a handout; they really want to work. But coordinating all their individual skills and abilities is a monumental task—in other words, it's going to take a lot of *work*. Why don't we give these eager teens the chance to do that work—for themselves?"

Puzzled, interested faces turned toward Cary.

"Some of us have money set aside for contributions. My company has about three thousand dollars, maybe more. Why couldn't we all chip in and pay a few of the kids to set up a sort of suburban employment agency to find jobs for each other?"

Thoughtful frowns began to replace puzzled looks on the faces around her.

"We could set up a jobs council—teenagers with an adult monitor. We'd pay the kids on the council a salary from our contributions. They would test applicants, run ads, sell skills, find jobs." Cary was getting excited about the idea.

"We could be our own special employment agency. We can draw up flyers and go door to door," cried an eager young voice.

"We could charge ten percent or something for helping the other students," added Brenda excitedly. "That way, we wouldn't be totally dependent on your charity for long."

There were nods and murmured approbation.

"I like your idea, Miss Blaine. How about the rest of you?" asked Hal Smith.

"It might work. Yes, I like it." The answers from the businessmen were unanimously positive. In one way, they were now off the hook; the ball was effectively in someone else's court. But this was an idea that actually might work. And they could still help—with money instead of their own previously unproductive ideas and artificially manufactured jobs that only increased tension for their other employees.

"Well, how much money have we got here tonight to start with?" Hal Smith went around the tables taking pledges. The final estimated figure was nearly a hundred thousand dollars.

"Miss Blaine, will you be our first monitor, since this whole thing was your idea?" he asked.

"Oh. Well, if everyone else agrees."

Cary should have expected the nomination. But it seemed everything was happening too fast. Everyone wanted a miracle and they wanted it now. And she seemed qualified for the role.

Quickly, the group approved her appointment without a single objection. Cary asked for Brenda Richardson to be her student liaison to help construct the council so that it fairly represented all of the schools in the city, including the parochial school.

Slowly, then with increasing speed, applause began to spread around the table. Cary was left standing alone as the others turned to face her and cheer her ideas and leadership. The forgotten cameras all moved in closer to film the ovation.

They were filming *her*! What would Mary Ellen say about all this? Cary hadn't cleared any of it with her supervisor, neither the funding or her time requirements. But it was all in the best interest of the teens, and Willingham would have the central role in a major community effort. Surely, the company couldn't object to that.

The cameramen were disconnecting their long extension cords now, and the board members were going around shaking hands with all the businessmen and businesswomen. A tall blond-haired young man detached himself from the camera with the KMKX logo and came over to Cary.

"Cary Blaine?"

"Yes. Do you need something?" she asked hesitantly. Cary hoped he wasn't going to ask her to answer any questions about her jobs council. Why, she'd only just thought up the idea ten minutes ago!

"I'm Phil Braden. I'm working the camera and recorders tonight for Hunter Pierce at KMKX. He wanted me to ask you to stay awhile. He's getting a statement from Mr. Smith right now, and he'd like to do your interview last. Oh, and be sure to watch his show tomorrow at six. That's when he's going to run your story."

"Oh!" Cary was dismayed. Hunter *was* here, and he wanted an interview! "I thought Hunter did only exposés, crime reports and things like that. Why is he interested in the jobs council?" she asked the young cameraman.

"Well, he likes to end the week with something upbeat, and boy, lady, you sure have cooked up some great stuff here tonight. Best of luck to you!" Phil started to walk off, but then he came back for a moment.

"And don't worry about being on 'Lineup.' Hunter doesn't cut everybody down—only the people who deserve it. I can guarantee he'll make you and this whole committee look like saints."

"Thanks." Cary's tone was mildly sarcastic. They certainly weren't saints, any of them. And they couldn't really expect any miracles to help accomplish their goals. It was going to be hard work all the way.

But she did feel good about the council, and she was proud that Hunter knew of her contribution. She was also glad to hear that he looked for "upbeat'' stories. He wasn't all crusader, then. There was more to his job than muckraking.

Fortunately no other crews seemed interested in interviews. They must have been satisfied with tapes of the commitee meeting itself. Well, at least she wouldn't have to face a multitude of questions from unfriendly, strange reporters.

There was only one potential problem she could see—cautious Mary Ellen, so touchy now with the pain of her ulcers and her unwarranted fear that Willingham might be trying to replace her. Cary only hoped she'd have time to call Mary Ellen in the morning and break the news to her before her supervisor heard about it from the media.

Most of the committee members had left the gymnasium when Phil Braden brought his camera over to her, followed closely by Hunter.

Tonight Hunter was wearing a light gray sweater and slacks. No wonder she hadn't spotted him in the crowd of denim-clad teens and casually dressed camera operators. Only the business people had dressed formally for the meeting.

While Phil adjusted his equipment, she spoke to Hunter of her concern about her employers' reaction to her voluntarism.

"Please, can we make this very short? Mary Ellen doesn't know anything at all about it, and I'm worried that she might think I've done this as some sort of publicity stunt."

"Why would she think that?" Under the weariness in Hunter's voice was a hint of the veteran reporter's steely reserve.

"Well, she's just very...sensitive right now. Because of her pain, you know. But she's not really an ogre or anything. I would just like a chance to explain why I volunteered—before she draws too many wrong conclusions from the news coverage."

"What kind of wrong conclusions? Is this a publicity stunt?"

Cary realized suddenly that the hardness in Hunter's voice was not strength but cold accusation. He, too, was going to think the worst!

"Oh, no. Hunter, how could you even ask such a question? I really believe in this jobs council and in what these kids can do to help themselves. I'm going to work as hard as I can to make it succeed."

"What do you think you can do on the council?"

"Well, at the beginning I suppose I'll have to work closely with the students to get them going, get them organized. But after the council is operational, I think they'll only need me as an advisor. It really is a good idea, Hunter. And I'm sure I can convince my company that what's good for Topeka is good for Willingham."

"Okay. Done!" Hunter was smiling broadly now, as he put his arms around Cary. "You handled that like a pro."

"What?" Cary was confused. She looked around to see Phil collapsing the camera and wheeling its stand off the gym floor. Was the interview over? Had she been talking to Hunter *on camera*?

"That's all there is, princess. See? It didn't hurt a

bit.'' Hunter was propelling her out of the gym, into the street. A large van with the KMKX 'Line-up' logo on the side was parked in front of the building. Phil was loading the last of his parapher-nalia into it.

"But...but, I was talking about Mary Ellen. You wouldn't...."

"Don't worry, Cary." Hunter gave her another quick kiss and climbed into the van's cab. "I'll edit that tape to pieces. There won't be anything about your supervisor on the air, I promise. In fact," he began, "how about coming down to the station with me right now. I can show you exactly what I do. Unless you'd rather get your beauty sleep."

"Oh, I'd love to come! I'll just trail your van."

"Great! See you in Kansas City in an hour." He climbed up beside Phil in the cab and waved to her.

Cary sped over to the Cutlass and drove it around to the front of the gym. She flashed her lights, and when the big van pulled out, she followed.

During the long drive, Cary had ample time to re-flect on her misgivings. She'd really been upset by Hunter's tricky interview. He could have mentioned the camera was rolling!

That hard, cold tone had been his reporter's voice—not the voice of accusation, but it had made her so defensive. Just what *had* she said to him any-way?

They pulled up outside a multistoried office building. Inside, a security guard hovered as they signed in, and then he followed them over to the elevators. The station was housed on the top floors of the building, with a magnificent view of the city's streets.

Hunter led Cary to a large room where several people were sitting in front of a bank of video screens. Though it was late at night, the room was brightly lit and full of noise.

"Those are our program-editing monitors. Wait just a minute and I'll run this tape onto the machine in the upper right." He fiddled with the black box he'd been carrying, took a large cartridge out of it and slipped it into something that looked like a tape deck.

On the high corner monitor, Cary now saw random shots of the participants at the meeting. Hunter handed her some earphones, and she heard the monotone roar of conversations. Then Hal Smith's voice echoed in the background, and she began to watch a replay of the actual conference.

But after a few moments, the screen went blank and Hunter reached for her headphones.

"See those reel-to-reel decks over there?" He pointed to a low table full of equipment along one wall. "That's where we cut and splice together the best pieces of each film to make a story. This one here will take me at least an hour to edit tomorrow. Now let me show you around the rest of the place."

Cary was disappointed that Hunter wasn't going to let her see just how he planned to "cut and splice'' the videotape. But she did want to see the rest of the station. . . .

"This is our news set," Hunter said, pointing to a very small wooden desk sitting in front of a garish blue wall.

Cary was puzzled. "I've seen your show, Hunter. And I don't remember that awful wall. Does it change color?"

Hunter laughed. "Watch here," he said, walking gingerly over cables to a large camera. He pointed it at the desk and then told Cary to look over at a monitor sitting off to one side.

What Cary saw was the empty desk—in front of the red-and-black KMKX logo!

"How are you doing that?"

"It's simple, really. That wall is a color this camera can't see. Another camera, in a little cubbyhole room, is aimed at our logo. We just superimpose this picture on that one and *voilà*!"

"Like the weather maps behind the meteorologist? And those film clips you run behind the news anchor's head sometimes?"

"Same thing, my dear. I'll bet you thought we had some kind of projection screen behind us. Most people do," he said, smiling. "Look, I can even do a bit of magic for you."

He picked up a piece of fabric, the same blue as the set wall, and draped it around Cary's shoulders. He made her stand in front of the desk and then told her to look at the monitor.

On the screen, her disembodied head floated near

the center. The cloth effectively made the rest of her invisible.

"Great fun, isn't it?" Hunter grinned. "Now you know why I got into television. I like to play games."

"Oh, I already knew that, Mr. Pierce. You have a ball becoming each of the different characters you play."

Hunter strode up to her and slowly pulled off her impromptu cape. "Not half as much fun as I have being myself around you, Cary Blaine." His voice dropped. "I don't have to play games around you. You're all the excitement I need."

He bent forward and kissed her. His lips were warm and inviting. How could she hold back? Her arms reached up to pull him into a stronger embrace.

Suddenly, his tongue invaded her mouth exploring, tantalizing and ravishing her.

She opened her mouth to his plundering and felt an urgent need to press against him, to somehow satisfy the rising ache that swelled her breasts. A need to have him touch her. She twisted against him and somehow slipped off the desk.

Her eyes flew open as she fell—and she saw the two of them, caught by the camera and displayed in full color on the monitor.

"Hunter! Stop!" she cried, startled. "Are you taping us? Is anyone watching?"

"No, you goose. That monitor is just hooked into the camera. It sees whatever the camera sees, even if there's no film behind the lens. Calm down. We're not being broadcast."

He bent to kiss her again, but Cary was completely unnerved by the experience of seeing their lovemaking on the screen. She pushed him away, laughing nervously.

With a shrug, Hunter helped her down from the set and led the way to other rooms, full of monitors and typewriters, down long hallways where people hurried with stacks of paper, and briefly past the weather room where a radar screen showed conditions around the Kansas City area.

It was getting late. After a quick cup of coffee in a tiny lunchroom, Hunter took Cary back past the security guard to her car.

"Thank you, Hunter. I really enjoyed that," she said, yawning.

"Be careful driving, princess. I'll see you... tomorrow. With no cameras to spook you. Just be sure to watch yourself on the six o'clock news."

He bent forward for a final kiss.

"I love you, Cary," he whispered.

Or was it something else he'd said? She looked up at him in surprise. But he just grinned and waved her on.

Cary's heart and her thoughts raced so wildly on the way home that she never once got sleepy. She was sure she had heard him correctly!

Sleep was elusive that night. Cary lay awake for hours, trying to reconstruct exactly how she had replied to Hunter's questions, worrying about what he meant by editing her comments.

In the gray light of early morning, as her alarm

intruded on her dreams, she remembered saying Mary Ellen wasn't an ogre. And she wasn't, was she?

A MESSAGE TO CALL her supervisor "immediately" lay on Cary's desk when she arrived at work the next day, beside a morning newspaper that had been folded to expose a photograph of Cary shaking hands with Hal Smith.

"May I have your autograph?" asked Marian, grinning.

Cary grimaced and then pretended to ignore her secretary completely, hoping she would go away. Cary wanted to get the call to Mary Ellen over with.

"You should have seen the early morning news on TV," persisted Marian. "You're now a local celebrity. We've had three calls already from people wanting to know where they can send money to help fund the jobs council."

"Already!" Cary was astounded and a little dismayed. She'd anticipated a month of setting up the council. She looked up at Marian's bright eager smile and shook her head. "You may think this is going to be fun, but I assure you, Marian Davies, we are all going to work our tails off!"

"Right, boss. Where do I start?"

Cary laughed. It was encouraging to see Marian so enthusiastic! Well, the call to Mary Ellen could wait a few more minutes.

"For starters," she began, "find out from our lawyers in St. Louis how to set up a nonprofit group like this one. Leave a message at the high school for Brenda Richardson to call me this afternoon. Then pack up everything in this room and see where you can store it. We can get four desks in here if we try. I'll move into the small office down the hall.''

"Roger. Where do I find the four desks?"

"From those contributors who called this morning. Or try salvage stores, secondhand shops. I don't care, and neither will the students. We'll use donations to buy typewriters and equipment.''

"Uh, pardon me for objecting, but from the little I know about nonprofit organizations, I think you'd better get a treasurer or something before you spend any money at all.''

Cary sighed. "You're probably right. I'll look through our applicant file first and see if anyone with that kind of experience is available right now—and willing to work for peanuts. We've got to get started fast though, or the people who are promising money today will lose interest.''

"I'll get to work on the lawyer and the office right away," said Marian. She scooped up the newspaper and scurried out to her own desk.

Now for Mary Ellen, groaned Cary. She dialed through and was lucky enough to find her supervisor free immediately.

"What's this I hear about Willingham founding a charity organization for high-school kids?" Mary Ellen sounded impatient and a little annoyed.

Not the best way to start the conversation, thought Cary with a sigh of resignation. She began to explain how she had been looking for ways to make Willingham charity contributions mean more to the community. As she described the meeting in the gymnasium, she could hear the nervous tapping of her supervisor's pen in the background. Quickly she summed up her proposal to the committee and her nomination to be the first monitor for the jobs council.

"So you've set up a nonprofit personnel agency to compete with us in finding jobs in Topeka. I can hardly believe it, Cary."

"Oh, they won't be competing with us. We couldn't possibly work on that level—finding baby-sitting and housecleaning jobs for teenagers. And think of all the good publicity we'll be getting free by directing and controlling the whole operation!"

"Well, yes. I see your point. But I have one... suggestion to make. I think you should limit your activities to current students. Under no circumstances should you try to find jobs for those who have already graduated. They are in the regular job market now and no other agency is going to thank you for stealing away those potential commissions. *Willingham* certainly wouldn't!"

"But the most recent graduates are—"

"Let's call that a 'firm' suggestion, shall we?" interrupted Mary Ellen. "I'll run it by management, but I think they'll agree with me. You've made a lot of commitments, Cary, which are going to cost Willingham a pretty penny in time—your *valuable* time. Those investments could eventually pay off for us. But if you want our sanction—at this late stage in the game—you'd better be prepared to play by corporate rules. Willingham doesn't just throw away potential clients.''

"Yes, Mary Ellen. I understand.''

"I hope you do. You've been taking on quite a lot of responsibility lately, Cary. I'd like to see that trend continued, and it can *if* you use a little discretion in your enthusiasm.''

Mary Ellen then reminded her that she still owed one more engineer to Omega and advised her to take care of that responsibility as soon as possible.

"Yes, I will,'' promised Cary. "Goodbye, then.''

Cary's mood when she hung up was less optimistic than it had been earlier in the morning. She'd really counted on being able to persuade Mary Ellen to wholehearted endorsement. But she should have anticipated the older woman's efficient, dispassionate attitude toward company policy. Even though they were talking about a serious community problem, the supervisor had seemed to say that if Willingham wasn't going to profit by the idea, then it might not get approval. But surely that wasn't the way to approach contributions and community involvement! It certainly wasn't the way Cary would like to see things handled.

She wondered if any of what Mary Ellen had said was the result of living with the constant pain of ulcers. No, she was probably right that Willingham management would back her up. In a major corporation, profit had to be the prime consideration, didn't it?

Cary stewed over Mary Ellen's comments and her own responses for some time. Later, she received a second call from St. Louis, from Dennis Forsythe. As Mary Ellen's superior, he represented Willingham Associates, the consulting firm that was the parent of Willingham Personnel Services and Executive Recruiting, and his reaction now to Cary's proposed jobs council was exactly the opposite of what her supervisor had told her to expect.

"This shows just the kind of initiative and enthusiasm we try to encourage in our field recruiters," he said with a sincere, booming voice.

"Thank you very much, Mr. Forsythe." Relief echoed in Cary's voice. "I'll be working hard to make the idea a success."

"I'm sure you will, Miss Blaine. By the way, I never have talked to you about the fine work you did when Miss Hughes was in the hospital. It didn't go unnoticed."

Sometimes, I wish it had, thought Cary ruefully.

"I would like you to be prepared to take over again, if Miss Hughes should have to go back for surgery," he continued.

"Is that likely?"

"Well, uh, between you and me, Miss Blaine, she does still seem to be in quite a bit of pain. She hasn't been able to handle a full work load without a great deal of effort. Everyone is quite concerned about her condition."

"That's too bad. I know she doesn't want to

go back into the hospital. She's always been so strong and this must really be difficult for her to handle.''

"Yes, well...." Dennis Forsythe hesitated. "That's very generous of you, Miss Blaine. I have heard that she has been...a little irritable as a result of her pain. Have you had occasion to notice such behavior?''

"I've always admired Mary Ellen Hughes very much, and I think she's handling her pain much better than I would," Cary said truthfully. "I also think she believes these ulcers are only a temporary thing. But I'm sure part of the problem now is her worry that a long stay in the hospital could damage her career.''

"Yes." Forsythe appeared to consider Cary's comment. "Perhaps that's why she's being so secretive about some of her accounts. She's trying to make certain we know she is indispensable.

"You've opened my eyes, Miss Blaine. I'll just have a little talk with Miss Hughes and let her know how much we all appreciate her. Her ulcers certainly won't heal as long as she's worried about that.''

"Perhaps someone else in her office could do the traveling-budget reviews, too," Cary suggested. "Mary Ellen looked so tired when she stopped by here last Friday.''

"Oh, has she started that already? Yes, I think we can find an alternative to so much travel this year. Speaking of travel—how's our aircraft-espionage case coming?''

"Just fine, so far. Mr. Pierce has been offered a job, starting next week."

"Sounds like you have that under control then, for the time being. Keep me informed. And thank you again for your wise suggestions, Miss Blaine."

Though he couldn't see her, Cary smiled at the warmth in Dennis Forsythe's rumbling voice. She was so glad he had called. And she was very pleased by his quick grasp of Mary Ellen's situation. Maybe he could ease things up for her, and everyone could get back to normal in St. Louis soon.

Things really are working out! she crowed inside.

Dwight Miller from the school board called late in the day to tell her they had received another sixty thousand dollars in pledges for the council. He also wanted to find out when detailed plans for the jobs council could be presented to the full board. Riding high on her wave of restored optimism and Marian's enthusiasm, Cary promised to have a draft plan available in two weeks.

"Our student coordinator, Brenda Richardson, has already started assembling a list of other students who want to work on the council."

"Good, good. I knew we had a winner when you agreed to spearhead this thing, Miss Blaine."

Cary glowed from the praise. Dennis Forsythe and Dwight Miller certainly made up for the cool reception from Mary Ellen! Cary laughed aloud to realize she was actually looking forward to hearing what good things Hunter would say about her ideas in his broadcast tonight. The rest of the afternoon seemed to fly by in a flurry of last-minute projects she had to finish before the week-end.

CHAPTER ELEVEN

CARY WAS A LITTLE LATE getting back to the apartment and barely had time to turn on her television set before the evening-news anchor began his introduction of Hunter. The "Lineup" segment began with some of the same facts about student unemployment Hal Smith had used to open the committee meeting.

"A serious problem for any community," Hunter summed up. "And only the community pulling together can come up with viable solutions.

"This meeting of school board, students and members of the business world in Topeka last night was called for that purpose. But in a typical big-business move, nearly everyone who could have helped backed away from the problem and refused to become involved."

Cary gasped. What followed were clips of the students, waving their hands and offering to "do anything" and shots of some of the business people claiming they had already tried everything possible to help. The picture Hunter painted was one of selfish moneyed professionals turning up their noses at the poor and unemployed.

But it wasn't that way! she wanted to shout. "You're leaving so much out!

"Finally, though, someone made a suggestions that met with general approval," continued Hunter.

Now Cary saw herself saying, "It's going to take a lot of work. Why don't we give these eager teens the chance to do that work—for themselves?"

She could hardly hear the rest of her speech as the deafening roar of her thoughts drowned out the words. *I sound just as bad! I'm coming across like I'm trying to pass the buck, to avoid doing anything helpful myself.*

"Relief was evident on many faces when Miss Blaine finished outlining her plan. Several students eagerly volunteered to work on the new jobs council. At least those few teens will be earning a salary soon."

The screen now showed Cary, embarrassed to be receiving the applause of the committee. Hunter's honeyed voice went on above the roar of the ovation.

"Executive Recruiter Caroline Blaine, from the Willingham Personnel agency in Topeka, is new to community involvement but she has just found out one of the standing rules. Don't come up with a new program unless you are prepared to run it. The members of the business community who were present, as well as the school board, lost no time in making Miss Blaine completely responsible for the success of the council. Fortunately for the students,

Caroline Blaine is willing to assume that responsibility.''

Cary's face again filled the screen. ''I really believe in this jobs council and in what these kids can do to help themselves. I'm going to work as hard as I can to make it succeed.''

The view cut back to Hunter's face at the studio.

''The Topeka Jobs Council sounds like the first concept we've heard about with real potential for success in solving the problem of unemployed teens in the Midwest. It deserves more support than money. At least it has Caroline Blaine, an imaginative, courageous young woman whom we wish the best of luck.

''This is Hunter Pierce for 'Lineup,' cable KMKX in Kansas City. Good night everyone, and have a good weekend.''

Cary rose from her couch and turned off the set. As if the act had been a prearranged signal, her doorbell rang a shrill summons.

Numbly, she opened the door. Hunter stood outside on the balcony, holding another pot of purple chrysanthemums. And Cary could only stare at him, her eyes round with a wounded look.

Wordlessly, Cary stepped back to let Hunter come inside. He set the flowers on her coffee table and then came over to where she stood beside the still-open door.

''You look tired, beautiful,'' he said, and then pulled her into a hungry embrace.

She felt unnatural; his arms did not warm her cold spirit, and his lips did not ignite a fire inside her soul. Instead she was even more empty now that his mouth was touching hers. She seemed to watch herself being unresponsive, and Hunter gradually realizing that she was not returning his kiss. She watched but was not really part of it—as though suddenly it was she and not this callous, hypocritical reporter who was the stranger.

She had loved him! No, she had wanted to love him. And her heart had tricked her into believing she knew and understood him. But it was all a lie.

"What's wrong, Cary?" His eyes seemed to feign worry and concern so well.

She couldn't find the words to answer him, though, and simply shook her head. Were there words for this feeling of desolation she felt?

"Is it your family? Or work?" he pressed her.

Still she answered mutely with only a shake of her head. How could she tell him, now that she had invited him to spend the night with her, now that she had said she had no more doubts, how could she tell him she'd been mistaken?

Hunter took a deep breath. His arms wrapped tightly around her and sealed her to his chest. "All right, princess. Tell me later, then, when you can. I hate to see you like this, so hurt. Whatever it is, I can help you through it—if you'll let me."

He moved so that her cheek lay against his shoulder. Perhaps he expected her to cry or to whisper of some terrible catastrophe but, though she could have done both, still neither tears nor words would come.

She knew about his work. She should have been

prepared. It was all part of his job. Nonetheless, she wanted to cry out, how could you have done this?

Hunter glanced at her silent television set. "You must not have seen my show," he remarked, smiling for her. "That would have cheered you up. Too bad you missed it."

She twisted out of his arms and walked away. "I saw it."

He could not mistake the flat, unenthusiastic tone of her comment. He couldn't fail to see. . . .

"What is it, Cary? What's wrong?" She turned her back on him as he spoke. "It has something to do with me, doesn't it?"

She wheeled on him, seeking strength in anger because there was no strength at all in her pain.

"How could you distort what happened? How could you make the cameras lie like that? How *could* you, Hunter?" Her last violent words were broken by the tears that would not come before. She was sobbing now, and Hunter—after a moment's hesitation—was holding her against him again as the tears spilled onto his shirt and tie. Her shoulders shook with the admission of her pain.

Strange, oh, how strange we are when love betrays us. Cary felt crushed by Hunter's glory-seeking debasement of the truth, and yet she leaned against his strong chest and huddled herself inside the protective circle of his arms. She wanted him to comfort her, to tell her that her fears were groundless and her interpretation wrong—though she knew his words would probably only be more lies. Yet still she wanted him to speak, to try to change the world back to *yesterday*.

When her tears were spent and the sobbing ceased to shake her, Hunter took her to the couch. He sat beside her and pulled her hands together between his own palms.

"Just listen. Close your eyes if you have to, Cary, but open your ears and your heart. You don't understand what that program was all about." He waited a moment for her response, and when it didn't come, he squeezed her fingers insistently. "Please?"

She nodded, but she couldn't look at him.

"That show wasn't about you, even though I'd love to tell the world all about you. It wasn't even about the jobs council, although that's what came out of the meeting. It was a story about something more important—a community getting together to solve a problem.

"Cary, listen to me. On my first station job, I covered auto accidents and city politics. Not important stories, just routine news. I knew what I wanted to do was crime reporting, but that wasn't my job. They said I was too young, but I knew they were wrong.

"One night after a city council meeting, I saw a dope transaction going down right on the corner near city hall. I got my cameraman over, and we filmed the whole thing. Then I went back to the station and cut in a voice-over story about dealing drugs in the council's backyard.

"The station manager killed the story. I was mad

and hurt, the way you are. I thought he was trying to put me down, and in doing that mean, personal thing he was also betraying the public trust and worse—I thought he was trying to avoid embarrassing any political bigwigs."

Cary felt Hunter's fingers caress her hands. But it was his voice that held her attention. The story he was telling seemed to have no relationship to his program tonight, and she considered each word desperately, needing to understand.

"Fortunately, I confronted my boss with my thoughts, and he set me straight. I hadn't checked out my story. The buyer in my film was an undercover narcotics officer. The seller was just a small fish, someone the police were hoping would lead them to the big man who ran the larger city-wide ring.

"If I had run that film, the whole carefully planned police operation would have fallen through."

He paused. "Do you see my point, Cary?"

She shook her head. *I want to,* she cried inside. *I want to, but I don't.*

"I felt I had a duty to tell people about the drug scene near city hall, expose the two men I saw breaking the law. But not running the story served a larger purpose—to stop the drug-dealing altogether. My boss could have run my story and perhaps one dealer would have been behind bars as a result. But he didn't run it, and eventually the police were led by that dealer to the man who brought the stuff into this country."

"But you didn't kill a story this time," Cary protested. "You deliberately twisted what went on to make everyone sound selfish and. . .mean."

"What would you say if I told you that was the way I saw it?"

"I'd say you were wrong! Narrow-minded and wrong!" Cary turned to face him, expecting to find her words had angered him. His eyes were steady, though, not shifting with guilt or uncertainty. In the face of his self-confidence, her anger flared.

"Cary, I'm not a news reporter; I don't just tell facts. My job involves giving my opinion of those facts and trying to rouse the emotions of our audience. I could have told a sweet story, the one you seem to think really happened, about how a group of concerned citizens got together and worked up plans to solve the problem of teenage unemployment. Everybody was enthusiastic, and the problem will probably disappear by next Sunday at the latest.

"But that wasn't what really happened, Cary. Believe in me for just this once. The big story I was trying to tell was about how a whole crowd of people ducked the issue they were supposed to be confronting. As a result of my broadcast tonight, many people will realize that you haven't received the help your outstanding idea deserves. They'll be afraid that if they don't do something themselves, your whole grand plan will fail. I'll be willing to bet that Monday morning your phone rings off the hook with offers from people who want to make sure your jobs council doesn't fail." His musical voice was rising, pleading with her to understand. The music fell false and flat for Cary, however.

"Yes, people will be concerned. But only because some very weary, busy people have been maligned and look like hypocrites!" Her outrage vibrated in every word. Hunter had made her a "saint" all right and made the business community seem like apathetic sinners. *No, that's an overreaction,* she cautioned herself. *Slow down.*

"I don't think what you did was fair," she said more evenly, trying to sort out her thoughts and sound less emotional. "You cut out all the talk about what those fine people on the committee had done before, all the different ideas they had tried that didn't work. You made them sound like they didn't care and that was only your opinion, not the truth."

"Are you sure about that?" Hunter was sitting stiffly, defensively. And that hard glitter of anger was there again, behind his glasses.

"What do you mean?"

Now his voice was charged with emotion, too. "They dumped on you, my sweet naive princess, and any impartial idiot could see that. The ideas they had tried before didn't work because no one gave anything but money to make them work. No one volunteered time or expertise—except you, Cary. And they jumped on your willingness like parasites, offering money again—not help. But they'll coast along to glory with you if your idea succeeds, and if it doesn't they can still say they tried.

"I told the story I felt the public deserved to know. The *real* story."

"Oh, Hunter. You make them all sound so cold and cruel! They do care, I know it." Cary shook with conflicting reactions to Hunter's denunciation. He believed what he said; but what he believed was all wrong! No matter how lofty his purpose sounded, the problem still boiled down to one thing: he had twisted what innocent people had said and done in order to make a story.

"But caring wouldn't have made as good a story for you, would it?" There! She'd said it.

Hunter did not move away. He put his arm around Cary's shoulders and turned her so that she fully faced him. He tilted her chin so that she looked directly into his eyes. And she allowed him to set the stage, because she wanted him to answer her. She desperately wanted to know if he could really explain everything to her and banish this cold, hard knot in her stomach. She didn't think he could.

At first, Hunter said nothing, he only looked into her eyes. His forehead was wrinkled with concentration or worry.

"That's what you really think, isn't it? You're making me out to be a callous liar, Cary. And I'm not. Oh, Cary! It's the truth I'm after. Can't you see that?" He searched her eyes, and his tense shoulders slumped.

"No, you can't. Princess, princess! We've each had a different experience of the world. You're still trusting of people like those lawyers and dentists and 'good citizens.' I'm not. Perhaps I'm too skeptical, though I doubt it. But as long as you haven't been hurt by the cold and calculating people out there, nothing I can say will make any sense to you. We're so much alike in our idealism, and so different in our methods. We might as well be talking gibberish to each other.''

''Then. . .there's nothing more to say. Is that what you're telling me?'' Cary asked. The distance between them seemed somehow unreal. Hunter was suddenly unreachable and untouchable.

''No. No, not at all, darling. There is still this.'' He bent to kiss her lightly. ''And this.''

Hunter pressed her against the cushions and kissed her again, a long ardent kiss that told her more about his perseverance than all the impassioned arguments he had given her before. She forced herself to turn away from him—but not completely. He brought her face back near his and kissed the tears that ran down her cheeks, then carefully brushed them away with his finger. She felt her fears drifting off at his tender touch. She shouldn't feel this way, but she did.

Yes, there was this. Could it be enough?

She knew the answer in the secret places of her heart. It would never be ''enough.'' She wanted it all. All or nothing. She laid her wet cheek on his shoulder.

When her tears had ceased and she was limp with spent emotion, Hunter drew away a little. ''Once you told me that you were rarely untruthful, Cary.

But there are all kinds of truth, aren't there? And some truths are unpleasant. I'll bet you haven't told your supervisor about the investigation yet, have you?''

Cary shook her head, and then thought bleakly of the cheerful optimism she showed to applicants, even when their prospects looked grim. She had even told Tommy not to worry, and that had only been the truth he had needed to hear.

"I haven't lied to you, Cary. And I wouldn't lie to my audience, either. They expect me to tell them the truth, and they would have me fired if I didn't."

"I know that," she admitted in a low voice. "I can even understand that you must believe the truth of your stories or you couldn't air them."

"Well, that's a step in the right direction!" He smiled.

"But I still think those businessmen didn't deserve what you did to them. The truth is they *were* trying, and now all their friends and associates will see them as uncaring shirkers."

"We'll see. Wait a few weeks before you try to come to that conclusion. You'll see I was right. I promise, princess. Everything will work out—for the jobs council and for us."

He bent once again to her, insistent, demanding. But she was not going to respond again on cue. She wasn't going to give him the satisfaction of seeing her weak and willing in his arms when she was still angry. . . but her lips were opening, welcoming his sweet invasion and her traitorous body was yielding to his assault.

Suddenly it seemed to Cary that if she could just give up and let go of her worries and doubts, the world would at last seem real again. She could wake up and find that everything was perfect once more.

She felt Hunter's warm breath, and her heart raced with pleasure. That uncontrollable fire in her soul had been rekindled once again by his butterfly kisses of reassurance and promise.

"I need your naive innocence, princess," he whispered. "And you need my lack of it. Perhaps I can teach you something new about the world. I know you can give back the joy of living in it."

Cary looked into his eyes and knew she couldn't ever feel hurt or anger when he looked at her that way. As long as he was with her....

Cary found she was smiling sadly. Yes, she could forget the world for a while in his arms.

Misinterpreting her smile, Hunter grinned, his expression irresistible. "Look. If your committee members surprise me and swamp you with job offers next week, I'll run an apology on my segment next Friday. How's that?"

Cary was crushed into his confident embrace, feeling the rough wool of his suit scratch gently against her cheek. "Fair enough," she answered, sighing.

"We'll get through this, princess. Just wait and see."

His hand softly caressed her hair, as he had done

so long ago at Lake Shawnee. His gentle tugs were like the soft plucking of a mandolin—they sent thrumming shivers down her spine and around her stomach.

Cary's thoughts went circling from the man and his motives to the incredible sensations he awakened in her. This was the man who had spent a whole night in the mud and debris to help strangers, the man who was playing a dangerous game of impersonation in order to help a company threatened by bankruptcy. Such a man wouldn't have deliberately tried to twist facts for personal gain. He wouldn't try to use her feelings for him? Would he?

"Oh, love me, Hunter! Love me now," she whispered, wrapping her arms around him. She didn't want to think any more now. She couldn't! Her body craved the honey of Hunter's kiss. But he only shook his head.

"Not now, sweetheart. Not like this. Last time was clouded by doubt. This time would be shadowed by. . . something else. It wouldn't work for either of us."

She pulled away, her eyes blank with surprise. "But, I thought you—"

"Later, love. Believe me."

That was the whole point, wasn't it? Either she believed in him and his motives completely or she didn't. *You can't have love without trust,* she thought, still trembling with unfulfilled desire.

Yet, why must it be Hunter who was right? Wasn't it just as possible—didn't she truly believe *she* was right? Maybe what they were waiting for was for Hunter to come to his senses, not her. She smiled tightly. Hunter certainly didn't see it that way!

"All right," she sighed. Her body still shook from the feelings that had coursed through her in such a short span of time. Bewilderment, pain, betrayal, hope, the overwhelming desire for physical release and then, finally, an exhausted emptiness that threatened to last for a long time, while they...waited.

"Let's go find someplace quiet for dinner," Hunter suggested, rising. He pulled Cary to her feet and into a soft embrace that was loving and full of confident promise.

"Yes. I'd like that," she answered.

Dinner was a difficult time, when their words flew about like frightened birds, and every look skittered away. The waiter had to repeat questions because neither of them was paying any attention to the meal. They were both trying to learn about each other and yet ignore the physical magnetism between them despite their mutual misgivings.

They were quick to contradict each other, even faster to seize on anything that seemed common ground.

"I guess your job has a lot of glamor," she offered dubiously.

"Glamor? Not really. It's mostly hard work finding stories and researching them. But if you mean meeting famous people, I guess there is a fair share of that. In fact, I really enjoy that aspect—getting to talk to politicians and leaders firsthand, getting to ask them questions I want answered."

"Sometimes I get to do that, too," she responded. "Every day I deal with corporate presidents and officers. Some of them are the real brains behind exciting new ideas and procedures. They just love to talk about their pet projects if you give them a chance. And sometimes a simple question will open up a whole new range of possibilities and creative ideas."

"That's exactly what I'm talking about! One of your state senators did just that for me yesterday— opened up a whole new area I didn't really know much about." Hunter's eyes sparkled with enthusiasm. "I asked him a straightforward question about next year's budget and got a minilesson in macroeconomics. I even understood it!"

Cary smiled. She understood his excitement. "That's what I love about my job. Learning, growing every day."

"Mine, too." Hunter paused and looked across at her seriously. "I've learned a lot from you, you know. About caring and sharing. And about believing in other people."

The last plates had been cleared and the check was ready to be paid, and Cary knew that soon a moment would come when they would have to deal with the unslaked hunger between them.

In the tiny Audi, though, where physical contact was impossible to avoid, Cary felt her need for Hunter grow and blossom as he moved beside her in the darkness, his long arms twisting the steering wheel and shifting gears only inches away from her thighs, brushing her legs occasionally with carefully controlled strength. . . .

At last they were standing before her front door. The key was opening the lock. And Hunter had taken Cary in his arms as she had imagined he would.

"I know I'm the one who said wait, Cary, but I can't." His voice was ragged. "Don't make me wait any longer."

All that was important to Cary was Hunter's kiss and his embrace. She gave in. "I won't," she promised him breathlessly.

His hands roamed across her back, pressing against her ribs. Her own hands were twined in the coils of his midnight hair, pulling his lips to her.

Cary swayed against his lean body, her hips pressed against his. He moaned when she continued her unconscious swaying.

"Princess. Oh, you beautiful princess!" Hunter whispered, breaking off the kiss to bury his mouth in her hair. He groaned. Then he laughed. "Shouldn't we go inside, before your neighbors see too much?"

They pushed open the door and were scarcely inside when the embrace began again, more intense than before.

Cary reached forward to the shirt that covered Hunter's chest. Her hands went up its slippery silk and unfastened his tie, then slowly pulled the tie off, still kissing him. Her mouth moved to his chin as she undid the top two buttons of the shirt, then to his neck as she opened two more, then down to the curling hairs of his chest as she pulled the cloth out of his pants and unfastened the last few buttons.

Hunter's breath was uneven and fast, gasping as she touched his skin lightly with her tongue.

"Cary," he said hoarsely, "I promised you I would go slowly, but I won't be able to keep that promise if you insist on doing this much longer."

Cary chuckled and reached up to remove his jacket and then his shirt. His hands grabbed at her and pulled her up tight against his naked shoulder. She could feel him panting and, below, his eagerness strained through both his clothing and hers.

"Cary!" he repeated. "Do you know what you're doing to me?"

"No," she whispered. "Tell me."

"You brazen wench! Don't ever tell me again that you don't lie. You know very well what you're doing!" He lowered his hands to her waist and tightened his grip there. In one swift, strong movement, he had lifted her up so that her head was above his and her hair hung down around his face.

"There's only one thing to do with a woman like you," he said, laughing. A few more inches and her waist was up as high as his shoulder.

"No! You wouldn't!" she cried.

"Oh yes I would!"

Suddenly her head was upside down behind his back, swaying as he strode toward the bedroom. He had put her across his shoulder like a sack of potatoes and was carrying her with the ease of a Tarzan.

She couldn't help it. She started giggling. It was all like some Cary Grant–Doris Day piece of fluff— only it was real and it was happening to her. And she loved it!

In only a few seconds she felt herself falling backward and found the bed beneath her, its pale blue-and-violet satin coverlet pillowing her fall. The game was over. Hunter leaned across and came to rest above her, supported by his arms on either side of her head. He was smiling, but not in his usual fashion.

Cary waited for him to come closer, but he didn't. He just looked at her, first at her face and then at her concealed but heaving breasts. Closing her eyes, she softly parted her lips to receive his kiss, but still he came no closer.

Her hands were free and finally she could wait no longer. She reached up to his hair and clutched at its coarse curls, pulling his face down to hers. She got more than she'd bargained for, though, because he fell on her completely then, covering her body with his.

She gasped.

Wordlessly, he rolled, pulling her with him, over him, beside him. His fingers swiftly loosened her ascot tie and undid the buttons of her blouse.

And then his lips were softly brushing her breasts as she arched toward him. Somehow the rest of their clothing disappeared, and their mutual desire overpowered everything else. The crashing tides of her passion roared in Cary's ears again and again and again. She would drown in the ecstasy that was pulsing through her.

Hunter, too, seemed driven by those tides to everswelling crests and falls until, at last, the flood of their passion reached its final crest and then slowly fell away back to the sea of sweet fulfillment.

"Oh, princess, princess!" Hunter breathed beside her ear so softly she almost couldn't hear. "You're all I ever want."

Damp with the heat of loving, Cary whispered softly. "I love you, Hunter Pierce."

He did not answer. Her heart quaked in sudden cold apprehension. Had she said it too soon?

Slowly Hunter rose on his arms again, until his face was inches above her own. "Say that again. I dare you." He was smiling, a broad pleased smile. No regret. No disgust.

"I love you. I love you. I love you, Hunter Pierce." Cary sang the words.

Suddenly, she was being crushed by a smothering bear hug. She kicked out and he released her, laughing.

"I love you, princess! I knew it! I knew you were the one!" He looked as if he alone had a monopoly on certainty. And then he yawned.

Cary got up to pick up all their jumbled clothes, and Hunter took his things from her to hang on a nearby chair. They wandered into the bathroom and took a shower together, without planning or agreement, because they both wanted the same thing—to be together. When she was dry and had on a robe, Cary went into the kitchen and began to make coffee. Hunter searched her small liquor supply for brandy to add to the hot coffee, and they sipped the combination on dining chairs pushed up tight beside each other. Hunter's hand was on her leg, and Cary's free arm was tucked around Hunter's, close beside his steadily beating heart.

Her grandmother clock chimed midnight, the witching hour, and Hunter yawned again.

"Sleepy?" she asked indulgently.

"You've worn me out, woman. Let's go to bed."

"That sounds like a contradiction in terms to me." She smiled and her eyes sparkled.

"Believe me, it isn't," Hunter managed to say as he yawned once more.

Cary put their coffee cups on the tile counter and thought of lying down to sleep beside Hunter. Of course she had done it once before—the night of the tornado—but tonight was different. He was awake and somehow she didn't believe that he would want to go straight to sleep.

She rinsed the crockery cups and turned out all the kitchen lights. But when she reached the bed, she found she'd been mistaken about Hunter's intentions. He lay on his stomach with a pillow loosely covering his head, presumably to shield his eyes from the lamp beside the bed, and his back rose and fell with even breaths.

Cary sighed in disappointment and then laughed silently at her reaction. Now that she had found the true pleasure of loving, she wanted so much more of it—and Hunter was asleep! She debated waking him, but finally turned off the lamp and settled for snuggling beside him in the darkness.

Her eyes remained open, however, as she considered what had happened to her this evening. She hadn't liked Hunter's program at all, and there would undoubtedly be many others in Topeka who would share her dislike. She could just barely see Hunter's point of view, though. He might even be right about the lack of real help that would be available from the business community.

But even if he was right, even if a greater purpose could be served by showing only part of the story, did that make his distortion of the truth correct? Yes, she accepted that Hunter believed in what he was doing. But did believing in yourself make you infallible? And if Hunter was morally wrong in twisting facts, what did that make her?

Her long legs tensed under the sheet at the memory of their lovemaking. She couldn't deny the pleasure that had produced the damp warmth of her body. She didn't want to give up the promise of a lifetime of such loving joy. It had seemed so right, so perfect that they should give each other such special soaring ecstasy. But pleasures of the senses weren't the only thing two people truly in love must share. If she was to risk loving, she had to be sure she could fully accept not just his body but Hunter's life as well, his career as a reporter who "interpreted" facts.

Now, not only her legs were tense, but her whole

body seemed a tight spring, ready to uncoil in a moment. She could not give him up! So who was the hypocrite—Hunter or herself?

Or *was* it hypocrisy to follow the simple, uncomplicated message of your heart if your mind was too confused or timid to make a decision?

She closed her eyes, but saw only rainbow fantasies, not answers.

CHAPTER TWELVE

THE FIRST THING Cary became conscious of was a movement beside her in the bed. She was lying on her back, her hands resting lightly on her stomach, and the motion caused her to roll slightly to the center of the bed. Her eyes flew open to see Hunter watching her, his own dark eyes barely half open in the morning sunlight.

"Good morning, beautiful," he said with all the melody of a symphony ringing in his voice. The slightly guttural tone of his voice reminded her of rumbling kettle drums.

"Good morning, handsome," she answered, smiling. "It's time to get up, isn't it?"

"No." He shook his sleep-wild locks and moved to rest closer to her. "You just close your eyes. I'll tell you when it's time to get up."

His sure, firm hand gently pulled at her short gown, tugging it up to her chin. She closed her eyes as he bent his head to kiss her.

With agonizing slowness, his lips began to brush the soft sensitive skin of her breasts, circling around her taut nipples before he finally took one, and then the other, into his mouth. It was exquisite torture that cried for some as yet unnamed relief.

Cary couldn't control the motion of her body as she surrendered to Hunter's unbearably arousing caress.

His kisses traveled down to her waist and she visualized his curls of black-and-silver hair against her ivory skin. He lifted her hands and raised them to lie beside her head on the pillow. He licked softly at each palm, teasing her. Then he kissed her stomach, and she tensed, as though his touch burned all the way through to some hidden core. His warm wet lips moved on to the hollow beside her left hipbone—and tickled!

"Oh!" she cried involuntarily. Her knee jerked up spasmodically and her eyes flew open.

In the act of raising his head in response to her cry, Hunter caught her knee squarely on the jaw. There was a crack as bone connected with bone.

Cary saw surprise flash across his face. Instantly, she sat up and reached out to him. With the suddenness of a shooting star, all thought of lovemaking vanished, replaced by concern for him.

"Oh, Hunter. I'm truly sorry. Did I hurt you?" Her hand caressed his face timidly.

His shocked look had given way to one of pain. "What was that for?" he asked, brushing aside her fingers and rubbing his jaw with his own hand.

Cary watched fearfully as Hunter opened and shut his mouth and wiggled his jaw back and forth. Relieved when nothing seemed to be broken, she leaned back on the pillows and chuckled. "Do you remember threatening to make me helpless with laughter by tickling me?'' she asked.

"Don't tell me," he answered dryly. "You're ticklish down there."

"Down there and under my arms and inside my knees and on the bottom of my feet, and. . . ."

Hunter groaned. "You weren't ticklish last night, as I recall."

"You just didn't happen to hit any of those particular spots," she protested. "I seem to recall you were in too much of a hurry, again, to do much exploring."

"Aha, she complains of *me* hurrying! We'll have to see about that! Nonetheless, I feel a little like Robinson Crusoe this morning, so go ahead and warn me where the booby traps and quicksand are—" he lowered himself back down to her chest and began his slow caresses again "—before I get kicked in a more sensitive place," he mumbled.

Cary laughed, but the sound died in her throat. It was as if the brief comic interlude had never happened. His touch was fire, igniting her every sense to hot desire.

Her eyes were open and she saw Hunter's wide smooth shoulders strained with the effort of holding himself above her. Her fingers traveled over the swell of his muscles, sliding over and around his arms as she marveled at the strength she found there.

In the morning sunlight, the silver in his hair glinted as if it were truly made of precious metal. So much silver—so many cares?

His lips again traveled down, but before they could reach the treacherous flesh beside her hips, she found she could not lie still any longer. She wriggled down, pushing her legs beneath his and forcing her way farther until his mouth was above hers and she could reach up to it and extract from it the honey-sweet kiss that she needed so.

Her arms reached up for his shoulders, and she pulled him down upon her, craving his body on hers.

"Hungry?" he whispered.

"Ravenous!" she cried and kissed his nose, his cheeks and his eyes, tasting the early-morning perspiration on his face and feeling the roughness of his new-dawn beard.

The fire inside her was building to a raging inferno, and she writhed as the temperature rose ever higher. Just as she realized it was not Hunter alone who had hurried them to ecstasy before, that it was she, too, who could not tolerate another moment of anticipation, Hunter moved to satisfy her growing need. The flames whipped around her, ever higher, until finally the blaze was quenched by the rivers of joy that Hunter poured for her.

"Oh, princess, I love you so!" Hunter said against her breast.

She knew it was so. And she knew that no doubt could conquer this feeling inside her, this knowledge that she loved him, too, despite her worries for the future.

Hunter groaned and sat beside her, rubbing his

jaw and stretching. She watched the leonine gesture, marveling again at the play of muscles under his smooth skin.

"Good morning."

"Yes, it was," he answered. "Very good." His hand now rested lightly on her thigh. He moved to trace the outline of her knee and smiled.

"Lady, this little knee is a lethal weapon. Ever consider registering it with the CIA?"

"Does it still hurt?" she asked softly.

"No, not very much at all." He rose and gathered up his clothes. "If I turn black and blue today, I'll consider it a badge of honor. Courage in the line of fire, or something like that. Any chance there might be some bacon and eggs left in that kitchen of yours?"

"Nope. But I had something better planned for us anyway."

"Great!" he answered, pulling on his shirt. "I'm beginning to look forward to your surprises. Now if I can only figure out how to protect myself when one comes in a little too fast...." He rubbed his jaw again suggestively.

Cary grinned and began to dress.

Hunter was so caring and so confident. She prayed silently that they could find a way to work out their differences—soon. Before doubts began to sabotage what they shared.

FOLLOWING CARY'S INSTRUCTIONS, Hunter drove through town until he came to Burlingame Road.

They turned down there, heading southwest out of Topeka toward Wichita, past Burnett's Mound.

"There are lots of legends associated with the mound," said Cary as they passed it. "Chief Burnett was a real person, a real *big* Indian, who was supposedly buried under the mound in a piano crate. I've seen a picture of him. The photographer had to prop him up because he was so large that he couldn't stand by himself."

"Sounds like an interesting guy. What are the legends?"

"Well, the most ironic was the one we all believed about the mound's ability to keep us safe from tornadoes. Even the meteorologists believed that a tornado that approached us from the southwest—and they almost all do—would just run right up the mound and jump over the city," she related.

"I take it that didn't happen."

"No. In 1966 a big one came in from the southwest. Some TV and radio people even went to the base of the mound to watch it come, believing they were safe. It never went up at all. It split and went around both sides of the mound, rejoined in greater strength and plowed straight through the city, destroying houses and university buildings, offices—everything in its way."

"What happened to the news people?"

"Most were lucky. One man had dirt and mud literally imbedded in his skin. Another reporter who coordinated all the live coverage for several days went on to become a well-known network newsman. His dedication and tireless energy impressed a lot of people."

"Where were you?" he asked.

"In a shopping mall. I never even knew it had hit until we tried to go home. But we didn't have any home left."

Hunter was silent for several miles. Cary assumed he was overwhelmed by her story. After all, he had seen the awesome devastation caused by a smaller tornado.

"I lost my home in Biloxi once, too, not long after you lost yours. But it wasn't quite so sudden for us—we knew it was going to happen. It was a hurricane. Camille."

"Oh!" So he, too, had been through disaster. Why then, had he been so surprised by the tornado's damage?

"You can see a hurricane coming for days," he continued. " The rain comes down in torrents and the wind picks up so strong you know nothing can stand in its way. But you have lots of warning; you can prepare for a hurricane. You can save what matters most to you. And the flooded houses can be rebuilt quickly. But what you all have suffered up here, from the instant carnage of these whirlwinds. . . ."

"It gives you strength," Cary responded to his unspoken question. "You learn to go on. And everybody helps."

"Yes, I can see that." He was silent again and the power lines were all the company they had on the lonely road. "Why aren't we taking the turnpike?" he asked suddenly.

"Because I have a surprise for you. Remember?"

"I hope it's food, 'cause I could eat a prairie dog right now—if I knew what one looked like and how to find one."

Cary watched the road for the small yellow sign of the turnoff. "Here!" she called at last. "Turn here for Grandma's Kitchen."

The small restaurant was really an old farmhouse, situated beside a long barn and surrounded with the machinery of a working farm. The smell of fresh hay surrounded them as they walked in the front door.

Inside, red-and-white checked tablecloths covered a dozen round tables, where only a few late-morning risers were enjoying breakfast. A young girl in jeans showed them a table by the window and asked if they wanted to see a menu.

"No, thank you," answered Cary for them both. "We'll have the buffet."

Hunter raised his brows, questioningly. Cary grinned.

"Follow me," she said, leading him to a long row of steaming pans and covered dishes. "You have to take a little of everything—I'll tell you what it is later."

Hunter picked up a tray and followed Cary, watching as she took a funny snowman-shaped roll from a covered basket, scrambled eggs, another square-shaped roll from a steam pan, a slice of what looked a little like an egg-and-meat loaf, a lumpy brown fried concoction and syrup to top both the loaf slice and the lumpy novelty.

"Will I recognize the coffee?" Hunter whispered.

Cary laughed and nodded. Back at their table she pointed out the zwieback, eggs, *Wurstgefüllte Brötchen*, scrapple and an apple fritter that Hunter had put on his plate.

"Translated, those are German twice-baked bread rolls, eggs, German sausage roll, a loaf made from scraps of pork, herbs and meal and a fried apple donut."

"I'm glad I asked," said Hunter dryly. But he cut into the scrapple bravely and declared it outstanding. His favorite turned out to be the sausage rolls, and he went back repeatedly to get "just one more."

"How did this fine German restaurant get way out here?" he asked between mouthfuls of sticky fritter.

"Kansas has always been a real melting pot, as international as New York, I guess. Germans, Spanish, Russians, Africans, English, and most recently, Cubans and Southeast Asians have all found a place here and thrived. Grandma Schwartz owns an apple orchard here, and her boys thought she ought to show the world some of her special recipes. So she opened her Kitchen six years ago and it's doing so well you have to have reservations for dinner.

"Not everything she cooks is German, by the way. The scrapple is an old cowboy recipe for trail rides."

"Mmm," replied Hunter. He was looking

around the large room at the antique spinning wheels, old plows and harnesses that decorated its simple white walls. "Do you know this 'grandma'?" he asked.

"I've met her," said Cary. "Would you like to meet her, too? Come with me. She loves to show off her kitchen."

Behind the buffet tables, in a large room full of gleaming stainless steel and copper, stood a very short, plump woman with iron gray hair bound in a bun. She was bending over a square table and humming softly to herself.

"Grandma Schwartz," called Cary. "May we come in?"

"Sure thing," returned the old woman. "Just let me finish my strudel and I show you around."

The table was covered with a checked cloth over which a thin pastry had been rolled out. The dough was so thin, the checks showed through. The old woman was distributing sliced apples, raisins, spices, coconut and sugar across the pastry. Then she lifted one end of the cloth beneath the mixture, wrapped her hands securely around its edge and yanked. The pastry and its contents rolled up perfectly as the cloth slipped out from under them.

"My strudel!" said grandma proudly. "I bake it for dinner tonight, to eat with fresh cream."

"I can hardly believe it," said Hunter in a low voice. "Can you do that again?"

Grandma laughed. "My dear boy. Ha! I do that every day."

She reached into a large refrigerator behind her

and pulled out two frosty glasses of amber liquid, which she set before Hunter and Cary.

"Fresh cider," she said, smiling. "Just pressed today."

"Thank you, grandma," said Hunter. He sipped the ice-cold apple drink, and his eyes widened in surprise. "This is really good!"

Cary and grandma laughed.

"Grandma, how would you like to have some free publicity?" Hunter asked.

"Oh, sure. Sure. Always I need the publicity," the old woman said.

"How would you like to be on television?"

"Me? Oh, you are joking, yes?"

"Oh, no, I'm not joking. I have a small show on cable television, and I would like to come out here and film you doing...whatever you did to that strudel."

"Oh, my!" Grandma Schwartz called over one of her sons to tell him about the television man.

Cary put her hand on Hunter's arm. "Hunter, she's not very sophisticated."

"I know. She's a real character, isn't she?" His eyes sparkled with enthusiasm. Cary knew he was already writing the story in his head.

"That's just it, Hunter, she isn't the kind of person you...."

"Hush, now. Here she comes. We can talk later." Hunter patted her hand abstractedly.

After only a few seconds' discussion, the family agreed to let a film crew come out on the following weekend.

"Right after church on Sunday," added grandma. "Not before."

"Not before," agreed Hunter.

Hunter's spirits, when he and Cary returned to the car, were high. He swept a low bow to Cary as he held open her car door, and whistled as he drove back to tie in to the turnpike for the rest of the trip to Wichita.

"Are you always looking for stories?" asked Cary, frowning slightly.

"Do you always look for potential employers?" Hunter returned, grinning. "I told you Burkham was paying most of my salary while I'm doing this investigation, but neither I nor the station can afford to have me disappear from the air completely. I still have to get three segments done each week— somehow. Mostly, Phil and I will have to do them on weekends, and I have a staff member who is trying to line up stories for me. But this! This is a gift from heaven. We'll film on Sunday and run the segment the following Friday."

He laid his hand comfortably, possessively, on Cary's knee. "You knew I'd love her, didn't you? Thanks."

Cary tried to stifle the uneasy feeling his swift maneuvering of grandma had produced. He was only doing his job.

The turnpike was long and straight, offering scant variety in scenery. Gradually they moved out of the wooded northeast corner of the state, south and west into the farmlands that made up most of

Kansas. Dark plowed earth lay on either side of the road.

Hunter frowned, looking at the neat rows of soil.

"I thought autumn was harvest time. But these fields look like they're ready for planting," he observed with a puzzled voice.

"You're right on target, Eagle Eye," answered Cary, glad of a safe topic. "Remember how I told you about all the immigrants who have come to Kansas over the decades? Well, a large group of Mennonites from Russia came here in 1874, bringing the seeds of a special kind of winter wheat grown on the steppes of their native land. The wheat is called Turkey Red. It's planted in the fall, lies dormant under the winter snow, and matures much earlier in the year than traditional summer crops. Itinerant harvesters begin reaping in May in Oklahoma and gradually move north as the wheat ripens up here."

Hunter was silent for several miles.

"You love this place, don't you?" he finally asked.

"Yes, I guess I do." Cary hadn't really thought about her feeling for Kansas. But Hunter was right. That was why she had felt her current assignment was a homecoming.

"Why? You've been so many other places. What's special about all...this?" He waved his arm expansively.

"I don't really know. It's open and free. People here are tolerant and warm. You can make your own way. There's so much opportunity."

"Even now? What about your high-school students who can't find jobs?"

"Oh, it's tight right now. But don't you see? No, perhaps you don't. Hunter, we came up with an idea to solve the problem, and people have already started calling in to offer help. They didn't resist the idea just because it was new and untried. Perhaps it appeals to them just because it is an experiment. There are still a lot of pioneers here, pioneers of the present."

"You make a very eloquent spokesman for them. . . for Grandma Schwartz and the wheat, the dentists and lawyers and for all the rest. Are you going to stay here?"

Cary felt another shadow cloud her horizon. "I don't know. Probably not. This is only a temporary assignment, you know."

"No. I didn't know." Hunter's voice was suddenly tightly controlled. "Am I temporary, too?"

"No. At least I hope not."

Hunter smiled. "Good. As long as that's settled, we'll just let the details work themselves out, huh?" He squeezed her knee.

Cary sighed. The relationship couldn't be as simple as his words implied, she knew. At least Hunter wasn't going to force a confrontation about her future assignments now. If he had, she didn't know how she would have replied. Her job at Willingham was a career she loved, with a firm she had always enjoyed being part of. But she really did not know what she would do if her vocation called her away from Hunter. It was one more problem she would have to face sooner or later, but she was glad it wouldn't be today.

Just now she was trying to set aside worry and doubt and concentrate on sunshine and loving and learning about Hunter.

She did not question why Hunter wasn't worrying.

LATE IN THE MORNING, Hunter slowed his car abruptly and brought it to a halt on the shoulder. He got out of the car and looked around him for several seconds.

"What is it, Hunter? Is something wrong?"

"Cary, there aren't any trees! Anywhere! Come out and look." His voice was strange, as if he had encountered something out of the *Twilight Zone*.

Cary laughed as she got out of the car.

"Haven't been this far West before, have you? These are the Flint Hills—the last of the true salt-grass prairies. Aren't they magnificent?"

"If you don't like variety, I suppose. There's nothing here but . . . nothing!"

"Yes. It's just the way the first pioneers found it. But they weren't looking for much—just good land and a chance. And they found both." She grinned at his quizzical look.

"Oh, if it's variety you want, Kansas does have that, too. You just have to drive around a bit to find it. In the southeast are the rolling hills and timbered valleys of our Ozark region, and bluffs over the Kansas River, eroded by wind and water over the last six hundred million years. Ten million years ago, glaciers carved out beautiful valleys and hills in the northeast. Parts of the central and western state were once the bottom of an inland sea and now have massive chalk pyramids rising from the valley floor. You see?''

"I see. I see a story here—not a news story. Something else.''

His eyes were unfocused, searching the horizon for something she couldn't define. Cary wandered off to the side of the road where large sunflowers nodded in the breeze. This part of Hunter did not belong to her. This part of him belonged primarily to the cameras and the lights, to his audience. Just as some aspect of her own personality was reserved for her own place in the world and couldn't be totally shared with Hunter.

They each had separate dreams and goals. Cary thought about their sweet morning lovemaking and knew that there, at least, they could meet and be completely one. And they both wanted to make the world a better place to live—each of them working for an ideal in a different way, but out of the same desire to assist other people. Could that attitude of service be the neutral territory where they could meet, love and live together?

At last, Hunter returned to the car. His eyes were alight with enthusiasm. He hugged Cary and kissed her a dozen times, then whirled her around on the pavement.

"Oh, honey! Am I glad I met you!'' He pressed her close and whispered in her ear. ''You're so good for me. I love you, princess.''

Hunter's joy was infectious. Cary felt her spirits soar like the cattle egrets wheeling above them. She could almost feel free of mundane concerns. Free to follow her true desires.

"Come over here," Cary said as she pulled Hunter toward the sunflowers. She wanted him to see the large flowers that were so much a part of the Kansas landscape. "This is my background, right here. Sometime you'll have to show me the south, just like this. It's not part of my recruiting region and I've never been there, you know."

"Of course I will," he answered, fingering the large orange yellow petals and the rough seed-filled center of the blossoms. "I'll show you my background—magnolias and wisteria, the bayous and the Spanish moss. We'll eat gumbo and hush puppies, red beans and cornbread. And we'll walk along the beach and swim in the Gulf of Mexico."

He turned away from the flowers, back to Cary. "We'll make a great team—you and I." It seemed to Cary that his eyes promised a future of incredible happiness together. He was so sure, so confident.

For long moments they stood beside each other on the empty prairie, looking out toward an infinitely distant horizon while the thick clouds of October gathered above them, blown by the fierce winds of the ever-changing Kansas skies.

WICHITA WAS COOL AND WET, smelling of damp earth. Hunter lost no time looking for an apartment. He had only three requirements: two separate bedrooms —for him and for David—, a large living room for entertaining, and a location near the Omega plant.

Cary was curious about his emphasis on entertaining.

"That's when David and I will hear secrets and gossip that will help in the investigation. They won't talk to me about bribes and stolen plans in the hallways of Omega Aircraft in the daytime. I have to bring them to me in a relaxed, informal setting. Then they'll talk."

Cary shivered at the cold logic behind his answer. She imagined Hunter sitting by a fireplace, a drink in one hand and a slightly tipsy engineer beside him. The two men would laugh in easy comradery, and then the engineer would begin bragging. In her imagination the engineer became Suzanne Foley.

Cary shook her head to banish the fancy. Hunter loved her and would not betray her, not even for the investigation. She believed in his honor.

Early in the evening, after walking for what seemed like miles, they found a beautiful apartment complex, across the street from a collection of small parks, near the river that ran through town. The exterior of the complex was English Tudor. Hunter found the apartments perfectly suited to his needs. Before eating, they decided to visit a furniture-rental store. The manager promised to deliver everything they selected by the following Wednesday.

At last, hours after darkness fell, they found a hotel where Hunter and David could stay until the apartment was ready. Cary and Hunter were so tired by this time that they booked a room and ordered a light meal from room service. Hunter yawned all through the meal and Cary could not even find the energy for conversation.

At last they switched off the lights and turned to each other in the soft, unfamiliar bed. Hunter kissed her and his hand caressed the swell of her hips and her upper thigh. Then he sighed and pulled her to him, so that her head could rest in the hollow between his arm and chest. His left hand lay lightly on her breast and stayed there, gently rising and falling with each breath she took, as they drifted to sleep.

CHAPTER THIRTEEN

CARY HAD IMAGINED she was feeling comfortable now with Hunter, but the sight of him clad only in pajama bottoms and sitting a scant yard away from her as he ate cold eggs and toast the next morning was enough to send her pulse racing wildly.

His every movement seemed to overwhelm her.

"You're going to starve if you don't eat something."

Cary looked down at her plate. The cold scrambled eggs looked like blobs of wet yellow rubber, and the single strip of undercooked bacon curled limply over the edge of her plate, dripping grease onto the small table she shared with Hunter.

She grimaced and pushed away the unappetizing meal. "I think I'll just feed my soul this morning, thank you," she said ruefully.

"Careful, woman. Them's rousin' words, them is," Hunter answered in a deep growl. His eyes fixed on hers with sudden intensity.

Cary parted her lips and smiled very, very softly. Her hand moved to the belt of her wraparound robe and slowly loosened it, allowing the front folds to separate and fall away from her full breasts.

"I can't explain it," said Hunter with a catch in

his voice. "Here I am almost finished with breakfast, and suddenly I'm hungrier than ever."

The flush that colored her face spread down Cary's body, lending a warm glow to her ivory complexion. She felt heat invading her and welcomed it as a newfound friend bringing sweet gifts of pleasure.

Cary chuckled mischievously and leaned forward so that her robe dropped completely away, revealing her nakedness.

"Come over here then," she invited him.

Hunter did not need coaxing. He covered her with tender-savage kisses.

Their lovemaking was playful, yet intense.

A sea of ecstasy rose around her, carrying her on cresting waves. And then suddenly she had risen above the tide. She was above Hunter, riding the surging wave of intense pleasure as he moved beneath her. Cary cried out with a newfound liberty, wondering at the change in herself.

Lying with his head between her breasts, Hunter was an integral part of her liberty. Gently, she rode the diminishing waves of desire as their breathing returned to its natural rhythm.

"What did I ever do to deserve you?" Hunter asked, looking at her languid body. "You're everything a man could ever want, princess."

"And you're the only prince this princess will ever need," she whispered in reply.

"Is that a promise?"

"That's complete, helpless capitulation, your highness. I surrender."

Hunter grinned. "I think I like surrender. But, on the other hand...."

His fingers gently brushed a treacherous spot near her hip, and she twisted away from him in one swift motion.

"On the other hand," he continued. "I told you once before I don't like docile women."

Cary grabbed at him, tickling Hunter mercilessly. With a howl, he jumped up from the bed, shielding himself with his arms. "Gotcha!" she sang out.

Hunter jumped back on top of her, imprisoning her wrists and using his tongue to inflict torturous kisses on every sensitive part of her. Her body thrashed back and forth as she begged him to stop.

"Say uncle!" he demanded.

"Never!" she gasped.

Suddenly, his mouth was no longer teasing. He kissed her breasts, above her eyes and circled her lips. Hunter no longer imprisoned her beneath his weight.

"I like you best like this," he whispered. "Not capitulating, but giving."

"Don't tell me you're hungry again?" she asked hoarsely.

"I forgot dessert last time," he answered.

And soon she was deafened with the roar of crashing tides. She rose again, one last time, above surging waves and then the world was quiet again, and she and Hunter lay together in silence.

Hunter was the first to rise—probably only because Cary couldn't have moved if she'd wanted to.

Hunter had collapsed on top of her, but his weight felt so good that she almost pulled him back when he began to get up. She smiled instead.

"Happy?" he asked.

"Mmm." Cary stretched lazily and nodded.

"You see? I told you everything would work out. All your crazy little doubts can't change what you feel inside, now can they?" His smile was triumphant.

But Cary's eyes changed subtly as his words brought back her nagging questions. "No," she said softly.

Hunter noticed the change in her. He stood beside the bed, towering over her, looking tense.

"Cary, you've—"

"No, Hunter! I don't want to talk about it now," she pleaded, tears beginning to glimmer in her eyes. "Not now."

Hunter whirled around so that she could only see his smooth, hard back. "Cary, don't do this to me. To us." He took a deep, ragged breath.

Suddenly he turned to face her. "Hell, woman! Why can't you just *let it be*!"

"I just don't want either of us to get hurt," she whispered.

"Cary, honey." He reached down to stroke her cheek. "What we're doing doesn't hurt anybody. It creates happiness."

For the first time, Hunter's touch did not warm her or comfort her or arouse her. The coldness inside her was too oppressive.

Oh, but he used words skillfully! He could play

on her emotions or her logic with equal ease. No matter what she said, he would have an answer for her. They would reach an impasse—as they had before—and more words would only be destructive or stupid. There was no point in it.

Cary smiled crookedly. Hunter seemed to accept her smile as agreement, because he bent down to kiss her again and then went off to shower. Slowly, she got up to join him.

But Cary began to change her opinion of his reaction the longer they spent together that day. There was something new in his eyes, something hard and hurt. He smiled, but suddenly it seemed as if he was using his professional wiles again, and every time Cary saw his artificial grin, she winced.

Together they explored a shopping mall, went to a late morning service in an unusual round church, ate lunch in a small café while rain drizzled down the window beside them and sloshed through wet grass to find a convenient jogging trail for Hunter.

They talked of commonplace things. Hunter never once mentioned the future, and Cary's spirits plummeted.

At three they drove out to the airport to meet David Thompson. The authentic engineer turned out to be very tall and blond, with the broad shoulders and massive muscles of an ex-football player. He shook hands with Hunter and seemed to dwarf the lanky reporter.

"And *this* is Cary," said Hunter.

"I've heard a lot about you, Cary. It's good to

meet you at last." David's voice had the flat twang of a born-and-bred Midwesterner.

"And I know a lot about you, too," said Cary, laughing. "At last I get to meet the real U.C.L.A. graduate. I'll bet *you* have even heard of Professor Holly," she added, with a pointed look at Hunter.

"Physics? Of course. I had the privilege of being a lab assistant for the professor one year. Great man, Holly. I was really sorry to hear about his death." David was about to continue talking to Cary when Hunter broke in.

"All right, all right. So you both speak the same language." He glowered with mock ferocity at the other man. "Just don't forget I saw her first."

Cary laughed and took Hunter's arm. He regarded her curiously, but put his hand on hers and left it there.

They took David to see the apartment and drove past the Omega plant. Then they all went out for dinner, and David explained how he planned to give Hunter bits and pieces of information about Burkham's current projects—not enough to compromise any of them, but hopefully enough to whet the appetite of Omega's management.

Back at the hotel, David plugged in his portable computer and showed Cary the three-dimensional plots he had worked up for the hypothetical new bleeding bolt. As he punched in commands, the subject of the drawing shed layers, rotated and was cut away to reveal its core. The material was impressive enough to fool an expert, if they could just get the nibble they would need to show it to someone.

"That's my department," explained Hunter. "I'm going to be such a friendly guy that people are going to seek me out just for a good time. But they'll be paying for that good time with every little piece of gossip and every little anecdote they tell about life at Omega."

Cary felt troubled. She refused, however, to give in to her doubts about Hunter in front of David. But her mood persisted.

How, how could she talk to Hunter about all her fears? She had an official responsibility to protect Willingham from unnecessary exposure and harm. And she felt personally responsible for all the innocent bystanders who might get in the way of Hunter's spying. He truly did believe in the necessity of what he was doing. If she confronted him, he would have to protect his pride. They would end up hurting each other in self-defense. How tangled it all was, she thought sadly.

David was looking at her, expecting her to say something.

"And when do you show them all this?" she asked, pointing to the slowly rotating diagram.

"As soon as they ask me if I'd like to earn a little higher salary."

"Which we hope will happen soon," added David.

Privately, Cary hoped that the investigation would move swiftly, also. It was the single most immediate cause of her doubt. And she was afraid for

Hunter's plans if someone should ask him too many of the wrong kind of questions. Despite her coaching and David's help he could not become an instant engineer.

David turned off the computer, and they packed up Cary's things for her flight back to Topeka. In the airport terminal, as they waited for her plane, Hunter told David about Grandma's Kitchen and his planned feature on her strudel-making. David asked if he could come along for the shooting.

"Of course. Grandma is something else! The audience will love her, don't you think, Cary?"

But Cary was silent. Later, when David left them alone to make their farewells, she decided to confront Hunter.

Taking a deep breath, she began, "Hunter, you wouldn't...look for all the cracks in the wall or ants on the floor, would you? Grandma's a very nice lady and her restaurant is very good. But she is...different. You won't make fun of her, will you? I'd...hate to see her hurt."

Hunter's lips pursed in a tight line. "I don't hurt people on purpose, Cary. I don't—"

He was silent for a long time. Cary hated herself for saying what she had. But she had to *know*!

Suddenly, Hunter pulled her into a seat near the gate. "Let's get this all straight, shall we? Right now?" he asked, in a tight angry voice. "You say you love me. Your body's not lying, I can tell. But what about the rest of you? You who prize truth so greatly, are you lying when you tell me that you love me?"

"No."

"Then why the third degree all the time? Why do you consistently take it for granted that I am some kind of two-faced monster who loves to destroy people's lives and reputations?"

"I don't think that, Hunter! I'm trying to understand what you do for a living. Believe me, I'm only trying to understand you."

"If you really loved me, you'd trust me to do the right thing no matter what," he said, and his voice sounded more hurt than angry.

"That's asking too much too soon," she answered. "I *do* love you and always will, I think, even if..."

He gripped her arm tightly, pressing her mohair sweater into her skin. "If what, Cary?"

"Even if I can't accept some of what you do to make a living. Hunter, please?" she cried out when he released her arm as violently as he had taken it. "You said yourself we see the world from different points of view. Yet you want me to understand yours—won't you please try to understand mine?"

"No, because yours seems to be narrow and bigoted and self-righteous."

Cary shivered under his glaring eyes.

For a long time, Hunter merely stared at her, while Cary watched the muscles of his face twitch as if he argued with himself. "Okay. What exactly is your point of view then," he asked abruptly. "Why do you distrust me so? It isn't just that little episode

I ran on your school-board committee meeting. You've been scared of me since...since the day I told you who I was.''

Yes, thought Cary. *Afraid of being drawn to you like an unsuspecting moth to a flame, and being somehow consumed by your passion for justice!*

But she didn't say that. Instead she said, ''You're so powerful in your red cardigan with the station logo. People let you form their opinions for them....''

''Only the fools.''

''And you consciously try to make people feel as you do. Not only the fools are guided by you. All the people who don't understand the world and who pessimistically believe somebody is out to get them—those people believe you, too, because you confirm their fears. You show them the face of their enemy and it looks...like their school board or their congressmen or the used-car salesman down the street.''

''I only expose the wrongs that other people really do. I protect people. I don't commit those wrongs myself just to get a story,'' Hunter protested.

''But don't you see? We all make mistakes, we all have wrongs to hide. You're our nemesis, the man who can find us out and tell the whole world about our sins,'' she finished, whispering. ''We're all afraid of you.''

''Am I your nemesis, too, Cary?'' he asked quietly.

"I don't know. But I can't help but feel that you're always looking for the dirt and shame around you—and that you will find it and expose it, even if there are roses growing in that dirt. You look for a story and don't really see the people in it."

"That's distorting the truth somewhat, isn't it? Cary, sometimes the story *is* more important than the handful of people involved in it. That's life, Cary. I didn't invent the rules."

"No, but you've lived by them for so long—while I've been living by another set—that I'm just not sure we can ever accept one another."

"Oh, honey, honey. That just isn't true. Oh, hell!" he cried out, smashing his fist against the back of the chair in front of him. "How can I make you see? We're the same, Cary. We want the same things in our world. We're both trying to help people. We just do it from different angles."

"Perhaps," Cary agreed slowly. "But those 'angles' could drive us apart, Hunter. They really could."

The loudspeaker announced that Cary's flight was boarding.

"You might as well go on now." He spoke flatly, unemotionally, reaching out for the chair back to steady him as he rose.

Cary reached out, too, to cover his hand and stop him from destroying what they had started to build by talking honestly.

"Please," she said urgently. "My mind isn't

closed. I told you I want to understand, and I truly do. Please help me, Hunter. Help us now.''

He stood still, facing her with questions furrowing his brow. ''I don't know, Cary. I don't have any problem accepting who and what you are. And I know that what I do is right, too, but your questions make me sound like a criminal or a hypocrite. Where is my self-respect if the woman I love is afraid of me and scorns my work?''

''Please, Hunter. Just explain it to me. Tell me again about your crusade and make me see the justice of it.''

His dark eyes were black now with some suppressed emotion that was not evident in his even, measured speech.

''No. I've said it all before. There's nothing new that I could add. You're the one who has to make the decisions now, but I can't offer you any new arguments. You just have to make up your mind whether you can live with what I am—with what you believe I am. That's all.''

Her topaz eyes were locked to his, held fast. There were no answers in the depths of Hunter's dark gaze, only reflections of passion given and returned. As long as she was near him, she could not resolve her dilemma.

''You know I can't think straight here so close to you,'' she whispered painfully, watching how his eyes reflected her pain.

''Then go home and work it out there. Let me know what conclusions you reach.''

''Yes, that would be best.'' She said the words,

and they felt like the very essence of defeat.

The plane trip back to Topeka and the cab ride to her apartment seemed to take forever. Slowly Cary trudged up the stairs and into the dim apartment. She sank down on the couch and let bewildering tears of regret flow down her cheeks, unheeded.

When the moon shifted out of her windows, Cary got up and began unpacking. Her thoughts were still confused, devoid of either solace or solutions. Not even sleep could comfort her.

ON MONDAY, she phoned Louise and won an invitation to a trout dinner. She stopped at a liquor store after work and bought a bottle of Riesling to complement the fish and to salve her conscience for using her sister's family to distract her from thoughts of Hunter.

Later, when she rocked Lynette to sleep, kissing the infant's peach-fuzz hair, Cary wished she had Hunter's head resting in her lap. When the baby was put in her cradle and all the dishes were washed, Louise took Cary into the long sewing workroom to show her some new blouses ordered for the shop.

Cary tried to pretend enthusiasm, but her attention wandered away from the silks and wools around her. "Louise, did you see Hunter's show last Friday night?"

Her sister put away a gaudy striped velour sweater and sat down on a three-legged stool. "Yes.

I thought it was a very romantic gesture—calling you a brave, courageous woman in front of a million people.''

Cary colored. ''But what did you think about the rest of the committee? About what they did at the meeting?''

''Why, I wasn't really paying that much attention. I guess I thought they were a little blind in not seeing that you would need more than money to make the jobs council work. I'll bet you were pretty disgusted that no one offered any real help.''

''But that's just the point! I didn't expect anything from them. I want the kids to go out and solicit all the help they need. Money is just fine right now.''

''Hmmph. I give you two months to change your mind—no, make that one month. Cary, what do you know about running an employment agency?''

Cary thought about her weeks in St. Louis. ''Just about everything, smarty pants,'' she replied.

But Louise wasn't flustered.

''What do you need besides a good, hard-working staff to make it work?''

''A clientele, of course. But that comes with time. You start out with a few contacts who are willing to give you the first few assignments....''

''Exactly. But have your kids been promised any assignments yet? No, just money. Have any of those big business corporations offered training, access to the contacts in their own recruiting files or anything but money? Have they offered to tell their employees' families about your plan or... *anything* that would actually help get the council moving?''

"No." Cary's voice was small. She rubbed her aching forehead with the back of her hand.

"What's the matter, Cary? What's this all about?''

"I guess I really don't know, Lou. I thought I did, once. But now I'm all confused.''

"Is it Hunter?''

"Yes. No. It isn't Hunter but what he does for a living. He has so much power! He twists facts and distorts the truth to make his audience see what he wants them to see. Sometimes people get hurt, and they're not all black-hatted villains, either. I'm afraid sometimes they just don't measure up to Hunter's standard of excellence, or he sees them as little fish in a much more important ocean. And I simply don't know if I can live with that! Oh, Lou, I don't know what to believe anymore!'' She leaned back against a bolt of heavy teal-colored fabric and closed her eyes.

"Has he told you why he does all this 'distorting'?''

"Yes,'' Cary whispered. "To warn gullible old ladies and trusting businessmen about the frauds and cheats who don't play by the rules. He feels it's his 'duty.' ''

"Do you believe him?''

"I told you. I don't know what to believe anymore. Yes, I think he's sincere, but does that excuse his methods?"

Louise got up and walked over to Cary. She put her arm around her sister and pulled her away from the fabric she rested on. "I can't answer that. I don't know how he lies, or what the truth is you claim he has distorted. But I do think you love him, don't you?"

"Yes," Cary said brokenly.

"Then I'd say for now you should believe your heart. Try to understand him all you can, but keep believing in your heart until your mind accepts it too, or...."

"Until my heart is broken?" asked Cary. "What cruel choices, Lou!"

"Well, there is one other choice. You can stop listening to your heart at all and live in cold security the rest of your life. You won't have love, but you won't have any doubts, either."

"Oh, Lou!" Cary bent her head onto her sister's shoulder and cried the final tears of loss. The last choice was too hard, too empty. She would have to face her doubts and risk the pain, for she wanted love—Hunter's love—more than anything in the world.

A few weeks ago, she hadn't even missed the lack of love in her life, but now that she had tasted its sweetness there was no going back to loneliness. She had to confront her fears and make the decisions Hunter had spoken of, or she could not live with herself.

Emotionally exhausted, she drove back to her apartment. Now she must figure out how to see the world from Hunter's point of view. There must be a way to answer all her own questions, without either Hunter or herself losing. *There must be!*

CHAPTER FOURTEEN

ON WEDNESDAY NIGHT, the need to hear Hunter's voice was too strong for Cary to overcome. She turned her television to KMKX and watched the full twenty minutes of news that preceded the "Lineup" segment.

And suddenly the professional Hunter was speaking to her—the man with the coal-black hair and no glasses. His eyes were looking straight at her, though he couldn't see her as she clenched her trembling hands together.

"The Whitley Motors used-car lot on Twelfth street in Booneville has a motto painted on the broken-down fence behind the office. It says, Where There's a Whitley, There's a Way.

"Mrs. Debra Lacey found that the only way is Whitley's way when she tried to return the car she purchased there—just one hour after she bought it."

Cary tried to follow the words of the story Hunter was telling, about how Mrs. Lacey had paid six hundred dollars for a car that died before traveling a mile. She tried to listen, but the words and the pictures of Mrs. Lacey were only getting in the way of Hunter's eyes.

She sought some message in those black eyes, an offering of forgiveness or understanding meant for her alone. But he was Hunter Pierce the reporter tonight. Once again, she realized this part of him that lived with cameras and microphones did not belong to her.

In fact, the program she was watching had undoubtedly been taped long before her argument with him. It was not even today's Hunter, just an electronic image, a media phantom.

Musical words continued to pour from her TV speakers. Apparently Mrs. Lacey had been offered three hundred for the "damaged" vehicle. But Hunter's caustic confrontation with Delbert Whitley secured the con man's promise he would refund the entire purchase price of the automobile. A tearful Mrs. Lacey thanked the reporter for his intervention.

And suddenly Hunter's face was gone, replaced by the news anchor who joked about "dirty tricks" played by some used-car salesman. Cary switched off the set and sat in the evening darkness recalling every feature of Hunter's face, every nuance of movement, every carefully articulated phrase he had used.

When Cary closed her eyes, his face was still before her. In her imagination his warm hands stole across her skin, igniting flames of desire. Memories of his voice telling the story of Mrs. Lacey to thousands of strangers twined in nonsense patterns with memories of his lovemaking and the sweet words of promise he whispered to her alone.

This was madness, she scolded herself. After all, she was no lovestruck teenager but a mature adult. Either she loved him or she didn't and if she loved him, couldn't she accept him?

At nine o'clock Cary gave up trying to answer her own question and dressed for bed. As she pulled up the coverlet, her phone rang, distant and tinny from the dark living room. She ran swiftly to answer it before the ringing stopped.

"Hello."

"Princess?"

There was something so tentative in his voice that her heart constricted with an excruciating pain.

"Hunter. I'm so glad you called. I...wanted to hear your voice again."

"Did you? Not more than I wanted to hear yours. I didn't know how to take...your silence."

What should she say? That with every day the answer to Hunter's question became less clear? "You're not talking," he prodded.

He would have to be given some response. Cary hoped she could offer the right one!

She laughed nervously. "You can't hear my heart pounding or you wouldn't call me silent."

Hunter's short laugh was polite. "You're avoiding the issue, Cary."

"I love you, Hunter."

He sighed. But he did not speak. He was waiting for something more.

"I saw your program tonight. It was very good."

Still he did not speak.

"Oh, Hunter," she cried, brokenly. "What more do you want? I love you!"

"I told you once before. I want all of it, Cary. Listen to me. I believe in you. I respect your strength, your dedication to what you believe in. I want you to say the same thing to me." He waited.

"This is important, darling," he continued urgently. "Answer me, please."

"I . . . can't, yet," Cary said in a small voice.

"Why not?" The question sounded as if it had been wrung from the very depths of Hunter's soul.

Cary sighed raggedly, only a breath away from tears. She knew what her refusal meant to him, yet . . . .

"I'm coming up to talk, Cary. We have to settle this. I won't let the only woman I have ever loved walk away thinking I'm some kind of cruel shyster. I know—I've said it all before, but maybe . . . maybe there's something I left out, or—hell, princess! Don't do this to us!" His voice cracked with emotion.

"I love you, Hunter. I truly, truly do," she whispered. "Please come."

"Oh, Cary!" he answered. "I wish there was some way I could come now, but it just isn't possible. Friday?"

"Friday's fine."

"Goodbye then, for now, darling. Promise me you'll try to understand."

"I promise with all my heart. Goodbye."

Her head filled with echoes of Hunter's voice, Cary went to bed. She had already cried all the tears of her loss, Monday night at Louise's house. So why did her shoulders shake so now, and her eyes ache? Why did she lie awake again, remembering all the loving and all the pain?

She wanted him to be the white knight on the white stallion, pursuing truth with a pure heart. But hadn't all the pure knights been corrupted? Hadn't they all failed in their ultimate quest because they were only human, after all—because they had succumbed to the temptation to search for glory and not for goodness? Wasn't the ultimate sin believing that a man could judge what was good and what was evil and mete out justice for other men?

And weren't the princesses all sad and lonely, left to their weaving of symbolic tapestries in isolated towers while the knights went off rescuing fair damsels in distress and beheading other knights who stood in the way? Might versus right—the age-old debate was the same today, for her.

She fought her own dragons every day—didn't everyone? But Cary fought with persuasion and reason and logic. And sometimes with emotion, as she worked to make people happy with their jobs.

Could she really object to Hunter's use of the bright sword of KMKX in his battles against even larger dragons? Could she? Or did she worry that the sword had become just a flashy way to manipulate facts and advance his career?

THURSDAY AFTERNOON, Cary questioned two more prospective engineers for Omega. They were both anxious to visit the plant for interviews. She made arrangements for the Omegajet to take them to Wichita, and then she called Hunter.

"David Thompson, please," she told the operator, feeling foolish as she spoke the false name.

"Thompson here."

"Hunter! Can you talk now?"

"Yes, my office is fairly private. What do you need, princess?"

"Well, I've got to make a trip to Omega tomorrow and I thought...I could come to you, instead of you traveling down here."

"That's wonderful, honey! When can you get here?"

"Oh, I'll be there early in the morning, but I'll have to stick around Henry Crandon until after lunch. Then I'll send the applicants back to Topeka and wait for you."

"Sounds great. That's a fine idea, Hank." Hunter's voice had risen and changed, suddenly. "I'll meet you then at the hotel on Friday."

"Is someone with you, Hunter?"

"Yes, yes. In the hotel lobby about five-thirty. Good to hear from you, Hank. Have a safe trip."

"Goodbye, Hunter. I love you."

"Duplicate!" he boomed, as if good-naturedly joking.

Cary laid down the receiver, thinking Hunter's visitor would surely be puzzled by that last remark. She smiled, enjoying the private message: I love you, too!

Cary packed a small traveling case in the morning and filled her briefcase with items that wouldn't fit in the bag. She wanted to be able to leave her things with Omega's receptionist to avoid provoking any embarrassing questions from Henry.

The interviews went smoothly, but neither Henry nor Omega's management was sufficiently impressed with the two candidates to even hint at a job offer. Cary had mixed emotions about their decision. On the one hand, she was earnestly trying to find the two men a good job. On the other hand, she was glad she would have at least one more excuse to fly down to Wichita. There'd been no more talk of changing to another agency—not since the hiring of Suzanne and "David."

After she had put the applicants back on their plane for Topeka, Cary took a cab to the hotel she and Hunter had used the previous weekend, hoping to take a nap in his room and change her clothes before five-thirty. But she'd forgotten that Hunter had arranged to move into his apartment on Wednesday. So she bought a romance novel in the hotel sundry shop and found a comfortable seat in the lobby to read and wait.

She was in the middle of the last chapter. The heroine had decided to leave the hero because she imagined him to be in love with another woman. Cary was disgusted that the heroine didn't ask a very simple question that would have cleared up the entire misunderstanding. She threw down the book just as Hunter walked in the door.

"Life is never simple in a book, is it?" he asked, smiling.

"No, but sometimes real life isn't simple," she answered, looking at his deep, dark eyes. Cary saw the passion and hunger in them. She felt the same passion rise within her, too, and she yearned to run to Hunter, to have him as close to her as a woman can have a man. But she held back.

Hunter, too, held back. He extended a hand to her and pulled her up, but not close. She gathered her purse and briefcase. He lifted the traveling case.

"Don't you want your book?" he asked.

"I know how it ends," she answered. *I only wish I knew how we would end!*

Hunter stowed her bags in the back of the Audi and headed into town.

He parked on a tree-lined street full of old houses and led Cary down a narrow alley to a door marked The Portobello Road. Low, heavy-beamed ceilings contrasted with white stucco walls inside the restaurant. Hunter and Cary were led to a table that was tucked into a secluded corner. Hanging lanterns and red glass spirit flames gave scant light to the dim dining room. In the shadows, Hunter reached across for her hand.

As always, his touch was magic. If there was to be only his touch in the world and nothing more, she would be content. But he wanted more. And so, if she was honest, did she.

"I have a membership here," he told her. "Would you like a drink?"

"Yes, a brandy sour, please." She was answering his simple question, but she was avoiding the need for other answers in his eyes.

A waitress brought them the drinks, a water goblet with a thin slice of lemon floating inside, and a menu full of wonderful surprises like beer-boiled shrimp, escargots, steak Diane, and other rich entrées and appetizers.

As she sipped the smooth, tangy drink, Cary felt the pull of Hunter's eyes, as surely as if they had been magnets pulling at her soul.

"Cary," he called to her. "We have to face this thing between us."

"Yes, I know."

"But I don't know what the difficulty is—it's *your* problem, and I can't help if you aren't honest. Tell me, darling. What's wrong between us?"

"I'm. . .not sure, Hunter. I love you, but I just can't seem to trust the reporter in you."

"Why? What's so bad about being a reporter?"

She took a deep breath. Here is where she either lost everything or gained something beyond measure.

"Hunter, I know someone has to do what you are doing. Someone has to expose the liars and cheats, and perhaps someone has to lie and cheat himself in order to do it. But is it always so clearly black and white for you? So clearly right or wrong? Don't you ever doubt? Can you see the other side, too?"

"What other side?" he asked. "The criminal's side?"

"Have you ever read *Les Misérables* by Victor

Hugo? Have you ever thought of the desperation that might drive someone to crime? Or how your pursuit, in front of millions of people, might turn a petty, trivial misdeed into something so huge that it would ruin a man's life?''

"My stories are not usually about the trivial, Cary. And men like Delbert Whitley are not desperate."

"No, perhaps not. But sometime someone might be, and what would your code of honor demand from you then? Would you still expose him, or would you have compassion for his pain?''

"I need to have compassion for the pain of his many victims first," he answered.

"I see."

"No, you don't see yet. I do think I would have to weigh that pain against that of the criminal, Cary. But I hope—I sincerely believe—I could do that, as well as any other human being could."

Cary was silent for a moment. Yes, of course he could. He was gentle and kind. She knew that. He was fond of people in general and devoted to helping them. She knew all that, too. Why, oh, why, could she not banish all her fears and doubts, then?

"What else is there, Cary? What else are you afraid of?''

"Perhaps of . . . manipulation?''

"Manipulation?'' Hunter frowned.

"You said once that I had never been hurt—that this was what made our perceptions of the world different. But that isn't exactly true. I've been hurt, and I've seen others torn apart by greedy people who don't play by the rules.

"But where it's made you hard, that kind of experience has only left me feeling very vulnerable and used."

"Can you tell me about it, princess? I want to know, to understand." He leaned forward, as if to share as much of her world as possible.

"It happened this summer, to me and to my supervisor, Mary Ellen Hughes. You've never met Mary Ellen, but she's such a strong person, such a dynamic leader. She's the kind of person every new recruiter should have for a teacher and a friend. I could always depend on Mary Ellen's support and encouragement and all of us knew she was headed for the top—until she took on the American Paper Company's business.

"I don't think she ever saw that American was not seriously considering her bid for a contract. Or, what is probably more accurate, she didn't want to see it."

As Cary told her story, she remembered the glint in Mary Ellen's eyes last spring when she had described her strategy to the four regional recruiters who would be involved in the planned coup.

"It's a plum, fellas. Ripe for the picking, if we do our job right," Mary Ellen had said with enthusiasm. "Joe Hartman, American Paper's senior V.P., tells me they are expecting to win some federal leases on the Western Slope, and then open a division office in Denver by the third quarter of this year.

"Many of the civil engineers, accountants and systems people they need for the new division will come through our regular personnel offices, but some—especially three key management positions—must come from this group here today. If we get the job."

Mary Ellen had paused then and looked directly at each of the four recruiters in turn. Unconsciously, her silver pen tapped out a staccato rhythm, reflecting some inner tension. How much tension and whether its source was the American Paper prospect, Cary could only guess. She speculated that Mary Ellen was not as confident of success as her tone of voice indicated.

Briskly, the older woman had continued. "I want each of you to make a list today of a half-dozen clients who will be good references. Remind them of past favors. Be gracious. Nose around and see if any of them has or knows of a restless genius or two just itching to move on to something better.

"And while you're working your other assignments, let's try to find some really fine carrots to dangle in front of Hartman—an outstanding financial manager, a brilliant systems analyst or maybe an exceptional plant manager or engineer. We find people Joe Hartman can't resist—even if he hasn't yet asked *us* for them—and we'll be in. I guarantee it."

"You see," explained Cary to Hunter. "Another agency, Dunfey and Crabb, had an exclusive contract with American Paper. Mary Ellen wanted that contract. That's the way she is, always going after the biggest and the best no matter who the competition is. Joe Hartman had told her he was thinking of switching firms. She thought she could win the contract if she could do a better job than Dunfey. I think I was the only one who was skeptical.''

Something about Mary Ellen's nervous tapping had communicated itself to Cary as doubt. And, of course, she had found out later that there had been good reason for her reservations.

Sometime during the summer, Mary Ellen must have begun to really worry, too. About then, her basketball coach was contacted by a big college on the West Coast. He'd asked her to quit Willingham and go away with him. She'd asked him to stay. Then Mary Ellen began to complain of stomach pains and indigestion. Her temper became short and her manner abrasive. Eventually the coach left, alone.

Cary recalled the Friday afternoon the recruiters had all assembled again in Mary Ellen's office. The weather in St. Louis had been grim and threatening, the silver pen ominously silent.

"Well, boys and girls," Mary Ellen had begun "We've been chasing a dream. The American Paper account is once more securely bound to Dunfey and Crabb Consultants." She had sighed and winced as if in pain, as everyone settled back wearily.

"Yesterday, American withdrew their bids on the Western Slope timber leases. So they no longer need a Denver division and—"

"What!" exploded the man next to Cary.

"Uneconomical. Or so says Joe Hartman. He says they never were very optimistic about opening the Denver office. He thanked me for all the work we put in and sent us packing."

"But why?" Cary was tired and frustrated, but even more she was curious to know the reasons behind this piece of maneuvering. "I thought they encouraged us to make a try for the contract. Was that a hoax? Would they file for timber leases just to give a recruiting agency the idea that they needed more personnel?"

Mary Ellen had smiled sardonically. "S.O.P. Standard operating procedure, if you are trying to beef up a stockholder report. Happens all the time."

"But that wasn't the whole story," Cary continued, watching for Hunter's reactions. This was the kind of story he would be interested in, but not even he could have done anything about it.

"My best friend, Joyce Mitchell, told me she had found out that American Paper wasn't trying to convince us they needed more people for a bigger operation. They were working to convince a shareholder group who had suspicions about the recent election of the company's new chairman. Dunfey and Crabb had supposedly found him and most of his new staff within only a few days of the old chairman's being kicked out for fraudulent stock manipulation. Some of the shareholders felt the timing was questionable—that the selection of potential candidates and possibly even the election of the new chairman himself were rigged by a management faction acting in collusion with Dunfey and Crabb.''

''Were they?'' asked Hunter.

''Mary Ellen didn't think so. Later she told me she had known Michael Dunfey a long time and was certain he wouldn't have knowingly been involved in anything like that. But that's beside the point, isn't it? We had all promised some outstanding people good jobs and suddenly our promises were all empty. There were no jobs. A few of the people had already given notice to their former employers and were left in desperate straits. And Willingham had spent a fortune recruiting those people.

''Mary Ellen sent us all on to new assignments. I came here to Topeka. And just a few weeks ago, she began hemorrhaging from the ulcers she had developed in the summer.''

Cary clasped her hands around her empty drink glass. ''When she found out about American's duplicity, Mary Ellen promised that she would never let something like that happen again. We were all hurt by it, and she swore she wouldn't accept any clients who weren't on the up and up.

''She was furious when I told her that Joe Hartman had tried to salve his conscience by paying us more than we had billed for our expenses.''

''How did you find out about that?'' Hunter asked.

''When I had to help out in St. Louis—while Mary Ellen was in the hospital.'' Cary mused aloud. ''Partly, she was angry that I had gotten involved in the matter. I think she would have liked to return that check to Joe Hartman in person and let him have a carefully worded piece of her mind, too.

"Do you see why I can't tell her about your investigation at Omega? And why I'm so suspicious of people who have that kind of power to manipulate and use people—like television reporters?"

Hunter reached across to take the empty glass from Cary's hand. Then he placed her tense fingers inside his own and gently held them in a firm grip.

"I see that you were as hurt as Mary Ellen, and that's something you will have to learn to deal with. But that needn't affect *us*, Cary."

"But it does!" she cried. "You can't deny that the day we met you were trying to manipulate me into getting you a job at Omega. And that night— don't tell me you had no ulterior motive in joining me for dinner!"

"All right, I won't tell you that. I did have an ulterior motive. I wanted to get to know the woman who so obviously took bribes from her clients."

"Wh-what?" Cary sputtered. "What are you talking about? I never—"

"Hold on, honey! I know *now* that you're as innocent as a babe. But I didn't know it then. All I knew was that you were procuring some questionable people for Omega Aircraft, and that you seemed to have a very cushy job at Willingham with some mysterious authority in their main office in St. Louis. You wore expensive-looking clothes that didn't jibe with your probable salary as a recruiter.

I was curious about you. Still am. Always will be, too.''

''My sister makes my clothes,'' Cary said slowly.

''I gathered that, when you told me about her boutique,'' replied Hunter. ''But I thought they were gifts, given in return for fraudulent references or spying. I even hinted directly to you that I thought you might be getting some extra compensation on the side, remember?''

''And I thought you were talking about going to bed with my clients!'' Cary laughed.

Hunter joined her in laughter and she stopped, just to hear the marvelous sound of joy issuing from him. Misunderstandings seemed so distant now, but even as she recalled the night they spoke of fondly, she was reminded that it was that evening she'd begun to doubt Hunter.

''But it's true. You did try to manipulate me for your own secret purposes and I...can't forget, or stop worrying that it might happen again.'' All the laughter was gone now. Cary watched Hunter close his eyes, then open them as if to concentrate all of his power on her.

''I was doing my job, Cary. You were only a suspect then. Now, you're so much more,'' he whispered. ''I promise I'll never use you again. Believe me, princess. Please,'' he pleaded.

''I believe you,'' she said. ''But what about all the others? Will you still....''

''I'll still keep trying to protect them from themselves, Cary. I won't change that. But I will try to see them as individuals more—you've convinced me of that, at least.''

For a long time they sat holding hands and looking at each other. Cary knew her emotions were obvious, but she didn't care. She could read Hunter's heart, too, and it matched her own perfectly. Love and pain mixed together. A bitter diet.

Then it was time to eat, though she scarcely tasted any of the rich food. But when the waitress asked if they wanted dessert, Cary remembered the afternoon Hunter had first kissed her, and she said, ''We'll have just one dessert, and share it.''

Hunter obviously remembered, too, for he smiled in such a way that Cary felt as if he was making love to her across the table. It was an apology of sorts and he knew it, accepted it. It didn't smooth things over completely, but it was a start.

The dessert was an Amaretto brandy ice-cream pie, heaped with whipped cream and shredded maraschino cherries. It took them a long time to eat it, licking the subtle flavors from a single fork.

When the bill was paid, and Cary was escorted to the Audi, her heart was pounding hopefully. They had talked, and neither had said anything to be regretted. Neither had walked away.

They were coming closer to the love they both desired.

CHAPTER FIFTEEN

DURING THE NIGHT, the temperature dropped quickly. The dawn was silver gray and wintery cold. Cary was glad of the wool layer inside her London Fog coat, but she still shivered at the unaccustomed chill of the outdoors.

Hunter had planned excursions for them today, explorations of the city and each other. But first he had brought her to this little park near his apartment complex, a narrow stretch of fading grass near the fork of the Arkansas River. Presiding over the fork was a giant metal sculpture of an Indian warrior, the *Keeper of the Plains*. And in the small park beside the water was a delicate bronze statue of Joan of Arc.

"Come look," called Hunter as he led the way to the little figure of the saint.

A plaque beside the statue explained that it was a gift from the city of Orléans, France. Orléans had sent this symbol of courage and bravery to its sister city, Wichita, where it had been placed to face outward from the river—out to the plains where other courageous and brave people had carved out a home and then a state.

"I can see her from my window, you know," said

Hunter softly. "And every time I see her, I think of you."

"Oh, Hunter! I'm no Joan of Arc. You're the one who fancies himself a crusader, not me!" Cary protested.

"Don't sell yourself short, princess. You're the other half of me—the part that nurtures and protects the people who are injured in the crusade. You care deeply about the people you work with, and you were willing to risk losing something very precious in your need to know the truth about me. Weren't you?"

"How did you know. . . how precious you are to me?" she asked.

"It's in your voice and in your eyes every time you look at me," he answered. "I'm right, aren't I? You do love me, Cary? In spite of everything?"

"Oh, yes, Hunter. Yes!" she cried. Her arms reached out for him and the chill of the morning was conquered at last by the warmth of their bodies meeting.

"You know I've been looking for a long time for someone like you. I can't give you up because of some hazy cloud that seems to hang between us. It will be gone tomorrow, I just know it. Cary, promise me you won't give up on us."

"I promise. I love you, Hunter Victor Pierce." She raised her mouth the fraction needed to bring it up to Hunter's, and drank from it his sweet visions of tomorrows without end.

They walked along the riverbank and scuffed up piles of fallen leaves. When the wind picked up and the sky turned dark, Hunter put his arm around her shoulders, and she was warm and content.

They ate lunch while it stormed, safe from the cold and wet in a bright cafeteria, drinking hot coffee and talking of the past. The future was still too sensitive and delicate a concept for much discussion and so they brought it up in roundabout fashion, casually mentioning safe things like vacation dreams, family and friends, the distances each traveled to work. Neither talked of possible conflict in job locale or the temporary nature of Cary's assignment. Such things might have spoiled the perfect happiness of the day.

Later, much later, after their legs grew weary from walking and the sun was low in the clear, storm-freshened sky, Hunter asked if she would like to go back to The Portobello Road. And of course, she agreed.

So they drove back to the small alley and went inside for espresso. It was early in the evening, and few people had sought out the place for dinner yet, so they were alone in this part of the dining room.

"Do you like diamonds?" Hunter asked.

"No," answered Cary, knowing what he had really asked. "I like amethysts and sapphires and rubies and tourmalines, and all the other colored stones."

"Shall we go looking then, for colored stones?" He asked, but did not wait for her answer. He led her out onto the tree-lined street and toward his car.

"Oh, wait!" she cried. "Look! We just missed the sunset."

Above them the sky glowed scarlet and gold, with deep purple clouds above the light. And in the clear pale lavender sky farther above, wisps of smoky, wind-driven contrails descended into the sunset.

They stood for a minute, watching the colors change and the contrails fade. The street darkened gradually, and they walked somberly to the Audi, sharing the beauty and knowing that the sharing itself was more momentous than the dying sun.

At a jeweler's in a modern mall, they found an opal shot with deep dark blue and fiery red. The colors of the sunset. Cary looked at it with longing, but Hunter studied the stone skeptically.

"Is it necessary to buy it in this setting?" he asked the saleswoman.

"No. We can have it reset for you, if you wish."

"I do," he answered firmly. "I want six of your deepest purple amethysts around it, and I want a gold wedding band made to fit beside it."

"Yes, sir. That sounds very simple, sir." The woman brought out a small case with loose stones on black velvet. She moved six small purple ones to the side and then handed them to Hunter.

The stones flashed pink and lavender and blue around their deeper core of violet. Cary gasped at their beauty.

"The opal for our sunset," said Hunter in her ear, "and the amethysts for your special color, princess."

"Yes. That will be very nice...someday." She smiled gently and firmly pushed the stones away.

"Today, Cary. I want you to have something to

remind you every minute that I'm waiting. Maybe the stones can speak to you for me, plead my case. Don't argue, princess. Just accept.''

Cary could only nod. Only a day ago, her world was as unstable as a bolt of lightning. Today even the future was fast becoming as tangible as Hunter's hand in hers, as real as the brilliance of these stones. Had her questions somehow been resolved, or were they just no longer quite so important?

On Sunday morning, the two of them left Wichita before the sun rose in order to be at Grandma's when the camera van arrived. David had been working all weekend on a special project Hunter had been assigned to research, and he reluctantly decided not to join them for the shooting.

Mrs. Schwartz and her sons were hard at work polishing chrome and setting fresh flowers on every table when Hunter and Cary pulled up in front of the farmhouse. The small square table in the kitchen had been laid out with strudel dough, ready for filling and rolling.

When the big KMKX van arrived, pandemonium broke loose. The Schwartz sons ran around trying to help Phil with the camera and to wait on their Sunday lunch customers at the same time. Hunter watched the confusion indulgently, until the camera was ready and Phil gave him a cue.

Then he began to direct. He motioned the camera to move slowly from the dining room into the kitchen, panning from side to side in order to capture the cheerful faces and bright conversation of the customers. In the kitchen, he placed Grandma

Schwartz at an angle to the lens and soothed her into losing her attack of jitters. He asked her to show him how to roll the strudel and promised that if they messed it up he would help her set it up to try again.

But she was so charmed by the melody of his voice that the strudel rolled perfectly the first time.

"Talk to me, grandma," he cajoled.

"You sure? I don't talk so good," she answered, laughing.

"Everyone loves the way you talk, grandma." He reassured her.

"Hunter, don't," interrupted Cary from the sidelines.

"It's all right, child," said the old woman. "I don't mind. Maybe people will come to hear me talk and stay to eat, *ja*?" She laughed and patted the doughy strudel. "That's fine with me!"

Hunter asked grandma a few more questions and then told Phil to film a couple of exterior shots of the farmhouse.

Only then did grandma become truly flustered. "You mean it's over?" she asked with a puzzled frown. "That's all? No 'Lights, Camera, Actioning'?"

"That's all, grandma." Hunter laughed. "You were outstanding!"

The older woman colored and laughed. "You come back, boy. You hear? I like you. I fix you the best strudel in the world!"

"It's a deal, grandma," Hunter answered, smiling.

He and Cary walked outside to where Phil was stowing away his gear.

"Phil, can you do me a favor?" Hunter called.

"Sure, boss."

"Will you take Miss Blaine on to Topeka with you? I really need to get back to Wichita."

"No problem. She can sit up here with me," Phil said, opening the passenger door of his cab.

"Wait a minute." Cary went over to the Audi and pulled out her traveling bag and her briefcase. "Can we stow these in the back?" she asked.

Phil stopped moving, whistled low and loud and then looked from Cary to Hunter and back several times. Cary began to feel a flush of heat rise from her neck up to her cheeks.

Hunter growled a sharp injunction to his cameraman and threw the bags into the rear of the van. Then he helped Cary up into the cab and glowered pointedly at Phil.

"Goodbye, princess. See you next weekend?" he asked softly.

"Of course. Call." She leaned down toward Hunter's face.

With a quick glance at Phil, Hunter reached up to kiss Cary on the lips. Phil gunned the motor into noisy life and then revved it even higher.

Hunter pulled away and shouted something at him above the roar, but Cary couldn't hear the words. Then they were off, down the dirt road that led back to the highway and to Topeka.

Phil was silent for several miles, but finally his curiosity overcame whatever reticence he had.

"You spent the weekend with our ace reporter?" he asked, nonchalantly.

There was no point in lying. She answered, "Yes," smiling.

Phil slapped his thigh. "Wouldn't have believed it if I hadn't seen it with my own eyes. That's a first, that is."

"A first?"

"Hunter hasn't ever let a woman spend the night—that I know of, that is. We've been taking bets among the crews, for weeks now, on when the rule would be broken."

Cary was embarrassed by the young man's casual attitude, but she was also secretly pleased to find out Hunter did not have a busy social life.

"They're gonna love this at the station," Phil concluded, chuckling. "They're just gonna love it."

She was a little worried about Hunter's attitude toward this gossipy method of telling his friends about her, but Cary couldn't think of any good reason to ask Phil to remain silent. Surely Hunter had considered the consequences of his request of Phil to drive her home—with luggage. Why, he had even kissed her in front of the cameraman.

Cary sat back and decided to enjoy Phil's conversation and leave the worrying to someone else. It was uncharacteristic of her, but then...she had become someone else today. Someone who belonged to Hunter Pierce. Even his exploitation of grandma's bad English hadn't upset her too much. She was willing to believe he would use discretion in his cutting and splicing.

The next days were hectic. There did not seem to be anyone willing to take on the job of treasurer for the jobs council at the low salary offered. Cary called the school board, but they had no recommendations, either. And she seemed to have run out of potential engineers to interview for Omega Aircraft. Each day, she worked harder than ever before but had nothing to show for all her efforts except aching muscles and frustration.

Hunter called every night. He, too, was frustrated. No one had approached him with an illegal proposition; few of the busy engineers wanted to spend time on week nights partying in his apartment; and he was finding it harder each day to maintain his façade as a knowledgeable aerospace engineer.

"Cary, I really need some time this weekend to set up some kind of informal gathering here at the apartment. Would you mind—" he asked on Thursday.

"Oh, no," she lied. "Go right ahead. Louise has asked me twice now to help her decorate and stock the boutique. She'll be really grateful for my help, I'm sure."

"Thanks, princess. If this doesn't work, I'm not sure what we'll have to try next." Hunter sounded exhausted and defeated.

"Don't all spies have little cameras hidden in their ball-point pens and microphones in their cuff links? Couldn't you just use your skeleton key some night to steal into the president's office and photograph all his secret documents?'' she asked, joking.

But Hunter wasn't in the mood.

"I sometimes wish I did have a few of those James Bond gadgets. Maybe they would help. Right now, I think I could use any help at all."

"I'll send you a rabbit's foot by courier," she offered, hoping he would see her levity as an attempt to cheer him up and not as a put-down of his problems. "And I'll think of you this weekend—every minute. I love you, Hunter."

"That makes it bearable. I love you, too, princess."

Somehow she never tired of hearing him say those words. But her body ached for his touch and even his beautiful, sensuous voice couldn't fill that void.

As she had predicted, Louise was grateful for her help. They spent all day on Saturday stripping old wallpaper from the shop walls, and all day on Sunday putting up fresh new paper. Tommy was building display racks and a raised platform just inside the front windows for manikins and seasonal decorations. Lynette slept in a large playpen in the center of the still-empty main sales room.

On Sunday night, the four of them went out for dinner and, for the first time all weekend, Cary thought of her own problems at Willingham. She'd been too busy trying to understand Hunter to give the agency much thought. But now, over coffee and a good steak, she spoke about the jobs council and her difficulty in finding a treasurer.

"But why do you need a full-time treasurer?" asked Tommy. "Couldn't you get by with a young college graduate in accounting and a consultant who could set up the nonprofit organization, audit your books and make reports to your board?"

Cary felt gears engage in her brain. Of course that was the solution! And she knew of one, no, *two* young accounting majors who might be perfect for the job. If she could just convince the board and if she could find a good consultant....

Tommy cleared his throat dramatically. "If you need a good consultant, I can recommend one," he said, loudly enough to break in on her reverie.

"You!" she exclaimed.

Louise sat beside her husband, holding their infant and beaming proudly.

"Well, two of the guys in my office are starting up a consulting firm and they want me to join them. I'm really tempted, but I'd like to make certain I can help bring in some business. This would be a good start, don't you think?"

He paused. "Unless you think your school board might object to your brother-in-law working on the same project with you?" His brow furrowed in worry.

Cary laughed. "You don't know how hard we've all been working to solve this dilemma of the treasurer. If I can sell them on the idea of the college grad, I'm sure they'll welcome whomever I choose as the consultant. And besides, I don't know that I'll be working with the jobs council for very long, anyway."

"Why not, Cary?" asked Louise.

"Oh, Brenda and the others won't need help for very long, I'm sure. And Mary Ellen doesn't really like the idea of my spending too much time outside the office, anyway."

"There's something else, though. Isn't there?" Louise persisted.

"No, nothing," Cary protested. But she felt the color rise in her cheeks as she thought of the opal-and-amethyst ring being fashioned in Wichita.

"Yes, there is, and it's something to do with Hunter," continued Louise. "I can tell. Here, are you ready to continue that burping lesson?" she asked, handing the baby over to Cary.

Laughing, Cary took Lynette and began to pat her on the back. She didn't want to deny Louise's guess, but she wanted them to meet Hunter and talk with him, love him as much as she did, before she told them of the ring.

So she merely laughed and let Louise go on guessing, while her secret throbbed away inside her heart.

On Monday, Cary met with Hal Smith to discuss the possibility of hiring a younger, less experienced person to fill the position of treasurer and using the services of a consultant to define his job and audit his performance.

The board president was enthusiastic, especially when Cary explained that they could have the job council's nonprofit status confirmed in a very short time, if they proceeded with her plan.

Not imposing any restrictions at all, Hal ap-

proved the plan and told Cary to "get cracking."
By Wednesday, she had hired Danny Boyles, a summer graduate from Washburn University and
moved him into her old office.

The lawyers in St. Louis were contacted, and they
began the process of securing nonprofit certifica-
tion. In anticipation of that approval, Marian and
Cary bought typewriters and calculators, installed
phones and set up desks for three student coor-
dinators.

Then they began the long hours of planning what
the council would do.

As Cary sat in the conference room, listening to
enthusiastic plans of the new council members, she
often thought of Hunter, alone at Omega, pretending to be someone he was not and looking for
elusive and perhaps nonexistent evidence. Cary
sympathized with Hunter's problems, and she
wished there was something she could do to help
him.

Cary no longer questioned the validity of his suspicions. Every conversation she had with Henry
Crandon made her more certain that Hunter had
been right all along. Henry was pressing her to find
another engineer. He seemed disappointed in
"David," though he refused to tell Cary why. She
had actually gone so far as to inquire after Suzanne
Foley, but Henry had been abrupt, even angry, at
the mention of her name.

No, none of the engineers Omega had spent a fortune to hire had given them the special help they
needed. That much was apparent. And the inven-

tion Dr. Racine had brought from Burkham had not been enough to ensure future prosperity. Omega, and Henry Crandon, were still looking for an unscrupulous genius.

And somehow "David" had either disappointed them, or they weren't sure how to approach him.

Hunter called on Thursday to say he would have to double up on his shooting schedule for KMKX that weekend. Did she mind that they would not have any time together, again?

Of course she minded, but Cary knew her demands would only increase the burdens of frustration Hunter already faced, and so she said no, she would be busy, too.

She went down to the boutique and worked on labeling and sorting Louise's inventory, but her head ached from the starch and sizing in the new fabrics, and her body ached with longing for Hunter's touch.

Finally, on the weekend of Halloween, Hunter came to Topeka. Like honeymooners, they went to the store and stocked up on enough supplies to last through Sunday. They closed all the curtains and unplugged the phone, and then they began to get to know each other all over again.

Cary had never believed such ecstasy was possible for mere mortals—that such tremendous power could be generated by the union of two bodies.

Hunter's gentle kisses led inevitably to paths of ever-increasing passion, to gentle kisses of fulfillment and repose. In Hunter's arms, Cary found that her surrender was always a victory and that

Hunter, too, surrendered a part of himself whenever he conquered her.

When they were not making love, they were enjoying being in love, offering each other bits of memories and tales of childhood that tied them together ever more securely.

But often Hunter would drift away, to stand alone on the balcony or stare at the leaping flames in the fireplace. Melancholy stole up on Cary at those times, stealing away a little of her happiness. She knew he worried about his investigation—and, because it was going badly, about the wisdom of his decision to get involved.

Hunter had begun to form attachments to some of his co-workers and, as a result, he was beginning to feel some of the same doubts that had troubled Cary earlier. It was ironic that now, when she had cast her own misgivings aside, they should return to plague Hunter. She was beginning to believe in his ability to handle the situation diplomatically. But suddenly he was just a bit unsure, just a fraction less confident. And they both knew that in the masquerade he was playing at Omega, supreme confidence was absolutely necessary to carry off the deception.

Once, when Hunter pulled aside the curtains and was staring outside. Cary stole up behind him and put her arms around him. She laid her head on his broad back and felt his breath come and go in gentle rhythm.

At first, he did not respond at all to her presence. But at last he sighed, a sound Cary both heard and felt through his chest.

"I don't know what to do next, princess. I'm all out of ideas."

"Maybe you just have to wait. Maybe someone will come to you next week, or the one after that," she said. Privately she recalled the hints Henry Crandon had dropped, and she was not optimistic.

Her words did seem to cheer him a little, though. He turned away from the window and sought her mouth. In a moment, Cary sensed that he had retreated again from her, though his mouth still pressed gently on her own.

"Hunter, is it that bad?" she asked, pulling away to look at him.

"I don't know!" he said savagely, turning away from her. "I don't know if we're any closer now than before we started. Something's wrong with what I'm doing, but I don't know what."

"You haven't learned anything at all?"

"No. Not a thing. At least, not anything I can use right now. If only you. . . . It's as if I'm being purposely excluded from whatever might be going on," he continued rapidly without explaining that one half-expressed thought. "No one comes to my parties, no one talks to me in the hallways, no one gossips at lunch with me. I think some of the more conservative ones believe I have a mistress somewhere because I disappear every weekend." He laughed thinly.

"Do you think anyone has guessed who you are?" she asked, worriedly.

"No. I'm fairly certain of that. But I just can't

tell if management is still testing me or if they're expecting me to make the first move.''

"Well, why not make the move and see what happens?''

"Because, my little hothead, if I make the wrong kind of move at the wrong time or to the wrong person, I'll be out so fast I'll never even know what hit me. End of investigation. End of Hunter Pierce.''

Cary reached up under Hunter's shirt and began to massage his tense back muscles. Her brain was whirling, searching for answers and possibilities. One solution kept returning to her mind, no matter how many times she brushed it aside.

"Hunter, what about Suzanne Foley?''

"What about her?''

"Henry Crandon was anxious to get her, remember? And you said she was very greedy, just the sort to be recruited by bribes. Have you talked to her?''

"Yes, and no dice. I think Henry and crew have had second thoughts about her military connection. They know that any secrets she might sell would amount to treason—not just industrial espionage. So far they haven't gotten that desperate.''

He laughed bitterly. "So far, I'm the only desperate one. But I'll find a way, come hell or high water. I promised.''

Cary kissed Hunter's smooth skin and pulled him around into her arms. In a few minutes, she made him forget all about his problems at Omega—at least temporarily.

But she did not forget, and over the next weeks

she tried to find a way to help Hunter. As the days wore by, one at a time, Hunter seemed no nearer to a solution, and Cary felt more and more the pain of his failure coming between them and their future.

Hunter came to Topeka for Thanksgiving vacation, to join Cary, Louise, Tommy and Lynette for the holidays. He played with the baby and went pheasant hunting with Tommy. He laughed with them and shared some of his own jokes, but behind his smiles Cary sensed a growing frustration that bordered on despair.

Not even the precious new ring of opal and amethysts could comfort her on Sunday night when Hunter left to go back to Wichita. She sensed that the desperation he had spoken of was eating at him and that she would lose a part of him forever if he was not able to come to grips with this lack of action.

The first Monday in December, Cary received a telephone call from Dennis Forsythe in St. Louis. Mary Ellen had begun bleeding again over the weekend and had been rushed into surgery. She was still in intensive care, but her condition was improving rapidly, and she would probably be moved to a convalescent ward soon. They needed Cary, and they wanted her right away.

Her first thought was pure panic. She would be so far away from Hunter! She hesitated before answering, but in the end she knew she had to go. She couldn't turn her back on Willingham now—and she couldn't do much to help Hunter, anyway.

"Good!" said the senior partner. "I know it's

short notice, but we'd like you to be up here by Wednesday and plan to stay at least a month.''

A month! she wailed inside. *So long?*

Her voice broke as she answered, ''Of course. I'll be there.'' What else could she say?

''I know your family is there in Topeka, and naturally you'll want to be with them at Christmas,'' Forsythe continued. ''We're really grateful for your help here. Would ten days of vacation at Christmas be enough break for you?''

Ten days! her heart echoed with a thrill. If Hunter could get away—

''Yes, of course,'' she answered calmly. ''That would be very nice. I know I used up most of my vacation earlier in the year when my niece was born. I'd. . .like those ten days very much.''

''Fine, fine. We'll see you day after tomorrow, then.''

''Goodbye, Mr. Forsythe.''

When she heard the dial tone Cary began to punch in the numbers for Hunter's office at Omega.

''Thompson here,'' came the familiar voice.

''Can you talk?'' she asked.

''Yes, princess. What can I do for you, a hundred seventy miles away from your beautiful body?''

''Just listen, and be understanding, please. I have to go to St. Louis. Mary Ellen's had emergency surgery, and they need me to take over for her.''

''How long will Mary Ellen be in the hospital?''

''At least a month, but they're giving me ten days vacation at Christmas,'' Cary added quickly.

"That's good, princess. That's good," he said slowly.

Something about his tone was wrong, though, and Cary felt her stomach tighten with worry. Would he feel she was deserting him?

"Cary, I don't know how to ask you this. Damn! I wish I was there to talk you through this slowly, but—"

"Hunter, what is it?" Now the worry was slipping into fear inside her.

"Listen carefully to me, darling. And don't interrupt for a while, okay?"

"Okay," she whispered.

"I want you to help me. I'm convinced that Mary Ellen Hughes knows all about this operation here at Omega, even if you don't. Now, you promised not to interrupt. I know how much you respect her and what she has done for you in the past. But I think she was a willing victim in that American Paper deal. I think that overlarge check was her payoff. And I think she's working hand in glove with Henry Crandon now."

He paused but Cary couldn't even protest. She was numb with shock. He *couldn't* believe that!

"Ask yourself, Cary. Why did she send you to Topeka instead of directly to Wichita? Because she didn't want you too close to Henry, but she did want some of the good people of Burkham, who were so conveniently near you in Topeka. How can she afford to send you on an assignment for just one client? Even when you were working that

American Paper ruse, you had your regular clients to service along with the special work. But Crandon is willing to pay handsomely for results, and so you have all the time you need. Except that you took on a volunteer project, the jobs council. I'm willing to bet Mary Ellen wasn't too happy about that, was she? It took you away from her gold mine at Omega.''

Cary felt his words strike her as if they were swift arrows. She could not find the answers to his questions, although surely there were answers. All those suspicions were unfounded. They had to be!

''Cary, has Mary Ellen ever mentioned Henry Crandon's name to you? They're good friends, you know. Her name and number are written inside the front cover of his desk calendar and in his secretary's phone index, and she's been to visit him twice since she left the hospital, though not in the last several weeks. I have a feeling she's somehow been prevented from coming out here and that may be what has put a damper on Crandon's approach to me. He may need her for courage.''

''How. . .did you find all that out?'' she asked, barely able to make the words audible.

''I'm a spy, remember?'' he answered harshly. ''I'm right about her, Cary. I've known about her for quite a while, but I just couldn't bring myself to hurt you by giving you the details, especially since there was nothing to be gained by telling you. But now. . .now you can use that information to help me win this thing, honey. If you just—''

"Hunter!" she cried in despair. "You promised me you would never use me!"

Hunter was silent for so long that Cary was afraid he had broken the connection. But at last he spoke, his smooth voice rough with suppressed anger and perhaps some other emotion.

"You've got to help me, Cary! I know what I promised, and this isn't easy for me to say. I don't want to use you, princess, but I have to. You're my only hope. I can't just let them get away with ruining Burkham, because I didn't want you to get involved. For heaven's sake, Cary! You *are* involved and you can't deny it."

Still Cary could not answer him. She felt that if she refused, their love would never be the same. But if she agreed, their relationship would be changed by that, too. Either way, she was doomed to lose—but one way, she might lose her self-respect, also.

"Come on, honey. You're strong. You're my Joan of Arc, my proud princess. You can do it." He was begging her, and Cary hated it.

"No, I can't. I *won't* do this to Mary Ellen behind her back. She deserves better than that from me. We've been friends—I'm the shoulder she cried on when her man left town. I'm the only one who understood how much American Paper hurt her pride.

"You're wrong about her, Hunter. And this time, by being wrong, you won't just ruin a drug bust. If you start accusing her of taking bribes, you just might kill her. I won't help you do that," she finished flatly.

Tears had welled in her eyes, blurring her vision. In her mind's eye she saw the painting of the Indian princess, cool and aloof in her courage. Hunter was wrong; she wasn't strong. Not strong at all.

Hunter didn't plead anymore. The line was quiet for so long that Cary finally placed the receiver in its cradle, not knowing if Hunter were still there or not.

She knew he would not call again.

He didn't.

CHAPTER SIXTEEN

IT WAS AGONY to pack for the lonely trip to St. Louis, for Cary sadly remembered packing for those two joyful weekends in Wichita. Cary left behind the black silk embroidered suit she had worn the night Hunter revealed his true name to her, as well as the pale purple suit she had worn the night they first made love. With trembling fingers she removed the opal-and-amethyst ring and placed it on her dresser.

On the wall above her couch, the Indian princess continued to gaze into the distance with calm determination. The last time Cary had gone to St. Louis, she had taken the painting with her. This time, she would leave the portrait behind for it, too, reminded her of Hunter.

She called Louise to tell her of the unexpected summons to Willingham's main office, but Cary refused her sister's dinner invitation. She wanted to be alone in her misery.

At the last moment, when her bags were packed and the door was locked behind her, Cary found she could not leave the ring. In seconds she had run inside, scooped it up into her purse, and dashed back to her car.

Her late-morning flight encountered no delays, and she landed in St. Louis with plenty of time to find the apartment Dennis Forsythe had rented for her. It turned out to be a small, plain set of rooms on the eleventh floor of a very stark, cold high-rise. Her minuscule balcony overlooked a parking garage roof and the distant spires of a Gothic-style church.

The rental car provided for her this time was a Mustang, which felt strange to drive, and steered differently. Cary was vaguely annoyed with the sensation of unfamiliarity it provoked in her.

She wanted her own car, her own house, her own rooms with always the same familiar furnishings. She wanted a home. She wanted Hunter.

But Hunter wanted a Joan of Arc, she thought dejectedly. He saw Cary as some sort of brave, heroic companion who would help him avenge the downtrodden and trample the wrongdoers and then pick up the broken pieces of the innocent victims of his quest.

With a soft, broken laugh, she acknowledged the irony of her situation. Here she was standing in the middle of her chilly living room grieving for the loss of something she had never truly possessed. Hunter had never belonged to her any more than he belonged to his audience. He was dedicated to a cause, and it possessed him wholly.

He measured the entire world by the standards of that cause—and Cary had refused to live up to its ideal. For her, the demands of Hunter's vision were too harsh and cold. She had always sought a different, kinder sort of purpose in her world—a purpose that seemed to be at odds with Hunter's.

Her life until now had been simple, directed toward the many people who needed her. Hunter's presence in her life had not changed that, but he had helped her expand her horizons. He had caused her to look inward, also, and begin to seek out what *she* needed.

Physically, she knew that she needed and wanted Hunter. But emotionally?

Perhaps those early doubts had been a warning she should have heeded. Something about Hunter Pierce had drawn her, but something else about him had repelled her from the moment they had first met. No, repelled was the wrong word. Frightened was more accurate.

Yes. That was it. All those doubts had really been fears of the pain it was in Hunter's power to induce. The hurt of exposure and humiliation—other people's pain. Love found and lost—her pain.

Cary looked around at the empty, impersonal walls that closed her in and felt that this fear of being hurt would haunt her for a long, long time.

In the morning, Anita Florez came to bring her up to date on Mary Ellen's activities.

"These files belong to candidates recently interviewed by our trainees. Mary Ellen was going to look them over and then confer with the trainees about possible leads. She had a staff meeting scheduled for this afternoon at one o'clock to go over the new expense-reporting procedure. And later, she had promised to make a report to the senior partners on the results of these surveys.''

Anita held out a stack of folders with neatly lettered headings—Placements, Rejections, Dismissals and Open.

Cary took the folders and reached down to slip them into the middle drawer of the desk in Mary Ellen's office. But the drawer seemed stuck.

"Oh, that's kept locked now." Anita reached over and opened a different drawer for Cary. "You can use this one for current projects. Miss Hughes has started using that other one for personal business. It's supposed to stay locked all the time.''

"Oh." Cary's thoughts accelerated. This was exactly the sort of thing Hunter would have expected her to pry into. She winced at the idea of searching through Mary Ellen's personal things, perhaps finding old love letters, or overdue bills from a dress shop, hidden away from curious eyes.

Yes, opening that drawer was almost certainly what Hunter would suggest, if he were here. But she had no intention of telling him about it or of opening it to satisfy her own curiosity.

Oh, how hurt Mary Ellen would feel to discover later that someone had violated her privacy while she was helpless in a hospital bed and that someone was a trusted employee! Cary could never willingly, knowingly wound her supervisor that way. No, she was glad she had chosen not to cooperate with Hunter's suggestion.

She'd thought about it long and hard. There was a completely innocent explanation for every one of his accusations. Mary Ellen had sent her to Topeka and not Wichita because there was room in the office there, and because she knew Cary had family close by. And she wasn't in Topeka for just one client; there were the community-relations projects and the budget, too. And—perhaps—Mary Ellen had dropped in on Henry while she was making a prebudget tour. As she had dropped in on Cary. After all, he was an important client.

No. She had no doubts about Mary Ellen.

Cary put the folders away in the second drawer and began to read through the applicant files. Hmm, the recruiter trainees were definitely getting better. These were very well composed notes indeed.

A knock sounded at her door.

"Come in," she said loudly.

Anita opened the door and then stood aside for someone else to enter. Cary could not see who it was because he or she was preceded by an enormous pot of pale purple chrysanthemums.

Tears pooled in Cary's eyes and she half rose, looking past the blossoms to the carrier. But it was only a deliveryman, garbed in khaki and struggling to get the bobbing flowers undamaged through the narrow door.

Taking them from him, Cary put the chrysanthemums on the corner of Mary Ellen's desk, where they dwarfed the round brass lamp.

"I have a message here for a Miss Blaine. Is that

you?'' asked the man. ''It's kinda strange.'' Cary accepted a folded sheet of stationery with the florist's logo at the top. The message began, ''Princess. I shouldn't have....''

Hurriedly, she reached for her purse and tipped the messenger, who shut the door behind him as he left with Anita.

''Princess,'' Cary read.

I shouldn't have asked you to help me. I know how much you admire and respect your friend—and I may be wrong about her involvement, anyway. I've explained everything to Suzanne Foley, and we have cooked up a scheme that should eliminate any need for your help. I'm sorry if I hurt you.

Hunter

Not a single word of love. So she was right to think it had all ended with her refusal to be his spy.

Cary read the message twice. It wasn't Hunter's handwriting, of course. But the words were his. Coldly professional and sharp.

It wasn't really a farewell letter, of course, but it might as well have been. She had disappointed Hunter deeply and betrayed his misplaced trust in her. She'd stepped right down from his pedestal and kept on walking. And Hunter—well, he had broken the only promise she'd ever asked him to make, never to use her in his cold pursuit of ''justice.''

They had nothing left to share now. Had there

ever really been anything, between them except passion?

Yes! her heart cried. *Oh, yes!*

But she silenced the affirmation by crumpling the letter and seizing the files that she needed. Driving herself, Cary finished her work, researched the topic of the staff meeting, and began her presentation for the firm's partners. In the next three hours she hardly thought of Hunter at all.

As Cary shuffled through the papers in front of her, she noticed that Mary Ellen's desk calendar was open to last Friday's date. She flipped through to Wednesday and then skipped ahead to see what her supervisor had planned for the next several days. Thursday, tomorrow seemed to be a round of meetings with various client corporations. Friday, she'd apparently been scheduled to take a day of vacation. Cary was relieved. That meant she could use all day on Friday to catch up on what was happening in the main office.

Cary called Anita to pull the files on each of the clients Mary Ellen had planned to visit, and to phone two of them requesting postponement until Friday. That done, she cleared her desk for lunch.

But before she could leave, Anita knocked again and brought in a stack of mail that had just been delivered. Sighing, Cary opted to send out for a sandwich and eat at her desk.

The mail contained routine correspondence, résumés and bills. There were also airline tickets, presumably for the three-day holiday Mary Ellen had planned. Without thinking, Cary ripped open the travel agent's envelope and withdrew the tickets. She would send them back for the refund as soon as possible.

Her heart stopped suddenly, leaving her cold and trembling. The ticket destination was Wichita. And the round trip had been paid for on an Omega Aircraft account.

Cary's numb fingers fumbled as she forced the tickets back inside the envelope.

There must be an explanation, she told herself, a perfectly innocent explanation for the trip. But, there wasn't. Again, Cary checked the page on Mary Ellen's calendar for Friday. There was no official trip to Omega written in there, but only a day for vacation.

Feeling like a thief, Cary sat in her office and waited impatiently until everyone else had left for lunch. Then she quietly checked the secretary's calendar to confirm her conclusions. And the office manager's, and the senior recruiter's. No one at Willingham knew of Mary Ellen's trip, and Omega's financing of it was probably a well-kept secret, also.

Could there be another explanation? Cary asked herself. Was it possible that she had trusted and valued the friendship of someone she really never knew—someone like the person Hunter thought Mary Ellen was?

Cary spent the rest of her lunch hour staring at the locked desk drawer. Hunter would have opened it.

The words echoed in her brain, over and over. *Hunter would have opened it.*

But in her imagination, she saw a once-strong woman now broken with pain, lying alone in a hospital bed, unable to eat or drink, without even the comfort of a loved one near. She saw a woman unable to defend herself against the prying eyes of strangers. Hunter would have opened the drawer, but then that was the difference between them, she told herself. For Hunter, truth was of paramount importance. For her, compassion and caring were far more precious than simple justice.

The staff meeting at one o'clock demanded her attention for a while. And then there was the report to the senior partners to prepare and deliver. At five o'clock, the envelope still lay in solitary isolation on Cary's desk, drawing her attention whenever she glanced away from the files she was trying to read.

Resolutely, she packed the files into her briefcase and turned her back on the envelope. She turned off the brass lamp and locked the office door behind her as she left.

It was sheer coincidence that she arrived at her bleak apartment a few minutes after six. Another coincidence that she was unfamiliar with the numbers of local stations available on her television set. A final coincidence that she found herself tuned in to the KMKX cable station out of Kansas City.

She reached for the dial to reset it, but drew back. The news was of a visit by the Pope to a South American country and she watched as thousands of

chanting people thronged to hear his message. She
fooled herself into thinking she was interested in the
news story, however, for an inner clock was ticking
away the minutes—counting off the seconds until
Hunter's voice and face would appear on the
screen. She watched the news, but later she remembered none of it.

When Hunter's face at last appeared, Cary's
breath caught at the sudden pain she felt inside.
He looked tired, or was that her imagination? His
velvet voice rolled on and on, telling of a newspaper ad that offered genuine diamonds and
emeralds at fabulous savings. Of course, it was a
scam. Cary did not even listen for the details,
knowing that Hunter was merely exposing another
fraud.

His segment would be short, Cary knew. And so
she drank in every view of him offered by the
camera. His head turned to the side in strong pro-
file. His dark hair bowed over a tiny gemstone. His
eyes seemed to look straight at her. And at last, he
smiled.

"This is Hunter Pierce for KMKX 'Lineup.'
Good night."

Her cheeks were wet, and it was dark inside her
living room when she turned off the set. Mechan-
ically, she fixed a light dinner, washed the dishes
and took a shower. Her mind refused to consider
the problem of Mary Ellen's tickets or the meaning
of the turmoil she'd experienced watching Hunter
on television.

Once in the unfamiliar bed, Cary lay still—staring at the ceiling and trying hard to think of nothing at all. Eventually, she slept.

ON THURSDAY, the troublesome envelope was still on her desk. Cary would be too busy to take care of it in the morning, but perhaps this afternoon she could take time to decide what to do with it.

But the afternoon was busy, also. At least too busy for disposing of the envelope. And so Cary left at five again, repeating her numb activities of the evening before. Except that Hunter's "Line-up" segment was not shown on Thursday, not while he was working as David Thompson in Wichita. It made the evening a little easier to stumble through.

Friday was not busy. The envelope screamed for her attention until finally Cary could ignore it no longer.

She had worried about the problem and had decided just to lock the tickets away. Cary hoped that when Mary Ellen returned, her supervisor would believe she had put them in the drawer herself. It was time she was buying. Time for Mary Ellen, and time for herself. But she no longer believed she could buy innocence for either of them.

Cary began a reluctant search for the key to her supervisor's locked drawer, part of her hoping she would not find it. But she did find it, lying in a small tray of paper clips on the credenza behind her chair.

She cursed silently when the key slipped into the lock easily.

Quickly, she opened the drawer and thrust the envelope inside. She slammed it shut and had begun to turn the key again, when her mind registered what she had seen in the split second of sliding out the drawer.

Just inside lay a file folder bearing the name of Joe Hartman, the vice-president of American Paper. But this was supposed to be a repository for Mary Ellen's "personal" business. What was such a file doing in there?

Slowly, Cary opened the drawer again. Beneath the Hartman folder was one for Henry Crandon at Omega and one for Solly Fenneman at Cooper Forge. And below them all was a slim checkbook, bound in navy and gilt-stamped with the name of M. E. Hughes.

She lifted out the Henry Crandon file, reluctantly, touching it gingerly. Inside were photocopies of checks made out to Mary Ellen personally from Omega Aircraft. There were also letters from Henry, thanking her for all her help. Heaven help that nervous man, but he had actually put in writing the kind of help Mary Ellen had given him!

And her supervisor had saved all the damning evidence in her own office!

There, in black and white, was the commission Mary Ellen had received for talking Dr. Racine into giving Omega the plans for the Burkham invention. There, too, was a discussion of how Mary Ellen had been prevented by Cary's suggestion to management from taking any more budget-review trips. She now planned to meet with "David Thompson"

on her own time to discuss the projects he'd been
working on for Burkham when he left.

Cary noted the date Mary Ellen had planned to
go for the talk with David. Today. The day of her
"vacation" in Wichita.

If Mary Ellen had not gotten so ill last week,
Hunter would have had his evidence today. The investigation would be over.

She closed the desk drawer and locked it. But she
did not return the key to its place among the paper
clips. Instead, she slipped it inside her coin purse,
where it came to rest with a clink against the opal-
and-amethyst ring.

Rapidly, Cary checked her watch. It was just
short of noon. She had one more client to visit today, and then she would be free to make the call
that would change the lives of so many people forever.

She buzzed Anita.

"I'm going out for lunch now. Then I'll be at
Midwestern Exterminators for a while. And then
I'm going home."

"Yes, Miss Blaine. Will you be here on Monday?"

"Of course. I'll be in...as usual," Cary said.
But nothing would ever be "usual" again, she
knew. The information about Mary Ellen's duplicity would have to be revealed soon to everyone at
Willingham. And the office would never be the
same.

Later, Cary sat in front of the phone in her apartment, trying to frame the words she would use to tell Hunter. She accepted completely that she would have to explain everything to him. There was no longer any question of proving Mary Ellen's guilt or innocence. After Hunter received her call, he could notify the authorities about Crandon and Dr. Racine. She would try to get as much time for Mary Ellen as possible, but at least Hunter would be able to close his investigation. That was what they had both wanted only a short time ago. Why then did she feel so defeated, now that the end was near?

"Thompson here."

Suddenly she couldn't speak. The rehearsed words stuck in her throat.

"Hello? Who's there?" he asked, annoyance ringing through his voice.

"Hunter, can you talk?" she finally managed.

"Yes, princess. What can I do for you?"

He was being jovial, a bad sign.

"How's. . . the investigation coming?"

"Good, real good. Suzanne has them convinced she knows about something so big they're seriously considering ignoring the military implications of trying to obtain it. I expect to have something concrete by the beginning of the week."

"Oh. That's good news." Cary's thoughts faltered.

"Yes. I'm sure we can conclude the investigation without any—"

"Without any help from me?" she asked.

"Honey, I know how you feel about Mary Ellen. I don't want you to do something against your conscience and then spend the rest of your life blaming me for it."

"I wouldn't do that, Hunter."

"Well, I don't want you to even think about it anymore. Just put it out of your mind. Next week I'm going to wrap this thing up, and then I'm going to come up to St. Louis to get us straightened out."

"What?"

"Princess. I was wrong to break my promise to you. This isn't your job; it's mine. I've kicked myself a thousand times since you hung up that phone. Did you get my flowers?"

"Yes," she answered. Her senses were reeling. He surely couldn't imagine they would be able to pick up the relationship as if nothing had changed!

"I wanted you to believe I understand now," he continued. "I do, Cary. Maybe I've just been working too long behind the cameras. I'd forgotten that I wasn't dealing just with crime but with people— people with loyalties and principles of their own. You've helped me get everything back into perspective, princess. In more ways than one." His voice was not bantering now, but husky with emotion.

Oh, he didn't know! He didn't know that she had been changed, too. She had become the very kind of person she'd accused him of being—driven to know the truth no matter how much or how many people it hurt. If only she hadn't opened that drawer!

"Cary?"

"Yes, Hunter?"

"I don't want you to even think about those things I said concerning Mary Ellen. Promise me you'll forget them?"

"I promise," she whispered. Now there was one more lie between them.

"I'll call you next week as soon as I know anything here. And I'll be up to see you on Saturday, no matter what. Goodbye, princess."

"Goodbye, Hunter."

Cary should feel relieved. There was no need for her to tell anyone about the contents of the locked drawer. The investigation would be concluded without involving her at all. But somehow that knowledge wasn't as comforting as it would have been a week ago.

Now she knew for certain that Mary Ellen was a criminal. Cary even had evidence that someone at American Paper and someone else at Cooper Forge were using the surreptitious services of Willingham's recruiting supervisor.

She hadn't told Hunter yet of her discovery, but sooner or later Dennis Forsythe would have to be told. Cary would have to describe how she had broken into Mary Ellen's private files, on a suggestion by the television reporter she was supposedly restraining from irresponsible acts.

Never once did she tell herself that what Mary Ellen had done could be excused, or that such a crime could remain hidden forever. Now Cary could see the situation through Hunter's eyes, as she had once longed to do. She knew the truth and had to tell it, though it might break her heart to do so.

The scenario of her confrontation with the Willingham executives played itself out in her mind several times during the dreary weekend. She went to movies, museums and even the zoo to keep herself occupied, but still she was plagued by visions of the future.

Not for a moment did she believe that Hunter wasn't disappointed in her refusal to help him investigate Mary Ellen. Of course when he found out she had actually gone ahead and done the spying, anyway, his disappointment would be gone. Yet it would still hang between them—for she did not regret her initial refusal. She had believed in Mary Ellen then. It was the opening of that drawer she wished had not occurred, wished with all her might.

On Monday, it was difficult to concentrate on the routine of running the regional office. Her report to the senior partners had brought to light several minor problems that needed to be solved, but Cary couldn't help but see any problem as trivial compared to Mary Ellen's betrayal. Several teleconferences needed to be arranged to go over the partners' recommendations, though, and Cary tried to keep busy with those details.

Anita came in at three o'clock to say that Mary Ellen was calling from the hospital, asking that some of her personal things be sent to her. One item on her list was the key to the locked drawer.

"Have you seen it?" asked Anita. "I'm sure she told me it was in the paper-clip tray. But I can't find it."

"Perhaps she was in some pain the last time she used it and wasn't thinking about where she laid it down. It might be anywhere." Cary wasn't ready yet to admit she had used the key, but she certainly couldn't surrender it to be sent to Mary Ellen.

"Yes, you're probably right. I'll just look for it a bit more and then tell her she can find the key when she gets back. Or I'll have a new lock put on the drawer for her, if she can't find that key."

"I'm sure that will be fine," agreed Cary.

When Anita had gone, Cary took out the key and opened the drawer once more. She forced herself to look into the file on American Paper and the one for Cooper Forge.

Anger began to replace the misery she had been nursing since last Friday. As she read the files, she realized that Mary Ellen's treachery had begun a long time ago, and Willingham had probably been damaged more than anyone would ever be able to calculate.

Mary Ellen had known from the start that American Paper had no plans to hire anyone found by her agency. In fact, she had helped Joe Hartman devise the story about leases in Colorado. There was even a copy of a letter from Dunfey and Crabb in the folder, a letter that would discredit them completely with the paper company's shareholders.

The file on Cooper Forge was older, almost five years old. Mary Ellen's special service to them had been to document the hiring of two executives who did not exist, in order to pad Cooper's expenses.

For any one of those crimes, Mary Ellen could be sent to jail. No wonder she developed ulcers, worrying about possible exposure.

And no wonder she had been upset when Cary spent several weeks working out of this office—sitting right next to all the damning evidence.

That had been a different Cary, however, a trusting friend with no suspicions. Mary Ellen had not needed to fear her. Then, Cary would not have pried into those files.

Now she was someone older, wiser and sadder, too. Now she knew that she and so many others had lived with treachery for a long time, and she would still be blindly naive if she had not done the very thing she'd accused Hunter of doing—pursued the truth without regard to the pain it might cause.

Dennis Forsythe and the other partners would be justifiably angered by her revelations. Cary's co-workers would be shocked and hurt by their own unwitting participation in Mary Ellen's schemes. Worst of all was what might happen to Mary Ellen herself. Cary knew the surgery the woman had undergone was not minor; she was still on heavy doses of medication for lingering infections in her abdominal cavity. So far, Mary Ellen had lost almost thirty pounds and was very weak. Her supervisor might not recover at all from a full-scale inquiry and subsequent prosecution.

Oh, how Cary longed to have Hunter's strong arms wrapped around her, sealing her away from the troubles that whirled about her! But she knew that whatever magic they had once shared was damaged irreparably now—torn apart by her own narrow accusations and Hunter's idealistic, impossible expectations.

She had lying and deceit on her conscience now, and the ruin of a beautiful love. Dear God, would she also have to live with the death of Mary Ellen if she followed the only honorable course open to her now?

CHAPTER SEVENTEEN

TUESDAY, WEDNESDAY, THURSDAY and finally Friday passed without a word from Hunter. The chrysanthemums were beginning to droop, and Anita had even cut a few of the drier blossoms off their scraggly stems. The remaining flowers wouldn't last much longer.

Somehow, Cary had gotten through the week. Each night had brought her less sleep than the night before and more inner conflicts. Whether Hunter was successful or not, she had committed herself to telling Dennis Forsythe of her discoveries on Monday.

Alone in her apartment Friday night, Cary waited with growing concern for news from Hunter. At eleven o'clock, there was a hesitant knock on her door.

She opened it slowly. Hunter stood outside with a large tan suitcase at his feet and a garment bag slung over his shoulder. He was slumped against the door frame, his whole body speaking of exhaustion and dejection.

"Hi, beautiful," he said, smiling weakly.

"Hunter! I thought you would call. You look awful!" she said, reacting without thinking to the dark circles under his eyes and the pallor of his skin. She reached out to draw him inside.

He came toward her, letting the garment bag slip from his fingers to the floor, unheeded. His arms closed around her, drawing her up and tight to his chest, while his mouth came down to hers in hungry need.

Each time Hunter released her lips, oh, so briefly, it seemed as if he was pulling Cary's passion from her, causing it to well up somewhere deep inside her, to rise and fill every ounce of her being and then spill out to flow around them both. Cary should have thought to fear Hunter's magic; she should have prepared her heart against the sweet invasion of his scent and his touch.

"Oh, princess, I've missed you so!" he whispered in her hair. "I need to hold you, kiss you. . . ."

His lips roamed over her face, lightly touching her eyes, her cheeks, her ears, her neck. And in between each tender soft caress, Hunter's voice continued weaving its melodic spell.

"I need your innocence. . . your goodness. Oh, my darling, I need your love."

Cary had never needed him more, either. His words denied all the fears that had surrounded her for days. He did not even know of her help, and yet he was as loving and wonderful as before her refusal.

Cary suddenly felt like laughing. If *this* was a disappointed man, then she was dreaming this whole scene!

Her fingers reached up to loosen his tie and unfasten the buttons on his shirt. She felt those powerful muscles in his arms tremble through the fabric. No, this was very, very real.

Hunter groaned against her as she pressed her palms to the bare, smooth place beside his left nipple where his heart beat hot and wild.

He gave a savage kick to his luggage, sending it sprawling inside the apartment. With one hand, he reached out to close and lock her door, while turning her around with his other hand. Gently prodding from the back, he pushed Cary straight into the bedroom.

Hunter closed that door, too, and turned off all the lights. In the deep black shadows he came to her, undressing her with a slow tenderness that made her limbs ache with fever. First the blouse and skirt, then her bra and the silky panty hose, until all that she wore was a strand of creamy pearls around her throat and beige lace briefs.

Infinitely gentle, his fingers slid beneath the lace, tugging the garment down over her abdomen and then her thighs, over her knees and off. Then he reached for the pearls, but did not remove them. Instead, to her indescribable delight, he lifted them only enough to kiss the tiny hollow at the base of her throat.

Fever spread across her skin, inching downward from that tiny kiss, licking at her breasts and then racing on down to where desire for Hunter throbbed unmercifully.

"Slowly, princess. Savor it," he whispered as her body arched and twisted with tension

Cary opened her eyes and looked full into his smiling face. There was no lingering anger there, no disappointment. Hunter was content—happy, she would have said.

Easing out from under his touch, Cary gently pushed him back into the pillows. He wanted it slow, hmm?

Using only one finger, she traced the outline of his nipples and then let her hand rove over the curling hairs between them, ruffling them gently. Her hands slipped down his chest, down to those tight muscles that corded either side of his navel. She felt them tense beneath her palm as she moved ever lower, watching his eyes all the time.

His lids lowered and his lips parted. Her hand moved lower yet and he groaned, arching toward her as she had moved toward him.

"Slower?" she asked, teasingly.

"No, Cary. No!" He rolled to her and crushed her to him, saying over and over, "I need you."

They moved around each other, over each other. His voice never stopped its litany of love, whispering between kisses of his need for her, his overwhelming love for every part of her.

"I love your softness here...and here," he said. "And I'll never have enough of the taste of you and the smell of you."

She was scarcely breathing as he said those words. Cary's head was reeling, and she felt dizzy with too many sensations all at once. Relief, happiness, new hope all filled her beyond her capacity for comprehension. This time, the magic in Hunter was a healing sorcery, a mystic medicine that cured her melancholy completely.

But soon, all the simpler emotions were swept aside by the complex, raging tide of desire that overwhelmed all other senses. Hunter, too, moved ever more swiftly with her to a level of passion that cried for release, and he kissed her ever faster, ever more hungrily.

At last, the surging crest broke over them, washing away the last remnants of questions and fears. There was nothing left but peace and weary joy.

"I love you so much more, princess," Hunter sighed. "Every day, I love you more. You don't know. I was so afraid—"

"Of what?"

"That I had lost you, by pushing you too hard. You didn't call. Not once."

"I know," she whispered. "I thought I had lost you, too. I thought you were. . .disappointed that I couldn't bring myself to help you."

"No, oh, no, darling," he protested softly. "I was angry at first. It would have made things so easy, if you had wanted to help. But I'm glad you stood up for what you believe. I told you once I loved you for your strength, and I meant it."

"Oh, Hunter," she cried, brokenly. "You don't know! I'm not strong. I didn't want to know about Mary Ellen's guilt—I tried to run away from knowing."

"Hush, now. That's all past. The investigation is over. We don't have to worry about it any more."

"It's all over? All of it?"

"Yes." He sighed deeply. "I gave up. Suddenly last week, everyone was even more secretive, more closemouthed than ever. If I didn't know any better, I would have thought they suspected my cover. But it's probably just that they are innocent, after all, and I made them very uncomfortable with my prodding and questioning."

Hunter reached across to move a damp curl from Cary's forehead. "Mary Ellen is probably innocent, too. I hope you can forgive me for all those terrible accusations I made about her."

Cary slipped away from him, off the bed. She gathered a sheer negligee about her and came round to sit beside him. This wasn't the way she had planned to tell him. She would have chosen another way, another time, different circumstances.

Before she could say anything, however, Hunter pulled her down for another long, loving kiss.

"I'm so glad you haven't changed, princess," he said, smiling.

"But I have, Hunter." She pulled away. "I've grown older since I saw you last. I've faced myself for the first time in my life."

"What are you talking about—older?"

"It wasn't right for me to run away from finding out the truth. I told myself I didn't want to hurt Mary Ellen, but I didn't fully realize that not exposing her guilt would hurt so many more people." Cary turned away, slightly, so that Hunter would not see the hardness she knew was in her eyes. "Mary Ellen is like a cancer, growing and spreading her disease among the healthy, honest people."

"What do you mean, Cary?" Hunter sat up beside her, sheltering her now trembling body in his arms.

"I found your evidence, Hunter. All of it. More, even, than you or anyone had dreamed of. For a while, I wasn't going to tell you or anyone else—you said you didn't need it, anyway. But gradually, I've come to realize that I do believe in what you're trying to do, and keeping that evidence secret is wrong."

"Oh, princess! Princess!" Hunter sighed against her hair. "What did I ever do to deserve you?"

Cary drew a ragged breath. "Just hold me and tell me I'm right. Keep reminding me that Willingham deserves to know about her treachery, and Henry Crandon deserves to be exposed. Oh, darling! I'm so new to this. I know I have to do it, but it . . . it hurts like hell!" she finished, sobbing.

Hunter pulled her tightly to him and let the tears course across his arms. He stroked her hair and kissed her forehead, murmuring the strengthening words she needed to hear.

At last he set her down beside him, drew the blankets over them both.

Spent, and secure beside the heat of Hunter's body, Cary closed her eyes and slept through the night for the first time in more than week.

HUNTER WAITED until after breakfast to ask for details of Cary's discovery. She told him about the locked drawer and the contents of the file folders inside it.

"What was in the checkbook?" he asked.

"I couldn't bring myself to look," she replied, feeling foolish.

"Hmm. How fast can you be packed and out of here?"

"Why? Where am I going?"

"I want to put this story on the air Monday night, princess. And I don't want you anywhere near here when the news breaks."

She shook her head. "No. I can't let you do it that way. I owe Willingham too much to let them find all this out from the headlines. I have to tell Dennis Forsythe myself and let him handle it the best way he can. He's known about you from the start. He made me. . .responsible for your actions. But now he's got to take over and try to preserve what he can of Willingham's reputation. He's a decent man, Hunter. He doesn't deserve to hear about this secondhand."

Hunter smiled. "Keep on teaching me, lady. I'm learning a lot about people from you. It's been too long since I remembered to put feelings instead of facts first."

He reached across the tiny table and laid his hand beside Cary's cheek. "Have I told you yet this morning that I love you?"

"Yes, but you can tell me again. If you really want to," she added. The weight of the opal-and-amethyst ring on her finger nudged slightly at her consciousness. How glad she was that she hadn't left it in Topeka.

"Can you call this Forsythe fellow today and set

up a meeting with him soon? I think you and I both need to get this thing out of the way as quickly as possible, and get on with the business of loving.''

Now she smiled, too. Yes, that was exactly what she needed.

''And don't worry,'' Hunter continued. ''You've been on camera once, so this time should be easy as pie for you.''

Cary's smile vanished. A chill breeze seemed to raise the hairs on her arms. What did he mean?

''Hunter, I'm not going to—''

''Oh, yes, you are!'' he insisted, reaching for her hands and holding them tightly. ''You're the one who knows all the answers. You're the star of this whole operation!''

''But I don't want to be the star!'' she protested. ''There isn't going to be an 'operation.' You can't put this on your show! Willingham is going to take care of everything!''

''It won't work that way. Neither one of us has a choice anymore, sweetheart. KMKX has invested thousands in this investigation, just to get a scoop. But without you, there's no story. Unless you want me to march into Mary Ellen's hospital room and confront her with our accusations?''

''No!'' she cried, horrified.

''Or put Dennis Forsythe on camera and then have the press plague him for more information— information only *you* possess?''

''N-no.''

''Well, I don't want to do that, either. And it isn't practical. I don't have the evidence. He doesn't have it. You do. You know, you're probably also going to have to testify in court when the time comes. Where are those documents now, by the way?''

"Back in the drawer. Locked.'' Her voice seemed foreign to her. How could she convince Hunter that she couldn't let him put any of her revelations on the air? Dennis Forsythe had to be allowed to handle everything very quietly. All Cary had planned to do herself was to give the senior partner the contents of the drawer, and her resignation.

Hunter didn't know about that last part. Somehow he still didn't understand about how much—and whom—this expose would hurt. Was she strong enough to use it—use his love for her against him? Could she really even consider using that precious love to destroy his dream of exposing a really big crime on his own show?

Cary pulled her hands away from his and walked across to the kitchen window, staring out at the foggy sky.

"Can you get into the drawer this weekend to show it to Forsythe, then?'' Hunter was asking.

"Yes,'' she said evenly. "But I won't go on your program, Hunter, and I won't let you have the contents of that drawer. Don't ask me to do it.''

"Dammit, Cary! Mary Ellen Hughes isn't worth all this devotion. She's the one who caused all this trouble—not you or me.

"Honey, you just have to cooperate. There's no story without you. What do you expect me to say? 'I know someone who has seen certain documents that implicate certain people. But I can't produce any witnesses.' Don't you see how ridiculous that sounds?

"Forsythe will want to hush this up as much as possible. Willingham doesn't want a scandal like this to get out. And Crandon won't admit anything if he knows neither of you will go public with it. By Tuesday morning, those precious files you saw may be ashes!"

Her shoulders sagged. "I know," she whispered. "But you just don't understand what's at stake." She would have to play out the game now, turning his love for her around to her purpose. How she hated herself.

Hunter rose and came to stand behind her. He put his hands on her shoulders and gradually forced her to turn and face him.

"Tell me, Cary. What don't I understand? Who else is there to protect besides Mary Ellen and Dennis Forsythe and all the fine folks at Willingham who surely aren't going to be put out of work? Who else are you afraid to hurt by telling the truth?"

"I'm going to resign, Hunter, when I tell Dennis Forsythe about Mary Ellen."

"You don't have to do that! I'll hit Willingham and Forsythe with everything in the book if they try to pressure you into leaving."

"No, no. They won't need to 'pressure' me. I lied to my superiors, I falsified a recommendation to a client, I knowingly sent a television reporter to a client with no solid evidence to back up his story, I broke into my supervisor's desk and looked into her personal papers...."

"You exposed a crime, Cary. One that needed to be exposed."

"You still can't see the human side of it, can you?" she returned, bitterly. For all his loving words, he hadn't really changed, after all.

"Every day now, my co-workers will be watching me, wondering which of them has a secret I might decide to investigate. They'll never trust me again. They will always wonder if I'm being honest and straightforward or if I'm lying again.

"Do you remember," she said softly, "when I said we all see investigators like you as our nemesis? Well, now I'm one, too."

"So you want to start over again someplace else. Is that it?"

"I don't want to. I have to." She moved away, restlessly needing something to do. Absentmindedly, she began to clear the breakfast dishes.

"And if I put you anywhere at all in the story, you may never get a chance to start over fresh. This thing will hang around you for a long time. Is that what you're thinking?"

Hunter did understand that part of it, at least. But Cary could sense in the harshness of his tone that he had trouble accepting it.

She nodded.

He didn't say any more. In silence, he helped her wash the dishes and put them away. They both dressed without speaking, and Cary went to sit on the lumpy sofa in her living room.

"I thought I knew you better," he said at last. "You're not trying to protect Willingham or anyone else but yourself. I'm going for a walk," he called angrily. And then she heard the sound of a door slam.

What else could she have said? Hunter would never accept her real reason for wanting to keep the story out of the news. He would never understand that, no matter how much she detested what the woman had done, she still owed a last measure of loyalty to Mary Ellen—at least enough to save her life.

She'd telephoned Dr. Hiram Boscoe, Mary Ellen's surgeon, yesterday and asked him for a frank assessment of her supervisor's condition.

"She's not healing well at all," had been the curt answer. "Her ulcers were brought on by chronic anxiety, and her nerves are no better now than when I first saw her three years ago. It's a wonder it took her this long to collapse."

"When will she be strong enough to face... going back to work?" Cary had asked.

"I don't know. I've told her to see a psychiatrist, but she won't listen to me. If she doesn't find some way to calm down—or if some major crisis occurs in her life—she may never go home."

"Never?" Cary asked in a small, shaken voice.

"Frankly, I don't think she can survive another operation. This one was too extensive and, as I said, she's not healing well at all."

Cary had hung up, feeling sick inside. It was just as she had feared. A major crisis might kill Mary

Ellen. And prosecution for fraud and conspiracy would certainly be a major crisis.

That's when she decided that, under no circumstances, would she let Hunter air Mary Ellen's guilt. She'd thought perhaps he would be satisfied merely to see the investigation concluded and the Omega "bad guys" discredited. That would have been enough for any true knight in shining armor.

But Hunter was no knight, any more than she was Joan of Arc. He had his career, his reputation, to consider. After all the time and money his station and Burkham had spent, he naturally wanted to give them the biggest possible show.

But she couldn't let him.

THROUGHOUT THE LONG MORNING, Cary searched her soul for a solution, finding none.

When Hunter returned, he went straight into the bedroom. She followed and saw that he was repacking his suitcase. The garment bag lay stuffed and zipped on the bed.

"What are you going to do?"

"What does it look like?"

"But where are you going, what are you going to do?"

"Look, princess. I told you once I was going to get this story, come hell or high water. I meant it. I'm going to see Henry Crandon now and confront him with what I know. Maybe he won't ask to see my evidence. Maybe he'll just come out with the whole story himself, and I won't need your precious testimony, after all."

Hunter wasn't looking at her. In fact, he was avoiding her gaze.

"Hunter, please." Cary reached out to touch his arm, but he shrugged it off.

"Don't say it, Cary. Right now, I just—"

He turned away from his packing to face her. The circles under his eyes were deeper, his cheeks white from clenched jaws. Cary felt her heart constrict.

"I thought—at last—you really believed," he said, and his eyes mirrored the hurt confusion in his voice. "I thought you were the kind of woman who stood up for what was right. I didn't know you'd turn your back on everything we've both been working for, because you were worried about what people might think about you.

"I guess I just didn't get to know you as well as I thought, Cary. Did I?"

Hunter's eyes searched hers, waiting for Cary to deny his words. She closed her own eyes against that look and bit her lip, holding in both pain and love and all the bitter certainty that she was doing the right thing.

Perhaps he would understand some day.

Hunter turned back to the bed and snapped shut the locks on his bag. He picked up his luggage and brushed past Cary, leaving the bedroom door open. Through it, she heard the apartment door sigh shut a few seconds later. Hunter was gone.

Woodenly, she returned to the living room. For a long time, she stared into space, not feeling, not thinking. The total silence of the room brought home to her that she was truly alone now.

Cary looked down at her lap, to where her hands rested on her lilac wool pants. Against the fabric, the opal-and-amethyst ring glinted, purple on purple, bright fire against dull sheen. A single teardrop fell on the stones, fracturing their brilliance.

She couldn't give him up. She couldn't let him leave believing she was a coward. Half rising from the couch, she looked up at the wall clock.

He'd left more than half an hour ago. It was too late to catch him and tell him she still loved him.

But not too late to do something about the reason for his departure, she thought, drawing purpose around her like a shield to ward off despair. But what could she do?

She reached for a pen and the pad of paper beside her phone. Tentatively at first, then gradually faster she began jotting down possible alternatives. There must be a way to give Hunter his story and yet protect Mary Ellen from bearing the full force of prosecution while she was still struggling for life. The woman was already suffering for her crimes—she did not need to die for them.

Dusk was falling when Cary finally put together the last details of the proposals she would make to Hunter and to Dennis Forsythe. Her heart was skipping rapidly, keeping time with the racing thoughts that whirled around her head.

One problem loomed. She must reach Hunter and prevent him from confronting Henry Crandon before she had time to put her plan into action. But Cary didn't know for certain where Hunter was.

She pulled out the telephone book and began calling.

She left one message at the St. Louis airport, another at Kansas City and one more at the Wichita airport. She left messages for Hunter to call his office at the hotel they had once used in Wichita and at Hunter's answering service in Kansas City. The phone had already been disconnected at his apartment in Wichita.

Next, she called KMKX in Kansas City. Hunter's boss was not in, but she left a very precise message to be given to him and also to Hunter, if he should call in.

"Have new evidence. Delay any action at Omega until Monday." Cary paused as the secretary read back the note. "That's just right. Now sign the first one with my name, Caroline Blaine, Executive Recruiter for Willingham Consultants. And sign the one for Mr. Pierce with 'Love, Princess.' Have you got that?"

"Yes, Miss Blaine. Pardon me, but are you the one Mr. Pierce spent the weekend with?"

Cary laughed. Phil had certainly been busy spreading the news!

"Yes, I'm the one. And if Hunter gets that message soon, I may get to spend a lot more time with him."

"I understand," the secretary said eagerly. "I'll make sure he gets this!"

Another possible lead to Hunter had occurred to Cary during the conversation.

"Can you tell me how to reach Phil Braden?" she asked.

"Yes, I'll give you his beeper number. Dial that and leave a message. When his beeper goes off, he'll call in and get your message."

Cary dialed the number and smiled as she left a cryptic message sure to win Phil's attention.

"This is Caroline Blaine. Call me immediately. Do not under any circumstances talk to Hunter before you call me. This is a life and death matter, Phil. I'm trusting you."

Then she sat down to wait.

In only a few minutes, Phil Braden called.

"What's up, Miss Blaine. Lovers' tiff?"

"No, not really, Phil. It's something much more serious. Has Hunter tried to reach you today?" she asked, anxiously.

"No, not yet. Is he going to?"

"I hope so. I hope he is going to want a cameraman to go along when he. . . . Never mind. I need to stall him, Phil. I've got some evidence to give him in the Omega investigation, and I don't want him to blow it by going to Henry Crandon before I have a chance to make some arrangements here."

"Got it. I'll tell him to call you."

"Well, that may not work," Cary replied, hesitantly.

"So there was a lovers' tiff!" Phil sang out gleefully. "Want me to beat some sense into him for you?"

"No," she answered, laughing. "Sounds to me

like you'd have too much fun! Just stall him, if you can, until Monday. Tell him you can't make it to Wichita this weekend. Anything. Just don't agree to film Crandon until Monday, please."

"Okay, Miss Blaine. I'll take care of it."

"Thanks. And call me Cary, Phil. I hope we'll be getting to know each other real well in the future."

Satisfied that she had done everything possible to prevent Hunter from breaking the story prematurely, Cary began work on the next items on her list.

Louise answered her call and wanted to know about the weather in St. Louis and Hunter and when Cary was coming for Christmas vacation. Cary tried to answer her questions naturally but quickly, evading the issue of Hunter. When the amenities were over, she asked to speak with Tommy.

"Hello, Cary. How goes the investigation?"

"Tommy, I need some advice. Could an auditor pick up on bonuses given to employees and travel payments made on a company account for someone who did not work for the company?"

"Perhaps. The bonuses would be easier to hide than the travel payments on the company account. Do you know the airline and the dates?"

"I know everything about one trip, and I can probably find out about some others, though they may be a couple of years old."

"No problem, then. This is Omega business, isn't it? Is Hunter about finished with his investigation?"

"Yes and no. I'll explain everything tomorrow night. I'm coming home."

If Tommy wondered at her sudden announcement, he didn't show it. He told her cheerfully that they would be looking forward to seeing her, and hung up.

There! Even if Hunter never saw the contents of the secret drawer, he would have something to use for evidence against Omega Aircraft—something to bargain with.

And now Cary had something to bargain with, too. If she could just pull her plan off, Hunter would have his big show, Burkham would get back its inventions and perhaps a hefty settlement as well, Henry Crandon and his associates would be sent to prison, and Willingham would still have the chance to protect its name—and Mary Ellen—from the press.

And perhaps she would have Hunter back—forever, this time.

CHAPTER EIGHTEEN

THROUGH THE NOISE of a shower later in the evening, Cary heard the phone ring. Quickly grabbing a towel, she ran out to the living room and snatched up the receiver.

"Hello!" she said, breathlessly. Shivering droplets of water were running down her back and legs, tickling her and making the chilly room seem drafty, too.

"Good grief, woman! Did you leave messages all over the United States?" Hunter's voice was demanding, but beneath it she sensed amusement.

"Where are you?" she asked, not really wanting to answer his question, in case she had misjudged his tolerance—or his anger.

"I'm in Wichita at the hotel. I was paged in Kansas City, paged at the Wichita airport, and then I found a message here at the hotel. You covered all the possibilities, didn't you?"

"I tried."

"What's this about new evidence? Have you changed your mind about coming on the show?"

"How tired are you?"

"Cary, just answer me! What's this all about?"

There was exasperation in his voice. She would have to choose her words very carefully.

"Hunter, if you're not too tired, I'd like you to come back to St. Louis tomorrow. I want you to sit in on my meeting with Dennis Forsythe. I think you'll get all the evidence you need then."

Would he fall for her bait? Her hands clenched around the receiver, waiting for his answer.

"Sure," he said slowly. "I can fly back into St. Louis. I'd like to meet your Mr. Forsythe. But what new evidence do you have? You haven't answered my questions yet."

"You'll just have to wait and see. I can't tell you about it over the phone," she said. *Or you'll know I'm bluffing,* she added silently.

"Okay, I'll be there." Now Hunter's voice was clipped and cold, no laughter bubbling behind his words. "Should I bring a cameraman along, or is this going to be a private showing?"

"No camera tomorrow. But I'm sure you'll need one on Monday."

Obviously, he hadn't called Phil yet. He would find one more sign of her frantic planning when he did. She hoped he wouldn't be too annoyed.

He grunted. "All right. Where do I go and when?"

"Just come here sometime before two o'clock. I'll take you to Willingham's."

"This better be good," he growled and then hung up.

"I love you," Cary whispered to the dead connection. "I love you."

She pulled the soggy towel closer, but it did little to ward off the chill that pervaded the room and her heart. Mental pictures of Hunter brought her no warmth or comfort now. She wanted to touch him again, to have that hot magic passion course through her. If she could only touch him, love him, everything would be all right.

No, that was only wishful thinking.

She had something to prove, to both Hunter and herself, before she could hope to have his love again. Tomorrow, they could start over....

Resolutely, Cary pushed her dreams aside. Now that Hunter had called, she could take care of the last thing on her list. Firmly, she punched out the numbers for Dennis Forsythe's home.

"Cary! What can I do for you? Surely you're not working on Saturday!"

"Mr. Forsythe, I need a very large favor from you. I need to see you tomorrow afternoon. It's urgent."

"Can I ask what it's all about?"

"No. I'm afraid it's something that can't be discussed over the phone. Please, will you meet me in your office tomorrow—at three o'clock?"

"All right, Cary. I'll be there. I hope this isn't as serious as your tone implies."

She didn't comment. Mary Ellen had created a situation far more serious than he could possibly imagine, but there was no point in telling him that now. She couldn't adequately prepare him for such bad news.

Shaking from the cold, Cary hung up the phone

and ran back to her hot shower. In spite of the water's warmth, however, she continued to tremble. So much depended on tomorrow!

HUNTER ARRIVED AT NOON, irritable and trying hard not to let it show. It was clear he wanted the story badly enough to cooperate with any eventuality, Cary thought wryly.

She took him to lunch at Stouffer's and then filled a half hour showing him the famous arch on the waterfront. There wasn't time to ride the little car inside to the top, but they did get out and walk around the huge base of one leg of the arch.

Hunter looked at all the sights like a dutiful child, his mind obviously racing ahead to the meeting with Forsythe. Once, he drew Cary around to face him.

"Can't you tell me what's going on? I've been a very patient man, but I can only take so much."

"I'll explain it all in just a little while. Trust me, please," she begged him.

Hunter's dark, forest-secret eyes were only inches away, fringed by lashes as ebony as the curls above his brow. The faint silver curls that lay mixed among his black ones were white in the winter sun. How softly they would coil around her fingers. Cary smiled at the thought.

"Trust you?" His voice was harsher than she had ever heard it. "Princess, I've tried that. I've tried believing in us. When you couldn't bring yourself to trust me, I was patient. I listened to you. I waited for you. I thought we had it all worked out," he added regretfully.

Cary reached up to touch his lips. "Hush, please," she pleaded. He would spoil it all. He would say something that neither of them could forget later. "I promise, Hunter. Everything will be all right. I love you."

"Do you, princess? Do you know what it means to really love someone so much that they become the sun and moon and stars to you? Do you, princess?"

Tears stood in his eyes. She had never hurt so much in all her life. He thought she had betrayed herself and him, and that she was going to do it again.

Only Cary's shaky confidence in her plan helped her stand still in front of his reproachful gaze instead of running as fast and as far away as she could. *Dear God,* she prayed. Her plan must work!

What was it she had told Hunter about the awful devastation of tornadoes? "It makes you strong," she'd said. Well, this ordeal should make her as strong as a granite monument!

She lifted Hunter's hand to her lips and kissed it tenderly. "It's time, now," she said. "We've got to go."

Hunter followed her silently back to her car. He didn't ask any more questions on the ride to the Willingham offices, but once she caught him looking at her—pain and confusion clouding his eyes.

She forced back her own tears and controlled an urge to floor the gas pedal.

Dennis Forsythe had unlocked the building and was waiting for them in his office. He was clearly surprised to see that Cary had brought someone with her.

"Hunter Pierce, this is Dennis Forsythe. Mr. Forsythe, Hunter is an investigative reporter, with KMKX in Kansas City. He has been looking into the allegations against Omega Aircraft Corporation—and Willingham."

Hunter removed his gray-rimmed glasses and put them in a pocket before he shook hands with the Willingham partner. Forsythe gave a start of recognition as the glasses were removed, but he betrayed no anxiety in meeting the newsman.

"Cary, what's going on?" he asked calmly.

"I'd like to show you some material I found in Mary Ellen Hughes's desk last week, Mr. Forsythe. Will you come with me to her office and take a look at them?"

She led the way down an unlit corridor to the supervisor's office, unlocked the door and turned on the brass lamp. Hunter leaned against the wall, watching every movement of hers with glittering eyes.

She unlocked the private drawer and withdrew the file on Henry Crandon.

"Will you please sit down over here and read through these papers?" she asked, trying to still the quaver in her voice and the trembling of her fingers. Oh, she was hating every minute of this ordeal!

In tense silence, she watched as the older man opened the folder and glanced through the letter on top. She saw him start, then look at her in amazement. Cary watched him, seeing his amazement turn to dismay as he continued reading.

The top letter had been the one in which Henry thanked Mary Ellen for her work in convincing Dr. Racine to give Omega the plans for Burkham's invention. Below it was the letter in which they confirmed her plans to visit Omega and discuss a similar arrangement with David Thompson.

As Forsythe finished reading the second document, he closed the file and laid it on his lap. He looked from Cary to Hunter, then back.

"Well. Do I need to tell you I knew nothing about this?"

"Oh, no, Mr. Forsythe. I know you didn't. It was entirely Mary Ellen's scheme. There's no doubt of that."

"What do you and this...reporter intend to do with this?" he asked.

Cary glanced at Hunter. His eyes were glued to the file, hungry to see its contents for himself.

"Before I tell you what I propose, you need to know that there is more."

"More?" Dennis Forsythe's voice rose.

Cary handed him the folders on American Paper and Cooper Forge, avoiding Hunter's surprised eyes. She waited while Forsythe read through them, seeing his confidence and control slowly fade. His hands, too, were shaking when he'd finished.

"I don't know what to say." He looked as if he had aged about ten years. "I've always had the utmost respect for Miss Hughes. I'll ask you again. What do you intend to do with these?"

"Nothing," answered Cary. She felt tension emanating from Hunter, even as she saw Dennis Forsythe look at her hopefully.

"Let me explain my proposition to you. I know you don't want to see Willingham destroyed by this, and I know Mary Ellen is too ill to stand trial right now. I'm giving these documents to you to handle as you see fit. But there are some conditions. I hope you will agree to handle this matter according to those conditions."

She had rehearsed the words so many times, they seemed to echo in her head. Now came the hard part.

"I asked Hunter to come along today because he has been involved in the investigation of Omega's espionage from the beginning. As you know, I... obtained a position for him at Omega as an engineer, under a false name. Since October, Hunter has been posing as the David Thompson you saw reference to in that file.

"I discussed with you the possibility of our cooperating with Hunter," she continued. "I didn't believe, at the time, that anyone at Willingham was involved. I made the discoveries about Mary Ellen just last week."

Cary's voice was quavering so badly that she had to take a deep breath every few words. Suddenly, Hunter was standing behind her, his hands resting lightly on her shoulders. She looked up at him quickly and saw him nod.

Surprised by his support before she had even come to the part that concerned him, Cary forgot for a moment what the next part of her speech was supposed to be.

"I—uh. Hunter, I mean Mr. Pierce, knows everything I do and I have made photocopies of everything in those files." She felt Hunter's presence as a warmth, steadying her. "But I don't want to see Willingham hurt any more than I want to see Mary Ellen have another attack."

"It might kill her, you know," Forsythe said.

"I know. That's my primary concern." Hunter's hands tightened on her shoulders. "I would like to suggest that you and Mr. Pierce visit Henry Crandon. Show him the letters, if you like. He's a very nervous man, and I think you can convince him to make a confession. If necessary, you can tell him the information in here can be confirmed by an official audit.

"It will be up to you to make sure he does not name Mary Ellen specifically. Mr. Pierce will use Crandon's confession on the air to expose Omega and make the public aware of Burkham's role as victim. Burkham may decide to prosecute. But if they do, it will be a long time before the case comes to trial and Mary Ellen's name, or Willingham's, is revealed. In the meantime, I suggest you do everything you can to assist the FBI in their investigation of the other two companies Mary Ellen did business with."

"I'm sure they'll keep Willingham out of it, if you cooperate as fully as possible," Hunter added. "And I'll do everything I can to prevent any leak to the media."

Cary was surprised and grateful for Hunter's comment. He was going to help her, as she had prayed he might.

"But what about Mary Ellen?" asked Forsythe.

Cary shook her head. "I'll leave that up to you. Her guilt is eating her alive right now. I don't think the FBI or anyone else will try to arrest her in her present condition. You'll just have to see what kind of immunity you can negotiate for her. You can destroy them, of course, but those papers—more than any audit—should give you some leverage in negotiating for her and Willingham."

Cary took a deep breath. What she said next was mostly for Hunter—to explain, if she could.

"I don't know why Mary Ellen did these things. Maybe she doesn't, either. She's always been a good friend and...a good supervisor. Her doctor told me he has recommended psychiatric help. Perhaps that would help all of us understand her better."

Dennis Forsythe rose slowly. He no longer trembled, but the strain was beginning to show in his face. He looked exhausted.

"Thank you, Miss Blaine, for being so generous. I'm very grateful it was you who found these things." He reached out to shake her hand.

Cary took one more deep breath. "I need to tell you, Mr. Forsythe, that I am resigning, effective immediately. I'm going home to Topeka tonight.''

The older man looked at her with sad, wise eyes. "I understand. I'm sorry to lose someone with your promise and sensitivity, but I do understand. Good luck, Miss Blaine.''

He shook her hand and Hunter's, then left.

Hunter had remained silent. He'd let Cary run the entire thing. Now he pulled her from her chair and turned her to face him.

He started to say something, but no words came. He just looked at her, and Cary knew that everything was finally, truly, all right.

She melted into his arms, feeling Hunter's strength not as a protection from the world now but as a support. As it should be. Her plan had worked. Now they could begin to love again.

Hunter bowed to touch her lips, gently confirming with his kisses that this was not an ending, but a beginning.

"I think I would have understood," he said softly.

"I know that now. I should have known it then. I'm sorry I didn't give you—us—the chance to prove it. I was. . .too mixed up, and hurt.''

"It's all over now, princess. No more apologies. No more hurt. Let's just go on from here, hmm?" Hunter's last word was muffled by her mouth as it closed on his to seal her agreement.

"What are you going to do now?" Hunter asked, several kisses later.

"Well, if Tommy can go into business as a consultant—when he's never been a consultant before—surely I can start a personnel agency of my own. I know the business inside out." Cary sounded much more confident than she felt, but after she had mulled over the idea for two days, it had begun to feel pretty comfortable.

"I can run it my way. I can make it really work for the community."

"I know you can, princess." Hunter kissed her lightly and pulled her into a bear hug. "You can do anything you want!"

"There's one thing I want to do before I set up the business, though," she said thoughtfully.

"What's that?"

"I want to make sure that wedding band fits this beautiful engagement ring."

Hunter *really* kissed her then, drawing from that well of passion deep inside her, causing wave after wave of joy to wash over her, drowning her in lovetide.

The security guard knocked softly at the door, questioning why they had not followed Mr. Forsythe out.

Hunter and Cary laughed.

"Let's go home, shall we?" he asked. "Your place or mine?"

"Mine," she answered. "I need to finish packing, anyway."

He squeezed her hand and they followed the guard down to the lobby and out into the sunshine.

At her apartment, Hunter phoned Phil and arranged to meet him early Monday morning at the Wichita airport. Then he and Cary closed the drapes and forgot about spies and all the other cares of the world.

MONDAY EVENING they sat in Louise's living room, watching the special taped "Lineup" segment with Tommy, Louise and David Thompson.

Henry Crandon had gone to pieces when Hunter had confronted him. His secretary had summoned Jack Beale and the confession had ended up coming from him, the principle instigator. The program was all Hunter, or KMKX, could have hoped for.

When it was over, Louise and Tommy applauded.

"Great work, Hunter!"

Hunter stood up and made a dramatic bow. "Thank you, ladies and gentlemen. But I owe it all to clean living, mom's apple pie and this lady right here."

He pulled Cary up and kissed her enthusiastically.

"Hunter!" she whispered. "You're forgetting somebody."

"Oh, and to this man—the real David Thompson! But if he thinks I'm going to kiss him, he's got another think coming!"

They all laughed, and even Lynette gurgled happily.

"So, when are you starting your agency?" asked Tommy. "I'll be glad to help if I can."

"Thanks, Tommy. But I'm going to take it slow and easy. I really want to do this right."

"Where is it going to be?" Louise asked, slyly.

"In Kansas City, I think," Cary answered, looking at Hunter.

"No question about it," he agreed. "We're going to stay close as close from here on in—for better or worse."

"Oh, Cary!" Louise came up to put her arms around her sister. "I'm so happy for you. I'm so glad you made up your mind."

"So am I," said Hunter. "So am I."

SIX WEEKS LATER, Cary felt morning sun bathe her face in its warmth as she floated on her back in the gently rocking tide. She closed her eyes against its glare. She could almost be floating in some secluded lagoon instead of this public beach and bay. She could be separated from the rest of the world by miles of empty tan sand and colorful coral. Her own palm-ringed Bali Hai, perhaps.

And striding across the glittering sand should be a tall, dark stranger. Ah, there he was. She positioned him in her fantasy, watching as he executed a perfect racing dive and swam with easy strokes to meet her. His head emerged from the clear deep water beside her, and he turned to look at her with. . . Hunter's dark brown spaniel eyes.

"Time to come in," he said.

"Really?" Cary opened her eyes a tiny bit. Yes, there he was beside her. This was no fantasy. The black curls were wet around his forehead and cheeks. Hunter.

Together the couple swam slowly back to the cabana and dried off. It was the last day of their stay on Maui. Tomorrow they would return to the snow and icy winds of Kansas—but today, there was nothing to do but lie in bed and do the things newlyweds always do in bed.

Hunter had just begun to nuzzle at Cary's left breast when a hesitant knock sounded on their door.

"Go away!" shouted Hunter. "Can't you read the Do Not Disturb! sign on the knob?"

"Telegram, sir," came the timid reply.

Hunter groaned and pulled on his slacks. Cary reached for the sheet and pulled it up to hide her nakedness.

She watched curiously as Hunter tipped the messenger and then ripped open the thin blue paper containing the telegram.

He smiled as he read the message and then laid it down on his dresser.

"What does it say?" Cary asked.

"I'll tell you later," Hunter answered. "Now, where was I a minute ago? Ah, there. . . ."

His lips found her nipple, and he began to tease it with his tongue until Cary moaned in ecstasy.

"You wicked, wicked deceiver," he crooned. "You tricked me."

"What . . . what are you talking about?" she managed to whisper, her mind fogged with joy.

"I told you I like strong women. So you tricked me. You put on that little show for Dennis Forsythe and made me think you were the strongest woman in the world And the smartest. But you deceived me."

As Hunter spoke, his fingers traced the outline of Cary's breasts, touching the nipples gently, pushing them together to form a dark shadowed valley between white mountains. His words made no sense to her, partly because her mind was full of the sensations of his touch, but partly because. . . they simply seemed nonsensical.

Cary shook her long back hair, and it flew out to lie across the pillow in silky strands of ebony on shiny white silk. "What do you mean?" she mumbled.

"You're not strong at all," he continued, his mellow voice purring like a kitten's. "You're all soft—here, and here, and here. . . ." He kissed her breasts, her stomach and then moved to kiss the swelling pleasure below her stomach.

"Ahh!" she cried. No, she wasn't strong at all. Not now. Now she was weak with craving, needing, wanting.

Her fingers clutched at his hair, and she pulled him toward her hungry mouth.

All at once, the enormity of their passion seized them and they moved to grasp its swelling force. *Now* Cary was strong! Now she could move mountains! Now they shared a power no one could ever take from them.

LATER, MUCH LATER, Cary asked Hunter again about the telegram, and he frowned.

"How much did you resent that 'someone' in your past who asked you to give up your job?" he asked, instead.

"Enough," she said, warily.

"Do you think you would mind very much postponing the opening of your new agency for one year—if it was for a very good cause?"

"What cause?"

"Your loving, wonderful husband has just been recruited."

"I'll say you have," she commented, dryly. "And this recruiter is pooped!"

"No, silly. I mean it. I've just been asked to go to work for one of the big networks, in Washington, to help them cover the elections this year."

"Wow!" she breathed. "I always knew you were good, but...."

"Hey, cut that out!" Hunter yelled as she reached over to tickle him. "Get serious, woman. Would you mind terribly?"

"No. I'd love Washington for a year. I told you before that I planned to go back and take a refresher course in accounting before I dive into starting a new business. I could take the course in Washington as easily as anywhere else. Maybe I could even see what help I can get from the Small Business Administration. Truly, dearest, I would love it. But what happens after that?"

"That's the best part. If they like what I do—and how could they not—I take over as their Midwest correspondent, based in Kansas City next year!''

"You know," Cary said. "You're a pretty lucky guy. You get me and a new job and Kansas, too. What more could you want?''

"Hmm. A little more of the first and less of the rest, right now," he answered, reaching to cup her breast again.

She arched up to meet his touch and then the tides of passion crested over them once more.

"Princess," he muttered, his voice sleepy beside her ear.

"Hmm?"

"I really am lucky, you know."

Cary thought of how many times they had come close to losing each other, battling an investigation that was too big for either of them.

"I know," she whispered thankfully. "We both are.''

ABOUT THE AUTHOR

"Perseverence pays," could be Donna Saucier's personal motto. Determined to see her first Superromance in print, Donna weathered a Texas hurricane and multiple family illnesses writing *Amethyst Fire*.

The author of a textbook, *Electricity and the Environment*, Donna wrote speeches, advertising copy and for technical fields before trying her hand at romance.

Born in Colorado and raised in Kansas and Missouri, Donna currently resides in Texas with her two children. The Great Plains state where she grew up serves as the backdrop for the love affair between Cary and Hunter in *Amethyst Fire*.

An exciting romantic saga
destined to become
the most talked-about book
of the decade!

By all-time bestselling
Harlequin author Charlotte Lamb—
writing as Sheila Holland.

Secrets
Sheila Holland

Sophia was torn between the love of two men—two
brothers who were part of a great and noble family. As
different as fire and ice, they were rivals whose hatred
for each other was powerful and destructive. Their
legacy to Sophia was a life of passion and regret, and
secrets that must never be told...

Begin a long love affair with

HARLEQUIN SUPERROMANCE.™

Accept LOVE BEYOND DESIRE **FREE.**

Complete and mail the coupon below today!

- -

FREE! Mail to: Harlequin Reader Service

In the U.S.
2504 West Southern Avenue
Tempe, AZ 85282

In Canada
P.O. Box 2800, Postal Station "A"
5170 Yonge St., Willowdale, Ont. M2N 5T5

YES, please send me FREE and without any obligation my
HARLEQUIN SUPERROMANCE novel, LOVE BEYOND DESIRE. If you do
not hear from me after I have examined my FREE book, please send me
the 4 new **HARLEQUIN SUPERROMANCE** books every month as soon
as they come off the press. I understand that I will be billed only $2.50 for
each book (total $10.00). There are no shipping and handling or any
other hidden charges. There is no minimum number of books that I have
to purchase. In fact, I may cancel this arrangement at any time.
LOVE BEYOND DESIRE is mine to keep as a FREE gift, even if I do not
buy any additional books.

NAME _____ (Please Print) _____

ADDRESS _____ APT. NO. _____

CITY _____

STATE/PROV. _____ ZIP/POSTAL CODE _____

SIGNATURE (If under 18, parent or guardian must sign.)   134-BPS-KAND
                                                          SUP-SUB-22